Mine

Books by Robert R. McCammon

Baal
Bethany's Sin
Blue World
The Night Boat
Stinger
Swan Song
They Thirst
The Wolf's Hour

Published by POCKET BOOKS

MINE

Robert R. McCammon

POCKET BOOKS

New York   London   Toronto   Sydney   Tokyo   Singapore

Thanks to Julie Keeton for the title inspiration.
And thanks also to Dale Davis for the technical help.

———————————————————

Grateful acknowledgment is made for permission to reprint lyrics from "Five to One," page 49. Written by Jim Morrison, Ray Manzarek, John Densmore and Robby Krieger. Copyright © 1968 Doors Music Company. All rights reserved. Used by permission.

 POCKET BOOKS, a division of Simon & Schuster Inc. 1230 Avenue of the Americas, New York, NY 10020

ISBN: 0-671-66486-7

First Pocket Books hardcover printing May 1990

10 9 8 7 6 5 4 3 2

POCKET and colophon are registered trademarks of Simon & Schuster Inc.

Printed in the U.S.A.

F MCLAMMON

To the survivors of an era
when the whole world was watching

What's Past Is...

The baby was crying again.

The sound roused her from a dream about a castle on a cloud, and set her teeth on edge. It had been a good dream, and in it she'd been young and slim and her hair had been the color of the summer sun. It had been a dream that she'd hated leaving, but the baby was crying again. Sometimes she regretted being a mother; sometimes the baby killed her dreams. But she sat up in bed and slid her feet into her slippers because there was no one else to take care of the child.

She stretched, popping her joints, and stood up. She was a big, heavy woman with broad shoulders, and she was six feet tall. Amazon

Chick, she'd been called. By whom? She couldn't remember. Oh, yes; it came to her. By him. It had been one of his pet names for her, part of their secret code of love. She could see his face in her mind, like a blaze of beauty. She remembered his dangerous laugh, and how his body felt hard as warm marble atop hers on a bed fringed with purple beads. . . .

Stop. It was torture; thinking of what used to be.

She said, "Hush, hush," in a voice raspy with sleep. The baby kept crying. She loved this child, better than she'd loved anything for a long time, but the baby did cry a lot. He couldn't be satisfied. She went to the crib and looked at him. Tears were rolling down his cheeks in the dank light from the Majik Market across the highway. "Hush," she said. "Robby? Hush, now!" But Robby wouldn't hush, and she didn't want to wake the neighbors. They didn't like her as it stood. Particularly not the old bastard next door, who knocked on the walls when she played her Hendrix and Joplin records. He threatened to call the pigs, and he had no respect for God, either.

"Quiet!" she told Robby. The baby made a choking sound, flailed at the air with fists the size of large strawberries, and his crying throttled up. She picked up the infant from his crib and rocked him, while he trembled with baby rage. As she tried to soothe his demons, she listened to the noise of eighteen-wheelers rushing past Mableton on the highway that led to Atlanta. She liked it. It was a clean sound, like water flowing over stones. But it made her sad, too, in a way. Everybody was going somewhere but her, it often seemed. Everybody had a destination, a fixed star. Hers had burned brightly for a time, flared, and dwindled to a cinder. That was a long time ago, in another life. Now she lived here, in this low-rent apartment building next to the highway, and when the nights were clear she could see the lights of the city to the northeast. When it rained, she saw nothing but dark.

She walked around the cramped bedroom, crooning to the baby. He wouldn't stop crying, though, and it was giving her a headache. The kid was stubborn. She took him through the hallway into the kitchen, where she switched on the light. Roaches fled for shelter. The kitchen was a damned mess, and anger burst in her for letting it get this way. She swept empty cans and litter off the table to make room for the child, then she laid him down and checked his diaper. No, it wasn't wet. "You hungry? You hungry, sweetie?" Robby coughed and gasped, his crying ebbing for a few seconds and then swelling to a thin, high keening that razored her skull.

She searched in vain for a pacifier. The clock caught her eye: four-twelve. Jesus! She'd have to be at work in little more than an hour, and Robby was crying his head off. She left him flailing on the table and opened the refrigerator. A rancid smell drifted from it. Something had gone bad, in there amid the cold french fries, bits of Burger King hamburgers, Spam, cottage cheese, milk, half-empty cans of baked beans, and a few jars of Gerber's baby food. She chose a jar of applesauce, then she opened a cupboard and got a small pot. She turned on one of the stove's burners, and she drew a little water from the sink's tap into the pot. She placed the pot on the burner and the jar of applesauce down into the water to heat it. Robby didn't like cold food, and the warmth would make him sleepy. A mother had to know a lot of tricks; it was a tough job.

She glanced at Robby as she waited for the applesauce to heat up, and she saw with a start of horror that he was just about to roll off the table's edge.

She moved fast for her one hundred and eighty-four pounds. She caught Robby an instant before he fell to the checkered linoleum, and she hugged him close as he squalled again. "Hush, now. Hush. Almost broke your neck, didn't you?" she said as she paced the floor with the crying infant. "Almost broke it. Bad baby! Hush, now. Mary's got you."

Robby kicked and wailed, struggling in her arms, and Mary felt her patience tattering like an old peace flag in a hard, hot wind.

She shoved that feeling down because it was a dangerous thing. It made her think of ticking bombs and fingers forcing bullet clips into the chambers of automatic rifles. It made her think of God's voice roaring commandments in the night from her stereo speakers. It made her think of where she'd been and who she was, and that was a dangerous thing to lodge in her mind. She cradled Robby with one arm and felt the jar of applesauce. Warm enough. She took the jar out, got a spoon from a drawer, and sat down in a chair with the baby. Robby's nose was running, his face splotched with red. "Here," Mary said. "Sweets for baby." His mouth was clamped shut, he wouldn't open it, and suddenly he convulsed and kicked and the applesauce spewed onto the front of Mary's plaid flannel robe. "Damn it!" she said. "Shit! Look at this mess!" The child's body jerked with fierce strength. "You're going to eat this!" she told him, and she spooned up more applesauce.

Again, he defied her. Applesauce dripped from his mouth down his chin. It was combat now, a battle of wills. Mary caught the infant's face with one large hand and squeezed the babyfat cheeks. "YOU'RE GOING TO MIND ME!" she shouted into the glistening blue eyes. The infant quieted for a second, startled, and then new tears streaked down his face and his wailing pierced Mary's head with fresh pain.

Robby's lips became a barrier to the spoon. Applesauce drooled down onto his sleepsuit, where yellow ducks cavorted. Mary thought of the washing she was going to have to do, a chore she despised, and the frayed thread of her temper broke.

She threw aside the spoon, picked up the infant, and shook him. "MIND ME!" she shouted. "DO YOU HEAR WHAT I SAID?" She shook him harder and harder, his head lolling and the high-pitched wail still coming from his mouth. She clamped a hand over his lips, and his head thrashed against her fingers. The sound of his crying went up and up, a crazy spiral. She had to get ready for work, had to put on the face she wore every day outside these walls, had to say "Yes ma'am" and "No sir" and wrap the burgers just so and the people who bought them never knew who she had been, they never guessed, no never never in a million years did they guess she would rather cut their throats than look at them. Robby was screaming, the apartment was filling up with screaming, somebody was knocking on the wall, and her own throat was raw.

"YOU WANT TO CRY?" she shouted, holding the struggling infant under one arm. "I'LL MAKE YOU CRY!"

She knocked the pot off the stovetop, and turned the burner up to high.

Still Robby, a bad seed, screamed and fought against her will. She didn't want to do this, it hurt her heart, but what good was a baby who didn't mind his mother? "Don't make me do it!" She shook Robby like a fleshy rag. "Don't make me hurt you!" His face was contorted, his scream so high it was almost inaudible, but Mary could feel its pressure sawing at her skull. "Don't make me!" she warned, and then she held him by the scruff of his neck and slapped his face.

Behind her the burner was beginning to glow.

Robby would not bend to her will. He would not be quiet, and somebody might call the pigs, and if that happened . . .

A fist was hammering on the wall. Robby flailed and kicked. He was trying to break her, and that could not be tolerated.

She felt her teeth grind together, the blood pulsing in her temples.

Little drops of crimson ran from Robby's nose, and his scream was like the voice of the world at the end of time.

Mary made a low, moaning sound, deep in her throat. She turned toward the stove and pressed the baby's face against the red-hot burner.

The little body writhed and jerked. She felt the terrible heat rising past him, washing into her own face. Robby's scream went on and on, his legs thrashing. She kept her hand pressed hard on the back of his head, there were tears in her eyes, and she was sick at heart because Robby had always been such a good baby.

His struggling ceased, and his scream ended with a sizzle.

The baby's head was melting.

Mary watched it happen as if she were outside her body looking down, a remote bystander cool in her curiosity. Robby's head was shrinking, little sparks of flame kicking up, and the pink flesh running in glistening strands. She could feel the heat beneath her hand. He was quiet now. He had learned who was in control.

She pulled him up off the burner, but most of his face stayed on the hot coils in a crisp black inside-out impression. Robby was dead.

"Hey, you crazy freak!" A voice through the thin wall. The old man next door, the one who went out on the highway collecting aluminum cans in a garbage bag. *Shecklett,* the name on his mailbox said. "Stop that hollerin' or I'll call the cops! Hear me?"

Mary stared at the black-edged hole where Robby's face had been. The head was full of smoke. Plastic sparked on the burner, and the kitchen was rank with the sickeningly sweet smell of another infant's death.

"Shut up and let a man sleep!" He struck the wall again, and the pictures of babies clipped from magazines and mounted in dimestore frames jumped on their nails.

Mary stood looking at the doll, her mouth half open and her gray eyes glassy. This one was gone. This one was ready for heaven. But he'd been such a good boy. She'd thought he was the best of them all. She wiped her eyes with a sluggish hand, and turned off the burner. Bits of plastic flamed and popped, a haze of blue smoke filming the air like the breath of ghosts.

She took the doll to a closet in the hallway. At the back of the closet was a cardboard box, and in that box were the dead babies. The signature of her rage lay here. Some of the dolls had been burned faceless, like Robby. Others had been decapitated, or were torn limb from limb. Some bore the marks of being crushed under tires, and some had been ripped open by knives or razors. All of them were little boys, and all of them had been her loves.

She peeled the sleepsuit with its yellow ducks off Robby. She held Robby with two fingers, like something filthy, and she dropped him into the box of death. She shoved the box into the back of the closet again, then she closed the door.

She put away the wooden crate that had served as a crib, and she was alone.

An eighteen-wheeler swept past on the highway, making the walls creak. Mary went into the bedroom with the slow gait of a sleepwalker. Another death freighted her soul. There had been so many of them. So many. Why didn't they mind her? Why did they always have to fight her will? It wasn't right that she fed them and clothed them and loved them and they died hating her in the end.

She wanted to be loved. More than anything in the world. Was that too much to ask?

Mary stood at the window for a long time, looking out at the highway. The trees were bare. Bleak January had gnawed the land, and it seemed that winter ruled the earth.

She dropped the sleepsuit into the clothes hamper in her bathroom. Then she walked to her dresser, opened the bottom drawer, reached under some folded-up sweaters, and found the Colt Snubnose .38. The shine had worn off, and in the six-bullet cylinder there was one shell.

Mary turned on the television set. The early morning cartoons from TBS were on. Bugs Bunny and Elmer Fudd. In the blue glow, Mary sat on the edge of her rumpled bed and spun the cylinder: once, twice, and a third time.

She drew a long, deep breath, and she pressed the Colt's barrel against her right temple.

"C'mere, ya cwazy wabbit!"

"Who, me?"

"Yeah, you!"

"Ahhhhhh, what's up, d—"

She squeezed the trigger.

The hammer clicked on an empty chamber.

Mary let her breath go, and she smiled.

Her heart was beating hard, driving the sweet adrenaline through her body. She returned the pistol to its place beneath the sweaters, and she slid the drawer shut. Now she felt so much better, and Robby was just a bad memory. But she couldn't survive long without a baby to care for. No, she was a natural mother. An earth mother, it had once been said. She needed a new baby. She'd found Robby in a Toys 'R Us in Douglasville. She knew better than to go to the same store twice; she still had eyes in the back of her head, and she was always watching for any sign of the pigs. So she'd find another toy store. No sweat.

It was almost time to get ready for work. She needed to relax, and put on the face she wore beyond these walls. It was her Burger King face, smiling and friendly, no trace of steel in her eyes. She stood before the mirror in the bathroom, the harsh incandescent bar of light switched on, and she slowly let the face emerge. "Yes ma'am," she said to the person in the mirror. "Would you like fries with that, ma'am?" She cleared her throat. The voice needed to be a little higher, a little dumber. "Yes sir, thank you sir! Have a nice day!" She switched her smile off and on, off and on. Cattle needed to see smiles; she wondered if the people who worked in slaughterhouses smiled before they smashed the skulls of cattle with big wooden mallets.

The smiley face stayed on. She looked younger than her forty-one years, but there were deep lines at the corners of her eyes. Her long hair was no longer as blond as the summer sun. It was a mousy brown, streaked with gray. It would go up in a tight bun when she got to work. Her face was square and strong-jawed, but she could make it look weak and afraid, like a cow who senses the breaking of skulls in the long line ahead. There wasn't much she couldn't do with her face if she wanted. She could look old or young, timid or defiant. She could be an aging California girl or a backwoods hick with equal ease. She could slump her shoulders and look like a frightened schmuck, or she could stand at her full Amazonian height and dare any sonofamotherfuckingbitch to cross her path. It was all in the attitude, and she hadn't gone to drama school in New York City for nothing.

Her real name was not the name on her Georgia driver's license, her library card, her cable TV bills, or any of the mail that came to her apartment. Her real name was Mary Terrell. She remembered what they used to call her as they passed the joints and the cheap red wine and sang songs of freedom: Mary Terror.

She had been wanted for murder by the FBI since the spring of 1969.

Sergeant Pepper was dead. G.I. Joe lived on. George Bush was president, movie stars were dying from AIDS, kids were smoking crack in the ghettos and the suburbs, Muslims were blowing airliners from the skies, rap music ruled, and nobody cared much about the Movement anymore. It was a dry and dusty thing, like the air in the graves of Hendrix, Joplin, and God. She was letting her thoughts take her into treacherous territory, and the thoughts threatened her smiley face. She stopped thinking about the dead heroes, the burning breed who made the bombs full of roofing nails and planted them in corporate boardrooms and National Guard armories. She stopped thinking before the awful sadness crushed her.

The sixties were dead. The survivors limped on, growing suits and neckties and potbellies, going bald and telling their children not to listen to that satanic heavy metal. The clock of the Age of Aquarius had turned, hippies and yippies had become preppies and yuppies. The Chicago Seven were old men. The Black Panthers had turned gray. The Grateful Dead were on MTV, and the Airplane had become a top-forty Starship.

Mary Terror closed her eyes, and thought she heard the noise of wind whistling through the ruins.

I need, she thought. *I need.* A single tear coursed slowly down her left cheek.

I need something to call mine.

She opened her eyes and stared at the woman in the mirror. Smile! Smile! Her smile ticked back on. "Thank you, sir. Would you like an ice-cold Pepsi with that burger?"

Her eyes were still hard, a chink in the disguise. She'd have to work on that.

She took off her plaid robe, stained by the applesauce that a convulsive jerk of her wrist had spilled upon it, and she looked at her nude body in the mean light. Her smile faded and went away. Her body was pale and loose, flabby around the belly, hips, and thighs. Her breasts sagged, the nipples grayish-brown. They looked empty. Her gaze fixed on the network of old scars that crisscrossed her stomach and her right hip, the ridges of scar tissue snaking down into the dark brown nest between her thighs. She ran her fingers over the scars, and felt their cruelty. What was inside her, she knew, were worse scars. They ran deep, and they had ravaged her soul.

Mary remembered when her body had been young and tight. He hadn't been able to keep his hands off her. She remembered the hot thrust of him inside her, when they were both flying on acid and the love went on forever. She remembered candles in the dark, the smell of strawberry incense, and the Doors—God's band—on the record player. Long time past, she thought. The Woodstock Nation had become the Pepsi Generation. Most of the outlaws had surfaced for air, had served their time in the cages of political restitution, put on the suits of the Mindfuck State, and joined the herd of cattle marching to the slaughterhouse.

But not him. Not Lord Jack.

And not her, either.

She was still Mary Terror down beneath the soft fastfood-puffed flesh. Mary Terror was sleeping inside her body, dreaming of what was and what might have been.

The alarm clock went off in the bedroom. Mary silenced the jangle with a slap of her palm, and she turned on the cold water tap in the shower and stepped into the bitter flood. When she had finished showering and drying her hair, she dressed in her Burger King uniform. She'd been working at Burger King for eight months, had reached the level of assistant day manager, and beneath her was a crew of kids who didn't know Che Guevara from Geraldo Rivera. That was all right with her; they'd never heard of the Weather Underground, or the Storm Front either. To those kids she was a divorced woman trying to make ends meet. That was all right. They didn't know she could make a bomb out of chicken shit and kerosene, or that she could fieldstrip an M16 or shoot a pig in the face with as little hesitation as flicking a fly.

Better that they stay dumb than be dead.

She turned off the TV. Time to go. She picked up a yellow Smiley Face button from atop her dresser and pinned it to the front of her blouse. Then she put on her brown overcoat, got her purse with its credentials that identified her as Ginger Coles, and opened the door into the cold, hated outside world.

Mary Terror's rusted, beat-up blue Chevy pickup was in the parking lot. She caught a glimpse of Shecklett, watching her from his window, pulling back when he realized he'd been seen. The old man's eyes were going to get him in trouble someday. Maybe real soon.

She drove away from the apartment complex, merged with the morning traffic heading into Atlanta from the small country towns around it, and none of the other drivers guessed she was a six-foot-tall time bomb ticking steadily toward explosion.

I

Scream of the Butterfly

1.

A Safe Place

The baby kicked. "Oh!" Laura Clayborne said, and touched her swollen belly. "There he goes again!"

"He'll be a soccer player, I'm telling you." Across the table, Carol Mazer picked up her glass of chardonnay. "So anyway, Matt tells Sophia her work is shoddy, and Sophia hits the roof. You know Sophia's temper. I swear, honey, you could hear the windows shake. We thought it was Judgment Day. Matt ran back to his office like a whipped puppy, but somebody's got to stand up to that woman, Laura. I mean, she's running the whole show over there, and her ideas absolutely—pardon my French—but they absolutely *suck."* She took a sip of wine, her dark brown eyes shining with the pleasure of a gossip well told. Her hair was a riot of black ringlets, and her red fingernails looked long enough to pierce to the heart. "You're the only one she's ever listened to, and with you off the track the whole place is falling to pieces. Laura, I swear she's out of control. God help us until you can get back to work."

"I'm not looking forward to it." Laura reached for her own drink: Perrier with a twist of lime. "Sounds like everybody's gone crazy over there." She felt the baby kick once more. A soccer player, indeed. The child was due in two weeks, more or less. Around the first of February, Dr. Bonnart had said. Laura had given up her occasional glass of wine the first month of her pregnancy, way back at the beginning of a long hot summer. Also forsaken, after a much harder struggle, was her habit of a pack of cigarettes a day. She had turned thirty-six in November, and this would be her first child. A boy, for sure. He'd displayed a definite penis on the sonogram. Some days she was almost stupid with happiness and other days she felt a dazed dread of the unknown perched on her shoulder, picking at her brain like a raven. The house was filled with baby books, the guest bedroom—once known as Doug's study—had been painted pale blue and his desk and IBM PC hauled out in favor of a crib that had belonged to her grandmother.

It had been a strange time. Laura had been hearing the ticking of her biological clock for the last four years, and everywhere she looked it seemed she saw women with strollers, members of a different society. She was happy and excited, yes, and sometimes she did think she actually looked radiant—but other times she simply found herself wondering whether or not she'd ever play tennis again, or what she was going to do if the bloat didn't melt away. The horror stories abounded, many of them supplied by Carol, who was seven years her junior, twice married, and had no children. Grace Dealey had ballooned up with her second child, and now all she did was sit around and wolf down boxes of Godiva chocolates. Lindsay Fortanier couldn't control her twins, and the children ran the household like the offspring of Attila the Hun and Marie Antoinette. Marian Burrows had a little red-haired girl with a temper that made McEnroe look like a pansy, and Jane Fields's two boys refused to eat anything but Vienna sausages and fish sticks. All this according to Carol, who was glad to help soothe Laura's fear of future shock.

They were sitting at a table in the Fish Market restaurant, at Atlanta's Lenox Square. The waiter came over, and Laura and Carol ordered lunch. Carol asked for a shrimp and crabmeat salad, and Laura wanted a large bowl of seafood gumbo and the poached salmon special. "I'm eating for two," she said, catching Carol's faint smile. Carol ordered another glass of chardonnay. The restaurant, an attractive place decorated in seagreen, pale violet, and pink, was filling up with the business crowd. Laura scanned the room, counting the power ties. The women wore their dark-hued suits with padded shoulders, their hair fixed in sprayed helmets, and they gave off the flashes of diamonds and the aromas of Chanel or Giorgio. This was definitely the BMW and Mercedes crowd, and the waiters hustled from table to table heeding the desires of new money and platinum American Express cards. Laura knew what businesses these people were in: real estate, banking, stockbrokerage, advertising, public relations—the hot professions of the New South. Most of them were living on plastic, and leasing the luxury cars they drove, but appearance was everything.

Laura suddenly had an odd vision as Carol talked on about the calamities at the newspaper. She saw herself walking through the doors of the Fish Market, into this rarefied air. Only she was not as she was now. She was no longer well-groomed and well-dressed, her nails French-manicured and her chestnut-brown hair drawn back with an antique golden clip to fall softly around her shoulders. She was as she had been when she was eighteen years old, her light blue eyes clear and defiant behind her granny glasses. She wore ragged bellbottom jeans and a blouse that looked like a faded American flag, and on her feet were sandals made from car tires, like the sandals the Vietnamese wore in the news films. She wore no makeup, her long hair limp and in need of brushing, her face adamant with anger. Buttons were stuck to her blouse: peace signs, and slogans like STOP THE WAR, IMPERIALIST AMERIKA, and POWER TO THE PEOPLE. All conversations of interest rates, business mergers, and ad campaigns abruptly ceased as the hippie who had once been Laura Clayborne—then Laura Beale—strode defiantly into the center of the restaurant, sandals thwacking against the carpeted floor. Most of the people here were in their mid-thirties to early forties. They all remembered the protest marches, the candlelight vigils, and the draft card burnings. Some of them, perhaps, had been on the front lines with her. But now they gaped and sneered, and some laughed nervously. "What happened?"

she asked them as forks slid into bowls of seafood gumbo and hands stopped halfway to their glasses of white wine. "What the hell happened to all of us?"

The hippie couldn't answer, but Laura Clayborne knew. We got older, she thought. We grew up and took our places in the machine. And the machine gave us expensive toys to play with, and Rambo and Reagan said don't worry, be happy. We moved into big houses, bought life insurance, and made out our wills. And now we wonder, deep in our secret hearts, if all the protest and tumult had a point. We think that maybe we could have won in Vietnam after all, that the only equality among men is in the wallet, that some books and music should be censored, and we wonder if we would be the first to call out the Guard if a new generation of protesters took to the streets. Youth yearned and burned, Laura thought. Age reflected, by the ruddy fireplaces.

". . . wanted to cut his hair short and let one of those rat-tail things hang down in back." Carol cleared her throat. "Earth to Laura! Come in, Laura!"

She blinked. The hippie went away. The Fish Market was a placid pool again. Laura said, "I'm sorry. What were you saying?"

"Nikki Sutcliff's little boy, Max. Eight years old, and he wanted to crop his hair and have a rat-tail. And he loves that rap junk, too. Nikki won't let him listen to it. You can't believe the dirty words on records these days! You'd better think about that, Laura. What are you going to do if your little boy wants to cut all his hair off and go around bald-headed and singing obscene songs?"

"I think," she answered, "that I'll think about it later."

The salad and the gumbo were served. Laura listened as Carol talked on about politics in the Atlanta *Constitution*'s Life and Style department. Laura was a senior reporter specializing in social news and doing book reviews and an occasional travel piece. Atlanta was a social city, of that there was no doubt. The Junior League, the Art Guild, the Opera Society, the Greater Atlanta Museum Board: those and many more demanded Laura's attention, as well as debutante parties, donations from wealthy patrons to various art and music funds, and weddings between old southern families. It was good that she was getting back to work in March, because that was when the wedding season began to blossom, swelling to its peak in mid-June. It sometimes puzzled her how quickly she'd gotten from twenty-one to thirty-six. She'd graduated with a degree in journalism from the

University of Georgia, had worked as a reporter on a small paper in her hometown of Macon for two years, then had come to Atlanta. The big-time, she'd thought. It took her over a year to get onto the copy desk of the *Constitution,* a period she'd spent selling kitchen appliances at Sears.

She'd always harbored hopes of becoming a reporter for the *Constitution.* A firebrand reporter, with iron teeth and eagle eyes. She would write stories to rip off the mask of racial injustice, destroy the slumlord, and expose the wickedness of the arms dealer. After three years of drudgery writing headlines and editing the stories of other reporters, she got her chance: she was offered a position as a metro reporter. Her first assignment was covering a shooting in an apartment complex near Braves Stadium.

Only they hadn't told her about the baby. No, they hadn't.

When it was all over, she knew she couldn't do it again. Maybe she was a coward. Maybe she'd been deluding herself, thinking she could handle it like a man. But a man wouldn't have broken down and cried. A man wouldn't have thrown up right there in front of the police officers. She remembered the shriek of an electric guitar, the volume turned up and roaring over the parking lot. It had been a hot, humid night in July. A terrible night, and she still saw it sometimes in her worst dreams.

She was assigned to the social desk. Her first assignment there was covering the Civitans Stars and Bars Ball.

She took it.

Laura knew other reporters, men and women who did their jobs well. They crowded around the distraught relatives of plane-crash victims and stuck microphones in their faces. They went to morgues to count bullet holes in bodies, or stood in gloomy forests while the police hunted for pieces of murder victims. She watched them grow old and haggard, searching for some kind of purpose amid the carnage of life, and she'd decided to stay on the social desk.

It was a safe place. And as she got older, Laura realized that safe places were hard to find, and if the money was good as well, then wasn't that the best a person could do?

She wore a dark blue suit not unlike the outfits worn by the other businesswomen in the restaurant, though hers was maternity-tailored. In the parking lot was her gray BMW. Her husband of eight years was a stockbroker with Merrill Lynch in midtown Atlanta, and together they made over a hundred thousand dollars a year. She used Estée

Lauder cosmetics, and she shopped for clothes and accessories in the tony little boutiques of Buckhead. She went to a place where she got manicures and pedicures, and another place where she took steambaths and had massages. She went to ballets, operas, art galleries, and museum parties, and most of the time she went alone.

Doug's work claimed him. He had a car phone in his Mercedes, and when he was home he was constantly making or receiving calls. That was a camouflage, of course. They both knew it was more than work. They were caring toward each other, like two old friends might be who had faced adversity and fought through it together, but what they had could not be called love.

"So how's Doug?" Carol asked. She'd known the truth for a long time. It would be hard to hide the truth from someone as sharp-eyed as Carol, and anyway, they both knew many other couples who lived together in a form of financial partnership.

"He's fine. Working a lot." Laura took another bite of her gumbo. "I hardly see him except on Sunday mornings. He's started playing golf on Sunday afternoons."

"But the baby's going to change things, don't you think?"

"I don't know. Maybe it will." She shrugged. "He's excited about the baby, but . . . I think he's scared, too."

"Scared? Of what?"

"Change, I guess. Having someone new in our lives. It's so strange, Carol." She placed a hand against her stomach, where the future lived. "Knowing that inside me is a human being who'll—God willing—be on this earth long after Doug and I are gone. And we've got to teach that person how to think and how to live. That kind of responsibility is scary. It's like . . . we've just been playing at being grown-ups until now. Can you understand that?"

"Sure I can. That's why I never wanted children. It's a hell of a job, raising kids. One mistake, and bam! You've either got a wimp or a tyrant. Jesus, I don't know how anybody can raise kids these days." She downed a hefty drink of chardonnay. "I don't think I'm the mothering type, anyway. Hell, I can't even housebreak a puppy."

That much was certainly true. Carol's Pomeranian had no respect for Oriental carpets and no fear of a rolled-up newspaper. "I hope I'm a good mother," Laura said. She felt herself approaching inner shoals. "I really do."

"You will be. Don't worry about it. You definitely *are* the mothering type."

"Easy for you to say. I'm not so sure."

"I am. You mother the hell out of me, don't you?"

"Maybe I do," Laura agreed, "but that's because you need some-body to kick you in the tail every now and again."

"Listen, you're going to be a fantastic mother. Mother of the year. Hell, mother of the century. You're going to be up to your nose in Pampers and you're going to love it. And you watch what happens to Doug when the baby comes, too."

Here lay the real rocks, on which boats of hope could be broken to pieces. "I've thought about that," Laura said. "I want you to know that I'm not having this baby so Doug and I can stay together. That's not it at all. Doug has his own life, and what he does makes him happy." She traced money signs on the misty glass of Perrier. "One night I was at home reading. Doug had gone to New York on business. I was supposed to cover the Ball of Roses the next day. It struck me how alone I was. You were in Bermuda, on vacation. I didn't want to talk to Sophia, because she doesn't like to listen. I tried four or five people, but everybody was out somewhere. So I sat there in the house, and do you know what I realized?"

Carol shook her head.

"I don't have anything," Laura said, "that's mine."

"Oh, right!" Carol scoffed. "You've got a three-hundred-thousand-dollar house, a BMW, and a closetful of clothes I'd die to get my hooks into! So what else do you need?"

"A purpose," Laura answered, and her friend's wry smile faded.

The waiter brought their lunches. Soon afterward, three women entered the restaurant, one of them pushing a stroller, and they were seated a few tables away from Laura and Carol. Laura watched the mother—a blond-haired woman at least ten years younger than herself, and fresh in the way that youth can only be—look down at her infant and smile like a burst of sunshine. Laura felt her own baby move in her belly, a sudden jab of an elbow or knee, and she thought of what he must look like, cradled in the swollen pink womb, his body feeding from a tube of flesh that united them. It was amazing to her that in the body within her was a brain that would hunger for knowledge. That the baby had lungs, a stomach, veins to carry his blood, reproductive organs, eyes, and eardrums. All this and so much more had been created inside her, had been entrusted to her. A new human being was about to emerge into the earth. A new person, suckled on her fluids. It was a miracle beyond the miraculous, and sometimes Laura couldn't believe it was really about to happen. But here it was, two weeks until a birth day. She watched the young mother smooth a white blanket around the infant's face, and then the woman glanced up at her. Their eyes met for a few seconds, and the two women passed a smile of recognition of labors past and yet to be.

"A purpose," Carol repeated. "If you'd wanted one of those, you could've come over and helped me paint my condo."

"I'm serious. Doug has his purpose: making money, for himself and his clients. He does a good job at it. But what do I have? Don't say the newspaper, please. I've gone about as far as I can go there. I know I'm paid well and I have a cushy job, but—" She paused, trying to put her feelings into words. "That's something anybody can do. The place won't fold if I'm not at my desk." She cut a piece of salmon but left it on her plate. "I want to be needed," she told Carol. "Needed in a way that no one else can match. Do you understand?"

"I guess so." She looked a little uncomfortable at this personal revelation.

"It doesn't have anything to do with money or possessions. Not the house, not the car, not clothes or anything else. It's having someone who needs you, day and night. That's what I want. And, thank God, that's what I'm going to have."

Carol was attacking her salad. "I still say," she observed, a shred of crabmeat on her fork, "that a puppy would have been less expensive. And puppies don't want to shave all their hair off except for a rat-tail hanging down in back, either. They don't like punk rock and heavy metal, they don't chase girls, and they won't get their front teeth knocked out at football practice. Oh, Jesus, Laura!" She reached across the table and gripped Laura's hand. "Swear you won't name him Bo or Bubba! I won't be godmother to a kid who chews tobacco! Swear it, okay?"

"We've decided on a name," Laura said. "David. After my grandfather."

"David." Carol repeated it a couple of times. "Not Davy or Dave, right?"

"Right. David."

"I like that. David Clayborne. President of the Student Government Association, the University of Georgia, nineteen . . . oh Lord, when would that be?"

"Wrong century. Try twenty ten."

Carol gasped. "I'll be ancient!" she said. "Shriveled up and ancient!

I'd better get some pictures made so David'll know how pretty I used to be!"

Laura had to laugh at Carol's expression of merry terror. "I think you've got plenty of time for that."

They veered away from talking about the forthcoming new arrival, and Carol, who was also a reporter on the *Constitution*'s social desk, entertained Laura with more tales from the trenches. Then her lunch break was over, and it was time for Carol to get back to work. They said good-bye in front of the restaurant as the valets brought their cars, and then Laura drove home while cold drizzle fell from a gray winter sky. She lived about ten minutes away from Lenox Square, on Moore's Mill Road off West Paces Ferry. The white brick house was on a small plot of land with pine trees in front. The place wasn't large, particularly in comparison to the other houses in the area, but it had carried a steep price tag. Doug had said he'd wanted to live close to the city, so when they found the property through the friend of a friend they'd been willing to spend the money. Laura pulled into the two-car garage, opened an umbrella, and walked back out to the mailbox. Inside were a half-dozen letters, the new issue of *The Atlantic Monthly,* and catalogues from Saks and Barnes and Noble. Laura went back into the garage and pressed the code numbers in on the security system, then she unlocked a door that led into the kitchen. She shed her raincoat and looked through the letters. Electric bill, water bill, a letter whose envelope read MR. AND MRS. CLEYBURN YOU HAVE WON AN ALL-EXPENSES-PAID TRIP TO DISNEY WORLD!, and three more letters that Laura held on to after she'd pushed aside the bills and the desperate come-on for the sale of Florida swampland. She walked through a hallway into the den, where she punched on the answering machine to check her messages.

Beep. "This is Billy Hathaway from Clements Roofing and Gutter Service, returnin' your call. Missed you, I guess. My number's 555-2142. Thanks."

Beep. "Laura, it's Matt. I just wanted to make sure you got the books. So you're going to lunch with Carol today, huh? Are you a glutton for punishment? Have you decided to name the kid after me? Talk to you later."

Beep. Click.

Beep. "Mrs. Clayborne, this is Marie Gellsing from Homeless Aid of Atlanta. I wanted to thank you for your kind contribution and the reporter you sent to give us some publicity. We really need all the help we can get. So thanks again. Good-bye."

And that was it.

Laura walked over to the tapedeck, pushed in a tape of Chopin piano preludes, and eased herself down in a chair as the first sparkling notes began to play. She opened the first letter, which was from Help for Appalachia. It was a note requesting aid. The second letter was from Fund for Native Americans, and the third was from the Cousteau Society. Doug said she was a sucker for causes, that she was on a national mailing list of organizations that made you think the world would collapse if you didn't send a check to prop it up. He believed most of the various funds and societies were already rich, and you could tell that because of the quality of their paper and envelopes. Maybe ten percent of contributions get where they're supposed to go, Doug had told her. The rest, he said, went to accounting fees, salaries, building rents, office equipment, and the like. So why do you keep sending them more money?

Because, Laura had told him, she was doing what she thought was right. Maybe some of the funds she donated to were shams, maybe not. But she wasn't going to miss the money, and it all came from her newspaper salary.

But there was another reason she gave to charities, and perhaps it was the most important one. Purely and simply, she felt guilty that she had so much in a world where so many suffered. But the hell of it was that she enjoyed her manicures, her steambaths, and her nice clothes; she'd worked hard for them, hadn't she? She deserved her pleasures, and anyway she'd never used cocaine or bought animal-skin coats and she'd sold her stock in the company that did so much business in South Africa. And had made a lot of profit from the sale, too. But Jesus, she was thirty-six years old! Thirty-six! Didn't she deserve the fine things she'd worked so hard for?

Deserve, she thought. Who really deserved anything? Did the homeless deserve to shiver in alleys? Did the harp seals deserve to be clubbed and slaughtered? Did the homosexual deserve AIDS, or the wealthy woman deserve a fifteen-thousand-dollar designer dress? *Deserve* was a dangerous word, Laura thought. It was a word that built barriers, and made wrong seem right.

She put the letters aside, on a small table next to her checkbook.

A package of four books had come in the mail yesterday, sent from Matt Kantner at the *Constitution.* Laura was supposed to read them and do reviews for the Arts and Leisure section over the next month or so. She'd scanned them yesterday, when she'd been sitting by the fireplace and the rain was coming down outside. There was the new novel by Anthony Burgess, a nonfiction book on Central America, a novel about Hollywood called *The Address*, and a fourth nonfiction work that had instantly caught her attention.

Laura picked it up from where it sat beside her chair with a bookmark in it. It was a thin book, only one hundred and seventy-eight pages, and not very well produced. The covers were already warping, the paper was of poor quality, and though the pub date was 1989, the book had a faintly moldy smell. The publisher's name was Mountaintop Press, based in Chattanooga, Tennessee. The title was *Burn This Book*, by Mark Treggs. There was no author's picture on the back, only an ad for another book about edible mushrooms and wildflowers, also written by Mark Treggs.

Looking through *Burn This Book* brought back some of the feelings that had surfaced when she was sitting in the Fish Market. Mark Treggs, as recounted in the slim memoir, had been a student at Berkeley in 1964, and had lived in Haight-Ashbury in San Francisco during the era of love-ins, long hair, free LSD, happenings, and skirmishes with the police in Peoples' Park. He wrote wistfully of communes, of crash pads hazed with marijuana fumes, where discussions of Allen Ginsburg poems and Maoist theories mingled into abstract philosophies of God and nature. He talked about draft card burnings, and massive marches against Vietnam. When he described the smell and sting of tear gas, he made Laura's eyes water and her throat feel raw. He made that time seem romantic and lost, a communion of outlaws battling for the common cause of peace. Seen in hindsight, though, Laura realized there was as much struggle for power between the various factions of unrest as there was between the protesters and the Establishment. In hindsight, that era was not as romantic as it was tragic. Laura thought of it as the last scream of civilization, before the Dark Ages set in.

Mark Treggs talked about Abbie Hoffman, the SDS, Altamont, flower power, the Chicago Seven, Charles Manson and the White Album, the Black Panthers, and the end of the Vietnam War. As the book went on, his writing style became more confused and less pointed, as if he were running out of steam, his voice dwindling as had the voices of the Love Generation. At the midpoint, he called for an organization of the homeless and a rising up against the powers of

Big Business and the Pentagon. The symbol of the United States was no longer the American flag, he said, it was a money sign against a field of crosses. He advocated demonstrations against the credit card companies and the TV evangelists; they were partners, Treggs believed, in the stupefaction of America.

Laura closed *Burn This Book* and laid it aside. Some people probably would heed the title, but the volume was most likely fated to molder in the cubbyhole bookstores run by holdover hippies. She'd never heard of Mountaintop Press before, and from the looks of their production work they were only a small regional outfit with not a whole lot of experience or money. Little chance of the book being picked up by mainstream publishers, either; this sort of thing was definitely out of fashion.

She put her hands to her stomach and felt the heat of life. What would the world be like by the time David reached her age? The ozone layer might be gone by then, and the forests gnawed bare by acid rain. Who knew how much worse the drug wars could get, and what new forms of cocaine the gangs could flood the streets with? It was a hell of a world to bring a child into, and for that she felt guilty, too. She closed her eyes and listened to the soft piano music. Once upon a time, Led Zeppelin had been her favorite band. But the stairway to heaven had broken, and who had time for a whole lotta love? Now all she wanted was harmony and peace, a new beginning: something real that she could cradle in her arms. The sound of amplified guitars reminded her too much of that hot July night, in the apartments near the stadium, when she watched a woman crazy on crack put a gun to a baby's head and blow the infant's brains out in a steamy red shower.

Laura drifted amid the piano chords, her hands folded across her belly. The rain was falling harder outside. The gutters that needed repairs would soon be flooding. But in the house it was safe and warm, the security system was on, and for the moment Laura's world was a sanctuary. Dr. Bonnart's number was close at hand. When the time came, she'd deliver the baby at St. James Hospital, which was about two miles from the house.

My baby is on the way, she thought.

My baby.

Mine.

Laura rested as the silvery music of another age filled the house and rain began to slam down on the roof.

* * *

And at a K-Mart near Six Flags, the clerk behind the counter in the sporting goods department was just selling a boy-sized rifle called a Little Buckaroo to a customer who wore stained overalls and a battered Red Man cap. "I like the looks of that one," the man in the cap said. "I believe Cory will, too. That's my boy. Saturday's his birthday."

"I wish I'd had me a squirrel gun like this when I was a boy," the clerk said as he got the rifle, two boxes of ammunition, and a small telescopic sight ready to go. "Nothin' better than bein' out in the woods doin' a little shootin'."

"That's the truth. Got woods all around where we live, too. And plenty of squirrels, I'm tellin' you." Cory's father, whose name was Lewis Peterson, began to write out a check for the amount. He had the work-roughened hands of a carpenter. "Yeah, I believe a ten-year-old fella can handle a rifle that size, don't you?"

"Yessir, it's a beauty." The clerk copied down the necessary information and filed the form in a little metal box behind the counter. When the Buckaroo was slid into its rifle case and wrapped up, the gun was passed across the counter to Lewis Peterson. The clerk said, "There you go. Hope your boy has a happy birthday."

Peterson put the package under his arm, the receipt in full view for the security guard up front to see, and he walked out of the K-Mart into the misting afternoon rain. Cory was going to be jumping up and down on Saturday, he knew. The boy had wanted a gun of his own for some time, and this little rifle was just the thing for him. A good starter rifle.

He got in his pickup truck, a shotgun in its rack across the back window. He started the engine and turned on the windshield wipers, and he drove home feeling proud and good, his son's birthday present cradled on the seat beside him.

2.

A Careful Shopper

The big woman in the Burger King uniform pushed a cart along the aisles of the Piggly Wiggly supermarket. She was at the Mableton Shopping Center about a quarter mile from her apartment. On her blouse she wore a yellow Smiley Face button. Her hair, shiny with smoke and grease from the grills, hung loosely around her shoulders. Her face was composed and calm, without expression. She picked out cans of soup, corned beef hash, and vegetables. At the frozen food section she chose a few TV dinners and a box of Weight Watchers chocolate fudge bars. She moved methodically and carefully, as if powered by a tense inner spring. She had to stop for a moment and breathe the chill air where the meat was kept, because she had the sensation that the store's air was too thick for her lungs. She smelled the blood of fresh slaughters.

Then Mary Terror went on, a careful shopper who checked prices and ingredients. Foods could be full of poisons. She avoided boxes with scraped sides or cans that had been dented. Every once in a while she paused to look over her shoulder and gauge who might be following her. The FBI bastards wore masks of human skin that they could peel on and off, and they could make themselves look young or old, fat or skinny, tall or short. They were lurking everywhere, like cockroaches in a filthy house.

But she didn't think she was being followed today. Sometimes the back of her neck tingled and goose bumps rose on her arms, and it was then she knew that the pigs were near. Today, though, there were only housewives and a couple of farmer types buying groceries. She checked their shoes. The pigs always wore shined shoes. Her alarm system was silent. Still, you never knew, and that was why she had a Compact Off-Duty Police pistol in the bottom of her purse that weighed twenty-eight ounces and packed four .357 Magnum bullets. She stopped by the wine section and picked a cheap bottle of sangria. Then it was on to select a bag of pretzels and a box of Ritz crackers. The next stop was an aisle over, where the jars of baby food were.

Mary pushed her cart around the corner, and before her was a mother with her baby. The woman—a girl, really, maybe seventeen or eighteen—had her child strapped into a bassinet in her cart. She had red hair and freckles, and the baby had a little shock of pale red hair, too. The child, dressed in a lime-green jump suit, sucked on a pacifier and stared out at the world through large blue eyes, hands and feet at war with each other. The mother, who wore a pink sweater and bluejeans, was choosing some baby food from the Gerber's shelf. That was also Mary's preferred brand.

Mary guided her cart in close and the young mother said, "Scuse me," and backed her cart off a few feet. Mary pretended to be searching for a certain food, but she was watching the red-haired infant. The girl caught her looking, and Mary snapped on a smile. "What a pretty baby," she said. She offered her hand into the cart, and the baby grasped her index finger.

"Thanks." The girl returned the smile, but uncertainly.

"Babies are a joy, aren't they?" Mary asked. She'd already checked the girl's shoes: scuffed-up sneakers. The child's fingers clenched and unclenched Mary's finger.

"Yes'm, I reckon they are. 'Course, when you got a kid, that's it, ain't it?"

"What's it?" Mary lifted her eyebrows.

"You know. A kid takes up an awful lot of time."

This was a child with a child, Mary thought. She could see the dark hollows under the young mother's eyes. You don't deserve to have a baby, Mary thought. You haven't paid your dues. Her face kept its smile. "What's his name?"

"Her name. She's a she. Amanda." The girl selected a few jars of assorted food and put them into the cart, and Mary worked her finger loose from the child's grip. "Nice talkin' to you."

"My baby likes the strained pears," Mary said, and took two jars of it off the shelf. She could feel her cheek muscles aching. "I've got a fine, healthy boy!"

The girl was already moving away, pushing the cart before her. Mary heard the soft wet noise of the baby sucking on her pacifier, and then the cart reached the end of the aisle and the girl turned to the right. Mary felt an urge to go after the girl, grab her by the shoulders, and make her listen. Tell her that the world was dark and full of evil, and it chewed up little red-haired baby girls. Tell her that the agents of Moloch Amerika lurked in every corner, and they could suck your soul out through your eyeballs. Tell her that you could walk through the most beautiful garden and hear the scream of the butterfly.

Careful, Mary thought. Be careful. She knew secrets that she should not share. No one at the Burger King knew about her baby, and that was for the best. She got control of herself, like the clamping down of a lid, and she chose a few more jars of various flavors, put them into the cart, and went on. Her index finger still had the heat of the infant's touch in it.

She paused at the magazine rack. The new *Rolling Stone* was in. On the cover was the picture of a band of young women. The Bangles. She didn't know their music. *Rolling Stone* wasn't the same magazine it used to be, when it folded over in the middle and had articles by Hunter Thompson and drawings by that weird Steadman dude who always showed people puking up their angry guts. She could relate to those drawings of rage and bile. Now *Rolling Stone* was full of glossy ads, and their politics sucked the bourgeois cock. She'd seen Eric

Clapton doing those beer commercials; if she had a bottle of it, she'd break it and cut his throat with the shards.

She put the *Rolling Stone* into her cart anyway. It was something to read, though she didn't know the new music or the new bands. Used to be she consumed the *Stone* from cover to cover, when it was a rag and the heroes were still alive. They had all burned out young, and that was why they were called stars. All young and dead, and she was still alive and older. She felt cheated sometimes. She felt as if she'd missed a train that would not come again, and she was still haunting the station with an unpunched ticket.

Through the checkout line. New cashier. Acne on her cheeks. Get out the checkbook, the checks in the name of Ginger Coles. Careful, keep the gun down in the bottom of the purse. Write out the amount. Damn, buying groceries fucks up a budget! Sign it. Ginger Coles. "There you go," she told the girl as she pushed the check and her driver's license forward. The license showed her smiling picture, her hair combed back and cut a little shorter than it was now. She had a strong face with a straight, narrow nose and a high forehead. Depending on the light and the clothes she wore, the color of her eyes shifted from pale green to frosty gray. She watched the cashier write down her license number on the back of the check. "Place of employment?" the girl asked, and Mary said, "United Parcel—" She stopped herself. A whirl of identities was spinning through her mind, like a little universe. No, not United Parcel Service. She'd worked there under another name from 1984 to 1986, at the shipping warehouse in Tampa. "Sorry," she said as the cashier stared blankly at her. "That's my old job. I'm the assistant day manager at a Burger King."

"Oh, yeah?" The girl's eyes showed a little interest. "Which one?"

A cold spear went through Mary's heart. She felt her smile slip a notch. "In Norcross," she said, which was a lie. She worked at the location on Blessingham Road, about six miles away.

"I just got this job," the cashier said, "but the pay ain't nothin'. You do the hirin' and all?"

"No." The acne might be makeup, Mary thought. The girl might not be as young or as dumb as she looked. "The manager does that." Her hand slid partway into her purse, and she could feel the chill of the pistol's metal with her fingertips.

"I don't like just standin' around. I like to be movin'. You need any help over there?"

"No. We've got all the help we need."

The girl shrugged. "Well, maybe I'll come in and fill out an application anyway. You get free burgers there, don't you?"

Mary sensed it. Someone coming up behind her. She heard a soft noise, like a gun coming out of an oiled leather holster, and her breath snagged.

She whirled around, her hand on the pistol's grip down in her purse, and she was a second away from drawing it when the red-haired young mother stopped her cart with the baby in it. The infant was still sucking wetly on the pacifier, eyes roaming back and forth.

"You okay?" the cashier asked. "Lady?"

The smile had left Mary Terror's face. For a small space of time the young mother caught a glimpse of something that made her pull the cart back and instinctively put her hand on her infant's chest in a protective gesture. What was standing before her she couldn't exactly say, because the sight was gone too soon, but she was left with the memory of the big woman's teeth clenched together and a pair of slitted eyes as green as a cat's. For those few stretching seconds the woman seemed to tower over her, and something cold came out of the big woman's skin like winter's mist.

Then it was over, as fast as a fingersnap. The clenched teeth and the slitted eyes were gone, and Mary Terror's face was bland and soft.

"Lady?" the cashier said.

"Such a pretty baby," Mary told the young mother, who didn't yet recognize what she was feeling as fear. Mary's gaze quickly scanned the area around the checkouts. She had to get out of there, and quickly. "I'm fine," she said to the cashier. "Am I ready?"

"Yeah. One sec and I'll get you sacked." The groceries went into two sacks. This was the dangerous time, Mary was thinking. If they were going to come after her, it would be when she had the groceries in her arms. She put away her license and hooked her purse over her shoulder. She left it unzipped, so she could get at the pistol in a hurry.

"My name's Toni," the cashier said. "Maybe I'll come in and fill out an application."

If she ever saw this girl again, Mary thought, she would kill her. From now on she would go to the Food Giant across the highway. She took the sacks in her arms and headed for the exit. A man in a camouflage jacket, the kind deer hunters wore, was walking across the parking lot in the nasty rain. Mary watched him carefully as she hurried to her pickup truck, but he didn't even glance at her. She put the groceries on the floorboard on the passenger side, next to the package from Art & Larry's Toys. Underneath the dashboard was a sawed-off shotgun secured by metal clips. She got behind the wheel, locked both doors, started the engine, and drove to her apartment by a circuitous route. All the time her hands were gripped hard on the steering wheel, her eyes ticking back and forth from the rearview mirror, and she hissed between gritted teeth: "Shit! Shit! Screwed up! Goddamn screwed up!" A light sheen of sweat was on her face. She took long, deep breaths. "Hold on. Take it easy, take it easy. Nobody knows you. Nobody. Nobody. Nobody knows you." She repeated it like a mantra, all the way to the red brick apartment building that had a trailer park on one side and a machine shop where truck engines were repaired on the other.

As Mary guided her pickup into her parking space, she saw a grizzled face peering out a window. It was the old man in the apartment next to hers. Shecklett was in his late sixties, and he rarely came out except to gather up the aluminum cans from the highway. He coughed a lot at night, too. She'd checked through the trash he'd brought out to the dumpster one night, and found an empty bottle of J. W. Dant bourbon, TV dinner trays, a *Cavalier* magazine with some of the ads clipped out, and pieces of a letter she'd taped together under a strong light. It was from a woman named Paula, and Mary remembered some of it: *I really would like to come visit. Would that be okay? Bill says it's fine with him. We were talking, and we can't understand why you don't come out and be with us. Ought to be ashamed, living the way you do with all that money you've saved from the store. Don't pretend you didn't. I know, Mom told me, so there. Anyway, Kevin asks about his grandpap every single day.*

As Mary pulled the handbrake up she saw Shecklett move away from the window, deeper into the darkness of his apartment. He watched her come and go as he watched the black woman upstairs and the young redneck couple on the other side of Mary's apartment. She would have wondered about the shine on his shoes if he hadn't been in the building long before Mary had moved in. Still, she didn't like being watched, being inspected and judged. When she decided it was time to leave, she might do something about Grandpap Shecklett.

Mary picked up the two sacks of groceries and took them inside. The apartment still smelled of burned plastic. The front room, paneled with pinewood, was neat and orderly; she never used it. A lava lamp cast a blue glow, the matter inside slowly coagulating and breaking apart. It made her think of semen searching for an egg. She laid the two sacks on the kitchen's countertop and flicked a dead roach off the scarred Formica. Then she went back out to get her new baby.

She heard the pickup's passenger door being opened before she reached the apartment's threshold. The door's hinges had a high, distinctive squeak. Her heart gave a violent kick, and she felt the blood swell in her face. Shecklett! He was rummaging in the truck! My baby! she thought, and she raced out the door with long, powerful strides.

Someone was leaning into the truck's passenger side. Mary grasped the door, slammed it against the offending body, and heard a wail of pain.

"Ow! Jesus Christ!" He came out of the truck, his eyes hazed with hurt, and his hand pressed against his side. "You tryin' to bust my fuckin' ribs?"

It was not Shecklett, though she was sure Shecklett was watching the drama from his window. It was Gordie Powers, who was twenty-five years old and had light brown hair that hung around his shoulders. He was as thin as a wish, his face long and gaunt, a stubble of beard on his cheeks and chin. He wore faded jeans and a flannel shirt under a battered black leather jacket decorated with metal studs. "Man!" he said. "You 'bout knocked the piss outta me!"

"I gave you a warning tap," she said. "What're you trying to steal?"

"Nothin'! I just drove up and saw you gettin' your groceries out! I thought I'd bring in the other sack for you!" He stepped away from the truck with a thin-lipped sneer. "That's what I get for bein' a Good Samaritan, huh?"

Mary glanced to the left and saw Gordie's silver Mazda sports car parked a few spaces away. She said, "Thanks anyway, but I'll get it." She picked up the package from the floorboard, and he saw the imprint ART & LARRY'S TOYS across the sack.

"What'cha gonna do?" Gordie asked. "Play games?"

Mary slammed the door and went into her apartment. Gordie followed, as she knew he would. He'd come to see her, after all. She'd placed an order last night, before Robby had been so bad. "Smells funny in here," Gordie commented as he closed the door and turned the latch. "You burn somethin'?"

"Yes. My dinner." Mary took the package into her bedroom and put it into the closet. Then, out of habit, she switched on the television set and turned it to the Cable News Network. Lynne Russell was on. Mary liked Lynne Russell because she looked like a big woman. The scene changed to a view of pig cars with their blue lights flashing, and a talking head saying something about somebody getting murdered. There was blood on a stretcher-sheet and the shape of a body. The images were hypnotic, a brutal pulse of life. Sometimes Mary watched CNN for hours on end, unable and unwilling to do anything but lie in bed like a parasite feeding off the torment of other human beings. When she was flying high on LSD, the scenes became three-dimensional and pushed into the room, and that could really be a heavy trip.

She heard the rustle of a sack. Then his voice: "Hey, Ginger! How come you got all this baby food?"

An answer had come to her by the time she walked back into the kitchen. "A cat comes around sometimes. I've been feeding it."

"A *cat?* Likes baby food? Man, I hate cats. Gimme the creeps." Gordie's beady brown eyes were always moving, invading private spaces. They found the crust of melted plastic on one of the oven's burners, registered the fact, and moved on. "Got roaches," he noticed. He walked around the kitchen as Mary put the groceries away. Gordie stopped before one of the framed magazine pictures of a smiling infant. "You got a thing about babies, huh?"

"Yes," Mary said.

"How come you don't have a kid, then?"

Keep the secret, Mary thought. Gordie was a mouse nibbling at a crumb between a tiger's fangs. "Just never did."

"You know, it's funny, huh? Been doin' business with you . . . what, five or six months? And I don't know nothin' about you." He pulled a toothpick from the pocket of his shirt and probed at his small yellow teeth. "Don't even know where you're from."

"Hell," she said.

"Whoaaaaaa." He shook his hands in the air in mock fear. "Don't scare me, sister. No, I ain't shittin'. Where're you from?"

"You mean where was I born?"

"Yeah. You ain't from around here, 'cause there ain't no Georgia peaches in your accent."

She decided she'd tell him. Maybe it was because it had been a long time since she'd said it: "Richmond, Virginia."

"So how come you're here? How come you ain't in Virginia?"

Mary stacked the TV dinners and put them in the refrigerator's freezer. Her mind was interweaving fictions. "Marriage went bad a few years ago. My husband caught me with a younger dude. He was a jealous bastard. Said he'd cut me open and leave me bleeding in the woods where nobody could find me. He said if he didn't do it, he had friends who would. So I split, and I never looked back. I kept on driving. I've been here and there, but I guess I haven't found home yet."

"Cut *you* open?" Gordie grinned around his toothpick. "I don't believe it!"

Mary stared at him.

"I mean . . . you're a mighty big lady. Take a hell of a man to get you down, huh?"

She put the jars of baby food into the cupboard. Gordie made a sucking sound on his toothpick, like the infant with the pacifier. "Anything else you want to know?" She closed the cupboard and turned to face him.

"Yeah. Like . . . how old are you?"

"Too old for any more bull shit," she said. "Did you bring my order?"

"Right here next to my heart." Gordie reached into his jacket's inside pocket and brought out a cellophane bag that held a small square of waxed paper. "Thought you might like the design." He handed the bag to Mary, and she could see what was on the paper.

Four small yellow Smiley Faces, identical to the button she wore, were spaced equidistantly on the square.

"My friend's a real artiste," Gordie said. "He can do just about any kind of design. Client wanted little airplanes the other day. Another dude asked for an American flag. Costs extra with all them colors. Anyhow, my friend enjoys his work."

"Your friend does a good job." She held the paper up against the light. The Smiley Faces were yellow with lemon-flavored food coloring, and the tiny black dots of the eyes were cheap but potent acid brewed in a lab near Atlanta. She got her wallet out of her purse, and removed the Magnum automatic, too. She laid the pistol on the countertop as she counted out fifty dollars for her connection.

"Nice little piece," Gordie said. His fingers grazed the gun. "I sure as hell got you a good deal on it, too." His hand accepted the money, and the bills went into his jeans.

Mary had bought the Magnum from him back in September, two months after she'd been steered to Gordie by a bartender in a midtown lounge called the Purple People Eater. The .38 in her drawer and the sawed-off shotgun had been purchased from other connections in the last few years. Wherever she went, Mary made the effort to find somebody who could supply her with two of her passions: LSD and guns. She'd always had a love affair with guns: their smell and weight thrilled her, their beauty dark and brooding. "Feminist cock envy" was how he'd put it, way back when. Lord Jack, speaking from the gray mist of memory.

The LSD and the guns were links to her past, and without them life would be as hollow as her womb.

"Okay. So that does it, right?" Gordie removed the toothpick and slid it back into his pocket. "Until next time?"

She nodded. Gordie started out of the kitchen, and Mary followed him with the acid-loaded Smiley Faces in her hand. When he left, she would give birth. The infant was in the closet in her bedroom, confined in a box. She would lick a Smiley Face and feed her new baby and watch the hateful world kill itself on CNN. Gordie was reaching toward the latch. Mary watched him move, as if in slow motion. She'd had so much LSD over the years that she could slow things down when she wanted to, could make them break into strobelike movements. Gordie's hand was on the latch, and he was about to open the door.

He was a skinny little bastard. A dope dealer and gun smuggler. But he was a human being, and Mary suddenly realized that she wanted to be touched by human hands.

"Wait," she said.

Gordie stopped, the latch almost thrown.

"You got plans?" Mary asked. She was ready for rejection, ready to curl back into her armored shell.

Gordie paused. He frowned. "Plans? Like plans for what?"

"Like plans to eat. Do you have anywhere to go?"

"I'm gonna pick up my girlfriend in a couple of hours." He checked his Swatch. "Give or take."

Mary held the Smiley Faces in front of his nose. "You want a taste?"

Gordie's eyes ticked from the offering to Mary and back again. "I don't know," he said. He'd caught an unspoken invitation—not for the LSD, but for something else. Maybe it was the way she crowded his space, or maybe it was the slight tilt of her head toward the bedroom. Whatever it was, Gordie knew the language. He had to

think about this for a minute; she was a client, and it was bad business
to screw clients. She wasn't a raging beauty, and she was old. Over
thirty, for sure. But he'd never sacked a six-foot-tall woman before,
and he wondered what it would be like to swim in that swamp of flesh.
She looked like she had a nice pair, too. Her face could be pretty if she
wore makeup. Still . . . there was something mighty strange about
her, with all these baby pictures on the walls and—

Hell! Gordie thought. Why not? He'd screw a tree if it had a
knothole big enough.

"Yeah," he said, his grin beginning to spread. "I guess I would."

"That's good." Mary reached past him, and double-locked the door
with its chain. Gordie smelled the aroma of hamburgers in her hair.
When she looked at him again, her face was very close and her eyes
were a shade between green and gray. "I'll make dinner, and then
we'll trip out. You like minestrone soup and ham sandwiches?"

"Sure." He shrugged. "Whatever." *Trip out,* she'd said. That was
an ancient expression. He heard it in old movies on TV about the
sixties and hippies and shit like that. He watched her as she went into
the kitchen, and in another moment he heard her run water into a
pot.

"Come in and talk to me," Mary said.

Gordie glanced at the latch and the doorchain. Still can go if you
want to. That big woman'll grind you down to white jelly if you don't
watch out. He stared at the lava lamp, his face daubed blue.

"Gordie?" Her voice was soft, as if she were speaking to a baby.

"Yeah, okay. You got any beer?" He took off his leather jacket,
threw it on the checkered sofa in the living room, and went into the
kitchen where Mary Terror was making soup and sandwiches for two.

3.

The Moment of Truth

Whbe is *this* junk?"

"What junk?"

"Here. *Burn This Book*. Have you been reading this?"

Doug walked into the kitchen where Laura had just slid the Oriental beef-and-onions casserole into the microwave. He leaned against the white counter and read from the book: " 'Like any disease, the credit card malady must be attacked with cleansing medicine. The first spoonful is a personal one: take a pair of scissors and destroy your cards. All of them. This minute. Resist the pleas of those who would have you do otherwise. Big Brother Business is watching, and you can use this opportunity to spit in his eye.'" Doug scowled and looked up. "Is this a joke, or is this Treggs guy a Communist?"

"Neither one." She closed the microwave's door and set the timer. "He was an activist in the sixties, and I think he's searching for a cause."

"Some cause! My God, if people really did this, the economy would collapse!"

"People do use their credit cards too much." She moved past Doug to the salad bowl on the countertop and began to mix the salad. "We certainly do, at least."

"Well, the whole country's heading toward being a cashless society. The sociologists have been predicting it for years." Doug paged through the book. He was a tall, slim man with sandy-brown hair and brown eyes, his face handsome but beginning to show the pressure of his work in lines and sags. He wore tortoiseshell glasses, suspenders —braces, they were called these days—with his pin-striped suits, and he had six different power ties on the rack in his closet. He was two years older than Laura, he wore a diamond pinky ring and his monogram on his shirts, he had a gold-tipped fountain pen, smoked an occasional Dunhill Montecruz cigar, and in the last year he'd begun to bite his fingernails. "We don't use our cards more than most people," he said. "Anyway, our credit's great and that's what it's all about."

"Could you get me the oil and vinegar, please?" Laura asked, and Doug reached up into the cupboard for her. She drizzled the salad and continued tossing it.

"Oh, this is ridiculous!" Doug shook his head and closed the book. "How does crap like this get printed?"

"It's from a small press. Based in Chattanooga. I've never heard of them before." She felt the baby move, a tiny movement, just a shift of weight.

"You're not going to review this, are you?"

"I don't know. I thought it might be different."

"I'd like to see what your advertisers would think of that! This guy's talking about an organized boycott of oil companies and major banks! 'Economic re-education,' he calls it." He snorted with derision. "Right, tell me another one. Want a glass of wine with dinner?"

"No, I'd better not."

"One won't hurt. Come on."

"No, really. You go ahead."

Doug opened the refrigerator, took the half bottle of Stag's Leap chablis out, and poured himself a gobletful. He swirled it around the glass, sipped at it, and then he got the salad plates down from their shelf. "So how was Carol today?"

"Fine. She filled me in on the latest trials and tribulations. The usual."

"Did you see Tim Scanlon there? He was taking a client for lunch."

"No, I didn't see anybody. Oh . . . I saw Ann Abernathy. She was there with somebody from her office."

"I wish I could take two-hour lunches." His right hand continued to spin the wine around and around the glass. "We're having a great year, but I'm telling you: Parker's got to hire another associate. I swear to God, I've got so much work on my desk it'll be August before I can get down to my blotter." Doug reached out and placed his left hand against Laura's belly. "How's he doing?"

"Kicking. Carol says he ought to be a good soccer player."

"I don't doubt it." His fingers touched here and there on her belly, seeking the infant's shape. "Can you see me being a soccer daddy? Going around town to all the games with a little rug rat? And softball in the summer. That t-ball stuff, I mean. I swear, I never pictured myself sitting in the bleachers cheering a little kid on." A frown worked itself onto Doug's face. "What if he doesn't like sports? What if he's a computer nerd? Probably make more money that way, though. Come up with a computer that teaches itself, how about that?" His frown broke, and a smile flooded back. "Hey, I think I felt him move! Did you feel that?"

"At real close range," Laura said, and she pressed Doug's hand firmly against her belly so he could feel David twitching in the dark.

They ate dinner in the dining room, where a picture window looked toward the postage-stamp-size plot of woods in back. Laura lit candles, but Doug said he couldn't see what he was eating and he turned the lights back on. The rain was still coming down outside, alternately hard and misty. They talked about the news of the day, how bad the traffic was getting on the freeways, and how the building spurt had to slow down sooner or later. Their conversation turned, as it usually did, toward Doug's work. Laura noted that his voice got tighter. She approached the idea of a vacation again, sometime in the autumn, and Doug promised he'd think about it. She had long since realized that they were not living for today any longer; they were living for a mythical tomorrow, where Doug's workload would be lighter and the pressures of the marketplace eased, their days relaxedly constructive and their nights a time of communion. She had also long since realized that it would never happen. Sometimes she had a nightmare in which they were both running on treadmills, with a machine that had teeth at their backs. They could not stop, could not slow down, or they would fall back into the teeth. It was a terrible dream because there was reality in it. Over the years she'd watched Doug climb from a junior position at his firm to a position of real responsibility. He was indispensable there. His term: indispensable. The work he brought home and the time he spent on the telephone proved it. They used to go out to dinner and the movies every weekend. They used to go dancing, and on vacations to places like the Bahamas and Aspen. Now they were lucky to get a day alone at home, and if they saw a movie it was on the VCR. The paychecks were more, yes: both his and hers had grown, but when did they have time to enjoy the fruits of their labors? She'd watched Doug age worrying about other people's portfolios, about whether they had enough long-term investments, or that international politics would drive down the dollar. He lived on a tightrope of quick decisions, above a sea of fluctuations. The success of his career was based on the worth of paper, of lists of numbers that could change dramatically overnight. The success of her own career was based on knowing the right people, on cultivating the path through the gilded gates of Atlanta's social set. But they had lost each other. They had lost the people they used to be, and that knowledge made Laura's heart ache. Which in turn made her feel incredibly guilty, because she had all the material things anyone could possibly want while people starved in the streets of the city and lived beneath overpasses in cardboard boxes.

She had lied to Carol today. When she'd said she wasn't having a baby for the reason of bringing Doug closer to her, it was a lie. Maybe it would happen. Maybe both of them would ease up, and find their way back to what used to be. The baby could do it. Having someone who was part of them could do it, and they'd find what was real again.

"I'm thinking of buying the gun tomorrow," Doug suddenly said.

The gun. They'd been talking about this for the last couple of weeks, ever since a house two blocks down the street was broken into when the family was at home asleep. In the past few months, Atlanta's crime wave had been washing closer and closer to their front door.

Laura was against having a gun in the house, but burglaries were on the rise in Buckhead and sometimes when Doug was gone at night she felt frighteningly vulnerable even with the alarm system.

"I think I'd better go ahead and do it, with the baby on the way," he continued as he picked at the casserole. "It won't be a big gun. Not a Magnum or anything." He gave a quick, nervous smile, because guns made him jumpy. "Maybe a little automatic or something. We can keep it in a drawer next to the bed."

"I don't know. I really hate the idea of buying a gun."

"I thought maybe we could take a class in gun safety. That way you'd feel better, and I would, too. I guess the gun shops or the police department teach a class."

"Great," she said with a little cynicism. "We can schedule gun class right after our prenatal class."

"I know having a gun around the house bothers you, and I feel the same way. But we've got to face reality: this is a dangerous city. Like it or not, we ought to have a gun to protect David with." He nodded, the issue settled. "Tomorrow. I'll go buy a gun tomor—"

The telephone rang. Doug had turned the answering machine off, and in his haste to get up and race to the phone in the kitchen he overturned his salad plate and spilled some of the oil and vinegar dressing on the front of his pinstriped pants. "Hello?" he said. "Yes, right here." Laura followed him into the kitchen, and she said, "Take off your pants."

"What?" Doug covered the mouthpiece. "Huh?"

"Your pants. Take them off. The oil'll set in if I don't put something on it."

"Okay." He unzipped them, unhooked the braces, and let his pants fall to his ankles. He was wearing argyle socks with his wingtips. "I'm listening," he said to the caller. "Uh-huh. Yeah." His voice was tight. He took off his shoes and then his pants and gave them to Laura. She went to the sink, ran the cold water, and rubbed some on the oil spots. The dry cleaner would have to repair the damage, but at least the oil wouldn't leave a permanent stain if she applied a little first-aid. *"Tonight?"* she heard Doug say incredulously. "No way! The paperwork isn't due until next week!"

Oh no, she thought. Her heart sank. It was the office, her constant rival. So much for Doug's night at home. Damn it, couldn't they leave him alone long enough for—

"I can't come in," Doug said. "No. Positively not." A pause. Then: "I'm at home having dinner, Eric. Cut me some slack, okay?"

Eric Parker. Doug's superior at Merrill Lynch. This was a bad sign.

"Yeah. All right." She saw his shoulders slump. "All right, just give me—" He glanced at the wall clock. "Thirty minutes. See you there." He hung up, let out a long breath, and turned toward her. "Well, that was Eric."

There was nothing she could say. Many nights he got telephone calls that stole him away from home. Like the rise of burglaries, that, too, was on the increase. "Damn," he said quietly. "It's something that has to be taken care of tonight. I'll try to be back by—" Another glance at his enemy the clock. "Two hours. Three at the most."

That meant four, Laura thought. She looked down at his less-than-muscular legs. "Better find another pair of pants, then. I'll take care of these."

Doug walked back to the master bedroom while Laura took the oil-spattered pants to the laundry room off the kitchen. She rubbed a little Gain on the spots and left Doug's pants on the dryer. Then she went to the dining room to finish her dinner, and in another moment Doug returned wearing khakis, a light blue shirt, and a gray Polo sweater. He sat down and wolfed his casserole. "I'm sorry about this," he said as he helped Laura carry the dishes into the kitchen. "I'll make it as quick as I can. Okay?"

"Okay."

He kissed her cheek, and as he leaned into her he placed his hand on her belly again. Then he was gone out the kitchen door to the garage; she heard the Mercedes start up and the garage door open. Doug backed out, the garage door closed with a *thunk,* and that was that.

She and David were alone.

"Well," she said. She looked at *Burn This Book,* there on the countertop where Doug had left it. She decided to finish it tonight and start on the Hollywood book. Then Laura scraped the dishes and put them into the dishwasher. Doug was being worked like a dog, and it wasn't fair. He was a workaholic anyway, and this pressure was only making it worse. She wondered what Eric Parker's wife, Marcy, had to say about her husband working so late on a rainy night. When had money become God? Well, there was no use fretting about it. She went into the laundry room and folded the pants over a wooden hanger. The creases weren't lined up exactly, and that imperfection would drive her nuts if she didn't correct it. Laura took the pants off the hanger and refolded them.

And something fluttered from a pocket.

It was a small green piece of paper. It came to rest on the linoleum tile near Laura's left foot.

She looked down at it.

A ticket stub.

Laura stood there with the pants halfway on the hanger. A ticket stub. She would have to pick it up, and that would require slow motion and a delicate balance. She leaned over, gripping an edge of the dryer, and retrieved the ticket. The muscles of her lower back spoke as she straightened up; they said *we've been kind with you so far, don't push it.* Laura started to throw the ticket stub into a trash can, but she paused with her hand halfway there.

What was the ticket for?

The theater's name was on it: Canterbury Six. Must be a shopping center cinema, she thought. One of those multiplexes. It was a new ticket. The green hadn't faded. Laura looked at the pants on the hanger. She reached into a pocket, found nothing but lint. Then the other pocket. Her hand brought out a third of a roll of peppermint Certs, a five-dollar bill, and a second ticket stub. Canterbury Six, it said.

She'd never been to the Canterbury Six in her life. Didn't even know where it was.

Laura wandered back into the kitchen, the two ticket stubs in her hand. Rain slapped against the windows, a brutal sound. She was trying to remember the last movie she and Doug had gone to see at a theater. It had been a couple of years, at least. She thought it had been *The Witches of Eastwick,* which was now old hat on HBO and Showtime. So why were these two ticket stubs in Doug's pocket?

She opened the phone book and looked up Theaters. The Canterbury Six was at a mall across town. She dialed the number and got a recorded message telling what films were showing: a mixture of teenage sex comedies, alien shoot-'em-ups, and Rambo clones. She put the receiver back into its cradle, and she stood staring at the clock on the kitchen wall.

Why had Doug gone to a movie and not told her? When did he have *time* to go see a movie? She knew she was skirting around the dangerous territory of the true question: whom had he gone with?

It was silly, she thought. There was a logical explanation. Sure there was. He'd taken a client to a movie. *Right.* Way across town for a drek picture? Hold it, she told herself. Stop right there, before you get crazy. There's nothing to this. Two ticket stubs. So what?

So . . . why had Doug not told her?

Laura turned on the dishwasher. It was fairly new, and made no noise but for a deep, quiet throbbing. She picked up *Burn This Book,* intending to go to the den and finish reading the philosophies and opinions of Mark Treggs. Somehow, though, she found herself at the telephone again. Nasty things, telephones were. They beckoned and whispered things that were better left unheard. But she wanted to know about the tickets. The tickets were as big as double Mt. Everests in her mind, and she couldn't see anything but their ragged edges. She had to know. She dialed the number of Doug's office.

Ring. Ring. Ring. Ring. Five times. Ten times. Then, on the fourteenth ring: "Hello?"

"Hello, this is Laura Clayborne. Is Doug there yet, please?"

"Who?"

"Doug Clayborne. Is he there yet?"

"Nobody's here, ma'am. Just us."

"Who are you?"

"I'm Wilbur," the man said. "Just us janitors here."

"Mr. Parker must be there."

"Who?"

"Eric Parker." Irritation flared. "Don't you know who works in that office?"

"There's nobody here but us, ma'am. We're just cleanin' up, that's all."

This was crazy! she thought. Even if Doug hadn't had time to get to the office yet, Eric Parker must be there! He'd called from the office, hadn't he? "When Doug Clayborne comes in," she said, "would you have him call his wife?"

"Yes ma'am, sure will," the janitor answered, and Laura said thank you and hung up.

She took *Burn This Book* into the den, put on a tape of Mozart chamber music, and sat down in a comfortable chair. Ten minutes later she was still staring at the same page, pretending to read but thinking *CanterburySixtwoticketsDougshouldbeattheofficebynowwhy hasn'thecalledwhereishe?*

Another five minutes crept past. Then ten more, an eternity. Doug's hurt! she thought. He might've had an accident in the rain! As she stood up, she felt David twitch in her belly, as if sharing her anxiety. In the kitchen, she phoned the office again.

It rang and rang and rang, and this time there was no answer.

Laura walked into the den and back into the kitchen in an aimless circle. She tried the office once more, and let the thing ring off the hook. No one picked up. She looked at the clock. Maybe Doug and Eric had gone out for a drink. But why would they do that if there was so much work to be done? Well, whatever was going on, Doug would tell her about it when he got home.

Just like he'd told her about the tickets?

Laura spun the Rolodex, and found Eric Parker's home number.

She was going to feel very dumb about this tomorrow, when Doug told her he and Eric had gone out to meet a client, or that they'd simply decided not to answer the phones while they were working. She was going to feel like crawling into a hole, for thinking—even minutely—that Doug might not be telling her the truth.

She was afraid to make the call. The gnawing little fear rose up and gripped her by the throat. She picked up the telephone, punched the first four numbers, and then put it down again. She phoned the office a third time; no answer, after at least twenty rings.

The moment of truth had arrived.

Laura took a deep breath and phoned Eric Parker's house.

On the third ring, a woman said, "Hello?"

"Hi. Marcy? It's Laura Clayborne."

"Oh, hi, Laura. I understand the time's growing near."

"Yes, it is. About two weeks, more or less. We've got the nursery all ready, so now all we're doing is waiting."

"Listen, enjoy the wait. After the baby comes, your life won't ever be the same."

"That's what I've heard." Laura hesitated; she had to go on, but it was tough. "Marcy, I'm trying to get in touch with Doug. Do you know if they went out to meet a client, or are they just not answering the phones?"

There was a few seconds of silence. Then: "I'm sorry, Laura. I don't know what you mean."

"Eric called Doug from the office. You know. To finish up some work."

"Oh." Marcy was silent again, and Laura felt her heart beating hard. "Laura . . . uh . . . Eric went to Charleston this morning. He won't be back until Saturday."

Laura felt the blood burn in her cheeks. "No, Eric called Doug from the office. About an hour ago."

"Eric's in Charleston." Marcy Parker gave a nervous laugh. "Maybe he called long distance?"

"Maybe." Laura was light-headed. The noise of the rain was a slow drumroll on the roof. "Listen . . . Marcy, I . . . shouldn't have called. I shouldn't have bothered you."

"No, it's all right." Marcy's voice was uneasy; she wanted to get off the phone. "I hope everything's fine with the baby. I mean, I know it will be, but . . . you know."

"Yes. Thank you. You take care."

"Good-bye, Laura."

Laura hung up.

She realized the music was over.

She sat in her chair in the den as rain streamed down the windows. Her hand gripped the two green ticket stubs, to a theater she'd never been to. Her other hand rested on her swollen belly, finding David's warmth. Her brain felt full of thorns, and it made thinking painful. Doug had answered the phone and talked to someone he called Eric. He'd gone to the office to work. Hadn't he? And if he hadn't, then where had he gone? Her palm was damp around the tickets. Who was Doug with if Eric was in Charleston?

Laura closed her eyes and listened to the rain. A siren wailed in the distance, the sound building and then waning. She was thirty-six years old, two weeks away from giving birth for the first time, and she realized she had been a child way too long. Sooner or later, the world would break you down to tears and regrets. Sooner or later, the world would win.

It was a mean place to bring a child into, but it was the only world there was. Laura's eyes were wet. Doug had lied to her. Stood right there and lied to her face. Damn him, he was doing something behind her back, and she was carrying their baby in her womb! Anger swelled, collapsed into sadness, built back again. Damn him! she thought. Damn him, I don't need him! I don't need any of this!

Laura stood up. She got her raincoat and her purse. She went out into the garage, grim-lipped, got into the BMW, and drove away, searching in the dark for a place where there were people, noise, and life.

4.

Mr. Mojo Has Risen

She tasted him in her mouth, like bitter almonds.

The first time, she'd wanted it because she missed it. The second time, she'd done it because she was thinking of how she could get a better rate on the acid. Now she stood in the bathroom, brushing her teeth, her hair damp around her shoulders. Her gaze followed the network of scars on her stomach, down to the ridges of scar tissue that ran between her thighs. *Freaky,* Gordie had said. *Looks like a fuckin' roadmap, don't it?* She'd been waiting for his response, steeling herself for it as she'd taken off her clothes. If he had laughed or looked

disgusted, she didn't know what she might have done. She needed
him, for what he brought her, but sometimes her anger rose up as
quick as a cobra and she knew she could reach into his eyeballs with
two hooked fingers and break his neck with her other hand before he
figured out what had hit him. She looked at her face in the mirror, her
mouth foamy with Crest. Her eyes were dark; the future was in them.

"Hey, Ginger!" Gordie called from the bedroom. "We gonna try
the acid now?"

Mary spat foam into the sink. "I thought you said you had to meet
your girlfriend."

"Aw, she can wait. Won't hurt her. I was pretty good, huh?"

"Far out," Mary said, and she rinsed her mouth and spat into the
sink again. She returned to the bedroom, where Gordie was lying on
the bed in the tangled sheet smoking a cigarette.

"How come you talk like that?" Gordie asked.

"Talk like what?"

"You know. 'Far out.' Stuff like that. Hippie talk."

"I guess because I used to be a hippie." Mary crossed the room to
the dresser, and Gordie's shiny eyes followed her through the haze of
blue smoke. On top of the dresser were the Smiley Face circles of acid.
She cut two of them away with a small pair of scissors, and she could
feel Gordie watching her.

"No shit? You used to be a hippie? Like with love beads and all
that?"

"Love beads and all that," she answered. "A long time ago."

"Ancient history. No offense meant." He puffed smoke rings into
the air, and he watched the big woman walk to the stereo. The way she
moved reminded him of something. It came to him: a lioness, silent
and deadly in one of those documentaries about Africa on TV. "You
into sports when you were younger?" he asked innocently.

She smiled slightly as she put a Doors record on the turntable and
switched on the power. "In high school. I ran track and I was on the
swim team. You know anything about the Doors?"

"The band? Yeah. They had a few hits, right?"

"The lead singer's name was Jim Morrison," Mary went on,
ignoring Gordie's stupidity. "He was God."

"He's dead now, right?" Gordie asked. "Damn, you've got a nice
ass!"

Mary set the needle down. The first staccato drumbeats of "Five to

One" began, and the raspy bass bled in. Then Jim Morrison's voice, full of grit and danger, snarled from the speakers: *Five to one, baby/ One in five/ No one here gets out alive/ You get yours, baby/ I'll get mine . . .*

The voice made memories flood through her. She had seen the Doors in concert many times, and had even seen Jim Morrison up close once, as he was going into a club on Hollywood Boulevard. She'd reached out through the crowd and touched his shoulder, felt the heat of his power course up her arm and shoulder like an electric shock, blowing her mind into the realm of golden radiance. He had glanced back at her, and for a brief second their eyes had met and locked; she had felt his soul, like a caged and beautiful butterfly. It screamed to her, wanting her to set him free, and then somebody else grabbed Jim Morrison and he was taken along in the surge of bodies.

"That's got a good beat," Gordie said.

Mary Terror cranked up the music a notch, and then she took the LSD to Gordie and gave him one of the yellow Smiley Faces. "Allll*right!*" Gordie said as he crushed his cigarette out in an ashtray beside the bed. Mary began to lick the circle, and Gordie did the same. In a few seconds the Smiley Faces were smeared and their black eyes were gone. Then Mary got onto the bed and sat in a lotus position, her ankles crossed beneath her and her wrists on her knees, her eyes closed as she listened to God and waited for the acid to work. The skin of her belly fluttered; Gordie was tracing her scars with his index finger.

"So you never said how you got all these. Were you in an accident?"

"That's right."

"What kinda accident?"

Little boy, she thought, you don't know how close you are to the edge.

"Must've been a bad one," Gordie persisted.

"Car wreck," she lied. "I got cut up by glass and metal." That much was true.

"Whoa! Heavy-duty hurt! Is that why you don't have any kids?"

Her eyes opened. Gordie's mouth was on his forehead, and his eyes were bloodred. Her eyelids drifted shut again. "What do you mean?"

"I wondered, 'cause of the baby pictures. I thought . . . you know . . . you must have a thing about kids. You can *have* kids, can't you? I mean . . . the accident didn't fuck you up, did it?"

Again, Mary's eyes opened. Gordie was growing a second head on his left shoulder. It was a warty mass just beginning to sprout a nose and chin. "You ask too many questions," she told him, and she heard her voice echo as if within a fathomless pit.

"Man!" Gordie said suddenly, his crimson eyes wide. "My hand's gettin' longer! Jesus, look at it!" He laughed, a rattle of drums that merged with the Doors' music. "My hand's fillin' up the fuckin' room!" He wriggled his fingers. "Look! I'm touchin' the wall!"

Mary watched the head taking shape on Gordie's shoulder. Its features were still indistinguishable, but the mass of flesh began to throw out cords of skin that looped around Gordie's other face, which had started to shrink and shrivel. As the Gordie-face dwindled, the new face tore itself loose and slithered across Gordie's shoulder, fastening itself onto the skull with a wet, sucking noise.

"My arms are growin'!" Gordie said. "Man, they're ten feet long!"

The air was filled with music notes spinning from the speakers like bits of gold and silver tinsel. The new face on Gordie's skull was becoming more defined, and a mane of wavy brown hair burst from the scalp and trailed down the shoulders. Sharp cheekbones pressed from the flesh, and a bastard's mouth with cruel, pouting lips. Dark eyes emerged under glowering brows.

Mary caught her breath. It was the face of God, and he said, "You get yours, baby. I'll get mine."

Jim Morrison's face was on Gordie's body. She didn't know where Gordie was, and she didn't care. She drew herself toward him, her lips straining for the pouting mouth that had spoken the truth of the ages. "Wow," she heard him whisper, and then their mouths sealed together.

She felt him slide into her, body and soul. The walls of the room were wet and red, and they pulsed to the music's drumbeat. She opened her mouth as he drove deeper into her, and a long silver ribbon trailed out that spun up and up. The air was vibrating, and she felt the notes of music prick her flesh like sharp little spikes. His hands were on her, melting into her skin like hot irons. She traced the bars of his ribs with her fingers, and his tongue came out of his face like a battering ram and tore up through the roof of her mouth to lick her brain.

His power split her, tearing her atoms asunder. He was burrowing into her as if he wanted to curl up inside her scarred belly. She saw his face again, amid a blaze of yellows and reds like a universe aflame. It was changing, melting, re-forming. Long sandy-blond hair replaced the wavy brown, and fierce blue eyes rimmed with green pushed God's eyes out of their sockets. The nose lengthened, the chin became sharper, like a spear's tip. A blond beard erupted from the cheeks and merged into a mustache. The mouth spoke in a gasp of need: "I want you. I want you. I want you."

It was him. After all this time. Lord Jack, here with her where he belonged.

She felt her heart pound and writhe, about to tear itself loose from its red roots. Lord Jack's beautiful face was above her, his eyes glowing like the sun on a tropical sea, and when she kissed him she heard the saliva hiss in their mouths like oil on a hot grill. He was filling her up, making her belly bulge. She clung to him as God sang for them. Then she was above him, grasping his stony flesh. The veins moved like worms below pale earth, and her mouth found velvet. She seized him deep, heard him groan like distant thunder, and she held him there as he twisted and drove beneath her. Then she drew back as Lord Jack convulsed and beads of moisture shivered on the flat plates of his stomach, and she watched him explode into the silver-streaked air.

He released babies: tiny, perfectly formed babies, curled-up and pink. Hundreds of them, floating like delicate pods from a wondrous flower. She grabbed at them, but they dissolved in her grip and trickled down her fingers. It was important that she catch them. Vitally important. If she did not hold at least one of them, Lord Jack wouldn't love her anymore. The babies glistened on her fingers and melted down her palms, and as she frantically tried to save at least one, she saw Lord Jack's hard flesh shrivel and withdraw. The sight terrified her. "I'll save one!" she said. Her voice crashed in her ears. "I swear, I'll save one! Okay? Okay?"

Lord Jack didn't answer. He lay on his back, on a field of tortured white, and she could see his skinny chest rising and falling like a weak bellows.

She looked at her hands. There was blood on them: dark red and thick.

She felt a sudden stabbing pain. She looked at her belly, and saw the scars ripping open and something reddish-black and hideous oozing through.

The blood was streaming from her in torrents, washing over the barren field. She heard her voice scream: "NO!" Lord Jack tried to sit up, and she caught a glimpse of his face: not Lord Jack anymore, but the pallid face of a stranger. "NO! NO!" Mary screamed. The stranger made a gasping, groaning noise and fell back again. She looked around, the red walls quivering and the music flaying her ears. She saw an open door and beyond it a toilet. The bathroom! she thought as her mind lurched toward reality. Bad trip! Bad trip!

She scrambled up, flooding blood from the widening wounds in her belly, and groped toward the bathroom. Her legs were rubbery, and her foot caught in a tangle of sheet. She fell, making the record skip as she hit. She couldn't stand up, and she gritted her teeth together and crawled toward the bathroom in a tide of blood.

Pulling herself across the tiles, she felt the madness beating in her brain like the wings of ravens. She gripped the edge of the bathtub with crimson fingers and hauled herself over into it. She wrenched on the tap; the showerhead erupted, stabbing her skin with cold water. Then she curled up beneath the flow, her body shivering and convulsing. Her teeth chattered, the blood flowing away down the drain, down the drain, down the drain drain drain . . .

Bad trip, she thought. Oh . . . bad fucking trip . . .

Mary Terror placed her hand against the scars. They had closed up again. The water was no longer red as it flowed away. Flowers were growing from the walls of the shower stall, but they were white and coated with ice. Mary drew her knees up against her chin and shivered in the chill. Dark batlike things spun around in the shower for a moment, and then they were caught in the spray and they, too, went down the drain. Mary offered her face to the water, and it flowed into her eyes, mouth, and through her hair.

She turned off the tap and sat in the tub. Her teeth clicked like dice. I'm all right, she told herself. Coming out of it now. I'm all right. The flowers on the walls were wilting, and after a while they fluttered down into the tub around her and vanished like soap bubbles. She closed her eyes and thought of her new baby, waiting in the closet to be born. What would she name him? Jack, she decided. There had been many Jacks, and many Jims, Robbys, Rays, and Johns, after God and his band. This one would be the best Jack of all, and look just like his old man.

When she could, she stood up. Still shaky. Hold on, wait a minute.

She got out of the tub, pulled a towel off the rack, and dried herself. Little squiggly things squirmed on the bathroom's walls like Day-Glo paisley amoebas. She was coming out of it, though, and she was going to be all right. She staggered into the bedroom, feeling her way along the wall. The music had stopped, and the needle was ticking against the record's label. Who was that sprawled in the bed? She knew his name, but it wouldn't come to her. Something with a G. Oh, right: Gordie. Her brain felt fried, and she could feel the little quivers of nerves and muscles in her face. The inside of her mouth tasted ratty. She walked toward the kitchen, her hands clinging to the walls and her knees still in jeopardy of folding, but she made it without going down.

In the kitchen, her vision began to go dark around the edges, as if she were peering into a tunnel. She opened the freezer and rubbed her face and eye sockets with ice cubes, and slowly her vision cleared up again. She got a beer from the fridge, popped the tab, and took a long, deep drink. Zigzagged blue and red lightning bolts played around her for a few seconds, as if she were standing at the center of a laser show. Then they faded, and Mary finished her beer and put the can aside. She felt the scars on her belly. Still stitched up tight, but damn, that had scared the hell out of her. It had happened a couple of times before, during other bad trips, and it always seemed so real even when she knew it wasn't. She missed her baby. It was time to get Gordie out of here so she could give birth.

The *Rolling Stone* was still on the countertop where she'd left it, the Bangles on its cover. She got the last beer from the fridge and started in on it, her mouth like a dustbowl. Then, by force of habit, Mary turned to the classified ads section at the back of the *Stone*. She looked at what was for sale: Bon Jovi T-shirts, Wayfarer sunglasses, Spuds MacKenzie posters, Max Headroom masks, and the like. Her gaze ticked to the section of personal messages.

We Love You, Robert Palmer. Linda and Terri, Your Greatest Fans.

Need Ride, Amherst MA. to Ft. Lauderdale FL. 2/9, willing to share all expenses. Call after 6 p.m. 413-555-1292, Greg.

Hi, Chowderhead!

Looking for Foxy Denise. Met you at the Metallica concert 12/28. Where'd you go? Joey, Box 101B, Newport Beach, CA.

Long Live the Rough Riders! See, we said we'd do it!

Happy Birthday, Liza! I Love You!

Mr. Mojo has risen. The lady is—

Mary stopped reading. Her throat tightened, her mouth full of beer. Swallowing was a major effort. She got the beer down, and then her eyes went back to the beginning of the message.

Mr. Mojo has risen. The lady is still weeping. Does anybody remember? Meet me there. 2/18, 1400.

She stared at the last four numbers. Fourteen hundred. Military time. Two in the afternoon, the eighteenth of February. She read the message again, and a third time. The Mr. Mojo was a reference to Jim Morrison, from a line in a song called "L.A. Woman." The weeping lady was—

It had to be. It had to be.

She thought maybe the acid was still freaking her mind, and she went to the fridge, got a handful of ice cubes, and bathed her face again. She was trembling, not only from the cold, when she looked at the *Stone* once more. The message had not changed. Mr. Mojo. The weeping lady. Does anybody—

"I remember," Mary Terror whispered.

Gordie opened his eyes to a shadow standing over him. "Whazzit?" he said, his mouth moving on rusted hinges.

"Get out."

"Huh? I'm tryin' to—"

"Get out."

He blinked. Ginger was standing beside the bed, staring down at him. She was naked, a mountain of flesh. Big ol' baggy tits, Gordie thought. He smiled, his brain still full of flowers, and reached up for one of her breasts. Her hand caught his, and held it like a bird in a trap.

"I want you gone," the woman said. "Right now."

"What time is it? Whoa, my head's spinnin'!"

"It's almost ten-thirty. Come on, Gordie, get up. I mean it, man."

"Hey, what's the rush?" He tried to pull his hand free, but the woman's fingers tightened. The force of her grip was beginning to scare him. "You gonna break my hand, or what?"

She let him go and stepped back. Sometimes her strength got away from her, and this would not be a good time for that to happen. "Sorry," she said. "But you'll have to go. I like to sleep alone."

"My eyeballs are fried." Gordie pressed his palms into the sockets and rubbed them. Stars and pinwheels exploded in the darkness. "Man, that shit's got a kick, don't it?"

"I've had stronger." Mary picked up Gordie's clothes and dumped them on the bed beside him. "Get dressed. Come on, move it!"

Gordie grinned at her, slack-lipped and red-eyed. "You been in the army or somethin'?"

"Or something," she answered. "Don't go back to sleep." She waited until he'd shrugged into his shirt and had started buttoning it before she put on her robe and returned to the kitchen. Her eyes took in the message once again, and her heart pounded in her chest. No one could've written this but a Storm Fronter. No one knew about the weeping lady but the Storm Front's inner circle: ten people of which five had been executed by the pigs, one had been killed in a riot at Attica, and the other three were—like her—fugitives without a country. The names and faces reeled through her mind as she stared at the black words on paper as if looking through a keyhole into the past: Bedelia Morse, Gary Leister, CinCin Omara, James Xavier Toombs, Akitta Washington, Janette Snowden, Sancho Clemenza, Edward Fordyce, and the Commander, Jack Gardiner, "Lord Jack." She knew who had died by the pig bullet and who still held to the underground faith, but who had written this message? She opened a drawer and fumbled around, searching for a calendar she'd gotten in the mail as a promotion from a furniture store. She found it, the days one white square after another. Today was the twenty-third of January. Thirty-one days in this month. Eight days to go. *Meet me there. 2/18, 1400.* She couldn't count right, the acid and her own excitement were screwing her up. Calm down, calm down. Her palms were slick. Twenty-six days before the meeting. Twenty-six. Twenty-six. She intoned it aloud, a soothing mantra but a mantra that was also ripe with dangerous possibilities. It could be Jack himself, calling the last of the Storm Front together again. She could see him in her mind, his blond hair wild in the wind and his eyes gleaming with righteous fire, Molotov cocktails gripped in both hands and a gunbelt around his waist. It could be Jack, calling for her. Calling, calling . . .

She would answer. She would walk through hell to kiss his hand, and nothing would stop her from answering his summons.

She loved him. He was her heart, ripped away like the baby she'd been carrying for him had been ripped from her womb. He was her heart, and without him she was an empty shell.

"Hey, what's in the *Stone?*" A hand reached past her and grabbed up the magazine from the countertop.

Mary Terror whirled toward Gordie. She felt it come out of her like the seething magma from a volcano. She knew what it was, had lived with it for what seemed like all her life. She had loved it, suckled it, embraced it, and fed on it, and its name was Rage. Before she could stop herself, she placed a hand around Gordie's stalky throat and pressed a thumb into his windpipe, at the same time slamming him so hard against the wall that some of the pictures of the precious infants jumped off their nails and clattered to the floor.

"Gaaak," Gordie said, his face reddening and his eyes beginning to bulge from the sockets. "Jesusgaaklemmegaaak . . ."

She didn't want to kill him. She needed him for what was ahead. Ten minutes ago she'd been a slug, its mind aglimmer with the bright wattage of LSD. Now the deep part of her that craved the smell of blood and gunpowder had awakened, and it was staring out at the world through heavy-lidded gray eyes. But she needed this young man for what he could bring her. She took the *Stone* from his hand and released his throat, leaving a red splotch of fingers on his pallid skin.

Gordie coughed and wheezed for a few seconds, backing out of the kitchen away from her. He was dressed except for his shoes, his shirttail hanging out. When he could get his voice again, he hollered, "You're crazy! Fuckin' crazy! You tryin' to fuckin' kill me, bitch?"

"No." That would have been easy enough, she thought. She felt sweat in her pores, and she knew she'd stepped very close to the edge. "I'm sorry, Gordie. Really. I didn't mean to—"

"You almost choked me, lady! Shit!" He coughed again and rubbed his throat. "You get your jollies outta shovin' people around?"

"I was reading," she said. She tore the page out and gave him the rest of the magazine. "Here. Keep it. Okay?"

Gordie hesitated, as if he feared the woman might gnaw his arm off if he reached for the *Stone*. Then he took it, and he said in a raspy voice, "Okay. Man, you almost put your thumb through my fuckin' throat."

"I'm sorry." That was the last time she would apologize, but she managed a cool smile. "We're still friends, right?"

"Yeah." He nodded. "Still friends, what the hell."

Gordie had the brains of an engine block, Mary thought. That was all right; just so he started up when she turned his key. At the front door Mary looked into his eyes and said, "I'd like to see you again, Gordie."

"Sure. Next time you want a score, just gimme a call."

"No." She said it purposefully, and let her mouth linger around the word. "That's not what I mean. I'd like you to come over and spend some time."

"Oh. Uh . . . yeah, but . . . I've got a girlfriend."

"You can bring her over, too," Mary said, and she saw the greasy light shine in Gordie's eyes.

"I'll . . . uh . . . I'll be callin' you," Gordie told her, and then he went to his Mazda in the nasty drizzle, got in, and pulled away. When the car was out of sight, Mary closed the door, locked it, and took a long, deep breath. She lit a cone of strawberry incense, put it in its burner, and stood with the blue coils of smoke rising past her face. She closed her eyes, thinking of Lord Jack, the Storm Front, the message in the *Rolling Stone,* and the eighteenth of February. She thought of guns and blue-uniformed pigs, pools of blood and walls of flame. She thought of the past, and how it wound like a sluggish river through the present into the future.

She would answer the summons. She would be there, at the weeping lady, on the appointed day and hour. There were lots of plans to be made, lots of strings to cut and burn. Gordie would help her get what she needed. The rest she would do by instinct and cunning. She went into the kitchen, got a pen from a drawer, and made a mark on the eighteenth square of February: a star, by which to fix her destination.

She was so happy she began to cry.

In the bedroom Mary lay on the bed with her back supported by pillows and her legs splayed. "Push," she told herself, and began breathing in harsh *whuffs.* "Push! Push!" She pressed against her scarred belly with both hands. "Push! Come on, push!" She strained, her face tortured in a rictus of concentrated pain. "Oh God," she breathed, her teeth gritted. "Oh God oh God ohhhhhh . . ." She shivered and grunted, and then with a long cry and a spasm of her thigh muscles she reached under one of the pillows and slid the new baby out between her legs.

He was a beautiful, healthy boy. Jack, she would call him. Sweet, sweet Jackie. He made a few mewling cries, but he was a good boy and he would not disturb her sleep. Mary held him close and rocked him, her face and breasts damp with sweat. "Such a pretty baby," she crooned, her smile radiant. "Oh such a pretty pretty baby." She offered a finger, as she had done to the infant in the shopping cart at the supermarket. She was disappointed that he didn't grasp her finger, because she longed for the warmth of a touch. Well, Jackie would learn. She cradled him in her arms and rested her head against the pillows. He hardly moved at all, just lay there against her, and she could feel his heart beating like a soft little drum. She went to sleep with Lord Jack's face in her mind. He was smiling, his teeth as white as a tiger's, and he was calling her home.

5.

Perpetrator Down

When Laura got home from the Burt Reynolds movie, she found a message on the machine.

Beep. "Laura, hi. Listen, the work's taking longer than we thought. I'll be in around midnight, but don't wait up. I'm sorry about this. I'll take you to dinner tomorrow night, okay? Your choice. Back to the salt mines." Click.

He didn't say *I love you,* Laura thought.

A wave of incredible sadness threatened to break over her; she could feel its weight poised above her head. Where had he called from? Surely not the office. Someone's apartment, maybe. Eric was in

Charleston. Doug had lied about that, and what else was he lying about?

He had not said *I love you,* she thought, because there was another woman with him.

She started to call his office, but she put down the phone. What was the point of it? What was the point of any of it? She wandered the house, not quite sure of her destination. She wound through the kitchen, the dining room, the living room, and the bedroom, her eyes taking note of their possessions: hunting prints on the walls, here a Waterford crystal vase, there an armchair from Colonial Williamsburg, a bowl of glass apples, a bookcase filled with Literary Guild best sellers neither of them had bothered to read. She opened both their closets, looked at his Brooks Brothers suits and his power ties, looked at her own designer dresses and her variety of expensive shoes. She retreated from there and walked into the nursery.

The crib was ready. The walls were light blue, and a Buckhead artist had painted tiny, brightly colored balloons around the room just below the ceiling. The room still smelled faintly of fresh paint. A mobile of plastic fish hung above the crib, ready to be tossed and jangled.

Doug was with another woman.

Laura found herself back in the bathroom, looking at herself in the mirror under an unkind light. She released the gold clasp that pinned her hair and let it fall free around her shoulders in a chestnut cascade. Her eyes stared at her eyes, light blue as the sky of April. Tiny wrinkles were creeping in around them, foretellers of the future. They were the briefest impressions of crow's feet now, but later they would become the tracks of hawks. Dark circles there, too; she needed more sleep than she was getting. If she looked hard enough, she would find too many strands of gray in her hair. She was nearing forty, the black-balloon year. She was already six years past that age you weren't supposed to trust anybody over. She regarded her face: sharp nose and firm chin, thick dark eyebrows and a high forehead. She wished she had the etched cheekbones of a model instead of chipmunk cheeks grown plumper with baby fluids, but those had always been so. She had never been an awe-inspiring beauty, and in fact she had been homely—a quaint word—until her sixteenth year. Not many dates, but many books had filled her time. Dreams of travel, and of the crusading reporter. She was very attractive with makeup, but her features took on a harder quality without the paints and powders. It was in her eyes, especially, when she didn't have on liner and eyeshadow: a chilly brooding, the light blue the color of packed ice instead of springtime. They were the eyes of someone who senses time being lost, time going into the dark hole of the past like Alice after her white rabbit.

She wondered what the girl looked like. She wondered what her voice sounded like when she spoke Doug's name.

Sitting in the theater with a big tub of buttered popcorn on her lap, Laura had realized there were things she had chosen not to see in the last couple of months. A long golden hair on a suit jacket, lying curled up like a question mark. A scent that was not her own. A flush of makeup smeared on a shirt cuff. Doug drifting into thought when she talked to him about the baby; to whom had he run in his dreams? He was like the invisible man, wrapped up in bandages; if she dared to unwrap him, she might find nothing at home.

Doug was with another woman, and David moved in Laura's belly.

She sighed, a small sound, and she turned off the bathroom light.

In the darkness, she cried a little. Then she blew her nose and wiped her eyes, and she decided she would not say a word about this night. She would wait, and watch, and let time spin out its wire for fools like her to dance upon.

She took off her clothes and got ready for bed. The rain outside was intermittent, hard and soft, like two instruments playing at odds. In the bed, she stared at the ceiling with a babycare book next to her on the bedside table. She thought of her lunch with Carol today, and her vision of the angry hippie who used to be.

Laura realized, quite suddenly, that she'd forgotten what a peace sign looked like.

Thirty-six, she thought. Thirty-six. She placed her hands on David's swell. A funny thing, all those people who said not to trust anyone over thirty. Real funny.

They had been right.

Laura turned out the light and searched for sleep.

She found it after twenty minutes or so, and then the dream came. In it, a woman held a shrieking baby by the back of its neck, and she screamed toward the sea of blue lights, "Come on, come on you pigfuckers, come on ain't gonna kiss your ass no more ain't gonna kiss nobody's ass!" She shook the baby like a ragged flag, and the sharpshooter on the roof behind Laura radioed on the walkie-talkie that he couldn't drop the woman without hitting the baby. "Come on, you bastards!" the woman shouted, her teeth glinting. Blood was splattered over the yellow flowers on her dress, and her hair was the color of iron. "Come on, fuck you! Hear me?" She shook the baby again, and its scream made Laura flinch and step back into the protection of the police cars. Somebody brushed past her and told her to get out of the way. Somebody else spoke over a bullhorn to the woman who stood on the apartment's balcony, the words like a rumble of dumb thunder across the sweltering projects. The woman on the balcony stepped over the dead man at her feet, his head shot open like a clay pot, and she held the pistol against the infant's skull. "Come on and take me!" she hollered. "Come on, we'll go to hell together, okay?" She began to laugh then, a cocaine giggle, and the inhuman tragedy of that hopeless laugh crashed around Laura and made her retreat. She bumped into other reporters, the TV people on the scene. They were grim and efficient, but Laura saw something darkly joyous in their eyes. She couldn't look in their faces without feeling shamed. "Crazy bitch!" somebody yelled, a man who lived in the projects. "Put down that baby!" Another voice, a woman's: "Shoot her 'fore she kills that baby! Somebody shoot her!"

But the madwoman on the balcony had found her stage, and she paced it with the pistol's barrel against the infant's skull and her audience spread out in the parking lot below. "Ain't gonna give him up!" she hollered. "Ain't gonna!" Her shadow was thrown large by the lights, and moths fluttered in the heat. "Ain't gonna take what's mine!" she shouted, her voice hoarse and cracking. "Told him! Told him! Ain't nobody gonna take what's mine away from me! Swear to Jesus, I told him!" A sob burst out, and Laura saw the woman's body tremble. "Ain't gonna! Oh my Jesus, ain't gonna take what's mine! Fuck you!" she roared at the lights and the police cars and the TV cameras and the snipers and Laura Beale. "Fuck you!" Someone began playing an electric guitar in one of the other apartments, the volume cranked up to earsplitting, and the noise of the bullhorn and the walkie-talkies, the reporters, the onlookers, and the raging of the madwoman merged into a single terrifying sound that Laura would forever think must be the voice of Evil.

The woman on the balcony lifted her face to the night, her mouth open in an animal scream.

A sniper fired. *Pop,* like a backfire.

Pop went the pistol in the woman's hand as the back of her head blew apart.

Laura felt something warm and damp on her face. She gasped, fighting upward through the dream.

Doug's face was over her. The light was on. He was smiling, his eyes a little puffy. She realized he had just kissed her.

"Hi," he said. "Sorry I'm so late."

She couldn't make her mouth work. In her mind she was still at the projects, on that hot night in July, and moths spun before the lights as the policemen stormed the building. *Perpetrator down, perpetrator down,* she heard a policeman saying into a walkie-talkie. *Three bodies up there, Captain. She took the kid out.*

"Got a kiss for me?" Doug asked.

She gave him one, on the cheek, and she smelled the scent that was not her own.

"Rainy out," Doug said as he unknotted his tie. "Traffic's pretty bad."

Laura closed her eyes, listening to Doug move around the bedroom. The closet opened and closed. The toilet flushed. Water ran in the sink. Brushing his teeth. Gargling, good old Scope. When would he realize about the tickets? she wondered. Or maybe he was past caring?

Her hands met over the bulge of her belly. Her fingers laced together and locked.

She slept, this time mercifully without dreams.

In her womb, David was still. Doug placed his hand against Laura's stomach, feeling the baby's heat, and then he sat on the side of the bed looking at his hand and remembering where it had been. Bastard, he told himself. Stupid, selfish bastard. He felt swollen with lies, bloated with them, and how he could look into Laura's face he didn't know. But he was a survivor and he had a silver tongue, and he would do what he had to do in a world where you took what you could get when you could get it.

He had a bad taste in his mouth. He left the bedroom and walked into the kitchen, where he opened the refrigerator and got out a carton of orange juice. He poured himself a glassful, and he was nearing the bottom of the glass when he saw the two ticket stubs next to the telephone. It hit him like a punch between the eyes: he'd forgotten to throw them away since he'd taken Cheryl to see a Tom Cruise movie across town a few nights ago. He almost choked on the orange juice, almost bit through the glass. The ticket stubs. There they were. Right there. From his pants pocket. The ones he'd taken off. Oh, *great!* Laura had found them. Damn it to hell, what was she doing going through his pockets? A man had a right to privacy! Hold on, don't lose it. Just hold on. He picked up the stubs, remembering when he'd pocketed them. Right after that, Cheryl had guided him to the snack bar for kingsize Cokes and Milk Duds. His eyes ticked back and forth from the telephone to the ticket stubs; he didn't like what he was thinking, but why were the stubs next to the telephone? He felt heat working in his face, and he started to throw the stubs into a trash can but stopped his hand. No, no; leave them where they were. Exactly where they were. Finish your juice. Go to bed. Think about it, and come up with a story. Right, right. A story. Client in town, wanted to see a movie. Uh-huh. Selling limited partnerships in movie companies, and a client wanted to check out a movie. Sure.

Laura wasn't dumb, that was for certain. He would have to work on the story. If she asked. If she didn't . . . he wouldn't volunteer anything.

Doug returned the ticket stubs to where they'd been. He drank down the rest of his orange juice; it was very bitter toward the end. Then he started back into the bedroom, where his wife lay sleeping and his son was curled up in her belly waiting to be born. Before he got there, he thought of something Freud had said, that nobody ever truly forgets anything. He set the alarm clock for an early hour, lay in the dark for a while listening to Laura breathe and wondering how he'd gotten here from the moment they had exchanged vows and rings, and finally sleep took him.

Seven miles could be the distance between worlds. It was that far—that close—to the apartment where Mary Terror slept with her new baby cradled against her. She made a soft, moaning noise, and her hand drifted down and pressed against her scars. The baby stared out at the world through painted eyes, his body giving off no warmth.

Rain fell on the roofs of the just and unjust, the saints and the sinners, those who knew peace and those in torment, and tomorrow began at a dark hour.

II

Unknown Soldier

1.

Bad Karma

The sun was shining, and Mary Terror was in the woods.

She ran on cramping legs through the wilderness, the breath pluming from her mouth in the chilly air, her body giving up moisture into the gray sweatsuit she wore. It had been a long time since she had run, and her legs weren't used to the effort. It angered her that she'd let herself get so out of shape; it was a weakness of the mind, a failure of willpower. As she ran through the sun-dappled Georgia forest about three miles from her apartment, she held the Colt .38 in her right hand, her index finger curled around the trigger guard. Sweat was on her face, her lungs beginning to labor though she'd barely gone a third of a mile at an easy pace. The ravines and hillocks were rough on her knees, but she was in training and she gritted her teeth and took the pain like an old lover.

It was just before two o'clock on Sunday afternoon, four days after she'd found the message in the *Rolling Stone*. Her pickup truck was parked at the end of an old logging road; she knew these woods, and often came here to practice her shooting. It had come upon her to run, to work up a sweat and make the hinges of her lungs wheeze, because the road to the weeping lady lay ahead. She knew the dangers of that road, knew that she was vulnerable out on the open byways of the Mindfuck State, where pigs of every description cruised for a killing. To reach her destination, she would have to be tough and smart, and she'd lived too long as Ginger Coles in a redneck cocoon for the preparations to be easy. Her body wanted to rest, but she pushed herself onward. As she went up a hill she caught sight of the highway to Atlanta in the distance, the sunlight sparking off the glass and metal of speeding cars; then she was going down again, through a pine tree thicket where shadows carpeted the earth, the breath burning in her lungs and her face full of heat. Faster! she urged herself. Faster! Her legs remembered the thrill of speed at a high school track meet, when she'd strained past the other runners toward the tape. Faster! Faster! She ran along the bottom of a wooded ravine, pushing herself to go all out, and that was when her left foot hit a snag and she went down on her belly in the dead leaves and kudzu. The wind whooshed out of her and her chin scraped along the ground, and she lay there puffing and listening to a squirrel chatter angrily in a nearby tree.

"Shit," Mary said. She sat up, rubbed her chin, found scraped skin but no blood. When she tried to stand, her legs didn't want to. She sat there for a moment, breathing hard, dark motes spinning before her eyes in the cold, slanting sunlight. Falls were part of the training, she knew. Falls were cosmic teachers. That's what Lord Jack used to say. When you knew how to fall, you truly knew how to stand. She lay on the ground, catching her breath and remembering the commando training. The Storm Front's headquarters had been hidden in woods like these, only you could smell the sea in the eastern winds. Lord Jack had been a hard taskmaster: sometimes he awakened them with whispers at four o'clock in the morning, other times with gunshots at midnight. Then he would run the soldiers through the obstacle course, keeping time with a stopwatch and shouting a mélange of encouragement and threats. Mary recalled the wargames, when two teams hunted each other in the woods armed with pistols that fired paint pellets. Sometimes the hunt was one-against-one, and those were the trials she'd enjoyed the most; she had never been tagged in all the dozens of hunts Lord Jack had put her into. She had enjoyed turning back on her adversary, coming around in a silent, stalking circle, and delivering the blow that finished the game. No one had ever beaten her at the hunt. No one.

Mary forced herself up. The pain in her bones reminded her that she was no longer a young firebrand, but low coals burned longer. She began running again, with long, steady strides. Her thighs and calves were aching, but she closed her mind to the pain. Make friends with agony, Lord Jack had said. Embrace it, kiss it, stroke it. Love the pain, and you win the game. She ran with the pistol held at her side, and she saw a squirrel dart from the brush and scramble toward an oak tree to her right. She stopped, skidding in a flurry of leaves, slowing the squirrel down into strobelike motions with the force of her concentration. The squirrel was going up the treetrunk, now leaping for a higher branch.

Mary lifted the pistol in a two-handed grip, took aim, and squeezed the trigger.

The crack of the shot and the explosion of the squirrel's head were almost simultaneous. The body fell into the leaves, writhed for a few seconds, and lay still.

She ran on, the sweet tang of gunpowder in her nostrils and the pistol warm in her hand.

Her eyes searched the shadowed woods. Pig on the left! she thought, and she checked her progress and whirled in a crouch with her gun ready, aiming at a scraggly pine. She ran again, over a hillock and down. Pig on the right! She threw herself to the ground, raising dust, and as she slid on her stomach she took aim at another tree and fired a shot that clipped a top branch and sent a bluejay shrieking into the sky. Then up again—quick, quick!—and onward, her tennis shoes gouging the ground. Another squirrel, drowsing in the sun, came to life and fled across her path; she tracked it, heading toward a group of pines. It was a fast one, desperate with fear. She fired at it as it clambered up a treetrunk, missed by a few inches to the left, but hit the squirrel in the spine with the second bullet. She heard it squeak as she passed on, a signature of blood across the treebark.

Pig to the right! She crouched again, taking aim at an imaginary enemy. Off in the forest, crows called to each other. She smelled woodsmoke as she ran again, and she figured houses must be near. She entered a tangle of thicket, the sweat trickling down the back of her neck and dead leaves snagged in her hair. As she fought through the growth, battering it aside with her forearms, she thought of Jack urging her on with his stopwatch and whistle. He had written the message from the underground; of that she had no doubt. He was calling the Storm Fronters together again, after all these years. Calling for her, his true love. There had to be a purpose behind his summons. The Mindfuck State was still full of pigs, and all the Revolution had done was make them meaner. If the Storm Front could rise up again, with Lord Jack holding its red banner, she would be the happiest woman on earth. She had been born to fight the pigs, to grind them down under her boots and blow their shitty brains out. That was her life; that was reality. When she got back to Lord Jack and the Storm Front was on the move again, the pigs would tremble at the name of Mary Terror.

She burst through the foliage, her face raked by thorns. Pig to the left! she thought, and she dove for the ground. She hit the clayey dirt on her shoulder, rolled through weeds, and contorted her body to the left, lifting the pistol to take aim at—

A boy.

He was standing maybe fifteen yards away, in a splash of sunlight. He wore bluejeans with patched knees and a camouflage-print windbreaker, and on his head was a dark blue woolen cap. His eyes were large and round, and in his arms he held a small, boy-sized rifle.

Mary Terror lay where she was, the gun aimed in the boy's direction. Time stretched, breaking only when the boy opened his mouth.

"You okay, lady?"

"I fell," she said, trying to assemble her wits.

"Yeah, I saw. You okay?"

Mary glanced around. Was the boy alone? No one else in sight. She said, "Who you out here with?"

"Just me. My house is over that way." He motioned with a turning of his head, but the boy's home was about a half-mile away, over a hill and out of sight.

Mary stood up. She saw the boy's eyes fix on the revolver in her hand. He was about nine or ten, she decided; his face was ruddy, the cheeks chill-burned. The rifle he held was a .22, and it had a small telescopic sight. "I'm all right," she told him. Again her gaze searched the woods. Birds sang, cars droned on the distant highway, and Mary Terror was alone with the boy. "I tripped," she said. "Stupid, huh?"

"You 'bout scared the life outta me, comin' through there and all."

"Sorry. Didn't mean to." She lifted her head slightly and sniffed the woodsmoke. Maybe a fire in the hearth at the kid's house, she thought.

"What're you doin' out here? Kinda far from the road." He kept his rifle pointed at the ground. The first thing his father had told him: never point a gun at a person unless you're gonna use it.

"Just hiking." She saw him look at the pistol again. "Target shooting, too."

"I heard some shots. That was you, I reckon."

"That was me."

"I'm squirrel-huntin'," the boy said, and he offered a gap-toothed grin. "I got me this here new rifle for my birthday. See?"

She had never run into anyone out here before. She didn't like this, didn't like it at all. A boy alone with a squirrel rifle. She didn't like it. "How come no one's with you?" she asked.

"My daddy had to go in to work. He said if I was careful I could come on out by myself, but I wasn't to go too far from the house."

Her mouth was dry. She was still breathing hard, but the sweat was drying on her face. She didn't like this; she could imagine this boy going home and saying to his parents *I saw a woman in the woods today. She had a pistol and she said she was out hikin'. She was a big, tall woman, and I can draw you a picture of what she looked like.*

"Is your daddy a policeman?" Mary asked.

"No, ma'am. He builds houses."

She asked if you were a policeman, Daddy, she could imagine the boy saying. *I can remember what she looked like. Wonder why she asked if you were a policeman, Daddy?*

"What's your name?" she asked him.

"Cory Peterson. My birthday was yesterday. See, I got this rifle."

"I see." She watched the boy's gaze tick to her .38 once more. *How come she had a pistol, Daddy? How come she was out there in the woods by herself and she don't even live around here?* "Cory," she said. She smiled at him. The sun was warm out here, but the shadows still trapped winter. "My name is Mary," she told him, and just that quick she decided it had to be done.

"Pleased to meet ya. Well, I guess I'd best be gettin' on now. I said I wouldn't be gone too long."

"Cory?" she said. He hesitated. "Can I have a closer look at your rifle?"

"Yes ma'am." He began walking toward her, his boots crunching on dead leaves.

She watched him approach. Her heart was beating hard, but she was calm. The boy might decide to follow her if she let him go; he might follow her all the way to her truck, and he might remember her license number. He might be a lot smarter than he looked, and his father might know someone who was a policeman. She was going to be leaving soon, after she'd gotten everything prepared, and she would worry about this boy if she didn't tie up the loose ends. *Daddy, I saw this woman in the woods and she had a pistol and her name was Mary.* No, no; that could screw up everything.

When Cory got to her, Mary reached out and grasped the rifle's barrel. "Can I hold it?" she asked, and he nodded and gave it up. The rifle hardly had any weight at all, but she was interested in the telescopic sight. Having it might save her some money if she ever bought a long-range rifle. "Real nice," she said. She kept her smile on, no trace of frost or tension around the edges. "Hey, you know what?"

"What?"

"I saw a place where a lot of squirrels are. Back that way." She nodded toward the thicket she'd broken through. "It isn't too far, if you want to see it."

"I don't know." Cory looked back in the direction of his house, then up into her face again. "I figger I'd better be gettin' on home."

"Really, it's not far. Won't take but just a few minutes to show you." She was thinking of the ravine where dead leaves and kudzu covered the bottom.

"Naw. Thanks anyway. Can I have my rifle back now, please?"

"Going to make it hard on me, huh?" she asked, and she felt her smile slip.

"Ma'am?" The boy blinked, his dark brown eyes puzzled.

"I don't mind," Mary said. She lifted her Colt and placed the barrel squarely in the middle of Cory Peterson's forehead.

He gasped.

She pulled the trigger, and with the crack of the shot the boy's head was flung backward. His mouth was open, showing little silver fillings in his teeth. His body went back, following the shock to his neck. He stumbled backward a few steps, the hole in the center of his forehead running crimson and his brains scattered on the ground behind him. His eyelids fluttered, and his face looked to Mary as if the boy were about to sneeze. He made a strangled little squeak, squirrellike, and then he fell on his back amid the detritus of winter. His legs trembled a few times, as if he were trying to stand up again. He died with his eyes and mouth open and the sun on his face. Mary stood over him until his lungs had stopped hitching. There was no use trying to drag the body away to hide it. She swept her gaze back and forth through the woods, her senses questing for sound and movement. The gunshot had scared the birds away, and the only noises were her heartbeat and blood trickling in the leaves. Satisfied that no one else was anywhere around, she turned away from the corpse and pushed back through the thicket again. Once clear of it, she began running in the direction she'd come, the .38 in one hand and the boy-sized rifle clenched in the other.

Her sweat turned cold. What she had just done fell upon her, and it made her stagger. But she regained her balance, her mouth grim-lipped and her eyes fixed toward the distant horizon. It had been his bad karma to cross her path, she thought. It had not been her fault that the boy was there; it was just karma, that's all. The boy was a minor piece of a larger picture, and that was what she had to focus on. His daddy might have wondered why a woman was stalking in the woods with a pistol on a Sunday afternoon. His daddy might have known a pig, or even a federal pig. One telephone call could start the pig machinery, and she'd hidden too long and been too smart to allow that to happen. The boy had to be laid low. Period.

A little whirlpool of anger had opened within her. Damn it! she raged. Shit! Why had that damned boy been there? It was a test, she thought. A karmic test. You fall down, and you stand up again. You keep going no matter what. She wished it were springtime, and that there were flowers in the woods. If there were flowers in the woods, she would've put one in the dead boy's hand.

She knew why she had killed him. Of course she did. The boy had seen Mary Terror without her mask. That was reason enough for execution.

She couldn't make it on the run all the way back to her truck. She walked the last three hundred yards, her lungs rasping and her sweatsuit soaked. She leaned the rifle against the seat and put the handgun on the floorboard beneath her legs. There were the marks of other tires in the dirt, so she didn't have to worry about brushing out the tracks. The pigs might get a footprint or two, but so what? They'd think it was a man's footprints. She started the engine, backed off the logging road to the paved highway where a sign said NO DUMPING and litter was everywhere. Then Mary drove home, knowing she had a lot of training to do but confident that she had not lost her touch.

2.

A Friend's Message

Laura slid the top drawer of Doug's dresser open, lifted up his sweaters, and looked at the gun.

It was an ugly thing. A Charter Arms .32 automatic, black metal with a black grip. Doug had shown her how it worked: the little metal thingamajig that held the seven bullets—the magazine clip, Doug had said—fit up into the grip, and you had to push the safety hickey with your thumb to engage the firing dololley. There was a box of extra clips, with the words Fast Loading and Rugged Construction on it. The gun was unloaded at the moment; a clip of bullets lay next to it.

Laura touched the automatic's grainy grip. The gun smelled faintly of oil, and she worried that the oil would leak onto Doug's sweaters. She ran her fingers over the cool metal. It was a dangerous, evil-looking beast, and Laura saw how men could become fascinated by guns: there was power in it, waiting to be released.

She put her hand around the grip and picked the gun up. It wasn't as heavy as it looked, but it was still a handful. She held it at arm's length, her wrist already beginning to tremble, and she sighted along the gun at the wall. Her index finger found the trigger's seductive curve. She moved her arm to the right, and sighted at the framed wedding picture of her and Doug atop the dresser. She aimed at Doug's smiling face, and she said, "Bang."

The little murder done, Laura put the automatic back under Doug's sweaters and slid the drawer shut. She left the bedroom, going to the den, where her typewriter was set up on a desk in a sunny spot. Her review of *Burn This Book* was about half finished. She switched on the TV, turned it to the Cable News Network, and sat down to work, the swell of her belly against the desk's edge. She'd written a few more sentences when she heard the words ". . . was found in a wooded area outside Atlanta on Sunday night . . ." and she turned around to watch.

It had been on the news all day, about the boy found shot to death in the woods near Mableton last night. Laura had seen the segment several times before: the sheet-covered corpse being put into the back of an ambulance, the blue lights flashing, a police captain named Ottinger talking about how the boy's father and neighbors had found the body around seven o'clock. There was a scene of reporters surging forward around a distraught-looking man in overalls and a Red Man cap, and a frail woman with curly hair and shocked, dark-hollowed eyes. The man—Lewis Peterson, the boy's father—waved the reporters away, and he and his wife went into their white frame house, the screen door banging shut behind them.

". . . senseless killing," Ottinger was saying. "Right now we have no suspects and no motive, but we're going to do everything in our power to find this young boy's killer."

Laura turned away from the television and went back to work. In the light of all the crime in the Atlanta area, having a gun made good sense. She would never have believed she could think that way, because she hated guns, but crime in the city was out of control. Well, it was out of control across the country, wasn't it? Across the world, for that matter. Things had turned savage, and there were beasts on the prowl. Take the example of that boy, for instance. A senseless killing, the police captain had said. The boy lived near those woods, had probably been down in there a thousand times. But on that particular day he'd met someone who had put a bullet through his head for no reason. A beast on the prowl, hunting for bloody meat. On Sunday, the paths of the boy and the beast had crossed, and the beast had won.

She focused on her review again. Mark Treggs and the echoes of the sixties. Writing sloppy in places, keen in others. The death of J.F.K. as a foreshadowing of dark disease in America. Free love was now AIDS, acid tripping was now crack. Haight-Ashbury, Patty Hearst, Timothy Leary, Abbie Hoffman, the Weather Underground, Days of Rage, the Storm Front, Woodstock and Altamont as the heaven and hell of the peace movement. Laura finished the review, judging *Burn This Book* as interesting but not necessarily incendiary, typed "30" at the end of it, and rolled the paper out of the Royal.

The telephone rang. After two rings, her own voice answered: "Hello, you've reached the residence of Douglas and Laura Clayborne. Please leave a message at the tone, and thank you for calling."

Beep. Click.

So much for that. Laura rolled another sheet of paper in, preparatory to doing her review of *The Address.* She paused to listen to the weather report: more clouds rolling in, and colder temperatures. Then she began on the first line of the review, and the telephone rang again. She kept working as her voice invited the caller to leave a message.

Beep. "Laura? It's a friend."

Laura stopped typing. The voice was muffled. Disguised, she thought it must be.

"Ask Doug who lives in Number 5-E at the Hillandale Apartments." *Click.*

And that was all.

Laura sat there for a moment, stunned. She got up, went to the answering machine, and played the message back. A woman's voice? Someone speaking with a handkerchief pressed against the receiver, maybe. She hit the playback button again. Yes, a woman's voice, but she couldn't tell whose it was. Her hands were trembling and her knees felt weak. When she played the message back a third time, she wrote down *5-E, Hillandale Apts* on a piece of paper. Then she opened the telephone book and looked up the address of the apartment complex. It was across town to the east. Very close to the Canterbury Six theaters, she realized. Well.

Laura erased the message from the answering machine. A friend, indeed. Someone who worked with Doug? How many people knew about this? She felt her heartbeat getting out of control, and David suddenly kicked in her belly. She forced herself to breathe slowly and deeply, one hand pressed to David's bulge. A moment of indecision: should she go to the bathroom to throw up, or would the nausea pass? She waited, her eyes closed and cold sweat on her cheeks, and the sickness did pass. Then she opened her eyes again, and she stared at the address on the piece of paper in her hand. Her vision seemed to blur in and out, her temples squeezed by what felt like an iron vise, and she had to go sit down before she fell down.

She hadn't said anything to Doug about the ticket stubs, though she'd left them out in full view. He hadn't said anything, either. The next night, Doug had taken her to the Grotto, an Italian restaurant that she particularly enjoyed, but he'd seen a client at a nearby table there and ended up talking to the man for fifteen minutes while Laura ate cold minestrone. He'd made an effort at being attentive, but his eyes wandered and he was obviously uncomfortable. He knows I know, Laura thought. She had hoped beyond hope that none of it was true, that he would explain away the tickets and tell her that Eric had somehow jetted back from Charleston for the day. She might have accepted the least little attempt at explanation. But Doug fumbled with his silverware and avoided eye contact, and she knew he was having an affair.

Anger and sadness warred within her as she sat in the den with the sunlight streaming through the Levolors. Maybe she would feel better if she got up and broke something, but she doubted it. Her mother and father were coming to Atlanta as soon as the baby was born, and that would start out fine at first but eventually she and her mother would wear on each other and the sparks would start to fly. Her mother would be of no help in this situation, and her father would want to baby her. She tried to stand up from the chair, but she felt very tired and David's weight hobbled her; she stayed where she was, one hand gripping the apartment number and the other clenched hard on the armrest. Tears suddenly welled up in her eyes, burning them, and Laura gritted her teeth and said, "No, damn it. No. No.

No." She couldn't will herself not to cry, though, and the tears streaked down her cheeks one after the other.

The inevitable questions came like hammerblows: Where did I fail? What did I do wrong? What is he getting from a stranger than I can't give him?

No answers, only more questions. "The bastard," Laura said quietly when her crying was done. Her eyes were red-rimmed and puffy. "Oh, the bastard." She lifted her hand and watched the sunlight glint off the two-carat diamond in her engagement ring, and her gold wedding band. They were worthless, she thought, because they meant nothing. They were empty symbols, like this house and the lives she and Doug had constructed. She could imagine the joke Carol would make about this: "So ol' Dougie went out and found a chick who doesn't have a cake baking in the oven, huh? See, like I told you: you can't trust men! They're from a different planet!" That might be so, but Doug was still part of her world, and he would be part of David's world, too. The real question was: where to go from here?

She knew the first step.

Laura stood up. She switched off the television and got her car keys. She found a map of the city, then judged the fastest way to get to the Hillandale Apartments.

The apartment complex, about twenty minutes from Laura's house, had a tennis court and a pool draped with a black cover. Laura drove around, searching for the E building. She found it after a circuitous route, and she parked the BMW and got out to check the names on the mailboxes.

The box for 5-E had *C. Jannsen* written on the little name tag in Flair pen. It was a feminine signature full of curves and squiggles, and it ended with a flourish.

It was a young signature, Laura thought. Her heart felt squeezed in a brutal grip. She stood in front of the door that had 5-E on it in brown plastic, and she thought of Doug crossing the threshold. In the center of the door was a little peephole, where the canary could peer out at the cat. She glanced at the door buzzer, put her finger on it and . . .

. . . did nothing.

On the drive back, Laura reasoned that C. Jannsen probably wouldn't have been home, anyway. Not at three o'clock on a Monday afternoon. C. Jannsen must work somewhere, unless—a horrible thought—Doug was keeping her. Laura racked her brain, trying to think of a C. Jannsen she might know from Doug's office, but she knew no one with that name. Someone *did* know about the girl, though; someone who had taken pity on Laura and called with the information. The more Laura thought about it, the more she decided the voice could have belonged to Marcy Parker. She had to figure out what to do now: to hit Doug with what she knew, or wait until after the baby was born. Unpleasant scenes were not to her liking, and her level of stress was already up in the stratosphere; a confrontation would shoot her blood pressure up and possibly hurt David in some way, and Laura couldn't chance it.

After David was born, she would ask Doug who C. Jannsen was. Then they would go on from there to whatever destination lay ahead. It would be a rocky and dangerous path, she knew. There would be tears and angry words, a clash of egos that might destroy the fictioned fabric of their lives, but one thought was paramount in Laura's mind: Doug has someone to hold, and soon I'll have mine.

Her knuckles were white around the steering wheel. Halfway home, she had to pull into a gas station, and in the bathroom the tears burst from her eyes and she threw up until there was nothing in her mouth but bitter.

3.

The Darker Heart

Mary Terror awakened in the dark, after the dream had passed. In it, she had walked toward a two-storied wooden house painted sky-blue, with gables and chimneys and a widow's walk. She knew that house, and where it stood: at the beginning. She had walked up the steps and across the porch into the house as the rays of white sunlight burned through the windows upon the pinewood floor. She had found him, in the room with bay windows that looked toward the sea. Lord Jack was wrapped in snowy robes, his blond hair down around his shoulders and his eyes keen and thoughtful as he watched her approach. She stopped just short of him, and in his presence she trembled.

"I called you," he told her. "I wanted you to come, because I need you."

"I heard you call," she said, her voice soft and whispery. It echoed in the large room, and she could smell the salt air in the walls. "I need you, too."

"We're going to do it again, Mary. All of it, again. We're going to raise the dead ones and bring the lost into the fold, and we're going to make sure that this time we win."

"This time we win," she repeated, and she reached out for his hand.

"Where's my child?" Lord Jack asked.

Mary's hand stopped in midair.

"My son," he said. "Where's my son?"

"I . . . I don't . . . know. . . ."

"You were carrying my son," he said. "Where is he?"

For a moment Mary couldn't speak. She heard the crash of surf against rocks, and she pressed her hands against her stomach. "I . . . got hurt," she told him. "You know I got hurt. The baby . . . I lost the baby."

Lord Jack closed his eyes. "I want a son." His head rocked back, and she could see the tears creeping down his cheeks. "You know I want a son, to carry my seed. Where's my son, Mary? Where's my son?"

The two words were the hardest she'd ever spoken: "He's dead."

Lord Jack's eyes opened, and looking into them was like peering into the center of the universe. Stars and constellations roamed in Jack's head, all the signs and symbols of the Age of Aquarius. "My son has to be alive," he said, his voice silken and pained. "Has to be. My seed has to go on. Don't you understand that? I gave you a great gift, Mary. And you lost that gift. You killed it, didn't you?"

"No! I didn't! The baby died! I got hurt, and the baby died!"

He lifted a thin finger and placed it against his lips. "When I called you, I wanted you to bring my son to me. That's part of all this. A very important part, if we're going to raise the dead and bring the lost ones back. Oh, Mary; you've hurt me so much."

"No!" Her voice cracked, and she heard dark laughter in the walls. "We can make another baby! Right now! Right now, okay? We can make another baby, just as good as the last one!"

He looked at her with his universe-filled eyes. Through her, into another dimension. "I want you to bring my son to me, Mary. The baby you and I made. If you can't bring me my son, you can't stay here."

As he said it, the walls began to fade. Lord Jack began to fade, too, like a dimming light. She tried to grasp his hand, but it whirled away from her like mist. "I don't . . . I don't . . ." Her throat was closing up with fear. "I don't have anywhere else to go!"

"You can't stay here," he repeated, a ghost in white. "Come to me with my son, or don't come at all."

The house went away. Lord Jack vanished. She was left with the smell of the sea and the noise of surf on rugged rocks, and that was when she awakened.

The baby was crying, a high, thin sound that drilled into her brain. Sweat glistened on her face, and she could hear the thunder of trucks on the highway. "Stop crying," she said listlessly. "Stop it right now." But Jackie wouldn't stop, and Mary Terror got out of bed and went to the cardboard-box crib where the baby lay. She touched the infant's skin. It was cold and rubbery, and the feel of it made the rage begin to beat within her like a second, darker heart. Babies were killers of dreams, she thought. They promised the future, and then they died.

Mary grasped the baby's hand and put her finger in it. Jackie wouldn't grip her finger like the baby in the shopping cart had done. "Hold me," she said. "Hold me." Her voice was getting louder, swelling with anger. "Hold me, I said!" The baby was still crying, a desperate sound, but he wouldn't grip her finger. His skin was cold, so very cold. Something was wrong with this baby, she realized. This was not Lord Jack's son. This was a crying, cold mass of flesh that was not of her loins. "Stop it!" she shouted, and she picked the baby up and shook him. "I mean it!"

The baby gurgled and choked, then came back to the high-pitched shriek. Mary's head was killing her, and the infant's crying was driving her crazy. She shook the baby harder, and saw his head loll in the darkness. "Stop it! Stop it! Stop it!"

Jackie wouldn't mind her. Mary felt the blood rush into her face. This baby was broken, something was wrong with him. His skin was cold, he wouldn't hold her finger, and his crying was strangled. None of the babies ever minded her, and that loss of control was what drove her into a frenzy. She gave them birth and love, fed them even when they didn't want to be fed, and she wiped the food from their mouths and changed their diapers, and still the babies were untrue. It was clear to her why that was, in the aftermath of the dream: none of them was Lord Jack's son, and none of them deserved to live. "Stop crying, goddamn it!" Mary shouted, but this infant wailed and thrashed in her hands, his rubbery body inching toward destruction. Jack wouldn't accept this child, she thought. No, no; he wouldn't let her stay with him if she brought this baby to him. This baby was wrong. Terribly wrong. Cold, rubbery, and in need of death.

The crying made her temples pound. A scream batted around in her mouth. She reached her breaking point, and with an animalish moan she held Jackie by the heels and swung him against the wall. The crying stuttered, came back again full force. "SHUT UP!" she roared, and bashed his head against the wall once more. "SHUT UP!" Against the wall. "SHUT UP!" The wall again, and this time she heard something break. The crying ceased. Mary swung the cold baby against the wall a last time, could feel the little body twitching and quivering in her hands. A banging. A banging. Someone's fist whamming the wall.

"Shut up, you crazy bitch! I'm gonna call the cops!"

The old man next door. Shecklett. Mary dropped the cold infant to the floor, and despair went through her like a floodtide. In a second it hissed and steamed and roared into rage as Shecklett kept hammering on the wall. "You're crazy, you hear me? *Crazy!*" He stopped, and Mary crossed the room to the dresser, opened the bottom drawer, and took out the .38 with which she'd executed Cory Peterson. There was only one bullet in the cylinder, and Mary fumbled with a box of shells and fed them into their chambers. She clicked the cylinder shut, and she walked to the wall between her apartment and Shecklett's and put her ear to the cheap paneling. She could hear Shecklett moving around the room. A door slammed. Water running. In the bathroom? Mary pressed the .38's muzzle against the wall, aimed toward where she thought the sound of running water was. Her heartbeat was slow and steady, her nerves calm, but she had had her fill of the old man's taunts and threats. She had killed another baby tonight; his body lay just a few feet away, his skull broken. Lord Jack would not let her come if she didn't bring a baby—his son—but none of the babies would let her love them. "Come on out," Mary whispered, waiting for the noise of the door opening. The water stopped. She heard Shecklett cough several times and spit, and a moment later the toilet flushed. Mary eased back the Colt's hammer. She was going to empty the cylinder through the wall, and then she was going to reload and empty another cylinder except for a single bullet. If she couldn't go to Lord Jack, she had nowhere else to go. She had no home, no country, no identity; she was no one, a walking blank, and she was ready to end the charade.

"Come on out," Mary said again, and she heard the hinges of the bathroom door squeak.

Her finger tightened on the trigger.

Bang bang.

It was not the noise of gunfire. It was the noise of a fist knocking on a door. Mary took her finger off the trigger. The knock came again, louder and more insistent. Her front door, she realized. She walked into the other room, the Colt still in her hand, and she peered furtively out the window. Two pigs stood there, and a pig car was out in the parking lot. She stood at the door, and she steeled her voice and said, "What is it?"

"Police. Would you open your door, please?"

Take it easy, she thought. Control. Control. The pigs are at the door. Control. Mary turned the lock and unhooked the chain. She kept her gun hand out of sight as she opened the door, and she peered out through the crack at the two pigs, one black and one white. "What's the problem?"

"We've had a call about a disturbance of the peace," the black one said. He clicked on a penlight and shone it into Mary's face. "Everything all right here, ma'am?"

"Yes. Fine."

"One of your neighbors called in to complain," the white pig told her. "Said there was a lot of yellin' comin' out of your apartment."

"I . . . was having a nightmare. I got loud, I guess."

"Would you open the door a little wider, please?" the black pig asked. Mary did, without hesitation; her gun hand was still hidden. The black pig played his penlight over her face. "What's your name, ma'am?"

"Ginger Coles."

"That's her!" Shecklett shouted from the doorway of his apartment. "She's crazy as hell, I'm tellin' you! You oughta lock her up before she hurts somebody!"

"Sir? Would you keep your voice down, please?" The black pig said something quietly to the white one, and the white pig walked over to Shecklett's door. Mary could hear Shecklett muttering and cursing, and she kept her gaze fixed on the black pig's eyes. He took a pack of

Doublemint gum from his jacket pocket and offered her a stick, but she shook her head. He popped one into his mouth and began to chew. "Nightmares can be weird, huh?" he asked. "They're so real, I mean."

Testing me, Mary thought. "Yeah, you're right about that. I have really bad nightmares sometimes."

"They must be bad if they make you shout so loudly." The penlight drifted across her face again.

"I was a nurse in Vietnam," Mary said.

The penlight stopped. Hung splashed across her right cheek for a few seconds. Then it went off with a small *click.*

"Sorry," the black pig said. "I was too young to go, but I saw *Platoon.* Must've been hell over there, huh?"

"Every day."

He nodded, and put his penlight away. "We're finished here, Phil," he said to the white pig. "Sorry to have bothered you, ma'am," he told Mary. "But I hope you can understand why your neighbor called this in."

"I can, yes. I usually take sleeping pills, but I didn't get my prescription refilled yet."

"She's crazy!" Shecklett insisted, his voice getting strident again. "Allatime hollerin' and raisin' the devil!"

"Sir?" The black pig walked to Shecklett's door. "Sir? I asked you to stop shouting, didn't I? This woman is a Vietnam veteran, and you ought to have some consideration for that fact."

"Is that what she told you? Shit! Make her prove it!"

"You going to settle down, sir, or are we going to take a ride in our car?"

There was a long silence. Mary waited, her hand tight around the .38's grip. She heard the black pig talking to Shecklett, but she couldn't make out the words. Then his door closed hard, and the two pigs came back to her door. "I think everything's understood now," the black one told her. "Good night, ma'am."

"Good night. And thank you so much, Officers," she said, and she closed the door, relatched it, and put the chain on. Behind the door, she said through clenched teeth, "Fuck you fuck you fuck you." She waited, watching out the window until the pigs had driven away, and then she went to the wall between her apartment and Shecklett's and she put her mouth against the paneling and said, "I'm going to fix you when I go. Going to fix you, hear me? Going to cut your eyeballs out and make you choke on them. Hear me, you old shit?"

She heard Shecklett coughing back in his bedroom. He made a ragged, gasping sound, and the toilet flushed again. Mary walked back to her own bedroom, and she switched on the light and stood looking down at the dead baby on the floor.

Its head was cracked and dented in, but there was no blood, no brains leaking from the skull. A doll, she thought. It's a doll. She picked the doll up by one leg, and she took it to the Heaven Box in the closet. Then she stood for a long time staring down at the other broken dolls, a pulse beating at her right temple and her eyes glazed over like pond ice.

All of them. Dolls. Not flesh and blood. Rubber and plastic, with painted eyes. They couldn't love her because they weren't real. That was the answer, and it stunned her that she hadn't seen it before. As much as she wanted them to be real, as much as she birthed them and fed them and gave them love, they were not real. She could see them as being flesh and blood in her mind, yes, but she eventually put them to death because she knew all along they were only rubber and plastic.

Lord Jack wanted a baby. A son. He had given her a baby, and she had lost the gift. If she did not go to Lord Jack with a baby, he would turn her away. That was the message of the dream. But there was a dangerous flaw here, like a crack in time. Jack's baby was dead. She had squeezed the corpse out of her body in a gas station bathroom near Baltimore, her stomach lacerated with glass and metal. She had wrapped the little mass of tissue in the swaddling clothes of paper towels and sailed it off into the current. It had been a boy. That's what Jack had hoped it would be. A boy, to carry his seed into the future. But how could she go to Jack with his son when his son was dead and washed away?

Mary sat on the edge of the bed, the pistol still in her hand, and she struck a Thinker pose. *What if.* She stared at a dead roach on the floor, lying on its back against the baseboard. *What if.*

What if she did have a baby boy to take to Jack?

A real baby boy. Flesh and blood. What if?

Mary stood up and paced around the room, the Colt in her grip. She walked from one wall to the other and back again, thinking. A real baby boy. Where would she get one of those? She could see herself going to an adoption agency, and filling out the application forms.

Killed six pigs that I know of, she would say. Killed a college professor and a dude who thought he was going to make a movie about the Storm Front. Killed a kid out in the woods, too. But I sure do want a baby boy, sure do.

That was out. Where else could you get a baby?

She stopped pacing. You could get a baby at the same place any mother did, she realized. You could get a baby at a hospital.

Right, she thought sarcastically. Sure. Just go in, shoot up a hospital, and take a kid out of the maternity ward.

Hold it.

I was a nurse in Vietnam.

It was a lie, of course. She'd used it before, and it always worked with the pigs. They were suckers when you mentioned Vietnam. She began pacing again, her mind roaming in fertile fields. A nurse. A nurse.

Costume stores rented nurse uniforms, didn't they?

Yes, but did the nurses at all hospitals wear the same color uniforms? She didn't know. If she was going to do this, the first thing would be to find a hospital and check it out. She got the telephone book, and looked up Hospitals. There were a lot of them, when you added in the health centers and clinics, as the directory did. There was a clinic near Mableton. Not big enough, Mary decided. Another hospital, Atlanta West, was maybe a mile or two away. That might do, she thought. But then her gaze fell upon another listing, and she said, "That's it."

It was St. James Hospital. An omen of good karma, Mary thought. A hospital named after Jim Morrison. She checked the address. St. James was over in Buckhead, the ritzy area of the city. It was a good distance from her apartment, but she thought that might work to her advantage: no one would possibly recognize her over there, and those rich people didn't eat Whoppers. She took a pen and circled the St. James Hospital listing. She had a metallic taste in her mouth; the taste of danger. This was like making plans in the old days, and the thought of taking a baby boy from the maternity ward of St. James Hospital—a rich bitch's kid, which made it even sweeter—caused her heart to pound and warm dampness to pulse between her thighs.

But she didn't know if it could be done or not. First she'd have to go to the hospital and check out the maternity ward. Check out the security, where the stairwells were, where the nurses' station was relative to the exits. Find out what the uniforms looked like, and how many nurses worked on the ward. There were other things that she wouldn't think of until she was there to see it for herself, and if it wouldn't work she'd find somewhere else.

It would not be Jack's son. That baby was dead. But if she went to Lord Jack with the offering of a new baby boy, wouldn't he be just as pleased? More pleased, she decided. She would tell him that the baby who'd died in her ripped-up belly had been a girl.

Mary put the pistol away. She lay down and tried to sleep, but she was too excited. Twenty days remained before her rendezvous at the weeping lady. She got up, put on her gray sweatsuit, and she went out into the midnight cold to run a mile and think.

4.

Thursday's Child

On Thursday night after dinner, the first of February, Doug put the newspaper aside and said, "I've got some work to do at the office."

Laura watched him stand up and walk back to the bedroom. Their dinner had been eaten in silence of the stoniest kind. It had been Monday afternoon when she'd driven out to the Hillandale Apartments, and since that day she had seen Doug's guilt in every movement and heard it in every word. Doug had asked her what was bothering her, and she'd said she didn't feel well, that she was ready to be unbloated again. That was partly true, but of course only partly;

Doug, acting on instincts that had begun to beep like a radar alarm the last few days, did not pursue the point. Laura immersed herself in reading or watching movies on the VCR, her body gathering strength for the rite ahead.

"I'll be back in about . . ." Doug glanced at the clock as he shrugged into his coat. "I don't know. I'll just be back when I'm through."

She bit her tongue. David was heavy in her belly tonight, and his kicking was a real irritation. She felt huge and lumpy, her sleep had been racked with bad dreams about the madwoman on the balcony for the last two nights, and she was in no mood for games. "How's Eric?" she asked.

"Eric? He's fine, I guess. Why?"

"Does he spend as little time at home as you do?"

"Don't start that now. You know I've got a lot of work, and the day isn't long enough."

"The night isn't long enough, either, is it?" she asked.

Doug stopped buttoning his coat. He stared at her, and she thought she saw a small flash of fear in his eyes. "No," he replied. "It's not." His fingers finished the job. "You know how much it costs to raise a child and send him to college?"

"A lot."

"Yes, a lot. Like more than a hundred thousand dollars, and that's today's rates. By the time David's ready for college, God only knows how much it'll cost. That's what I think about when I have to go to work at night."

She thought she might either burst into tears or laughter, she didn't know which. Her face ached to collapse, but she kept her expression calm by force of will alone. "Will you be home by midnight, then?"

"Midnight? Sure." He pulled his collar up. "Want me to call if I'm going to be too late?"

"That would be nice."

"Okay." Doug leaned over and kissed her cheek, and Laura realized he had dashed his face with English Leather. His lips scraped her flesh, and then they were gone. "See you later," he said. He got his briefcase and headed for the garage door.

Say something, Laura thought. Stop him in his tracks. Stop him from going out that door, right now. But terror hit her, because she didn't know what to say and—worst of all—she feared that nothing she could say would stop him from leaving.

"The baby," she said.

Doug's steps slowed. He did stop, and he looked back at her from a slice of shadow.

"I think it's going to be only a few more days," she told him.

"Yeah." He smiled nervously. "I guess you're good and ready, aren't you?"

"Stay with me?" Laura asked, and she heard her voice quaver.

Doug took a breath. Laura saw him look around at the walls, a pained expression on his face, like a prisoner judging the width and breadth of his confinement. He took a couple of steps toward her, and then he stopped again. "You know, sometimes . . . this is hard to say." He paused a few seconds and tried again. "Sometimes I see what we have, and how far we've come, and . . . I feel really strange inside, like . . . is this it? I mean . . . is this what it's all about? And now, with you about to have the baby . . . it's like the end of something. Can you understand that?"

She shook her head.

"The end of just us," he went on. "The end of Doug and Laura. You know what I had a dream about last week?"

"No. Tell me."

"I dreamed I was an old man. I was sitting in that chair." He motioned to it with a tilt of his chin. "I had a gut and I was balding and all I wanted to do was sit in front of the television set and sleep. I don't know where you and David were, but I was alone and everything was behind me, and I . . . I started crying, because that was a terrible thing to know. I was a rich man, in a fine house, and I was crying because—" He had trouble with this, but he forced it out. "Because the journey's what it's all about. Not the being there. It's the fight to make it, and once you get there . . ." He trailed off, and shrugged. "I guess I don't make much sense, do I?"

"Come sit down," she urged him. "Let's talk about it, okay?"

Doug started to walk toward her. She knew he wanted to come, because his body seemed to tremble, as if he were trying to break away from some force that pulled at him. He balanced toward her for a few precious seconds, and then he lifted his arm and looked at his Rolex. "I'd better go. Got a heavy client first thing in the morning, and there's paperwork to clear up." His voice was stiff again, all business. "We'll talk tomorrow, all right?"

"Whenever," Laura said, her throat tight. Doug turned away from her and, briefcase in hand, he walked out of the house.

Laura heard the Mercedes' engine growl. The garage door went up. Before it ratcheted down again, Laura got to her feet. She winced and put a hand to her lower back, which had been hurting since early morning. Her bones ached as she walked across the den, and she picked up the keys to her BMW from the little silver tray. She went to the closet and got her overcoat and purse. Then she walked out— hobbled was more the correct term—to the garage, slid behind the BMW's wheel, and started the engine.

She had made up her mind that she was going to follow Doug. If he went to work, fine. They would talk about the future honestly, and decide where to go from here. If he went to the Hillandale Apartments, she was going to call a lawyer in the morning. She pulled out of the garage, turned off the driveway onto Moore's Mill Road, and drove toward the complex, hoping for the best but fearing the worst.

As she merged into the traffic on the expressway, she realized what she was doing as if seeing it from a distance, and its audacity surprised her. She hadn't known she still had any true toughness left in her. She'd thought all her iron had melted in the blast furnace of murder on that hot night in July. But following Doug—tracking him as if he were a criminal—shamed her, and she began to slow the car to take the next exit ramp off and circle back for home. *No,* she thought. A stern inner voice, commanding her to keep going. Doug *was* a criminal. If he had not already slaughtered her heart, he was hacking steadily at it. Savaging their lives together, tearing them asunder, making a mockery of the vows they'd taken. He was a criminal, and he deserved to be tracked like one.

Laura put her foot to the accelerator and sped past the exit.

At the Hillandale Apartments, Laura cruised around the building where C. Jannsen lived, looking for Doug's car in a parking slot. There wasn't a Mercedes in sight, only the low-slung, jazzy sports cars of younger people. Laura found an empty space just down from the building, and she pulled into it to wait. He's not here and he's not coming, she thought. He left before I did. If he was coming here, he'd be here already. He went to work, just as he said. He really did go to work. Relief rushed through her, so strong she almost put her head against the steering wheel and sobbed.

Lights brushed past the car. Laura looked behind her and to the right as the Mercedes moved by like a shark on the prowl. Her breath snagged on a soft gasp. The Mercedes pulled into a parking space eleven cars away from Laura. She watched as the lights were switched off and a man got out. He began to walk toward C. Jannsen's building. It was a walk Laura recognized instantly, sort of a half-shamble, half-strut. In Doug's hand was no longer the briefcase, but a six-pack of beer.

He'd stopped at a package store, she realized, and that was why she'd gotten there first. Rage flared within her; she could taste it in her mouth, a burnt taste like the smell of lighter fluid on charcoals. Her fingers were squeezed around the wheel so hard the veins were standing up in relief on the backs of her hands. Doug was on his way to see his girlfriend, and he was swinging the six-pack like an excited schoolboy. Laura reached for the door's handle and popped the door open. She wasn't going to let him get to that apartment thinking he'd pulled another one over on his dimwitted, compliant wife. Hell, no! She was going to fall on him like a sack of concrete on a slug, and when she was through with him, C. Jannsen would need a pooper-scooper to scrape him up.

She stood up, her face flaming with anger.

Her water broke.

The warm fluid flooded between her thighs and down her legs. The shock registered in her mind by the time the fluid reached her knees. What she'd been experiencing as back pain and occasional cramping all day long had been the first stage of labor.

Her baby was about to be born.

She watched Doug turn a corner, and he went out of sight.

Laura stood there for a moment, her panties drenched and the first real contraction beginning to build. The pressure soared into the realm of pain like a powerful hand squeezing a deep bruise, and Laura closed her eyes as the contraction's pain slowly swelled to its zenith and then began to subside. Tears rolled down her cheeks. Time the contractions, she thought. Look at your watch, stupid! She got back into the BMW and checked her watch by the courtesy light. The next contraction began to build within eight minutes, and its force made her clench her teeth.

She could not stay there much longer. Doug had someone. She was on her own.

She started the engine, backed out of the parking slot, and drove away from her husband and the Hillandale Apartments.

Two contractions later Laura pulled off the expressway and stopped at a gas station to use the phone. She called Dr. Bonnart, reached his answering service, and was told he'd be paged by his beeper. She waited, gripping the telephone as another contraction pulsed through her, sending pain rippling up her back and down her legs. Then Dr. Bonnart came on the line, listened as she told him what was happening, and he said she should get to St. James Hospital as soon as she could. "See you and Doug there," Dr. Bonnart told her, and he hung up.

The hospital was a large white building in a parklike setting in northeast Atlanta. By the time Laura had done the paperwork in Emergency Admitting and was moved into the LDR room, Dr. Steven Bonnart showed up in a tuxedo. She told him he hadn't needed to dress for the occasion. Formal dinner party for the hospital's new director, he explained as he watched the monitor that fed out a display of Laura's contractions. Wasn't much of a party anyway, he said, because everybody there wore beepers and the place sounded like a roomful of crickets.

"Where's Doug?" Dr. Bonnart asked as Laura had known he would.

"Doug's . . . not able to be here," she answered.

Dr. Bonnart stared at her for a few seconds through his round tortoiseshell glasses, and then he gave directions to one of the nurses and he left LDR to get changed and scrubbed.

A Demerol drip was inserted into the back of Laura's hand with a sharp little stab. She was in a green hospital gown with an elastic belt around her waist that fed wires to the monitor, and she sat up on a table with her weight bent forward. The smell of medicine and disinfectant drifted into her nostrils. The nurses were fast and efficient, and they made chatty small talk with Laura but she had trouble concentrating on what they were saying. Everything was becoming a blur of sound and movement, and she watched the monitor's screen blip as the contractions built inside her, swelled and cramped, and finally ebbed again until the next one. One of the nurses began talking about a new car she'd just bought. Bright red, she said. Always wanted a bright red car. "Easy breaths," one of the others told Laura, laying her hand on Laura's shoulder. "Just like they taught you in class." Laura's heart was beating hard, and that showed up in erratic spikes on another monitor. The contractions were like trapped thunder; they shook through her body and foretold a storm. "First child?" the nurse with the red car asked as she looked at Laura's chart. "My goodness, my goodness."

Dr. Bonnart reappeared, green-gowned and professional, and he parted Laura's legs to check her dilation. "You're working on it," he told her. "Still have a ways to go yet. Hurting much?"

"Yes. A little." Did apples hurt when they got cored? "Yes, it's hurting."

"Okay." He gave directions to Red Car about ceecee something, and Laura thought, *Time for the big needle, huh?* Dr. Bonnart went to a table and came back with a small item that resembled a spring in a ballpoint pen, a wire trailing from it to a high-tech white machine. "A little invasion," he said with a quick smile, and he reached up into her with his gloved fingers. The spring-looking thing was an internal fetal monitor; she knew that from her class. Dr. Bonnart found the baby's head, and he slid the device under the flesh. The high-tech machine began to put out a ticker tape of David's heartbeat and vital signs. Laura felt a scraping at her lower back. The nurse was preparing her for the epidural. At least she wouldn't have to look at the needle. The force of the contractions was powerful now, like a fist beating at a bruise on her spine. "Breathe easy, breathe easy," someone urged. "Little sting now," Dr. Bonnart told her, and she felt the needle go in.

A little sting for him, maybe. The wasps were bigger where she came from. Then it was over and the needle was out, and Laura felt the skin on her lower back prickle. Dr. Bonnart checked the progress of her dilation once more, then he checked the ticker tape and her own signs. In another moment she thought she could taste medicine in her mouth, and she hoped the epidural worked because the contractions were fierce now and she felt sweat on her face. Red Car mopped her brow and gave her a smile. "All that waiting for this," the nurse said. "Amazing how it happens, isn't it?"

"Yes, it is." Oh, it's hurting. Oh God, it really does hurt now! She could feel her body, straining open like a flower.

"When it's time, it's time," the nurse went on. "When a baby wants to come out, he lets you know about it."

"Tell him that," Laura managed to say, and the nurses and Dr. Bonnart laughed.

"Hang in there," Dr. Bonnart told her, and he left the room. Laura had a moment of panic. Where was he going? What if the baby came right this minute? Her heartbeat jumped on the monitor, and one of the nurses held her hand. The pressure built within her to what seemed like a point of sure explosion. She feared she might rip open like an overripe melon, and she felt tears burn her eyes. But then the pressure faded again, and Laura could hear her own quick, raspy breathing. "Easy, easy," the nurse advised. "Thursday's child has far to go."

"What?"

"Thursday's child. You know. The old saying. Thursday's child has far to go." The nurse glanced up at a clock on the wall. It was almost nine-fifteen. "But he might wait until Friday, and then he'll be fair of face."

"Full of grace," Red Car said.

"No, Friday is fair of face," the other contended. "Saturday is full of grace."

This line of argument was not Laura's primary concern. The contractions continued to build, pound within her like waves on rugged rocks, and ebb again. They were still painful, but not so much so. The epidural had kicked in, thank God, only the ceecee was not strong enough to mask all sensation. The pain was lessened, but the fist-on-bruise pressure was just as bad. At just after nine-thirty, Dr. Bonnart came into the room again and checked everything. "Coming along fine," he said. "Laura, can you give us a little push now?"

She did. Or tried, at least. Going to split open, she thought. Oh, Jesus! Breathe, breathe! How come everything had been so neat and orderly in class and here it was like a VCR tape running at superfast speed?

"Push again. Little harder this time, okay?"

She tried once more. It was clear to her that this was not going to be as simple as the classes had outlined. She could see Carol's face in her mind. *Too late now, toots,* Carol would say.

"Push, Laura. Let's see the top of his head."

Another face came into her mind, behind her closed eyelids as she strained and the pressure swelled at her center. Doug's face, and his voice saying *The end of just us. The end of Doug and Laura.* She saw the Hillandale Apartments in her mind, and Doug's car sliding into the parking space. She saw him walking away from her, carrying a six-pack of beer. *The end of just us. The end.*

"Push, Laura. Push."

She heard herself make a soft moan. The pressure was too much, it was killing her. David had hold of her guts, and he didn't want to let go. Still she tried, her body quivering, and she saw Doug walking away on the shadowfield of her mind. Walking away, farther and farther away. A distant person, becoming more of a stranger with every step. Her cry grew louder. Something broke inside her; not David's grip, but at a deeper level. She gritted her teeth and felt the warm tears streaking down her cheeks, and she knew it was over with Doug.

"There, there," Red Car said, and mopped her cheeks. "You're doing just fine, don't you worry about a thing."

"All right, take it easy." Dr. Bonnart patted her shoulder in a fatherly fashion, though he was about three or four years younger than she. "We've got the top of his head showing, but we're not quite ready. Relax now, just relax."

Laura concentrated on getting her breathing regulated. She stared at the wall as Red Car mopped her face, and the time alternately speeded up and crawled past on the clock, a trick of wishes and nerves. At ten o'clock, Dr. Bonnart asked her to start pushing again. "Harder. Keep going, Laura. Harder," he instructed her, and she gripped Red Car's hand so tightly she thought she might snap the woman's sturdy fingers. "Breathe and push, breathe and push."

Laura was trying her hardest. The pressure between her legs and in the small of her back was a symphony of excruciation. "There you go, doing fine," another nurse said, looking over Red Car's shoulder. Laura trembled, her muscles spasming. Surely she couldn't do this by herself; surely there was a machine that did this for you. But there was not, and surrounded by monitors and high-tech equipment, Laura was on her own. She breathed and pushed, breathed and pushed as she gripped Red Car's hand and the sweat was blotted from her cheeks and Dr. Bonnart kept encouraging her to greater effort.

Finally, at almost twenty to eleven, Dr. Bonnart said, "All right, ladies, let's take Mrs. Clayborne in."

Laura was helped onto a gurney, with what felt like a fleshy cannonball jammed between her thighs, and she was rolled into another room. This one had green tiles on the walls and a stainless steel table with stirrups, a bank of high-wattage lights aimed down from the ceiling. A nurse covered the table with green cloth, and Laura was positioned on the table on her back, her feet up in the stirrups. Light gleamed off a tray of instruments that might have found a use during the Inquisition, and Laura quickly averted her gaze from them. She was already feeling exhausted, with about as much strength as a wrung-out washrag, but she knew the most strenuous part of the birthing process still lay ahead. Dr. Bonnart sat on a stool at the end of the table, the tray of instruments close at hand. As he examined her and the position of the baby inside her, he actually began to whistle. "I know that song," one of the nurses said. "I heard it on the radio this afternoon. You hear it and it really gets in your mind, doesn't it?"

"Guns and Roses," Dr. Bonnart said. "My son loves 'em. He walks around wearing a baseball cap turned backward, and he's been talking about getting tattoos." He shifted the position of his fingers. Laura felt him prodding around inside her, but she was as numb down there as if she were stuffed with wet cotton. "I told him one tattoo and I'd break his neck. Could you lift your hips just a bit, Laura? Yes, that's fine."

Red Car turned on a videotape camera on a tripod, its lens aimed between Laura's legs. "Here we go, Laura," Dr. Bonnart said as the other nurse put a fresh pair of surgical gloves on his hands. "You ready to do a little work?"

"I'm ready." Ready or not, she thought, she would have to do it.

The nurse tied a surgical mask over Dr. Bonnart's nose and mouth. "Okay," he said, "let's get it done." He sat down on the stool again, Laura's gown folded back over her knees. "I want you to start pushing, Laura. Push until I say stop, and then rest for a few seconds. He's crowning very nicely, and I believe he wants to come on out and join us, but you're going to have to give him a shove. Okay?"

"Okay."

"All right. Start pushing right now."

She began. Damned if she didn't have that Guns and Roses tune snagged in her brain.

"Push, push. Relax. Push, push." A cloth mopped her face. Breathing hard. David wasn't coming out. Why wasn't he coming out? "Push, push. That's good, Laura, very good." She heard the silvery click of an instrument at work, but she could feel only a slight tugging. "Push, Laura. Keep pushing, he wants to come out."

"Doing just fine," Red Cap told her, and squeezed her hand.

"He's stuck," Laura heard herself say; a stupid thing. Dr. Bonnart told her to keep pushing, and she closed her eyes and clenched her teeth and did what he said, her thighs trembling with the effort.

Near eleven-ten, Laura thought she felt David begin to squeeze out. It was a movement of maybe an inch or two, but it thrilled her. She was wet with sweat and her hair was damp around her shoulders. It amazed her that anybody had ever been born. She pushed until she thought her muscles would give out, then she rested for a little while and pushed again. Her thighs and back rippled with cramps. "Oh, Jesus!" she whispered, her body strained and weary.

"You're doing great," Dr. Bonnart said. "Keep it up."

A surge of anger rose within her. What was Doug doing right now, while she was laboring under spotlights? Damn him to hell, she was going to sue his ass for divorce when this was over! She pushed and pushed, her face reddening. David moved maybe another inch. She thought she must surely be about to bend the stirrups from their sockets; she pushed against them with all her strength as Red Car swabbed her forehead.

Click, click went the instrument in Dr. Bonnart's hand. *Click, click.*

"Here he comes," Dr. Bonnart said as the clock ticked past eleven-thirty.

Laura felt her baby leaving her. It was a feeling of great relief mingled with great anxiety, because in the midst of the wet squeezing and the beep of monitors Laura realized her body was being separated from the living creature who had grown there. David was emerging into the world, and from this point on he would be at its mercy like every other human being.

"Keep pushing, don't stop," Dr. Bonnart urged.

She strained, the muscles of her back throbbing. She heard a damp, sucking sound. She glanced at the wall clock through swollen eyes: eleven forty-three. Red Car and the other nurse moved forward to help Dr. Bonnart. Something snipped and clipped. "Big push," the doctor said. She did, and David's weight was gone.

Slap. Slap. A third quick *slap.*

His crying began, like the thin, high noise of a motor being jump-started. Tears sprang to Laura's eyes, and she took a long, deep breath and released it.

"Here's your son," Dr. Bonnart told her, and he offered her something that was wailing and splotched with red and blue and had a froggish face in a head like a misshapen cone.

She had never seen such a beautiful boy, and she smiled like the sun through clouds. The storm was over.

Dr. Bonnart laid David on Laura's stomach. She pressed him close, feeling his heat. He was still crying, but it was a wonderful sound. She could smell the thick, coppery aromas of blood and birth fluids. David's body, still connected to her by the damp bluish-red umbilical cord, moved under her fingers. He was a fragile-looking thing, with tiny fingers and toes, the bump of a nose, and a pink-lipped mouth. There was nothing, however, fragile about his voice. It rose and fell, an undulation of what might have been adamant anger. Announcing himself, Laura thought. Letting the world know that David Douglas Clayborne had arrived, and demanding that room be made. As the umbilical was clipped off and tied, David trembled in a spite of infant fury and his wailing grew ragged. Laura said, "Shhhh, shhhh," as her fingers stroked the baby's smooth back. She felt the little shoulder blades and the ridges of his spine. Skeleton, nerves, veins, intestines, brain; he was whole and complete, and he was hers.

She felt it kick in then. What other women who'd had babies had told her to expect: a warm, radiant rush through her body that seemed to make her heart pound and swell. She recognized it as a mother's love, and as she stroked her baby she felt David relax from rigid indignation to soft compliance. His crying eased, became a quiet whimper, and ended on a gurgling sigh. "My baby," Laura said, and she looked up at Dr. Bonnart and the nurses with tears in her eyes. "My baby."

"Thursday's child," the nurse said, checking the clock. "Far to go."

It was after midnight when Laura was in her room on the hospital's second-floor maternity ward. She was drained and energized at the same time, and her body wanted to sleep but her mind wanted to replay the drama of birth again and again. She dialed her home number, her hand trembling.

"Hello, you've reached the residence of Douglas and Laura Clayborne. Please leave a message at the tone, and thank you for calling."

Beep.

Words abandoned her. She struggled to speak before the machine's timer clicked off. Doug wasn't home. He was still at the Hillandale Apartments, still with his girlfriend.

The end, she thought.

"I'm at the hospital," Laura forced out. And had to say it: "With David. He's eight pounds, two ounces."

Click: the machine, turning a deaf ear.

Laura, hollowed out, lay on the bed and thought about the future. It was a dangerous place, but it had David in it and so it would be bearable. If that future held Doug or not, she didn't know. She clasped her hands to her empty belly, and she finally drifted away to sleep in the hospital's peaceful womb.

5.

Gaunt Old Dude

The voice of God was singing in Mary Terror's apartment, at thirty-three and a third revolutions per minute. She was sitting on the bed, using a dark blue marker on the white size extra-large uniform she'd rented from Costumes Atlanta on Friday afternoon. The uniforms of the nurses on the maternity ward at St. James had dark blue piping around the collars and the breast pockets, and their hats were trimmed with dark blue. This uniform had snaps instead of buttons, as the real uniforms did, but it was all she could find in her size.

It was near seven o'clock on Saturday morning. The wind had picked up outside, scudding gray clouds over the city. The third of February, Mary thought: fifteen days until her meeting at the weeping lady. She was patient and careful at her work, making sure the ink didn't run or smear. She had a jar of white-out nearby in case of mistakes, but her hand was steady. On the table beside her bed was a dark blue plastic name tag with white letters: JANETTE LEISTER, in memory of two fallen comrades. She had gotten it from a place in Norcross that made plastic tags and novelties "While U Wait." It was the same colors as the name tags the nurses at St. James wore. Her white shoes—size 10EE—had also come from the costume rental, and she'd bought white stockings at Rich's department store.

She'd gone to the hospital yesterday, changing from her Burger King uniform after work and putting on jeans and a sweater under a baggy windbreaker. Had taken the elevator up to the maternity ward and walked around. Had gone to the big glass window to look at the babies, and she'd been very careful not to make eye contact with any of the nurses but she'd made mental notes of the dark blue piping on the white uniforms, the white-on-blue plastic name tags, and the fact that the elevator opened right onto the nurses' station. There had been no security people in sight on the maternity ward, but Mary had seen a pig with a walkie-talkie in the lobby and another one strolling around in the parking deck. Which meant that the parking deck was a scrub; she'd have to find another place to leave her truck, close enough to walk to and from the hospital. Mary had checked out the stairwells, finding one at either end of the long maternity ward corridor. The one on the building's south wing was next to a supply room, which could make for an unpleasant confrontation; the one on the north wing would have to do. A problem here, though: a sign on the stairwell door said FIRE ESCAPE. ALARM WILL SOUND IF OPENED. She couldn't check out where the stairwell led to, so she had no idea where she would come out. She didn't like that, and it was enough to call the whole thing a scrub until she saw an orderly pop the very same door open with the flat of his hand and walk through. There wasn't a peep. So was the alarm turned off at some times of the day, was the sign a phony, or was there some way to cheat the alarm? Maybe they'd had trouble with it going off, and they'd shut it down. Was it worth the risk?

She'd decided to think about it. As she looked through the window at the babies, some sleeping and some crying soundlessly, Mary knew she could not take a child from this room because it was too close—twenty paces—to the nurses' station. Some of the perambulators were empty, though they were still tagged: the babies were in the rooms with their mothers. The corridor took a curve between the nurses' station and the north stairwell, and on almost every door there was a pink or blue ribbon. The last four doors next to the stairwell were promising: three of the four ribbons were blue. If a nurse went into one of those rooms and found a baby with his mother, what reason might she have for going in? *Time to feed the baby.* No, the mother would know the feeding times, and what were breasts for? *Just need to check the baby for a minute.* No, the mother would want something more specific. *Time to weigh the baby.*

Yes. That would work.

Mary walked to the north stairwell door and back to where the corridor curved again. A woman's laughter trailed from one of the rooms. A baby was crying in another one. She noted the numbers of the three rooms with the blue ribbons: 21, 23, and 24. The door to 21 suddenly opened, and a man walked out. Mary turned away quickly and strode to a nearby water fountain. She watched the man walk in the opposite direction, toward the nurses' station; he had sandy-brown hair, and he wore gray slacks, a white shirt, and a dark blue sweater. Polished black wingtips on his feet. Rich bastard, father of a rich kid, she thought as she took a sip of water and listened to his shoes click on the linoleum. Then she walked back to the stairwell's door and looked at the warning sign. She would have to know where this led if she was going to do it, because she couldn't come up in the elevator. There was no choice.

Mary popped the door open with the flat of her hand, as the orderly had done. No alarm sounded. She saw black electrical tape holding down the door's latch, and she knew somebody had decided it was better to cheat the alarm than wait for the elevator. It was a good sign, she thought. She stepped into the stairwell and closed the door behind her.

She started down. The next door had a big red one on it. The stairwell continued down, and Mary followed it. At the bottom of the stairwell the door was unmarked. Through its glass inset, Mary could see a corridor with white walls. She opened it, slowly and carefully. Again there was no alarm and no sign of warning on the other side. She walked along the hallway, her senses questing. At a crossing of corridors, a sign pointed to different destinations: ELEVATORS, LAUNDRY, and MAINTENANCE. The smell of fresh paint lingered in the air, and pipes clung to the ceiling. Mary kept going, in the direction of the laundry. In another moment she heard someone humming, and then a husky black man with close-cropped white hair came around the corner, wheeling a mop in a bucket-and-wringer attachment. He wore a gray uniform that identified him as a member of the hospital's maintenance crew. Mary instantly put a mask on her face: a tightening of features, a coolness of the eyes. The mask said she was where she was supposed to be, and she had some authority. Surely a maintenance man wouldn't know everyone who worked in the hospital. His humming stopped. He was looking at her as they neared each other. Mary smiled slightly, said, "Excuse me," and walked past him as if she were in a hurry to get somewhere—but not too much of a hurry.

"Yes'm," the maintenance man answered, drawing his bucket out of her path. As she walked on around the corner she heard him start humming again.

Another good sign, she thought as the tension eased from her face. She had learned long ago that you could get into a lot of places you weren't supposed to be if you stared straight ahead and kept going, and if you masked yourself in an aura of authority. In a place this big, there were a lot of chiefs and the Indians were more concerned with the work at hand.

She came upon an area where there were several laundry hampers standing about. The voices of women neared her. Mary figured one woman alone might not ask questions, but someone in a group possibly would. She stepped around another corner and waited, pressed against a door, until the voices had gone. Then she went on, concentrating on her path and how to get back to the stairwell. She passed through a room full of steam presses, washers, and dryers. Three black women were working there, folding linens on a long table, and as they worked they were talking and laughing over the thumping noise of laboring washing machines. Their backs were to Mary, who moved past them with a fast, powerful stride. She came to another door, opened it without hesitation, and found herself standing on a loading dock at the rear of St. James Hospital, two panel trucks pulled up close and a couple of handcarts left untended.

When she closed the door behind her, she heard the click of a lock. A sign read PRESS BUZZER FOR ADMITTANCE. AUTHORIZED PERSONNEL ONLY. She looked at the buzzer's white button beside the door grip.

There was a dirty thumbprint on it. Then she walked down a set of concrete steps to the pavement, and she began the long trek around to the parking deck, her gaze alert for security guards.

Joy sang in her heart.

It could be done.

As she worked on the uniform, Mary began to think about her pickup truck. It was fine for around here, but it wasn't going to do for a long trip. She needed something she could pull onto a side road and sleep in. A van of some kind would do. She could find a van at one of the used car dealers and trade her pickup for it. But she'd need money, too, because the trade surely wouldn't be even-steven. She could sell one of her guns, maybe. No, she didn't have papers on any of them. Would Gordie buy the Magnum from her? Damn, she hadn't given any thought to money before. She had a little over three hundred dollars in the bank, and a hundred more stashed around the apartment. That wasn't enough to last her very long on the road, not with a van needing gas and a baby needing food and diapers.

She got up and went to the bedroom closet. She opened it and brought out the boy-sized Buckaroo rifle and telescopic sight she'd taken from Cory Peterson. Maybe she could get a hundred dollars for this, she thought. Seventy would be all right. Gordie might buy this and the Magnum. No, better keep the Magnum; it was a good concealment weapon. He might buy the sawed-off shotgun, though.

As Mary returned to the bed, she caught sight of a figure walking out on the highway in the dim gray light. Shecklett was wearing an overcoat that blew around him in the wind, and he was picking up crushed aluminum cans and putting them into a garbage bag. She knew his routine. He'd be out there for a couple of hours, and then he'd come in and cough his head off on the other side of the wall.

Ought to be ashamed, living like you do with all that money you've saved.

Paula had said that. In the letter Mary had taken from Shecklett's trash and taped together.

All that money you've saved.

Mary watched Shecklett pick up a can, walk a few paces, pick up a can. A truck rushed past, and Shecklett staggered in its cyclone. He fought the garbage bag, and then he picked up another can.

All that money.

Well, it would be in a bank, of course. Wouldn't it? Or was the old man the type who didn't trust banks? Maybe kept money stuffed in his mattress, or in shoeboxes tied up with rubber bands? She watched him for a while longer, her mind turning over the possibility like an interesting insect pulled from underneath a rock. Shecklett never had any visitors, and Paula—his daughter, Mary supposed—must live in another state. If something were to happen to him, it might be a long time before anyone found him. She could easily do it, and she didn't plan on sticking around very long after she took the baby. Okay.

Mary walked into the kitchen, opened a drawer and got a knife with a sharp, serrated blade. A knife used for gutting fish, she thought. She laid it on the countertop, and then she returned to the bedroom and the work on the nurse's uniform.

She was long finished with the job by the time she heard Shecklett coughing as he passed her door. Aluminum cans clanked together; he was carrying the garbage bag. Mary stood at her door, dressed in jeans, a brown sweater, her windbreaker, and a woolen cap. She listened for the clicking of Shecklett's keys as he slid the right one into his door. Then she went out into the cold, her .38 gripped in her right hand and the knife slipped down in her waistband under the windbreaker.

Shecklett was a gaunt man with a pockmarked face, his white hair wild and windblown, and his skin cracked like old leather. Shecklett barely had time to register the fact that someone was beside him before he felt the gun's barrel press against his skull. "Inside," Mary told him, and she guided him through the open door and slid the key out of the lock. Then she picked up the garbage bag full of cans and brought that in, too, as Shecklett stared at her in shock, his pale blue eyes red-rimmed with the chill.

Mary closed the door and turned the latch. "Kneel," she told him.

"Listen . . . listen . . . wait, okay? Is this a joke?"

"Kneel. On the floor. Do it."

Shecklett paused, and Mary judged whether to kick him in the kneecap or not. Then Shecklett swallowed, his big Adam's apple bulging, and he knelt on the thin brown carpet in the cramped little room. "Hands behind your head," Mary ordered. *"Now!"*

Shecklett did it. Mary could smell the fear coming out of the old man's skin, what smelled like a mixture of beer and ammonia. The window's curtains were already drawn. Mary switched on a lamp atop the TV. The room was a dreary rat's nest, newspapers and magazines lying in stacks, TV dinner trays strewn about, and clothes left where they'd been dropped. Shecklett trembled and had a coughing fit, and he put his hands to his mouth but Mary pressed the Colt's barrel against his forehead until he laced his fingers behind his head again.

She stepped away from him and glanced quickly at her wristwatch. Nine-oh-seven. She was going to have to get this done fast so she could find a good deal on a van before she changed to the uniform and made the drive to St. James.

"So I called the cops. So what?" Shecklett's voice shook. "You'd have done the same thing if you heard somebody hollerin' next door. It wasn't nothin' personal. I won't do it again. Swear to God. Okay?"

"You've got money," Mary said flatly. "Where is it?"

"Money? I don't have money! I'm poor, I swear to God!"

She eased back the Colt's hammer, the gun aimed into Shecklett's face.

"Listen . . . wait a minute . . . what's this all about, huh? Tell me what it's all about and maybe I can help you."

"You've got money hidden here. Where?"

"I don't! Look at this place! You think I've got any money?"

"Paula says you do," Mary told him.

"*Paula?*" Shecklett's face bleached gray. "What's Paula got to do with this? Jesus, I never hurt you, did I?"

Mary was tired of wasting time. She took a breath, lifted the Colt, and brought it down in a savage arc across Shecklett's face. He cried out and pitched onto his side, his body shuddering as the pain racked him. Mary knelt down beside him and put the gun to his pulsing temple. "Shit time is over," she said. "Give me your money. Got it?"

"Wait . . . wait . . . oh, you busted my face . . . wait . . ."

She grasped him by the hair and hauled him up to his knees again. His nose had been broken. The ruptured capillaries were turning dark purple, and blood rushed from his nostrils. Tears were trickling down Shecklett's wrinkled cheeks. "Next time I'll knock out your teeth," Mary said. "I want your money. The longer you screw around, the more pain I'm going to give you."

Shecklett blinked up at her, his eyes beginning to swell. "Oh God . . . please . . . please . . ." Mary lifted the Colt again to hit him in the mouth, and the old man flinched and whined. "No! Please! In the dresser! Top drawer, in my socks! That's everything I've got!"

"Show me." Mary stood up, backed away, and held the gun steady as Shecklett staggered up. She followed right behind him as he went through a hallway into the bedroom, which looked like a tornado had recently roared through. The bed had no sheets. On the walls hung yellowed, framed black-and-whites of a young Shecklett with a dark-haired, attractive woman. There was a picture atop the dresser of Shecklett wearing a tasseled fez and standing amid a group of smiling, paunchy Shriners. "Open the drawer," Mary said, her insides as tight as a crushed spring. "Easy, easy."

Shecklett opened it in fearful slow motion, blood dripping from his nose. He started to reach in, and Mary stepped forward and pressed the gun's barrel against his head. She looked into the drawer, saw nothing but boxer shorts and rolled-up socks. "I don't see any money."

"It's there. Right there." He touched one of the rolled-up socks. "Don't hurt me anymore, okay? I've got a bad heart."

Mary picked up the wad of socks he'd indicated. She closed the drawer and gave the socks back to him. "Show me."

Shecklett unwadded them, his hands trembling. Inside the socks was a roll of money. He held it up for her to see, and she said, "Count it."

He began. There were two hundred-dollar bills, three fifties, six twenties, four tens, five fives, and eight dollar bills. A total of five hundred and forty-three dollars. Mary snatched the cash from his hand. "That's not all of it," she said. "Where's the rest?"

Shecklett held his hand to his nose, his puffed eyes shiny with fear. "That's all. My social security. That's all I've got in the world."

The lying bastard! she thought, and she almost smacked him across the face again but she needed him conscious. "Stand back," she told him. When he obeyed, she pulled the dresser drawers out one after the other and dumped their contents onto the bed. In a couple of minutes it was all over; the pile contained Shecklett's T-shirts, sweaters, copies of *Cavalier, Nugget,* and *National Geographic,* handkerchiefs, a full bottle of J. W. Dant and one half killed, and other odds and ends of a solitary life but no money to speak of except for the errant few quarters, dimes, and pennies.

Mary Terror turned to face the old man, who had crushed himself up against the wall, and she said, "Paula thinks you've saved a lot of money. Is it true or not?"

"What do you know about Paula? You've never even *met* my daughter!"

Mary went to the bedroom closet, opened it, and ransacked it as Shecklett kept asking her how she knew his daughter. Mary overthrew the mattress and then the entire bedframe, finding nothing but TV dinner trays and old newspapers under the bed. She bulldozed through the bathroom's medicine cabinet and tore into the kitchen cabinets, and when her search was over she realized she knew Shecklett a lot better than Paula did.

"There's no more, is there?" she asked, training the Colt on him.

"I said there wasn't! Jesus Christ, look what you did to my place!"

"Give me your wallet."

Shecklett fished it from his pants and handed it over. There were no credit cards, and the wallet held a five and three ones. "Listen," Shecklett said as Mary pocketed the cash and tossed the wallet aside, "you've got every cent now. Why don't you just get out?"

"Right. The faster I get out, the faster you can call the pigs, huh?"

Shecklett's gaze dropped to the gun. He looked up from it into Mary's face, then back to the gun again. His Adam's apple wobbled. "I won't tell anybody," he said.

"Take off your clothes," Mary ordered.

"Huh?"

"Your clothes. Off."

"My *clothes?* How come you want me to—"

She was on him before he could utter another word. The gun rose and fell, and the old man dropped to his knees with his jaw broken and three teeth loose. Moaning with pain, he began to take his clothes off. When he was finished, his bony white body nude, Mary said, "Get up." He did, his eyes deep-sunken and terrified. "Into the bathroom," she told him, and she followed him in. "Get in the bathtub on your hands and knees." He balked at this, and began to beg her to leave him alone, that he wouldn't tell anybody, wouldn't ever tell anybody. She pressed the gun's barrel against the staircase of his spine, and he got into the tub in the position she'd demanded.

"Head down. Don't look at me," she said. Shecklett's skinny chest heaved, and he coughed violently for maybe a minute. She waited until his coughing was done, and then she slid the knife from her waistband.

"Swear I won't tell a soul." His chest heaved again, this time in a sob. "God, please don't hurt me. I never did anything to you. I won't tell anybody. I'll keep my mouth shut, I swear to—"

Mary picked up a washrag from the sink and jammed it into Shecklett's mouth. He gasped and gagged, and then Mary leaned over his naked body. She thrust the knife into one side of Shecklett's throat, her knuckles scraping the sandpaper of his skin. Before

Shecklett could fully realize what she was doing, Mary cut his throat from ear to ear with the serrated blade, and crimson blood fountained into the air.

Shecklett tried to scream around the washrag. As the blood sprayed into the bathtub from his severed carotid artery, Shecklett grasped at his throat with his one hand and started to rise to his knees. Mary put her foot into the small of his back and jammed him down again. His body thrashed and writhed under Mary's strength, blood spewing into the tub as if released from a pulsing faucet. "My name is Mary Terrell," she told him as he bled and died. "Soldier of the Storm Front. Freedom fighter for those without rights in the Mindfuck State, and executioner of the state's pigs." He was trying to get up again, his knowledge of death affording him a last surge of power. She had to bear down hard on him, and his adrenaline flood ceased in a few seconds. He writhed at the bottom of the tub as if doing a breast stroke in his own gore. "Defender of the just. Protector of the weak. Crusher of the Mindfuck mentality, and keeper of the faith."

He had a lot of blood for a gaunt old dude.

Mary sat on the edge of the tub and watched him die. There was something about him that made her think of a baby swimming through a sea of blood and mother's fluid to reach the light. He died not with a shudder or a moan or a final desperate thrashing; he simply got weaker and weaker, until the weakness killed him. And there he lay in the tub with his life going down the drain, his eyes open, and his skin the color of a fish Mary had once seen washed up and swollen-bellied on a gray beach.

Mary stood up. She slashed the mattress open in the bedroom, just to make sure no money was hidden inside. Cotton wadding puffed out, and it served to clean the blade. Then she left Shecklett's apartment and closed the door behind her, richer by five hundred fifty-one dollars and some change.

The uniform was ready. She took a shower with God cranked up on the speakers, the bass pounding at the walls like an eager fist. Before the day was done, she would be a mother. She scrubbed spatters of blood from her hands, and she smiled in her veil of steam.

6.

Big Hands

On Saturday morning just after eleven o'clock, Doug stood at the window of Room 21. He watched the clouds move in the pewter sky, and he thought about the question Laura had just asked him.

How long has the affair been going on?

Of course she knew. He'd seen yesterday that she knew; it was in her eyes when he'd told her he hadn't been able to get away from work until long after midnight Friday morning. Her eyes had looked right through him, as if he were no longer truly there. "I don't want to hear it," she'd said, and she'd lapsed into silence. Every time he spoke to

her, he was met with the same wall of words: "I don't want to hear it."
He'd known she'd be upset because he wasn't there at David's birth,
and that fact gnawed at his guts like little piranhas that meant to
devour him to the bones, but then he realized there was more to it.
Laura knew. Somehow, she knew. How much she knew he wasn't
sure, but just knowing was bad enough. All day yesterday and all night
last night it had been either "I don't want to hear it" or cold silence.
Laura's mother, who'd come to Atlanta yesterday with Laura's father
to see their grandson, had asked him what was wrong with Laura, that
she didn't want to talk, that all she wanted to do was hold the baby
and croon to David. He hadn't been able to say because he didn't
know. Now he did, and he watched the pewter sky and wished he
could think of something to say.

"The truth," Laura said, reading his mind in the stiff reluctance of
his body. "That's what I want."

"An *affair?*" He turned from the window, a salesman's smile
plastered to his mouth. "Laura, come on! I can't believe you—" He
stopped speaking because his son was down the hall in the maternity
window, and he couldn't carry off the lie.

"How long?" she prodded. Her face was wan and pale, her eyes
tired. She felt light of body and leaden of spirit. "A month? Two
months? Doug, I'd like to hear it."

He was silent. His mind was searching for cracks like a mouse who
hears a footstep in the dark.

"She lives at the Hillandale Apartments," Laura went on. "Apartment 5-E. I followed you there on Thursday night."

Doug's mouth opened. Hung open. A small gasp escaped his chest.
She saw the color bloom in his cheeks. "You . . . *followed* me? You
actually . . . my God, you actually *followed* me?" He shook his head
incredulously. "Jesus! I can't believe this! You followed me
like . . . like I was some kind of . . . common criminal or something?"

"STOP IT, DOUG!" The thunder crashed out of her before she
could contain it. She was not a yeller—far from it—but the anger
sprang forth seemingly from every pore in her body like scalding
steam. "Stop the lies, all right? Just stop lying, right now!"

"Keep your voice down, will you?"

"Hell, no, I won't keep my voice down!" The expression of shocked
outrage on Doug's face was like kerosene on her charcoals. The flames

leapt high, out of her control. "I *know* you've got a girlfriend, Doug! I found the two tickets! I found out Eric was in Charleston the night he was supposed to have called you to the office! Someone called me and told me what her address was! You'd better believe I followed you, and by God I was hoping you wouldn't go to her, but there you were! Right there! How was the beer, Doug?" She felt her mouth contort in a bitter twist. "Did you two enjoy the six-pack? My water broke right there in the parking lot, while you were walking to her door! While our son—*my* son—was being born, you were shacked up with a stranger across town! Was it good, Doug? Come on, tell me, damn you! Was it good? Was it really really good?"

"Are you finished?" He was grim-lipped and stoic, but she saw the shiny fear in his eyes.

"NO! No, I'm not finished! How *could* you do something like this? Knowing I was about to have David? How? Don't you have a conscience? My God, you must think I'm so stupid! Did you think I'd never know? Is that it? Did you think you could have this secret life forever, and I'd never figure it out?" Tears burned her eyes. She blinked them back, and they were gone. "Come on, let's hear it! Let's hear how you figured you'd have your little piece of cake at home and your little piece of . . ." She couldn't say the word she was thinking. "Your little girlfriend at the Hillandale Apartments and I'd never find out!"

The bloom had faded from Doug's cheeks. He stood there, just staring at her with his eyes that glinted like false coins, and he seemed very small to her. He seemed to have shrunken in the space of a minute or so, until his Dockers khaki trousers and his Polo sweater hung on a framework of bones and lies. He lifted his hand and touched his forehead, and Laura saw his hand tremble. "Someone *told* you?" he asked; even his voice had gotten small. "Who told you?"

"A friend. How long has it been going on? Will you tell me that, or not?"

He drew a breath and let it leak out. He was deflating, right in front of her. His face had gotten pasty and pallid, and he spoke with what seemed a great effort: "I . . . met her . . . in September. I've been . . . I've been seeing her since . . . the end of October."

Christmas. All through Christmas Doug had been sleeping with another woman. For three months as David grew inside her, Doug had been making his heated runs to and from the Hillandale Apartments. Laura said, "Oh my God" and pressed her hand to her mouth.

"She's a secretary at a real estate agency," Doug went on, flaying her with a small, hushed voice. "I met her when I was doing some work for one of the realtors. She seemed . . . I don't know, cute, I guess. I asked her out to lunch. She said okay. She knew I was married, but she didn't mind." Doug turned away from Laura, his gaze scanning the clouds again. "It happened fast. Two lunch dates in a row, and then I asked her out to dinner. She said she'd make dinner for me at her apartment. On the way over there I pulled off the road and just sat and thought. I knew what I was doing. I knew I was stepping on you and David. I knew it."

"But you did it anyway. Very thoughtful of you."

"I did it anyway," he agreed. "I have no reason for it other than an old tired one: she's twenty-three, and when I was with her I felt like a kid again. Just starting out, no responsibilities, no wife, no child on the way, no house payments, no car payments, nothing but the wild blue yonder ahead. That sounds like bullshit, doesn't it?"

"Yes."

"Maybe so, but it's the truth." He looked at her, his face ancient with sorrow. "I meant to stop seeing her. It was just going to be a one-time thing. But . . . it got away from me. She's studying for her real estate tests, and I helped her with her homework. We drank wine and watched old movies. You know, talking to somebody that age is like talking to a person from another planet. She's never heard of Howdy Doody, or Steppenwolf, or Mighty Mouse or John Garfield or Boris Karloff or . . ." He shrugged. "I guess I was trying to reinvent myself, maybe. Make myself younger, go back to how I used to be before I knew what the world was all about. She looked at me and saw somebody you don't know, Laura. Can you understand that?"

"Why didn't you show that person to *me?*" she asked. Her voice cracked, but she held the tears at bay. "I wanted to see you. Why didn't you let me?"

"You know the real me," he said. "It was easier to fool her."

Laura felt the crush of despair settle upon her. She wanted to rage and scream and throw something, but she did not. She said, in a quiet voice, "We did love each other once, didn't we? The whole thing wasn't a lie, was it?"

"No, it wasn't a lie," Doug answered. "We did love each other." He wiped the back of his hand across his mouth, his eyes glazed and unfocused. "Can we work this out?" he asked.

Someone knocked on the door. A nurse with curly red hair came in, carrying a small human being wrapped up in a downy blue blanket. The nurse smiled, showing big front teeth. "Here's the little one!" she said brightly, and she offered David to his mother.

Laura took him. His skin was pink, his skull—reformed into an oval by Dr. Bonnart's gentle hands—covered with light brown fuzz. He made a mewling noise, and blinked his pale blue eyes. Laura smelled his aroma: a peaches-and-cream smell that she'd caught the first time David was brought to her after being cleaned. Around his pudgy left ankle he wore a plastic band that had Boy, Clayborne, Room 21 typed on it. His mewling became a hiccupy sound, and Laura said, "Shhhhh, shhhhh," as she rocked him in her arms.

"I think he's hungry," the nurse said.

Laura unsnapped the top of her hospital gown and guided David's mouth to one of her nipples. One of David's hands closed on the flesh of her breast and his mouth went to work. It was a feeling ripe with satisfaction and—yes—sensuality, and Laura sighed deeply as her son fed on the mother's milk.

"There we go." The nurse offered a smile to Doug, then reclaimed it when she saw his sallow face and sunken eyes. "Well, I'll leave him with you for a while," she said, and then she left the room.

"His eyes," Doug said, leaning over the bed to look down at David. "They look like yours."

"I'd like you to leave," she told him.

"We can talk about this, okay? We can work everything out."

"I'd like you to leave," Laura repeated, and in her face Doug found no mercy.

He straightened up, started to speak again, but saw no use in it. She paid him no further attention, all her attention being focused on the baby cradled against her breast. After a minute or so in which there was no sound but that of David's mouth sucking on Laura's swollen nipple, Doug walked through the door and out of her sight.

"Make you big and strong," she crooned to her son, a smile relighting her face. "Yes it will. Make you big and strong."

It was a hard world, and people could burn love to cinders and crush the ashes. But in this moment of time the mother held her son close and spoke softly to him, and all the hardness of that world was shunted aside. Laura didn't want to think about Doug and what was ahead for both of them, so she did not. She kissed David's forehead and tasted his sweet skin, and she traced the faint blue lines of veins in the side of his head with a forefinger. Blood was rushing through them, his heart was beating, and his lungs were at work: the miracle had come true, and it was right there in her arms. She watched him blink, watched the pale blue eyes search the realm of his sensations. He was all she needed. He was everything she needed.

Her parents returned in another fifteen minutes. Both of them were gray-haired, Miriam firm-jawed and dark-eyed and Franklin a simple, jocular smiler. They didn't seem to want to know where Doug was, possibly because they smelled the smoke of her anger lingering in the room. Laura's mother held David for a while and koochy-kooed him, but she gave him back when he started to cry. Her father said David looked as if he was going to be a big boy, with big hands fit for throwing a football. Laura suffered her parents with polite smiles and agreements as she held David close. David cried off and on, like a little switch being tripped, but Laura rocked him and crooned to him and soon the infant was sleeping in her arms, his heart beating strong and steady. Franklin settled down to read the newspaper, and Miriam had brought her needlepoint. Laura slept, David nestled against her. She winced in her sleep, dreaming of a madwoman on a balcony and two gunshots.

At one twenty-eight, an olive-green Chevy van with rust holes in the passenger door and a cracked left rear window pulled to the loading dock behind St. James Hospital. The woman who got out wore a nurse's uniform, white trimmed with dark blue. Over her breast pocket her plastic tag identified her as Janette Leister. Next to the name tag was pinned a yellow Smiley Face.

Mary Terror spent a moment pulling a smile up from the depths of her own face. She looked fresh-scrubbed and pink-cheeked, and she'd put clear gloss on her lips. Her heart was hammering, her stomach twisted into nervous knots. But she took a few deep breaths, thinking of the baby she was going to take to Lord Jack. The baby was up there on the second floor, waiting for her in one of three rooms with blue bows on the doors. When she was ready, she climbed the steps to the loading dock. A laundry hamper and a handcart had been left there. She guided the hamper to the door and pressed the buzzer, and then she waited.

No one answered. Come on, come on! she thought. She pressed the buzzer again. Damn it, what if no one could hear the buzzer? What if a security guard answered? What if someone instantly saw through the disguise and slammed the door in her face? She was wearing the right uniform, the right colors, the right shoes. Come on, come on!

The door opened.

A black woman—one of the laundry workers—peered through.

"I locked myself out!" Mary said, her smile fixed and frozen. "Can you believe that? The door closed and here I am!" She started to push the hamper before her through the doorway. There was a second or two when she thought the woman wasn't going to give way, and she said merrily, "Excuse me! Coming through!"

"Yes ma'am, come on, then." The laundress smiled and backed away, holding the door open. "Blowin' up a rain out there!"

"It sure is, isn't it?" Mary Terror took three more long strides, the hamper in front of her. The door clicked shut at her back.

She was inside.

"You sure 'nuf must be lost!" the laundress said. "How come you to be down here?"

"I'm new. Just started a few days ago." Mary was moving away from the woman, guiding the hamper down a long hallway. She could hear the whisper of steam and the *thunk-thunk-thunk* of washing machines at work. "Guess I don't know my way around like I thought I did."

"I hear you! 'Bout have to carry a map to get around this big ol' place."

"You have a good day, now," Mary said, and she abandoned the hamper next to a group of other hampers parked near the laundry room. She picked up her pace, heading deeper into the hospital. The laundress said, "Bye-bye," but Mary didn't respond. She was focused on the path that would take her to the stairwell door, and she walked briskly through the corridor, steam pipes hissing above her head.

She came around a curve and found herself about twenty paces behind a female pig with a walkie-talkie, going in the same direction as she. Mary's heart stuttered, and she stepped back out of sight for a minute or two, giving the she-pig time to clear out. Then, when the corridor was clear, Mary started toward the stairwell again. Her eyes ticked back and forth, checking doorways on either side of the corridor; her senses were on high alert, and her blood was cold. She heard voices here and there, but saw no one else. At last she came to the stairwell, and she pushed through the door and started up.

As she ascended past the first floor, she faced another challenge: two nurses coming down. She popped her smile back on, the two nurses smiled and nodded, and Mary passed them with damp palms. Then there was the door with a big two on it. Mary went through it, her gaze checking the black tape that held down the latch and cheated the alarm. She was on the maternity ward, and there was no one else in the corridor between her and the curve that led to the nurses' station.

Mary heard a soft chimes that, she presumed, signaled one of the nurses. The crying of babies drifted through the hallway like a siren song. It was now or never. She chose Room 24, and she walked in as if she owned the hospital.

A young woman was in bed, breastfeeding her newborn. A man sat in a chair beside the bed, watching the process with true wonder. They both turned their attention to the six-foot-tall nurse who walked in, and the young mother smiled dreamily and said, "We're doing just fine."

The man, woman, and their son were black.

Mary stopped. She said, "I see you are. Just checking." Then she turned and walked out. It would not do to take Lord Jack a black child. She went across the hall into Room 23, and there found a white woman in bed talking animatedly with another young couple and a middle-aged man, joyful bouquets of flowers and balloons arranged around the room. The woman's baby wasn't with her. "Hi," she said to Mary. "Could I have my baby, do you think?"

"I don't see why not. I'll go get him."

"You're a big one, aren't you?" the middle-aged man asked, and his grin flashed a silver tooth.

Mary gave him a smile, her eyes cold. She turned away, walked out of the room and to the door that had a blue bow and the number 21 on it.

She was nervous. If this one didn't work out, she might have to scrub the mission.

She thought of Lord Jack, awaiting her at the weeping lady, and she went in.

The mother was asleep, her baby cradled against her. In a chair by the window sat an older woman with curly gray hair, doing needlepoint. "Hello," the woman in the chair said. "How are you today?"

"I'm fine, thanks." Mary saw the mother's eyes start to open. The baby began to stir, too; his eyelids fluttered open for a second, and

Mary saw that the child's eyes were light blue, like Lord Jack's. Her heart leapt; it was karma at work.

"Oh, I drifted off." Laura blinked, trying to focus on the nurse who stood over the bed. A big woman with a nondescript face and brown hair. A yellow Smiley Face button on her uniform. Her name tag said Janette something. "What time is it?"

"Time to weigh the baby," Mary answered. She heard tension in her voice, and she got a grip on it. "It'll just take a minute or two."

"Where's Dad?" Laura asked her mother.

"He went down to get another magazine. You know him and his reading."

"Can I weigh the baby, please?" Mary held her arms out to take him.

David was waking up. His initial response was to open his mouth and let out a high, thin cry. "I think he's hungry again," Laura said. "Can I feed him first?"

Couldn't chance a real nurse coming in, Mary thought. She kept her smile on. "I won't be very long. Just get this over with and out of the way, all right?"

Laura said, "All right," though she yearned to feed him. "I haven't seen you before."

"I only work weekends," Mary replied, her arms offered.

"Shhhhh, shhhhh, don't cry," Laura told her son. She kissed his forehead, smelling the peaches-and-cream aroma of his flesh. "Oh, you're so precious," she told him, and she reluctantly placed him in the nurse's arms. Immediately she felt the need to grasp him back to her again. The nurse had big hands, and Laura saw that one of the woman's fingernails had a dark red crust beneath it. She glanced again at the name tag: *Leister.*

"There we go," Mary said, rocking the infant in her arms. "There we go, sweet thing." She began moving toward the door. "I'll bring him right back."

"Take good care of him," Laura said. Needs to wash her hands, she thought.

"I sure will." Mary was almost out the door.

"Nurse?" Laura asked.

Mary stopped on the threshold, the baby still crying in her arms.

"Would you bring me some orange juice, please?"

"Yes, ma'am." Mary turned away, walked through the door, and saw the black father from number 24 just leaving the room to go toward the nurses' station. She put her index finger into the baby's mouth to quiet his crying, and she went through the stairwell's door and started down the stairs.

"She had dirty hands," Laura said to her mother. "Did you notice that?"

"No, but that was the biggest woman I ever laid eyes on." She watched Laura position herself against her pillows, and Laura winced at a sudden pain. "How're you doin'?"

"Okay, I guess. Hurting a little bit." She felt as if she'd delivered a sack of hardened concrete. Her body was full of aches and pains, the muscles of her back and thighs still prone to cramps. Her stomach had lost its bloat, but she was still sluggish and heavy with fluids. The thirty-two stitches between her thighs, where Dr. Bonnart had clipped the flesh of her vagina open to allow extra room for David's head to slide through, was a constant irritation. "I thought the nurses had to keep their hands clean," she said when she'd gotten herself comfortable again.

"I sent your father downstairs," Laura's mother said. "I think we need to talk, don't you?"

"Talk about what?"

"You know." She leaned forward in her chair, her gaze sharp. "About what the problem is between you and Doug."

Of course she'd sensed it, Laura thought. Her mother's radar was rarely wrong. "The problem." Laura nodded. "Yes, there's sure a problem, all right."

"I'd like to hear it."

Laura knew there was no way to deflect this conversation. Sooner or later, it would have to be spoken. "Doug's been having an affair since October," she began, and she saw her mother's mouth open in a small gasp. Laura began to tell her the whole story, and the older woman listened intently as Laura's son was being carried through a corridor where steam pipes hissed like awakened snakes.

Mary Terror, her index finger clasped in the baby's mouth, strode through the corridor toward the loading dock's door. Before she reached the laundry area, she stopped where the hampers were parked. One of them had towels at the bottom, and she put the baby down amid them and covered him up. The infant gurgled and mewled, but Mary grasped the hamper and started pushing it ahead of her. As she passed through the laundry where the black women were working, Mary saw the laundress who'd allowed her in.

"You still lost?" the woman called over the noise of washers and steam presses.

"No, I know where I'm going now," Mary answered. She flashed a quick smile and went on. The baby began to cry just before Mary reached the exit, but it was a soft crying and the noise of the laundry masked it. She opened the door. The wind had picked up, and silver needles of rain were falling. She pushed the hamper out onto the loading dock and scooped the infant out, still wrapped in a towel. Then she hurried down the concrete steps to her van, which she'd traded for her truck and three hundred and eighty dollars at Friendly Ernie's Used Cars in Smyrna about two hours before. She put the crying baby onto the floorboard on the passenger side, next to her sawed-off shotgun. She started the engine, which ran rough as a cob, and made the entire van shudder. The windshield wipers shrieked as they swept back and forth across the glass.

Then Mary Terror backed away from the loading dock, turned the van around, and drove away from the hospital named after God. "Hush, now!" she told the baby. "Mary's got you!" The infant kept crying.

He'd just have to learn who was in control.

Mary left the hospital behind, and swung up onto a freeway, where she merged into a sea of metal in the falling silver rain.

7.

A Hollow Vessel

Hi." The nurse had red hair and freckled cheeks, and she beamed a smile. Her name tag identified her as Erin Kingman. She glanced quickly at the empty perambulator beside the bed. "Where's David?"

"Someone took him to be weighed," Laura said. "I guess that was about fifteen minutes ago. I asked her for orange juice, but maybe she got busy."

"Who took him?"

"A big woman. Janette was her first name. I hadn't seen her before."

"Uh-huh." Erin nodded, her smile still there but the first butterfly flutters beginning in her stomach. "All right, I'll go find her. Excuse me." She hurried out of the room, leaving Laura and Miriam to their conversation.

"Divorce." It had a funeral-bell sound, coming from the older woman's mouth. "Is that what you're saying?"

"Yes."

"Laura, it doesn't *have* to be divorce. You could go to a counselor and talk things out. Divorce is a messy, sticky thing. And David's going to need a father. Don't think just of yourself and not of David."

Laura heard what was coming. She waited for it without speaking, her hands clenched under the sheet.

"Doug's given you a good life," her mother went on in that earnest tone of voice used by women who knew they'd traded love for comfort long ago. "He's been a good provider, hasn't he?"

"We bought a lot of things together, if that's what you mean."

"You have a history. A life together, and now a son. You have a fine house, you drive a fine car, and you're not wanting for anything. So divorce is a drastic option, Laura. Maybe you could get a good settlement, but a thirty-six-year-old woman with a baby on her own might have a hard time—" She stopped. "You know what I'm saying, don't you?"

"Not exactly."

Her mother sighed, as if Laura had the brains of a wooden block. "A woman your age, with a baby, might have a hard time finding another man. That's important to think about before you make any rash decisions."

Laura closed her eyes. She felt dizzy and sick, and she clamped her teeth down on her tongue because she couldn't trust what she might say to her mother.

"Now I know you think I'm wrong. You've thought I was wrong before. I'm looking out for your interests because I love you, Laura. What you've got to figure out is why Doug decided to play around, and what you can do to make up for it."

Her eyes opened. "Make *up* for it?"

"That's right. I told you a long time ago, a headstrong man like Doug needs a lot of attention. And he needs a loose rope, too. Take your father. I've always held him on a loose rope, and our marriage is the better for it. These are things a woman learns by experience, and no one can teach her. The looser the rope, the stronger the marriage."

"I can't . . ." Words failed her. She tried again, knocked breathless. "I can't believe you're saying these things! Do you mean . . . you want me to *stay* with Doug? To look the other way if he ever decides to"—she used her mother's term—"play around again?"

"He'll outgrow it," the older woman said. "You have to be there for him, and he'll know that what he has at home is priceless. Doug is a good provider and he's going to be a good father. Those are very important things in this day and time. You need to be thinking about healing the wound between you and Doug instead of talking about divorce."

Laura didn't know what she was about to say. Her mouth was opening, the blood was pounding in her face, and she could feel the shout beginning to draw power from her lungs. She longed to see her mother cringe before her voice, longed to see her get up from that chair and march out of the room in a practiced sulk. Doug was a stranger to her, and so was her mother; she didn't know either of those pretenders to her love. She was about to shout in her mother's face, though she didn't yet know what she was going to say.

She would never know.

Two nurses—one of them Erin Kingman and the other an older, stockier woman—entered the room. Following behind them was a man in a dark blue blazer and gray slacks, his face round and fleshy and his brown hair receding from a high globe of a forehead. He wore black horn-rimmed glasses, and his shoes squeaked as he approached Laura's bed.

"Excuse me," the older nurse said to Laura's mother. Her name tag read: Kathryn Langner. "Would you go with Miss Kingman for just a few minutes, please?"

"What is it?" Laura's mother stood up, her radar on full alert. "What's wrong?"

"Would you come with me, please?" Erin Kingman stood at the woman's side. "We'll just step out into the hall, all right?"

"What's going on? Laura, what's this all about?"

Laura couldn't answer. The older nurse and the man moved in to take positions on either side of the bed. A foreboding of horror swept like a cold tide through Laura's body. Oh Jesus! she thought. It's David! Something's happened to David!

"My baby," she heard herself say frantically. "Where's my baby?"

"Would you wait in the hall, please?" The man spoke to Miriam in a flat tone that said she would, whether she liked it or not. "Miss Kingman, close the door on your way out."

"Where's my baby?" Laura felt her heart pounding, and there was a fresh twinge of pain between her legs. "I want to see David!"

"Out," the man told Laura's mother. Miss Kingman closed the door. Kathryn Langner grasped one of Laura's hands, and the man said in a quieter, steady voice, "Mrs. Clayborne, my name is Bill Ramsey. I'm on the security staff here. Do you remember the name of the nurse who took your child from this room?"

"Janette something. It started with an L." She couldn't recall the last name, and her brain was sluggish with shock. "What's wrong? She said she was going to bring my baby right back. I'd like him back now."

"Mrs. Clayborne," Ramsey said, "no nurse with that first name works on the maternity ward." Behind his glasses, his eyes were as black as the frames. A pulse beat at his balding left temple. "We think the woman may have taken your child from the premises."

Laura blinked. Her mind rejected the last three words. "What? Taken him where?"

"From the hospital," Ramsey repeated. "Our people are checking all the exits right now. I want you to think carefully and tell me what this woman looked like."

"She was a nurse. She said she worked on weekends." The blood was roaring in Laura's head. She heard her voice as if at the far end of a long tunnel. I'm about to faint, she thought. Dear God, I'm really about to faint. She squeezed the nurse's hand and was met by forceful pressure.

"She wore a nurse's uniform, is that correct?"

"Yes. A uniform. She was a nurse."

"Her first name was Janette. Did she tell you that?"

"It was . . . it was . . . on her name tag. Next to the Smiley Face."

"Pardon me?"

"The . . . Smiley Face," Laura said. "It was yellow. A Smiley Face button."

"What color was the woman's hair and eyes?"

"I don't—" Her thinking was freezing solid, but there seemed to be pulsing heat trapped in her face. "Brown hair. Shoulder-length. Her eyes were . . . blue, I think. No, gray. I can't remember."

"Anything else about her? Crooked nose? Heavy eyebrows? Freckles?"

"Tall," Laura said. "A big woman. Tall." Her throat was closing up, dark motes spun before her eyes, and only the pressure of the nurse's hand kept her from passing out.

"How tall? Five nine? Five ten? Taller?"

"Taller. Six feet. Maybe more."

Bill Ramsey reached under his coat and pulled out a walkie-talkie. He clicked it on. "Eugene, this is Ramsey. We're looking for a woman in a nurse's uniform, description as follows: brown shoulder-length hair, blue or gray eyes, approximately six feet tall. Hold on." He looked at Laura again, whose face had gone chalky except for red circles around her eyes. "Heavyset, slim, or medium build?"

"Big. Heavyset."

"Eugene? Heavyset. Got a name tag that identifies her as Janette, last name begins with an L. Copy?"

"Copy," the voice crackled over the walkie-talkie.

"The button," Laura reminded him. She was about to throw up, the nausea hot in her stomach. "The Smiley Face button."

Ramsey clicked the walkie-talkie on again and gave Eugene the extra information.

"I'm going to be sick," Laura told Kathryn Langner, tears burning trails down her cheeks. "Would you help me to the bathroom, please?"

The nurse helped her, but Laura didn't make it to the bathroom before she expelled her lunch. Laura, cold as death, slipped from the woman's grasp and fell to her knees onto the floor, and when she splayed there she felt the raw pain of the stitches tearing between her thighs. Someone was called to clean up the mess, Laura was returned to bed shivering and dazed with shock, and Ramsey allowed her mother back into the room with Miss Kingman. The young nurse had already told Laura's mother what was happening, and Ramsey sat beside the bed and directed more questions at both of them. Neither could recall the woman's last name. "Lewis? Logan?" Ramsey prompted. "Larson? Lester?"

"Lester," Laura's mother said. "That was it!"

"No, it wasn't that," Laura disagreed. "It was something close to Lester."

"Think hard. Try to see the name tag in your mind. Can you see it?"

"It *was* Lester!" the older woman insisted. "I know what it was!"

Her face flamed with anger. "Jesus Christ, is this your way of running a hospital? Letting crazy people come in and steal babies?"

Ramsey paid her no attention. "See the name tag," he told Laura while the nurse pressed a cold washrag against her forehead. "Look at the last name. Something like Lester. What is it?"

"*Lester,* for God's sake!" Miriam insisted.

Laura saw the name tag in her mind, white letters on a blue background. She saw the first name, and then the last name came clear of its fog. "Leister, I think it was." She spelled it out. "L-e-i-s-t-e-r."

At once Ramsey was on his walkie-talkie again. "Eugene, Ramsey. Call down to records and have them check a name: Leister." He spelled it, too. "Get me a printout when it's done. Metro on the way?"

"Double quick," the disembodied voice answered.

"I want my baby back," Laura said, her eyes deep with tears. Her mind wasn't truly registering what was happening; this had to be a gruesome, hideous joke. They were hiding David from her. Why were they being so cruel? She hung to sanity by the pressure of a nurse's hand. "Please bring my baby back. Right now. Okay? Okay?"

"You'd better find my grandson!" Laura's mother was right up in Ramsey's face. "You hear me? We'll sue your asses off if you don't find my grandson!"

"The police are on their way." His voice was brittle with tension. "Everything's under control."

"Like hell it is!" the older woman shouted. "Where's my grandson? You people had better have a damned good lawyer!"

"Be quiet," Laura rasped, but her voice was lost in her mother's anger. "Please be quiet."

"What kind of security do you have around here? You don't even know who's a nurse and who's not a nurse? You let just anybody off the street come in here and take babies?"

"Ma'am, we're doing the best we can. You're not helping things."

"And *you* are? My God, there's no telling who's got my grandson! It could be any kind of lunatic!"

Laura began to cry, hopelessly and in great pain. Her mother raged on as Ramsey took it with a tight-lipped stare and rain slashed at the window. His walkie-talkie beeped. "Ramsey," he said into it, and Miriam stopped shouting.

The voice said, "Need you down in the laundry, pronto."

"On my way." He clicked the walkie-talkie off. "Mrs. Clayborne, I'm going to have to leave you for a little while. Is your husband in the hospital?"

"I don't . . . I don't know . . ."

"Can you get in touch with him?" he asked her mother.

"We'll take care of that! You just do your job and find that baby!"

"Stay with them," Ramsey told the two nurses, and he hurried out of the room.

"Get away from my daughter!" Laura heard her mother command. The nurse's grip relaxed and fell away, leaving Laura with an empty hand. Her mother stood over her. "It's going to be all right. Do you hear me, Laura? Look at me."

Laura lifted her face and looked at her mother through blurred and burning eyes.

"It's going to be all right. They'll find David. We're going to sue this damned hospital for ten million dollars, that's what we're going to do. Doug knows some good lawyers. By God, we'll break this hospital, that's what we'll do." She turned away from Laura and picked up the telephone, dialing the house on Moore's Mill Road.

The answering machine came on. Doug wasn't home.

Laura lay on the bed and pulled herself into the fetal position, grasping a pillow against her. "I want my baby," she whispered. "I want my baby. I want my baby." Her voice broke, and she could speak no more. Her body, a hollow vessel, ached for her child. She squeezed her eyes shut, blocking out all light. Darkness filled her. She lay at the mercy of God, or fate, or luck. The world spun with her curled up in a tight, hurting ball and her baby stolen from her, and Laura struggled to hold back a scream that she feared might shred her soul to bloody ribbons.

She lost.

III

Wilderness of Pain

1.

Pigsticker

*Y*ou're absolutely certain you've never seen the woman before?
"Yes. Certain."
Did she speak your first or last name?
"No, I don't . . . no."
Did she speak the baby's name?
"No."
Did she have an accent?
"Southern," Laura said. "But different. Somehow. I don't know."
She was answering these questions through a tranquilized haze, and

the voice of the police lieutenant named Garrick seemed to be floating to her along an echoing tunnel. Two other men were in the room: Newsome, the craggy-faced chief of security for the hospital, and a younger policeman taking notes. Miriam was being questioned in another room, while Franklin and Doug—who'd returned from a drinking bout in a bar near his office—were down in the administration office.

Laura had to concentrate hard on what Garrick was asking her. The drugs had done a strange number on her, relaxing her body and tongue while her mind was racing, going up inclines and speeding down into troughs like a runaway roller-coaster.

A southern accent? Different how?

"Not deep south," she said. "Not a Georgia accent."

Could you describe the woman for a police artist?

"I think so. Yes. I can."

Newsome was called out of the room by a third policeman. He returned in a few minutes accompanied by a boyish-looking man in a dark gray suit, a white shirt, and a black tie with tiny white dots on it. There was a hushed conference, Garrick got up from his chair beside the bed, and the new arrival took his place. "Mrs. Clayborne? My name is Robert Kirkland." He showed her a laminated identification card. "Federal Bureau of Investigation."

Those words made fresh panic surge through her, but the drugs kept her expression calm and dreamy. Only the wet glint of her eyes betrayed her stark terror. Scenarios of ransom notes and murdered kidnap victims wheeled through her brain like evil constellations. "Please tell me," she said. Her tongue was leaden, the taste of the tranquilizers sour in her mouth. "Please . . . why did she take my baby?"

Kirkland paused, his pen hovering over a yellow legal pad. He had eyes, Laura thought, that resembled one-way blue glass, giving no hint of what went on within. "The woman was not a nurse at this hospital," he told her. "There's no Janette Leister on staff, and the only person with that last name who worked here was an X-ray technician in 1984." He checked his prewritten notes. "A black male, aged thirty-three, who now resides at 2137 Oakhaven Drive in Conyers." His one-way stare returned to her. "We're checking the records of other hospitals. She may have been a nurse at one time, or she may have simply bought or rented the uniform. We're checking uniform and costume-rental stores, too. If she did rent the uniform and a clerk got her address from her driver's license—and it's a correct address—we're in luck."

"Then you can find her fast, is that right? You can find her and my baby?"

"We'll act as soon as we get the information." He checked his notes again. "What's working for us here is the woman's size and height, both out of the norm. But bear in mind that the uniform might belong to her, so she wouldn't turn up on a rental list. She might have bought it a year ago, or rented it outside the city."

"But you'll find her, won't you? You won't let her get away?"

"No ma'am," Kirkland said. "We won't let her get away." He didn't tell her that the woman had been allowed into the hospital by a laundry worker, and evidently had spirited the baby out in a linen hamper. He didn't tell her that there was no description of a car, that the laundress was vague about the woman's face, but that two things stuck out: the woman's six-foot height and the yellow Smiley Face button pinned to her breast pocket. It had occurred to Kirkland that the woman had pinned the button there so it would draw attention away from her own face. She had moved fast and known what she was doing; it was no off-the-street patchwork job. His notes told him she'd been wearing a white uniform with navy blue piping, the same colors as the real nurses wore. That was the uniform they were trying to track down. She had acted, as Miriam Beale had put it, "in charge." The laundress had said "she looked like a nurse and she acted like one, too." The woman must've cased the hospital first, because she'd known how to get in and out in a hurry. But there was an interesting point: the woman had gone to rooms 24 and 23 as well. Had she come expressly for the Clayborne infant, or was she gunning in the dark for a child to steal? Was it important that she steal a boy? If so, why?

Kirkland spent about twenty minutes with Laura, replowing old ground. It was obvious to him that she could offer nothing new. She was drifting in and out of shock, becoming less coherent. Twice she broke into tears, and Kirkland asked Newsome to go get her husband.

"No." The strength and ferocity of her voice surprised him. "I don't want him in here."

On Kirkland's drive to his office, his car phone chirped. "Go ahead," he answered.

It was one of the other agents on the case. A clerk at Costumes

Atlanta had rented an extra large nurse's uniform—solid white, with no navy piping—to a "big woman" on Friday afternoon. The address, taken from a Georgia driver's license, was Apartment 6, 4408 Sawmill Road in Mableton. The name was Ginger Coles. Kirkland said, "Get me a search warrant and some backup and meet me there." He hung up and turned the Ford around, wipers beating at the steady rain.

Forty minutes later, Kirkland and two more FBI agents were ready to move on Apartment 6 in the dismal little complex in Mableton. The clock had ticked past four, the sky plated with low gray clouds. Kirkland checked his service revolver. He'd been sitting in the parking lot watching the door of Apartment 6 and had seen no movement, but being less than cautious got you killed. "Let's go," he said over his walkie-talkie, and he got out of his car and walked with the other two men through the rain toward Apartment 6.

Kirkland knocked. Waited. Knocked again. No answer. He tried the doorknob. Locked, of course. Who would have the key? The apartment manager? "Let's try this one," he said, and he went to the next door. Knocked. Waited. Repeated it a little louder. No one home? He tried the knob, and was surprised when the door opened.

"Hello!" he called into the gloom. "Anybody in there?" He smelled it, then: the coppery, unmistakable reek of blood. He had no search warrant for this apartment, and walking in would be asking for an ass-rip. But he could see the result of tumult in the place, could look right through into the guts of the bedroom and see the mattress overturned and cotton ticking strewn about. "I'm going in." He went in with his hand on the butt of his gun.

When he emerged less than three minutes later, Robert Kirkland had aged. "Got a homicide in there. Old man in the bathtub with his throat cut." *Deep shit,* he thought. "We need a key! Find me a manager, fast!"

The manager was not at home. The locked door of Apartment 6 stared Kirkland in the face. Kirkland walked back to his car and used the phone to place a call to the metro police. Then he dialed FBI Central in Atlanta, requesting information on a Coles, Ginger. The computer came up empty. The name Leister, Janette also drew a blank. Both aliases? he wondered. Who would need an alias but a fugitive? And what did the old man in the bathtub have to do with the kidnapping of a baby boy from St. James Hospital in Buckhead?

Deep shit, he thought.

Within an hour, as the metro police questioned the other residents of the complex and a specialist team hunted for fingerprints and evidence in the debris, the wind picked up. It swirled around the trash dumpster, and lifted from its depths the crumpled picture of a smiling infant. The wind blew it away from the policemen and the FBI agents, and it floated north on a cold current before it snagged in the pines.

The apartment complex's manager, it was learned from a resident who'd just arrived home, worked at a Kinney's shoe store at a nearby mall. Two policemen were assigned to go get him, and he arrived in their custody around five-thirty to find the place acrawl with officers in dark raincoats. He unlocked the door to Ginger Coles's apartment with a trembling hand, reporters armed with minicams beginning to swoop in like vultures on the death scent.

"Step back," Kirkland told the man. Then he turned the knob and opened the door.

As the door came open, Kirkland heard a small *click.*

He saw what was waiting for him, and he had a split second to think: *Deep sh—*

The picture-wire trigger pull coiled around the doorknob did its work very well. The sawed-off shotgun that had been positioned on a chair, its barrel carefully uptilted, went off with a hollow *boom* as its trigger was yanked, and the full force of the lead shot almost tore Robert Kirkland in half. The pellets ripped through a second FBI agent's throat and blew the manager's right shoulder apart in a cascade of flesh, blood, and bone for the TV minicams. Kirkland staggered back, minus his heart, lungs, and much of what held him together, and fell in a twitching heap. The policemen hit the wet pavement on their bellies, the reporters yelled and screamed and backed off but not too far away to lose the pictures. Somebody started firing into the apartment, another scared policeman started shooting, too, and in another moment pistols were being emptied through the doorway and windows of Apartment 6 as plaster and woodchips danced in the air. "Cease fire! Cease fire!" the remaining FBI agent shouted, and gradually the shooting died down.

Finally, two brave—or foolish—policemen rushed into the bullet-riddled apartment. A lava lamp had been hit, the glop spattered all over the walls. Open kitchen cupboards, chipped by bullets, were empty. A stereo and a TV remained, along with some records. If the police had known to look, they would have found no Doors albums among them. There were marks on the walls where pictures had been hung, but there were no pictures. In a closet was found a cardboard box filled with mutilated plastic and rubber dolls, and behind that was a boy-sized rifle minus its sight. The closets held no clothes, and the dresser drawers had been emptied.

The ambulances were on the way. Someone had already put a raincoat over Kirkland's corpse. His blood was collecting in a pothole on the pavement, one arm sticking up from the folds of the coat and the fingers curved heavenward into claws. The reporters shoved to get the best camera angles. Already, on CNN, the network was about to start a live feed from the Mableton apartments.

Over a hundred miles northeast of Atlanta, on Interstate 85, an olive-green Chevy van puttered along at fifty miles an hour in a heavy rain. While her new baby slept in a little cardboard box on the floorboard, wrapped up in his blue blanket, Mary Terror sang "Age of Aquarius" in a low voice and wondered who would find the pigsticker she'd left cocked and ready in her front door. She was no longer wearing the nurse's uniform; she had changed at the apartment, put the uniform in a trash bag and thrown it over a bridge into a wooded creek, and the name tag had been tossed away twenty miles out of the city. But the pigs would find out where she'd rented the uniform soon enough, and they would have her Ginger Coles name and her address. It couldn't be helped, because she hadn't had time to come up with a false driver's license. No matter; she was leaving the wasp's nest behind her, and she had her baby, and everything would be great when she met Lord Jack at the weeping lady.

A siren. Flashing lights. Mary's heart jumped, and she started to put her foot to the brake, but the highway patrol car pulled past her and disappeared in the swirling rain and mist ahead.

She had a long way to go. She had her fist-sized Magnum and her Colt, and her clothes and groceries in the back. Plenty of diapers, plenty of formula. A plastic thermos she could pee into so she wouldn't have to make any stops. Messy, but adequate. She'd topped the gas tank before leaving Atlanta, and she'd checked the tires. She wore her Smiley Face on her paisley-print blouse. She was in high cotton.

Who would find the pigsticker, and when? she wondered. It would be worth the loss of the shotgun to take down a really big Mindfucker, to blow the shit out of some superpig with medals on his chest. She glanced down at the little pink thing in its cardboard box, and she said, "I love you. Momma loves her baby, yes momma does."

The tires thrummed on the rain-slick interstate. Mary Terror, a careful driver who observed all speed limits and rules of the road, went on.

2.

Armed and Dangerous

The man in Michigan could not sleep.

He checked his watch. The luminous hands read seven minutes after midnight. He lay in bed awhile longer, but the metal plate in his jaw was picking up radio noise. He opened his mouth, and he could hear the gnashing of rock and roll guitars. This was going to be a very bad night.

Nothing to be done but to get drunk, he decided, and he got up in the dark.

The wind was whistling outside, the cold borne across the Great

Plains on the back of buffalo winter. The woodframe house shivered and moaned, also unable to sleep by reason of turbulence. The man, gray hair all over his chest and matting his back, walked in his pajama bottoms to the chilly kitchen, where he opened the refrigerator. Its dim light fell upon his death's head of a face, all hollowed cheekbones and deep-socketed eyes. Something was wrong with the left eye, and his jaw was crooked. His breathing was a slow, hoarse bellows. He reached for the four remaining cans of Bud in their plastic harness, and he took them all with him to the den.

In his sanctuary of walnut paneling, his bowling plaques on the walls and his marksmanship trophies standing around like Greek sculptures, he turned on the TV and settled himself into his butt-worn, old plaid recliner. He used the remote control to go to ESPN first, where two Australian teams were playing their brand of football. He drank most of one of the beers, putting it down in a few long swallows. In his mouth someone sang underwater. His head was pounding, too, a slow, excruciating pain that began at the crown of his bald skull and trickled like hot mercury down to the nape of his neck. He was a connoisseur of headaches, as some men know wines or butterflies; this headache would fill him with delicious pain, and leave an aftertaste of gunsmoke and metal.

He finished a second beer and decided the Australians didn't know squat about football. His big-knuckled hand moved on the remote control. He was in the realm of movies now: *The African Queen* on one station, *Easy Rider* on another, *Godzilla vs. Megalon* on a third. Then into the jungle of talking heads, people selling cellulite cream and promising hair growth for desperate men. Women were wrestling on the next channel: GLOW. He watched that for a while, because the Terrorist knocked him out. Then he went on, searching the electric wilderness while his head sang and his skull vibrated with bass notes.

He came to Headline News, and he stopped his impatient finger to watch the nuts in Beirut blow themselves to pieces. He was about to move on, toward religious territory, when the newscaster said: "A bizarre scene today just outside Atlanta, when police officers and agents of the FBI walked into a trap set by a woman who may have stolen an infant from an area hospital."

The third can of Bud hung poised at his lips. He watched the jerky cameras record a scene of carnage. *Boom* went a gun. Shotgun, it sounded like to him. People screamed and backpedaled. Someone was on the ground, writhing in agony. Whoever was holding the camera fell to his or her knees. More gunfire: pistol shots this time. "Get down, damn it!" somebody yelled. The camera angle went down to pavement level, and raindrops splashed the lens.

"The suspect," the newscaster said, "identified by the FBI as Ginger Coles, is thought to have taken a baby boy from St. James Hospital at approximately two o'clock on Saturday afternoon. FBI agents and policemen tripped a wire-fired shotgun at her apartment, killing FBI agent Robert Kirkland, thirty-two, and critically wounding another agent and a young man."

The man in the chair gave a soft grunt. The scene showed a sheet-covered body being put into an ambulance.

"The suspect, also known as Janette Leister, may still be in the Atlanta area."

Leister, the man thought. *Janette.* Oh, Jesus! He sat bolt upright, his headache forgotten, and beer streamed from the Bud can onto the carpet.

"Coles is also implicated in the murder of a neighbor, sixty-six-year-old Grady Shecklett, and she's considered to be armed and extremely dangerous. We'll have more on this story as it develops. Stay tuned for sports news next."

Leister. Janette. He knew those names, but they didn't go together. A tick bothered his right eye. *Gary Leister. Janette Snowden.* Yes, those were names he knew. Two dead members of the Storm Front. Oh, Christ! Could it be? *Could it be?*

He stayed where he was until the story came around again thirty minutes later. This time he had his VCR on, and he taped it. The house shuddered under the onslaught of winter winds, but the man's attention was riveted to the violent drama on his television set. When it was over, he played it back once more. Walked into a trap. A wire-fired shotgun. Ginger Coles. Janette Leister. Taken a baby boy. May still be in the Atlanta area. Armed and extremely dangerous.

You can bet your life on it, the man in the plaid recliner thought.

His heart was racing. The wire-fired shotgun was something she'd come up with, all right. A little extra effort to nail the first person through the door. But still in the Atlanta area? That he seriously doubted. She was a night traveler. Even now she was probably on the road. But going where? And why with the baby?

He reached over beside his chair. He picked up a cord with prongs on one end, the other end connected to a small black box with a speaker in it. He fit the prongs into a flesh-colored socket on his throat, and he held the black box in his right hand and clicked it on. There was a low humming noise.

"It's you, isn't it, Mary?" the metallic voice said through the speaker. The man's lips moved only a bit, but his throat convulsed with the words. "It's you, Mary. Mary, Mary, quite contrary, how does your garden grow?"

He ran the tape back and watched it a third time, his excitement mounting.

"With shotgun shells and walking hell and dead men all in a row," he finished.

He unplugged his throat socket to save the batteries. They were expensive, and he lived on a budget. There were tears in his eyes: the bright, standing tears of great joy. He opened his mouth to laugh, and what came out was heavy metal thunder.

3.

When the Candles Went Out

R eady?" Newsome asked.

Laura nodded, her eyes tear-swollen behind sunglasses as Newsome grasped the back of her wheelchair.

The elevator reached the first floor. Ramsey kept the Door Closed button pressed, but they could hear the murmur of voices beyond the door. Newsome drew a long breath, said, "Let's do it, then," and Ramsey released the button.

The elevator door slid open, and Newsome wheeled Laura out into the knot of reporters.

144

It was Sunday afternoon, almost twenty-four hours since David had been stolen. Laura was leaving the hospital without him, the torn stitches between her legs still oozing a little blood and her insides crushed with grief. In the wee hours of the morning, between three and four, her anguish had turned monstrous, and she might have taken her own life if she'd had a gun or pills. Even now, every movement and breath was a labor, as if gravity itself had become her enemy. The rain had ceased, but the sky was still plated with gray clouds and the wind had turned viciously cold. The glaring lights of minicams caught her in their crossfire. Laura ducked her face as Newsome said, "Give her room, please. Step back now," and the security officers in the lobby tried to get between Laura and the reporters.

"Mrs. Clayborne, look this way!" someone shouted. She didn't. "Over here, Laura!" someone else insisted. The questions were flung at her: "Has there been a ransom note yet, Laura?" "Do you think Ginger Coles was stalking you?" "Are you going to sue the hospital?" "Laura, are you afraid for your baby's safety?"

She didn't answer, and Newsome kept pushing the chair. Though she'd lost David's weight, she'd never felt so burdened down. Cameras whirred, driven by electric motors. "Mrs. Clayborne, look up!" to her left. On her right, the hot focus of a minicam in her face. "Get back, I said!" Newsome demanded. Laura looked at the floor. She had been instructed by both Newsome and her own lawyer not to answer any questions, but they flew about her like squawking birds nipping at her ears. "What about the baby box?" a reporter shouted over the din. "Did you know about the burned dolls?"

The burned dolls? she thought. What was that about burned dolls? She looked up into Newsome's face. It was closed, like a piece of stone, and he kept guiding her onward through the human sea.

"Did you know she cut an old man's throat before she took your baby?"

"What're you feeling right now, Laura?"

"Is it true she's a member of a satanic cult?"

"Mrs. Clayborne, did you hear that she's insane?"

"Back off!" Newsome growled, and then they'd reached the hospital's front doors and Doug's Mercedes was waiting beyond. Doug was striding toward her, his face drawn from lack of sleep, and her mother and father were in the car. More reporters were waiting outside, converging on her with a glee that was almost wolfish. Doug reached out to help her from the chair, but Laura ignored him. She got into the backseat with her mother, and Doug slid behind the wheel. He accelerated so quickly, a news team from the ABC station had to scatter to keep from being run down, and one of the men lost his toupee in the Mercedes' backblast.

"They're at the house, too," Doug said, racing away from the hospital. "Bastards are crawling out of the woodwork."

Laura saw that her mother wore a black dress and pearls. Was she in mourning? Laura wondered. Or dressed up for the cameras? She closed her eyes, but she saw David behind them and so she lifted the lids again. She felt as if she were bleeding internally, growing weaker and weaker. The engine drone lulled her, and sleep was a sweet refuge: her only refuge.

"The FBI's bringing over some pictures in an hour or so," Doug told her. "They took the police sketch you helped them with and put it into a computer that matches photos from their files. Maybe you can identify the woman."

"She might not be in their files," Miriam Clayborne said. "She might be a lunatic escaped from an asylum."

"Hush!" her father said. Good for him, Laura thought. Then he added, "Sugarplum, let's don't upset Laura anymore."

"Don't upset her? Laura's half crazy with worry! How can it be helped?"

Talking about me like I'm not even here, she thought. I'm invisible, gone bye-bye.

"Don't bite my head off, hon."

"Well, don't sit up there telling me what to do and what not to do! My God, this is a *crisis!*"

Dark things stirred in Laura's head, like beasts pulling themselves free of swamp mud. "What about the burned dolls?" she asked, her voice as raw as a wound.

No one answered.

It's bad, Laura knew. Oh Jesus oh God oh it's bad very bad. "I want to know. Please."

Still, no one would rise to the challenge. Pretending I don't know what I'm saying, she thought. "Doug?" she said. "Tell me about the burned dolls. If you don't, I'll find out from a reporter at the house."

"It's nothing." Her mother spoke up. "They found a doll or two at the woman's apartment."

"Oh, Christ!" Doug slammed a fist against the wheel, and the

Mercedes briefly swerved from its lane. "They found a box of dolls in a closet! They were all torn up, some of them burned and others . . . crushed and stuff. There! You wanted to know! All right?"

"So . . ." Her mind was starting to shut down again, guarding itself. "So . . . the police . . . think she might . . . hurt my baby?"

"Our baby!" Doug corrected her fiercely. "David is *our* child! I've got a stake in this, too, don't I?"

"The end," she said.

"What?" He looked at her in the rearview mirror.

"The end of Doug and Laura," she said, and she uttered not another word.

Her mother clasped her hand with cold fingers. Laura pulled away.

The reporters were at the house, waiting. The vans were out in full force, but the police were there, too, to keep order. Doug put his hand on the horn and bellowed his way into the garage; the garage door slithered down and they were home.

As Miriam took Laura back to the bedroom to get her settled, Doug checked the answering machine. The voices he'd expected were there: NBC, CBS, ABC, *People* magazine, *Newsweek,* and other magazines and newspapers. All of them were hooked to the tape recorder left by the police to monitor a possible ransom call. But there was one voice Doug hadn't expected. Two quick words: "Call me." Cheryl's voice had gone into the tape recorder, too.

He looked up, and saw Laura's father staring at him.

Laura stood in the nursery. Miriam said, "Come on, let's get you to bed. Come on now."

The nursery was a haunted place. Laura heard the ghost-sounds of a baby, and she touched the brightly colored mobile over the crib and sent it gently twirling. She was crying again, the tears stinging on her chapped cheeks. She heard David crying, too, his voice waxing and falling in the little room. Stuffed animals grinned from the crib. Laura picked up a teddy bear and held it against herself, and she sobbed quietly onto its brown fur.

"Laura!" her mother said right behind her. "Come to bed this minute!"

That voice, that voice. Do what I say when I say it. Jump, Laura! Jump! Be successful, Laura! Marry someone with money and social standing! Stop wearing those awful tie-dyed blouses and bluejeans! Fix your hair like a lady! Grow *up,* Laura! For God's sake, grow *up!*

She knew she was stretched to her limit. One more small stretch and she would snap. David was with an insane woman named Ginger Coles, who'd slashed an old man's throat on Saturday morning and killed an FBI agent on Saturday evening. Between those two events, Laura had given her baby to murderous hands. She remembered the red crust under a fingernail. Blood, of course. The old man's blood. That thought alone was enough to rip her off her hinges and send her shambling to a madhouse. Hang on! she thought. Dear God, hang on!

"Did you hear me?" Miriam prodded.

Laura's crying stopped. She wiped her tears on the teddy bear, and she turned to face her mother. "This is . . . my house," she said. "My house. You're a guest here. In my house, I'll do what I please when I please."

"This isn't the time to act fool—"

"LISTEN TO ME!" she screamed, and Miriam was knocked backward by the power of her daughter's voice as surely as if she'd been punched. "Give me some room to breathe! I can't breathe with you on my neck!"

The older woman, a scrapper, regained her cool composure. "You're out of control," she said. "I understand that." Doug and Franklin were coming along the corridor. "I think you need a sedative."

"I NEED MY BABY! THAT'S WHAT I NEED!"

"She's losing her mind," Miriam said matter-of-factly to her husband.

"Get out! Get out!" Laura shoved her mother, who gasped with horror at the touch, and then Laura slammed the nursery door in their three stunned faces and turned the latch.

"Want me to call the doctor?" she heard Doug ask as she leaned against the door.

"I think you'd better." Franklin speaking.

"No, let her alone. She wants to be alone, we'll let her be alone. Good God, I always knew she had an unstable temper! Yes, we'll let her be alone!" Her voice was raised for her daughter's benefit. "Franklin, call the Hyatt and get us a room! We won't stay here and breathe down her neck!"

She almost unlocked the door. Almost. But no, it was quiet in here. It was calm. Let them go to the Hyatt, and let them sulk. She needed space, even if it had to be within these four haunted walls.

Laura sat on the floor with the teddy bear, dim light drifting through the window blinds. She had given David to a murderess. She had put her child into bloodstained hands. She closed her eyes and shrieked inside, where no one but herself could hear.

An hour or so later, there was a tentative knock at the door.

"Laura?" It was Doug. "The FBI's here with the pictures."

She got up, her legs in need of blood, and unlocked the nursery. The teddy bear remained clamped under her arm as she went out. In the den, she found a middle-aged man in a pin-striped suit, his hair sandy brown and cut to a stubble on the sides. He had warm brown eyes and a good smile, and Laura saw him glance quickly at the teddy bear and then pretend he hadn't seen it. Her father had remained at the house, but her mother had retreated to the Hyatt; the battle of wills had begun.

The FBI agent's name was Neil Kastle, "with a K," he told her as she sat down in a chair. He had some photographs, both color and black and white, he wanted her to look at. He opened a manila envelope with large fingers not used to small tasks, and he spread a half-dozen pictures out on the coffee table next to a book on Matisse. They were all pictures of women, some of them face-on—mug shots—and others at an angle. There was one picture of a big, heavyset woman aiming a rifle at a bank clerk. Another showed a husky woman glancing back over her shoulder as she was getting into a black Camaro; light glinted off a pistol in her hand.

"These are women from our Most Wanted list," Kastle told her. "Six of them who match Ginger Coles in size, age, and build. We put the police sketch in our computer and assigned the variables, and that's what we came up with."

One of the women, tall and blond-haired, wore bell bottoms, an American-flag belt, and a green paisley blouse. She was grinning broadly, and she held a hand grenade. "Some of them are old," Laura said.

"Right. They go back . . . oh . . . twenty years or so."

"You've been looking for some of these women for twenty years?" Franklin asked, peering over Laura's shoulder.

"One of them, yes. One's from the late seventies, one's from 1983, and the other three are from 1985 to the present."

"What crimes did they do?" Franklin persisted.

"An assortment," Kastle said. "Look at those good and hard, Mrs. Clayborne."

"They look alike to me. All of them: same size, same everything."

"Their names and statistics are on the back."

Laura turned over the picture of the bank robber. *Margie Cummings, AKA Margie Grimes AKA Linda Kay Souther AKA Gwen Becker. Height 5 feet 10½, hair brown, eyes blue-green, birthplace Orren, Kentucky.* She looked at the back of the black Camaro picture: *Sandra June McHenry, AKA Susan Foster, AKA June Foster. Height 5 feet 9, hair brown, eyes gray, birthplace Ft. Lauderdale, Florida.*

"Why do you think it might be one of these women?" Franklin asked. "Couldn't it just be . . . like . . . a crazy woman or somebody you don't even know about?"

"The city police are putting their own list of mug shots together. That'll include local fugitives. The reason we decided to go back into our Most Wanted file was because of the shotgun."

"What about it?"

"Ginger Coles knew we'd find her apartment. She set the trap to take out the first man through the door. That means she has a certain . . . shall we say . . . mindset. An aptitude for such things. She scrubbed her apartment down pretty well, too. All the doorknobs and drawer grips were wiped clean. Even her records were wiped. We did get some partial prints off a rifle we found in a closet, and a good thumbprint off the shower head."

"So does that print match any of these women?" Doug asked.

"I can't say," Kastle answered. "They haven't let me know yet."

Laura turned over another photo. *Debra Guesser, AKA Debbie Smith, AKA Debra Stark. Height 6 feet, hair reddish-brown, eyes blue. Birthplace New Orleans, Louisiana.* She looked closely at that face: it was similar to the face of Ginger Coles, but there was a small scar on her upper lip that put a sneer in her smile. "This one . . . maybe," she said. "I don't remember the scar."

"That's okay. Look hard and take your time." He didn't tell her that he was testing her. Three of the women, including Debra Guesser, had been convicted and were now in federal prisons. A fourth, Margie Cummings, had died in 1987.

Laura turned over the picture of the bell-bottomed girl. *Mary Terrell, AKA Mary Terror. Height 6 feet, hair brown, eyes gray-blue, birthplace Richmond, Virginia.* "This says she has brown hair, but her hair's blond in the picture."

"Dyed blond," Kastle said. "The statistics are based on family records, so they might appear a little different in the photos."

Laura stared at Mary Terrell's face. The woman—fresh-faced and innocent, in a way—wore a relaxed, toothy grin, and the grenade dangled from a finger. "This is the oldest one?" she asked.

"Yes."

"Ginger Coles is . . . harder looking. This woman's close, too, but . . . I don't know."

"Put about twenty years of rough living on that woman's face," Kastle suggested.

"I don't know. I can't see it."

"How can a woman hide from the FBI for twenty years?" Franklin took the photo and Laura went on to the next. "It seems impossible!"

"It's a mighty big country. Plus there's Canada and Mexico to consider. People change their hair and clothes, they create new identities, and they learn how to walk and talk differently. And you'd be amazed at what some of the fugitives get away with: we found one who'd been a park ranger at Yellowstone for about seven years. Another was the veep of a bank in Missouri. I know of a third who became a fishing boat captain in the Keys, and we got hold of him when he ran for mayor of Key West. See, people don't really look at other people." He sat down in a chair opposite Laura. "Folks are trusting. If somebody tells you something, you're likely to believe it. In every city there's somebody who'll take money, no questions asked, to forge you a new driver's license, birth certificate, anything you want. So you get yourself a job where they don't care to ask too many questions, and you burrow underground like a smart little mole." He folded his hands together as Laura started through the photos again. "These Most Wanted fugitives grow eyes in the backs of their heads. They learn to smell the wind and listen to the railroad tracks. They probably don't sleep too well at night, but they keep their smarts sharp. See, most people—law officers included—have a big failing: they forget. The FBI never forgets. We've got computers to keep our memories up-to-date."

"Who's this in the background?" Doug asked, looking at the photo of Mary Terrell.

Kastle took it, and Laura looked, too. Mary Terrell was standing on dewy green grass, her feet in clunky sandals. A blue sky, somewhat faded, was overhead and the camera operator's slim shadow lay on the grass. But in the background atop a small green rise stood a blurred figure, one arm cocked to throw a yellow Frisbee.

"I don't know. Looks like the picture was taken in a—"

Laura took the photo from Kastle's hand. She had been looking at the woman's face, and she'd not noticed this before. Still, it was blurry and hard to make out. "I need a magnifying glass."

Doug got up. Kastle leaned forward, squinting. "What're you looking at?"

"There. The Frisbee. See it?"

"Yeah. What about it?"

"Right there. You can see the top of the Frisbee, the way it's angled. See?" Her heart was pounding. Doug brought her a magnifying glass, and she held it over the yellow Frisbee. She positioned the glass out to its highest magnification from the picture, just about to lose its focus altogether. "There," she said. "There it is. Look."

Kastle did. "I see it," he said.

Two black dots of eyes and a semicircle of a mouth had been painted on the Frisbee's lid. It was a Smiley Face, about to be spun to an unknown destination.

Laura held the magnifying glass over Mary Terrell's face, studied it carefully.

She knew her enemy.

Time had changed this woman, yes. It had made her heavier and broken the smoothness of her skin; it had razored her prettiness down to the raw mean. But the real resemblance was in the eyes, those gray-blue soul mirrors. You had to have a magnifying glass, and even then you had to look hard and close. The eyes had a dead, hot hatred in them. They didn't go with the blond hippie locks or the Crest-white smile. The eyes were the same ones that had looked down upon her as Laura had given up her baby to bloodstained hands. Yes. Yes. They were the same, but older. Yes. The same.

"It's her," Laura said.

At once Kastle was kneeling beside her, looking at the photo from Laura's perspective. "Are you sure?"

"I . . ." No doubts. Those eyes. Big hands. The Smiley Face in the background. No doubts. "It's Ginger Coles," she said.

"You're identifying Mary Terrell as the woman who took your infant?"

"Yes." She nodded. "Yes. It's her. This is the woman." She felt a double shattering within her: relief and horror.

"May I use your telephone?" Kastle took the photograph and went into the kitchen. In another moment, Laura heard him say, "We've got a positive ID. Hold on to your hat."

When Kastle returned, Laura was sitting gray-faced, her arms huddled around herself and Franklin stroking her back. Doug stood at a window across the room, like an outcast. "All right." Kastle sat down again, and put the photo on the coffee table. "We're getting a file together on Mary Terrell. All available pictures, prints, family whereabouts, relatives, everything. But I guess there are things you ought to know that I can tell you right now."

"Just find my baby. Please. That's all I want."

"I understand that. I have to tell you, though, that Mary Terrell—Mary Terror—probably killed a ten-year-old boy in the woods around Mableton just recently. She took his rifle, and we matched the serial numbers with the seller. So that makes three people she's killed that we know about, not counting the others."

"The others? What others?"

"As I recall, six or seven police officers, a university professor and his wife, and a documentary filmmaker. All those murders took place in the late sixties and early seventies. Mary Terrell was a member of the Storm Front. Do you know what that was?"

Laura had heard of it before, yes. A militant terrorist group like the Symbionese Liberation Army. Mark Treggs had talked about it in *Burn This Book.*

"I was in the Miami bureau when it was going on, but I kept up with it," Kastle continued. "Mary Terrell was a political killer. She believed that she was an executioner for the masses. The whole bunch of them did. You know how that used to be: a group of hippies stoned all the time and listening to weird music, and sooner or later they started thinking about how much fun it might be to kill somebody."

Laura nodded vacantly, but part of her was recalling that she had been a hippie who got stoned and listened to weird music, though she'd never wanted to murder anyone.

"The Bureau's been looking for her since the early seventies. Why she broke cover now and took your baby, I don't know. Now I guess I'm getting ahead of myself, because we won't be certain until we match some fingerprints, but I have to tell you this: Mary Terrell is very, very dangerous." He didn't tell her that Mary Terrell was held in such awe that there was a target dummy in her likeness at the FBI's Quantico firing range. Nor did he tell her that less than an hour before he'd left the office, the Washington Bureau had come back with a four-point match on the shower-head thumbprint with Mary Terrell's right thumbprint. But he'd wanted Laura's positive ID on the photo to clinch it. Funny he hadn't noticed the Smiley Face Frisbee. The big chiefs in Washington had to be chewing their pencils for action on this one, particularly since a fellow agent had been murdered. "We're going to do everything we can to find her. Do you believe that?"

She nodded again. "My baby. She won't hurt my baby, will she?"

"I don't see why she would." He turned the thought of the baby box with its mutilated dolls out of his mind. "She took your baby for a reason, but I don't think she plans on hurting him."

"Is she insane?" Laura asked.

This was a difficult question. Kastle shifted his position in the chair, thinking it over. The baby box said she might very well be crazy, like an animal that's lived too long in a hole gnawing on old bones. "You know," he said quietly, "I wonder about some of those people from the sixties. You know the ones I mean: they hated everything and everybody, and they wanted to break the world apart and start it all over again in their image. They fed on hate, day and night. They breathed it, in their attics and cellars, while they burned their incense and candles. I wonder what they did with that hate when the candles went out."

Kastle began to put away the photographs, and he closed the envelope. "I suppose I'll go out and face the reporters now. I won't give them much, just enough to whet their appetite. You work for the *Constitution*, don't you?"

"Yes."

"You understand what I mean, then. I won't ask you to come out with me. That'll be for later. The longer we can keep the press interested, the better chance we have of finding Mary Terrell quickly. So we have to play them a little bit." He smiled. "Such is life. Mr. Clayborne, would you come outside with me?"

"Why me? I wasn't even in the room!"

"Right, but you're a good human interest angle. Plus you can't answer any question in detail. I'll handle all the detail work. Okay?"

"Okay," Doug said reluctantly.

Kastle stood up, and Doug braced himself for the onslaught. There was a question Laura had to ask: "When . . . when you find her . . . David won't be hurt, will he?"

"We'll get your baby back for you," Kastle said. "You can count on it." Then he and Doug went out front to where the reporters waited.

Laura's father held her hand and talked quietly and reassuringly to her, but Laura barely heard him. She was thinking of a madwoman holding a baby on a balcony, and a SWAT sniper sighting in for the kill. She closed her eyes, remembering the double *pop pop* of two shots, and the baby's head exploding.

It couldn't happen to David that way.

No.

It couldn't.

No.

She put her hands to her face and wept heartbroken tears, and Franklin sat there, not knowing what to do.

4.

Hope, Mother

In the big red brick house in Richmond that had been built in 1853, the telephone rang.

It was approaching nine o'clock on Sunday night. A large-boned woman with silver hair, her face broken by lines and her nose as sharp as a Confederate sword, sat in a high-backed leather chair and stared at her elderly husband through chill gray eyes. One of the new Perry Mason series shows was on television, and both the woman and her husband Edgar enjoyed watching Raymond Burr. The man sat in a wheelchair, his body shrunken in blue silk pajamas, his head lolled

156

over to one side and a pink flap of tongue showing. His hearing was not what it used to be before the stroke six years earlier, but the woman knew he could hear the telephone because his eyes had widened and he was shaking more than usual.

They both knew who was calling. They let it ring.

The phone stopped ringing. After a pause of less than a minute, it began again.

The ringing filled the mansion and echoed through its twenty-three rooms like a voice crying in the dark.

Natalie Terrell said, "Oh dear God," and she got up and crossed the black and crimson Oriental rug to the telephone table. Edgar's gaze tried to follow her, but his neck wouldn't swivel past a certain point. She picked up the receiver with wrinkled, diamond-ring-adorned fingers. "Yes?"

No answer. Breathing.

"Yes?"

Then it came. Her voice: "Hi, Mother."

Natalie stiffened. "I don't care to talk to—"

"Don't hang up. Please don't. All right?"

"I'm not going to talk to you."

"Are they watching the house?"

"I *said* I'm not going to talk—"

"Are they watching? Just tell me that."

The elderly woman closed her eyes. She listened to the sound of her daughter breathing. Mary was their only child, since Grant had committed suicide when he was seventeen and Mary was fourteen. Natalie struggled for a moment, right against wrong. But which was which? She didn't know anymore. "There's a van parked down the street," she said.

"How long has it been there?"

"Two hours. Maybe longer."

"Do they have the line tapped?"

"I don't know. Not from inside the house. I don't know."

"Anybody hassle you?"

"A reporter from the local paper came this afternoon. We talked awhile and he left. I haven't seen any policemen or FBI, if that's what you mean."

"FBI's in that van. You can believe it. I'm in Richmond."

"What?"

"I said I'm in Richmond. At a pay phone. Have I been on TV yet?"

Natalie put a hand to her forehead. She felt faint, and she had to lean against the wall for support. "Yes. All the networks."

"They found out faster than I thought they would. It's not like it used to be. They've got those laptop computers and shit. It's really Big Brother now, isn't it?"

"Mary?" Her voice quavered and threatened to break. *"Why?"*

"Karma," Mary said, and that was all.

Silence. Natalie Terrell heard the thin crying of a baby through the receiver, and her stomach clenched. "You're crazy," she said. "Absolutely crazy! Why did you steal a baby? For God's sake, don't you have *any* decency?"

Silence, but for the crying baby.

"The parents were on television today. They showed the mother leaving the hospital, and she was in such shock she couldn't even speak. Are you smiling? Does that make you happy, Mary? *Answer me!"*

"It makes me happy," Mary said calmly, "that I have my baby."

"He's *not* yours! His name is David Clayborne! He's not your baby!"

"His name is Drummer," Mary said. "Know why? Because his heart beats like a drum, and because a drummer sounds the call to freedom. So he's Drummer now."

Behind Natalie, her husband gave an incomprehensible shout, full of rage and pain.

"Is that Father? He doesn't sound good."

"He's not. You've done it to him. That should make you happy, too." About eight months after the stroke, Mary had called out of the blue. Natalie had told her what had happened, and Mary had listened and hung up without another word. A week later, a get well card had arrived in the mail with no return address and no signature, postmarked Houston.

"You're wrong." Mary's voice was flat, without emotion. "Father did it to himself. He mindfucked too many people and all those bad vibes blew his head out like an old lamp. Does all his money make him feel better now?"

"I'm not going to talk to you anymore."

Mary waited in silence. Natalie did not put down the phone. In a few seconds she could hear her daughter cooing to the baby.

"Let that baby go," Natalie said. "Please. For me. This is going to be very bad."

"You know, I'd forgotten how cold it can be up here."

"Mary, let that child go. I'm begging you. Your father and I can't stand any more." Her voice snagged, and the hot tears came. "What did we ever do to make you hate us so much?"

"I don't know. Ask Grant."

Natalie Terrell slammed the telephone down, the tears blinding her. She heard the labored squeaking of the wheelchair as Edgar pushed himself across the Oriental carpet with all the strength in his spindly body. She looked at him, saw his face contorted and his mouth drooling, and she looked away quickly.

The telephone rang.

Natalie stood there, her head and body slumped like a broken puppet dangling from a nail. Tears raced down her cheeks, and she put her hands to her ears, but the telephone kept ringing . . . ringing . . . ringing.

"I'd like to see you," Mary said when Natalie picked up the receiver again.

"No. Absolutely not. No."

"You know where I'm going, don't you?"

The mention of Grant had told her. "Yes."

"I want to smell the water. I remember it was always a clean smell. Why won't you meet me there?"

"I can't. No. You're a . . . you're a criminal."

"I'm a freedom fighter," Mary corrected her mother. "If that's criminal, to fight for freedom, then yeah, okay, I plead guilty. But I'd still like to see you. It's been . . . Jesus . . . it's been over ten years, hasn't it?"

"Twelve years."

"Blows my mind." Then to the child: "Hush! Mama's on the phone!"

"I can't come there," Natalie said. "I just can't."

"I'll be here for a few days. Maybe. I've got some things to do. If you'd come see me, I'd be . . . you'd make me feel real good, Mother. We're not enemies, are we? We've always understood each other, and we could talk like real people."

"I talked. You never listened."

"Like real people," Mary plowed on. "See, I've got my baby now and there are things I have to do, and I know the pigs are hunting me but I've got to go on because that's the way it is, that's how things stand. I've got my baby now, and that makes me feel . . . like I belong in the world again. Hope, Mother. You know what hope is, don't you? Remember, we talked about hope, and good and evil, and all that stuff?"

"I remember."

"I'd like to see you. But you can't let the pigs follow you, Mother. No. See, because I've got my baby. I'm not going to let the pigs take me and my Drummer. We'll go to the angels together, but the pigs won't take us. Can you dig it?"

"I understand," the older woman said, her hand tight around the receiver.

"Gotta change Drummer's diaper," Mary said. "Bye, Mother."

"Good-bye."

Click.

Natalie backed away from the phone as one might retreat from a particularly deadly snake. She bumped into Edgar's wheelchair, and he said something to her that sprayed spittle.

Perhaps thirty seconds passed. The phone began to ring once more. Natalie didn't move.

It rang and rang, and finally Natalie stepped forward, reached out, and picked up the receiver. Her face had gone deathly pale.

"We've got it on tape, Mrs. Terrell," one of the FBI agents in the white van said. She thought it was the younger of the two, the one who'd shown her the phone-tracing device that automatically printed out a caller's number. "It was from a pay phone inside the city limits, all right. We're getting a precise location on it now, but your daughter'll be long gone by the time we get a car there. Do you know where she's going, Mrs. Terrell?"

Natalie had an obstruction in her throat. She swallowed and swallowed, but she couldn't make it go away.

"Mrs. Terrell?" the young man urged.

"Yes," she answered with an effort. "Yes, I do know. She's . . . going to our beach house. In Virginia Beach. The address is . . ." She couldn't get her breath, and she had to stop for a moment. "The address is 2717 Hargo Point Road. It's a white house with a brown roof. Is that all you need?"

"Do you have a phone number, please?"

She gave it to him. "Mary won't answer the phone, though."

"You're sure about this, then?"

"Yes." Again, the breathless sensation. "I'm sure."

"How?"

"She mentioned Grant, her brother. He committed suicide at the beach house. And she said she wanted to smell the water." Natalie felt a sharp stab in her heart. "That's where we used to take her when she was a little girl."

"Yes, ma'am. Excuse me, please." There was a long pause. Talking it over, Natalie surmised. Then the younger man came back on the line. "Okay, that does it. Thank you for your cooperation, Mrs. Terrell."

"I—" Her throat closed up.

"Ma'am?"

"I . . . oh God, I don't . . . want anything to happen to that baby. You heard her. She said she'd kill the baby and herself, too. That's what she meant. You heard her, didn't you?"

"Yes, ma'am."

"What are you going to do, then? Go in after her?"

"No, ma'am, we'll put the house under surveillance first. We'll wait until daylight and try to pinpoint her position and the infant's position in the house. If we have to, we'll evacuate the other houses around it. We won't go storming in like you see in the movies; all that does is get people killed."

"I don't want that baby's blood on my hands. Do you hear me? I couldn't stand to live if I thought I'd helped kill that child."

"I hear you." The young man's voice was calm and sympathetic. "We'll stake the house out for a while, and then we'll see what has to be done. Just pray to God your daughter decides to listen to reason and give herself up."

"She'll never give up," Natalie said. "Never."

"I hope that's where you're wrong. We're going to sit here awhile longer and make some calls, so if you think of anything, you know our number. One more thing: do you mind if we leave the tap on your line?"

"No, I don't mind."

"Thank you again. I know this hasn't been easy."

"No. Far from easy." She hung up, and her husband made a gibbering sound.

At ten-thirty, Natalie put Edgar to bed. She kissed his cheek and wiped his mouth, and he gave her a weak, helpless smile. She pulled the covers up to his throat, and she wondered where her life had gone.

The white van left a little after eleven. From an upstairs window Natalie watched it go, the room dark behind her. She presumed another team of agents now had the beach house under watch. She let one more hour slip past, to make sure.

Then, bundled in an overcoat against the raw cold, Natalie left the house and went to the garage. She got into the gray Coupe de Ville, started the engine, and drove away into the night. For fifteen minutes or so she drove through the streets of Richmond, her speed slow, and she obeyed all traffic signs though there were hardly any cars out. She stopped at a Shell station on Monument Avenue to fill up with gas, and she bought a diet drink and a candy bar to calm her nervous stomach. She left the station and drove in aimless circles again, and all the time she watched her rearview mirror.

She pulled into an area of warehouses and railroad tracks, and she stopped the Cadillac next to a chain-link fence and watched a freight train speed past. Her gaze swept the dark streets around her. As far as she could tell, she was not being followed.

They believed her. Why wouldn't they? She was the woman who'd vehemently said, in a 1975 interview on the Dick Cavett Show along with the families of other wanted criminals, that she hoped the police locked her daughter in a cage where she belonged and tossed the key into the Atlantic Ocean.

The quote had gotten a lot of newsprint. The FBI knew she was willing to help them in any way possible. She still felt that way. But now there was a vital difference: Mary had a baby.

Around one o'clock, Natalie Terrell turned the Cadillac up onto a ramp of I-95, and she headed north toward the wooded hills.

5.

Into the Vortex

It was bad, the nightmare.

In it, Laura gave David into the hands of the murderess, and she saw drops of blood falling from the woman's fingers, falling like scarlet leaves through October air, falling to spatter on white sheets as ridged and rumpled as snowswept badlands. She gave David up, and the murderess and David became shadows that slipped away along a pale green wall. But something had been given in exchange; something was in Laura's right hand. She opened her fingers, and saw the yellow Smiley Face pinned to the flesh of her palm.

Then the scene changed. She was in a parking lot on a hot and humid night, the blue lights of police cars spinning around her. Voices bellowed through bullhorns, and she heard the sharp clickings of bullet magazines being snapped into automatic rifles. She could see a woman standing on a balcony, caught in a white light, and one hand held a pistol while the other gripped David by the back of the neck. The woman wore a green paisley blouse and bell-bottom trousers with an American-flag belt, and she was raving as she held David in the air and shook him. Laura could feel his crying more than hear it, like a razor blade drawn along the folds of her labia. "I want my baby!" she told a shadowy policeman who passed on without speaking. "My baby! I want my baby!" She grasped at someone else; he looked blankly at her. She recognized Kastle. "Please!" she begged. "Don't let my baby be hurt!"

"We'll get your baby back for you," he answered. "You can count on it."

Kastle pulled away and disappeared into the vortex of shadows, and as Laura saw the snipers taking their positions she realized with a jolt of horror that Kastle had not promised to get David back alive.

"Hold your fire until I give the signal!" someone commanded through a bullhorn. She saw Doug sitting on the hood of a police car, his head slumped forward and his eyes half closed, as if all this had no meaning to him whatsoever. A spark of light caught her attention. She looked up at the corner of a rooftop, and there she could make out a shadowy shape aiming a rifle at Mary Terror. She thought the man was bald-headed—slick bald—and that something might be wrong with his face, but she couldn't tell for sure; she thought she might know him, but that, too, was uncertain. The man was lifting his rifle to take aim. He wasn't waiting for the signal; he was going to shoot Mary Terror, and his would be the bullet that made the madwoman fire her gun and blow David's head apart.

"NO!" Laura screamed. "STOP IT!" She began running toward the building the sniper perched on, but the concrete mired her feet like fresh tar. She heard the click of his rifle, a bullet slipping into the chamber. She heard the insane raving of Mary Terror's voice, and the shrill, frantic crying of her son. A doorway was ahead of her. She started through it, fighting the earth, and that was when two muscular dogs with flaming eyes leapt from the darkness at her.

She heard two shots, a split second apart.

The scream started to come out. It swelled in her throat and burst from her mouth, and someone was over her saying, "Laura? Laura, wake up! Wake up!"

She came up out of the hot darkness, sweat on her face. The lamp beside the bed was on. Doug was sitting on the bed beside her, his face furrowed with worry, and behind him stood Doug's mother, who'd arrived from her home in Orlando earlier in the evening.

"It's all right," Doug said. "You were having a nightmare. It's all right."

Laura looked around the room, her eyes wide with fear. There were too many shadows. Too many.

"Doug, can I do anything?" Angela Clayborne asked. She was a tall, elegant woman with white hair, and she wore a dark blue Cardin suit with a diamond brooch on the lapel. Doug's father, divorced from Angela when Doug was in his early teens, was an investment banker in London.

"No. We're okay."

Laura shook her head. "We're not okay. We're not okay." She kept repeating it as she pulled away from Doug and huddled up under the blanket again. She could feel sticky wetness between her thighs: the oozing stitches.

"Do you want to talk?" he asked.

She shook her head.

"Mom, would you leave us alone for a minute?" When Angela had gone, Doug stood up and walked to the window. He peered through the blinds, out into the rainy dark. "I don't see any reporters," he told her. "Maybe they called it a night."

"What time is it?"

He didn't have to look at his watch. "Almost two." He came back to her side. She smelled a stale aroma wafting from him; he hadn't taken a shower since David had been stolen, but then, neither had she. "You *can* talk to me, you know. We still live in the same house."

"No."

"No what? No we don't live in the same house? Or no you can't talk to me?"

"Just . . . no," she said, using the word like a wall.

He was silent for a moment. Then, in a somber voice: "I screwed it up, didn't I?"

Laura didn't bother to answer. Her nerves were still jangled by the nightmare, and she clung to the blanket like a cat.

"You don't have to say anything. I know I screwed up. I

just . . . I . . . well, I guess I've said everything I can say. Except . . . I'm sorry. I don't know how to make you believe that."

She closed her eyes, blocking out his presence.

"I don't want . . . things to be like this. Between you and me, I mean." He touched her arm under the blanket. She didn't pull away, nor did she respond; she just lay there without moving. "We can work it out. I swear to God we can. I know I screwed up, and I'm sorry. What more can I say?"

"Nothing," she answered without emotion.

"Will you give me a second chance?"

She felt like something that had been thrown off a ship in a heavy sea, thrashed from wave to wave and left stranded on jagged rocks. He had turned his back on her when she needed him. She had given up her son—*her* son—to the hands of a murderess, and all she wanted to do was turn off her mind before she went insane. Would God grant *her* a second chance, to hold her baby again? That and only that was what she steered toward, and everything else was wreckage in the storm.

"The FBI's going to find David. They'll take care of everything. It won't be long, now that they've got her name and picture on television."

Laura wanted desperately to believe that. Kastle and another FBI agent had come to the house at seven o'clock, and Laura had listened as Kastle told her more about the woman she'd come to identify as Mary Terror. Born on April 9, 1948, to wealthy parents in Richmond, Virginia. Father in the railroad freight business. One brother who'd hanged himself when he was seventeen. Attended Abernathy Prep, honors student, active in student government and editor of the school newspaper. Went to Penn State for two years, political science major, again active in student government. Evidence of drug use and radical leanings. Left college and resurfaced in New York City, where she enrolled in drama at NYU. Evidence of radical student involvement at NYU and Brandeis University. Then across the country to Berkeley, where she became involved with the Weather Underground. At some point she met Jack Gardiner, a Berkeley radical who introduced her into a Weather Underground splinter group designated the "Storm Front." On August 14, 1969, Mary Terrell and three other members of the Storm Front broke into the home of a conservative Berkeley history professor and his wife and knifed them to death. On December 5, 1969, a bomb attributed to the Storm Front exploded in the car of a San Francisco IBM executive and tore both his legs away. On January 15, 1970, a second bomb exploded in the lobby of the Pacific Gas and Electric building and killed a security guard and a secretary. Two days later, a third bomb killed an Oakland attorney who was defending a winery owner in a civil liberties case involving migrant workers.

"There's more," Kastle had said when Laura had lowered her face.

On June 22, 1970, two policemen in San Francisco were shot to death in their car. Witnesses put Mary Terrell and a Storm Front member named Gary Leister at the site. On October 27, 1970, a documentary filmmaker who'd evidently been doing a film on the militant underground was found with his throat slashed in a trash dumpster in Oakland. Two of Mary Terrell's fingerprints were discovered on a roll of exposed film. On November 6, 1970, the chairman of a police task force on the Storm Front was ambushed and shotgunned to death while leaving his home in San Francisco.

"Then the Storm Front moved east," Kastle had told her, the thick file folder on the coffee table between them. "On June 18, 1971, a policeman was found with his throat cut and hanging by his hands from nails in an abandoned warehouse in Union City, New Jersey, a communiqué from the Storm Front in his shirt pocket." He looked up at her. "They were declaring total war on what they called—and excuse me for my language—'pigs of the Mindfuck State.'" He continued on, along the trail of terror. "On December 30, 1971, a pipe bomb exploded in the mailbox of a Union City district attorney and blinded his fifteen-year-old daughter. Three months and twelve days later, four police officers eating lunch in a Bayonne, New Jersey, diner were shot to death and a taped communiqué from the Storm Front—with Jack Gardiner's voice on it—was delivered to area radio stations. On May 11, 1972, a pipe bomb crippled the assistant chief of police in Elizabeth, New Jersey, and again a taped communiqué was delivered. Then we found them."

"You found them?" Doug had asked. "The Storm Front?"

"In Linden, New Jersey, on the night of July 1, 1972, there was a shootout, an explosion, and fire, and in the smoke Mary Terrell, Jack Gardiner, and two others got away. The house they were living in was an armory. They'd stockpiled weapons, ammunition, and bomb apparatus, and it was apparent they were about to do something very big and probably very deadly."

"Like what?" Doug was working a paper clip around and around, nearing its breaking point.

"We never found out. We think it was timed to happen on the Fourth of July. Anyway, since 1972 the Bureau's been looking for Mary Terrell, Gardiner, and the others. We had a few leads, but they went nowhere." He closed the file, leaving the picture of Mary Terrell out on the table. "We came close to finding her in Houston in 1983. She was working as a cleaning lady at a high school under the name Marianne Lakey, but she cleared out before we got an address. One of the teachers was an undergrad at Berkeley, and she recognized her but not soon enough."

"So why haven't you been able to catch her in all this time?" Laura's father stood up from his chair and picked up the photograph. "I thought you people were professionals!"

"We do our best, Mr. Beale." Kastle offered a thin smile. "We can't be in all places at all times, and people do get through the net." He returned his attention to Laura. "One of our agents on the scene that night in 1972 saw Mary Terrell at close range. He said she was pregnant and badly wounded, bleeding from the abdomen."

"Well, why the hell didn't he shoot her right then and there?" Franklin asked.

"Because," Kastle said evenly, "she shot him first. One bullet in the face, one in the throat. He retired on disability. Anyway, we thought for a while that Mary had crawled off somewhere and died, but about a month later a letter with a Montreal postmark was delivered to the *New York Times*. It was from Jack Gardiner: 'Lord Jack,' he called himself. He said Mary Terrell and the two others were still alive, and that the Storm Front's war against the pigs wasn't over. That was the last communiqué."

"And no one's ever found Jack Gardiner?" Doug asked.

"No. The underground swallowed him up and the others, too. We think they must've split up, and were planning to converge again at some prearranged signal. It never happened. The reason I'm giving you all this background is that you're going to be hearing it on the newscasts every day, and I wanted you to hear it from me first." He stared at Laura. "The Bureau's releasing Mary's file to the networks, CNN, and the newspapers. You'll probably start hearing the first stories on the late news tonight. And the longer we can keep the press interested, the better our chances of someone spotting Mary Terrell and leading us to her." He lifted his eyebrows. "You see?"

* * *

"They'll find her," Doug said, sitting on the bed beside Laura. "They'll bring David back. You've got to believe it."

She didn't answer, her eyes staring at nothing. The shadows of the nightmare swarmed in her mind. After hearing what Kastle had to say, she knew Mary Terror would never surrender without a fight. It wasn't in the psychology of such a person to surrender. No, she would choose the martyr's death, by gun-battle execution. And what would happen to David in that hell of bullets?

"I want to sleep," she said. Doug stayed with her awhile longer, helpless to soothe her silent rage and pain, and then he left her alone.

Laura was afraid of sleep, and what might be waiting for her there. Rain tapped at the window, a bony sound. She got up to get a drink of water from the bathroom, and she found herself opening the dresser drawer where the gun rested.

She picked it up. Its evil, oily smell came to her. A small package of death, there in her hands. Mary Terror must know a lot about guns. Mary Terror lived by the gun and would die by the gun, and God help David.

Their pastor from the First United Methodist Church had come to see them that evening and had led them all in prayer. Laura had hardly heard the words, her mind still bombarded with shock. She needed a prayer now. She needed something to get her through this night. The thought that she might never hold her child again was about to drive her crazy with grief, and the idea of that woman's hands on him made her grip the gun with bleached knuckles.

She had never thought she could kill anyone before. Never in a million years. But now, with the gun in her hand and Mary Terror on the loose, she thought she could squeeze the trigger without flinching.

It was a terrible feeling, the desire to kill.

Laura put the gun back into the drawer and slid it shut. Then she got down on her knees and prayed for three things: David's safe return, that the FBI found that woman quickly, and that God would forgive her thoughts of murder.

6.

Belle of the Ball

As Laura prayed in Atlanta, a gray Coupe de Ville slowed on a forested road sixty miles northwest of Richmond. The car took a curve off the main road onto one that was narrower, and continued another half mile. Its headlights glinted off the windows of a house on a bluff, nestled amid pines and century-old oaks. The windows of the house were dark, and no smoke rose from the white stone chimney. Telephone and electric lines stretched from here to the highway, a rugged distance. Natalie Terrell stopped her car before the steps of the front porch, and she got out into the bitter wind.

A half moon had broken free of the clouds. It threw sparks of silver onto the ruffled water of Lake Anna, which the house overlooked. Another road snaked down the hill to a boathouse and pier. Natalie saw no other car, but she knew: her daughter was there.

Shivering, she walked up the steps to the porch. She tried the doorknob, and the door opened. She walked inside, out of the wind, and she started to reach for the light switch.

"Don't."

She stopped. Her heart had given a vicious jolt.

"Are you alone?"

Natalie strained to see where her daughter was in the room, but couldn't find her. "Yes."

"They didn't follow you?"

"No."

"Don't turn on the lights. Close the door and step away from it."

Natalie did. She saw a shape rise up from a chair, and she stood with her back against a wall as it passed her. Mary stared out a window, watching the road. Her size—her largeness—made pure fear leech to Natalie's stomach. Her daughter was taller than she by about four inches, and much broader through the shoulders. Mary stood motionless in the dark, her gaze on the road as her mother shrank back from her presence.

"Why didn't they follow you?" Mary asked.

"They . . . went somewhere else. I sent them. . . ." Fear had her by the throat and wouldn't let her speak. "I sent them to the beach house."

"They had a tap on the line."

"Yes."

"I figured they'd have one of those new phone-tracer gizmos. That's why I didn't call from here. Like I said, Big Brother's in action, huh?"

Mary's face turned toward her mother. Natalie couldn't make out her features, but something about her face was brutal. "So how come you didn't tell them I was coming here?"

"I don't know," Natalie answered. It was the truth.

"Mother," Mary said, and she walked to her and gave her a cold kiss on the cheek.

Natalie couldn't suppress a shudder. Her daughter smelled unclean. She felt Mary's hand rest against her shoulder; there was something gripped in it, and Natalie realized Mary was holding a gun.

Mary stepped back, and mother and daughter stared at each other in the dark. "It's been a long time," Mary said. "You've gotten older."

"No doubt."

"Well, so have I." She wandered to the window again, peering out. "I didn't think you'd come. I figured you were going to send the pigs after me."

"Then why did you call?"

"I've missed you," Mary said. "And Father, too. I'm glad you didn't bring the pigs. I saw your car pull in, and I knew pigs don't drive Cadillacs. But I'm parked down at the boathouse, and if I saw somebody following you I was going to take my baby and get out on the lake road." The lake road was a trail, really, that wound around much of Lake Anna before joining the main road. This time of year a gate closed the trail off, but Mary had already broken the gate off its hinges to allow a quick escape.

My baby, Mary had said. "Where's the child?" Natalie asked.

"Back bedroom. I've got him wrapped up in a blanket so he'll be all comfy-cozy. I didn't want to start a fire. You never can tell who might smell the smoke. The rangers' station is still a couple of miles north, isn't it?"

"Yes." The lake house, constructed for summer use, had no furnace but there were three fireplaces for cool nights. Right now the house was as chilly as a tomb.

"So why didn't you bring the pigs?"

Natalie could feel her daughter watching her, like a wary animal. "Because I knew you wouldn't give up if they caught you. I knew they'd have to kill you."

"But isn't that what you want? You said it in the papers: you wouldn't cry if I was dead."

"That's right. I was thinking of the baby."

"Oh." She nodded. Her mother had always loved babies; it was when they got older that she turned her back in boredom. Mary had taken a gamble, and it had worked. "Okay, I can dig it."

"I'd like to know why you stole him from his mother."

"I'm his mother," Mary said flatly. "I told you. I've named him Drummer."

Natalie moved out of the corner. Mary's gaze tracked her across the room, and her mother stopped near the cold fireplace made of fieldstones. "Stealing a baby is a new one for you, isn't it? Murders, bombings, and terrorism weren't enough for you? You had to steal an innocent child not two days old?"

"Talk, talk," Mary said. "You're still the same, talking that shit."

"You'd better listen to me, damn it!" Natalie snapped, much louder than she'd intended. "By God, they're going to hunt you down for this! They'll kill you and drag your body through the street! Sweet Jesus, what's in your mind to make you do such a thing?"

Mary was silent for a moment. She set the Colt down on a table, close enough to get it fast if she needed it. The coast was clear, though; the pigs were sniffing around the family's beach house by now. "I always wanted a baby," Mary told her. "One of my own, I mean. From my own body."

"And so you steal another woman's child?"

"Talking shit," Mary chided her mother. Then: "I almost had a baby once. Before I got hurt. That was a long time ago, but . . . sometimes I still think I can feel the baby kick. Maybe it's a ghost, huh? A ghost, up inside me trying to get out. Well, I let the ghost out. I gave him bones, skin, and a name: Drummer. He's my baby now, and no one in this mindfucked world's going to take him away from me."

"They'll kill you. They'll hunt you down and kill you, and you know it."

"Let them try. I'm ready."

Natalie heard a sound that made her sick with anguish: the thin noise of a baby crying, from the guest bedroom. Mary said, "He's a good kid. He doesn't cry very much."

"Aren't you going to go get him?"

"No. He'll go back to sleep in a few minutes."

"He's hungry!" She felt her cold cheeks redden with anger. "Are you letting him starve to death?"

"I've got formula for him. Don't you get it, Mother? I love Drummer. I'm not going to let anything hap—"

"Balls," Natalie said, and she strode past her daughter into the hallway. She reached out, found a light switch, and turned on the overhead light. It stung her eyes for a few seconds, and she heard Mary pick up the gun again. Natalie continued into the guest bedroom, turned on a lamp, and looked at the crying, red-faced baby wrapped in a coarse gray blanket on the bed. She wasn't prepared for the sight of such a small infant, and her heart ached. This child's mother—Laura Clayborne they said her name was—must be ready for an asylum by now. She picked up the crying infant and held him against her. "There, there," she said. "It's all right, everything's going to be all—"

Mary came into the room. Natalie saw the animal cunning in her daughter's eyes, the years of hardscrabble living etched on her face. Mary once was a beautiful, vivacious young woman, the belle of the ball in Richmond society. Now she resembled a bag lady, used to living under train trestles and eating out of cast-iron pots. Natalie looked quickly away from her, before her eyes were overpowered by the waste of a human being. "This child's hungry. You can hear it in his crying. And he needs his diaper changed! Damn it, you don't know the first thing about taking care of a baby, do you?"

"I've had some practice," Mary said, watching her mother rock Drummer with a gentle motion.

"Where's the formula? We're going to warm some up and feed this child, right this minute!"

"It's in the car. You'll walk down to the boathouse with me, won't you?" It was a command, not a question. Natalie hated the boat-house; it was where Grant had hanged himself from an overhead rafter.

When they returned, Natalie switched on the kitchen stove and warmed a bottle of formula. Mary sat at the small table and watched her mother feed the freshly diapered Drummer, the Colt near at hand. The shine of light on her mother's diamond rings drew Mary's attention. "That's right, that's right," Natalie crooned. "Baby's having a good dinner now, isn't him? Yes, him is!"

"Did you ever hold me like that?" Mary asked.

Natalie ceased her crooning. The baby sucked noisily at the nipple.

"What about Grant? Did you hold him like that, too?"

The nipple popped out of the infant's mouth. He made a little wailing sound of need, and Natalie guided the nipple back into his cupid's-bow lips. What would Mary do, she wondered, if she were to suddenly turn away, walk out of this house with David Clayborne, and get into the car? Her gaze fixed on the Colt and then skittered away.

Mary read it. "I'll take my son now," she said, and she stood up and lifted Drummer away from her mother. Drummer kept feeding, staring up at her with big, unfocused blue eyes. "Isn't he pretty? I almost had a wreck looking at him. He's so pretty, isn't he?"

"He's not your son."

"Talking shit," Mary crooned to Drummer. "Talking shit shit shit, yes she is."

"Please listen to me! It's not right! I don't know why you did this, or what . . . what's in your mind, but you can't keep him! You've got to give him up! Listen to me!" she insisted as Mary turned her back. "I'm begging you! Don't put this child in danger! Do you hear me?"

Silence, but for the sucking. Then: "I hear you."

"Leave him with me. I'll take him to the police. Then you can go on wherever you want to, I don't care. Lose yourself. Go underground. Just let me take that child back where he belongs."

"He's already where he belongs."

Natalie glanced at the pistol again, lying on the table. Two steps away. Did she dare? Was it loaded, or not? If she picked it up, could she use it if she had to? Her mind careened toward a decision.

Mary held the baby with one hand and retrieved the gun with the other. She tucked it down in the waistband of her faded denims. "Mother," she said, and she looked into Natalie's face with her cold, intense eyes in that hard and bitter face, "we don't live in the same world. We never did. I played the game for as long as I could stand it. Then I knew: your world would break me if I didn't fight back. It would grind me down, put me in a wedding dress and give me a diamond ring, and I would look across the dining room table at some stupid stranger and hear the screams of injustice every day of my life, but by then I'd be too weak to care. I'd live in a big house in Richmond with foxhunt paintings on the walls, and I'd worry about finding good help. I'd think that maybe we should have nuked Vietnam, and I wouldn't give a shit about whether the pigs billy-clubbed students in the streets and whether the Mindfuck State got fat on the bodies of the uneducated masses. Your world would have killed me, Mother. Can't you understand?"

"All that is past history," Natalie answered. "The fighting in the streets is over. The student rebellions, the protests . . . all of it is gone. Why can't you let it go?"

Mary smiled thinly. "It's not gone. People just forgot. I'm going to make them remember."

"How? By committing more murders?"

"I'm a soldier. My war didn't end. It'll never end." She kissed Drummer on the forehead, and her mother flinched. "He's part of the next generation. He'll carry on the fight. I'll teach him what we did for freedom, and he'll know the war's never over." She smiled into the baby's face. "My sweet, sweet Drummer."

Natalie Terrell had thought for over twenty years that her daughter was unbalanced. Now it came at her in a savage rush: she was standing in a kitchen with a madwoman who held a bottle of formula to an infant's lips. There was no way to reach her; she was beyond touching, a resident of a world of twisted patriotism and midnight slaughters. For the first time, she feared for her own life.

"So you sent them to the beach house," Mary said, still looking at Drummer. "That was motherly of you. Well, they'll find out soon enough that I'm not there. The pigs won't be kind to you, Mother. You may get a taste of the whip."

"I did it because I didn't want to see that child hurt, and I hoped—"

"I know what you hoped. That you could put me in your fist and mold me, like you tried to mold Grant. No, no; I won't be molded. I suppose I can't stay here much longer, can I?"

"They'll find you wherever you go."

"Oh, I've done pretty well up until now." She looked at her mother, and saw she was afraid. It made her feel both elated and very sad. "I'll take one of your rings."

"What?"

"One of your rings. I want the one with the two diamonds side by side."

Natalie shook her head. "I don't know what you—"

"Take off that ring and put it on the table," Mary said; her voice had changed. It was a soldier's voice again, all daughterly pretense gone. "Do it right now."

Natalie looked at the ring Mary meant. It was worth seven thousand dollars, and had been given to her as a birthday gift by Edgar in 1965. "No," she said. *"No.* I won't."

"If you don't take it off, I'll do it for you."

Natalie's chin lifted, like the prow of a battleship. "All right, come ahead."

Mary moved fast; she held Drummer in the crook of her left arm and was upon Natalie before she could back away. Mary's hand grasped her mother's. There was a fierce pull, some pain as skin was torn and the finger was almost wrenched from its socket, and the ring was gone.

"Damn you to hell," Natalie rasped, and she lifted her right hand and slapped Mary Terror across the face.

Mary smiled, a handprint splayed across her cheek. "I love you, too, Mother," she said, and she put the ring with its double diamonds into her pocket. "Would you hold my baby?" She gave Drummer to Natalie, and then she walked purposefully into the den and yanked the telephone from its wall socket. She flung the telephone against the wall and smashed it to pieces as Natalie stood with tears in her eyes and the baby in her arms. Mary offered her mother another smile as she passed her on the way out the front door. She drew her pistol, put the first bullet through the Cadillac's left front tire and the second bullet through the right rear tire. She returned to the house, bringing with her a whiff of gunsmoke. When they'd walked down to the boathouse to get the formula, Mary had made her mother stand far enough away so Natalie couldn't tell she was in a van, not a "car," what make it was or what color. That was for the best; when her mother got back to civilization, she would sing like a little teakettle to the pigs. Mary took Drummer back from Natalie's trembling hands, her mother's face drawn and pallid. "Will you stay in the house, or do I have to take your shoes?"

"What would you do? Tear them off my feet?"

"Yes," Mary said, and her mother believed her. Natalie sat down in a chair in the den and listened to the squeal of air leaving the Cadillac's tires. Mary squeezed the last drink of formula into the baby's mouth, then she held him against her shoulder and patted his back, trying to draw forth a burp.

"Lower," Natalie said quietly. Mary moved her hand and kept patting. In a few seconds Drummer did his thing. He yawned in the folds of his blanket, getting sleepy again.

"I wouldn't try to walk to the ranger's station in the dark," Mary advised. "You could break an ankle. I'd wait until the sun comes up."

"Thank you for your concern."

Mary rocked Drummer, a motion as soothing to her as it was to the infant. "Let's don't say good-bye as enemies. Okay?"

"Everyone's your enemy," Natalie told her. "You hate everything and everybody, don't you?"

"I hate what tries to kill me, body or spirit." She paused, thinking of something else to say though it was time to get going. "Thanks for helping me with Drummer. Sorry I had to take the ring, but I'm going to need some money."

"Yes. Guns and bullets *are* expensive, aren't they?"

"So is gas. It's a long way to Canada." There's a morsel to feed the pigs, she thought. Maybe they wouldn't be so hard on her. "Tell Father I asked about him, will you?" She started to turn away, to go out through the back door the same way she'd entered the house, using the key that always remained hidden on the doorjamb's ledge. She hesitated. One more thing to say. "You can be proud of me for this, Mother: I never gave up what I believed in. I never quit. That counts for something, doesn't it?"

"It'll make a fine epitaph on your gravestone," Natalie said.

"Good-bye, Mother."

And she was gone.

Natalie heard the creak of the back door opening. The *thunk* of its closing. She stayed where she was, her hands folded in her lap as if awaiting the soup course at a formal dinner. Perhaps five minutes slipped past. And then a sob broke in the woman's throat, and she lowered her face and began to cry. The tears fell from her cheeks onto her hands, where they glittered like false diamonds.

Mary Terror, behind the van's wheel with Drummer swaddled and warm on the floorboard, saw the last of the house's light in her rearview mirror before the skeletal trees got in the way. She felt weakened; her mother had always had the knack of draining her. Didn't matter. Nothing mattered but being at the weeping lady at two o'clock on the afternoon of the eighteenth, and giving Drummer to his new father. She could imagine the radiance of Lord Jack's smile.

Today was Monday, the fifth. She had thirteen days. Time enough to find a cheap motel off the highway, lay low for a while and make some changes. Have to smell the wind and be sure the pigs weren't near. Have to disappear for a while, and let the heat drift past. She said to the sleeping Drummer, "Mama loves you. Mama loves her sweet, sweet baby. You're mine now, did you know that? Yes you are. Mine forever and always."

Mary smiled, her face daubed green by the dashboard glow. The van made a rocking motion, almost like a cradle. Mother and baby were at peace, for now.

The van sped on, its tires tracking across the dark land.

IV
Where the Creatures Meet

1.

Shards

On the fourteenth day of February, two things happened: a TWA jet carrying two hundred and forty-six people exploded in the air above Tokyo, Japan, and a deranged man with an AK-47 assault rifle opened fire in a shopping mall in La Crosse, Wisconsin, killing three people and wounding five others before he took refuge in a J.C. Penney's. Both these news items together drove the last nails into the flagging Mary Terror drama, dooming it to that part of the newscasts and papers known as "the coffin corner": dead items.

The fifteenth dawned. Laura Clayborne awakened sometime

around ten, after another restless night. She lay in bed for a while, getting her bearings; sometimes she thought she was awake when she was still dreaming. The sleeping pills tended to do it. Everything was confused and uncertain, an entanglement of reality and delusion. She gathered her strength to face another day, a monumental effort, and she got out of bed and peered through the blinds. The sun was shining, the sky was blue. It was windy outside, and it looked very cold. There were, of course, no more reporters. The reporters had trickled away, day after day. The press conferences held by the FBI—which were really only attempts to keep the story newsworthy —had ceased luring the reporters in. The press conferences had stopped. There was never any news. Mary Terror had vanished, and with her had vanished David.

Laura went to the bathroom. She didn't look at her face in the mirror because she knew it would be a terrible sight. She felt as if she'd aged ten years in the twelve days since David had been stolen. Her joints throbbed like an old woman's, and she constantly had headaches. Stress, the doctor had told her. Perfectly understandable in this situation. See this pink pill? Take half of one twice a day and call me if you need me. Laura splashed cold water into her face. Her eyelids were swollen, her body bloated and sluggish. She felt warm wetness between her thighs, and she touched down there. Watery reddish fluid on her fingertips. The stitches had pulled loose again; nothing would hold her together anymore since her baby was gone.

It was the weight of not knowing that was killing her. Was David dead? Murdered and thrown into the weeds by the roadside? Had she sold him on the black market for cash? Was she planning to use him in some kind of cultish rite? All those questions had been pondered by Neil Kastle and the FBI, but there were no answers.

Sometimes the urge to cry suddenly overwhelmed her, and she was forced back to bed. She sensed it coming now, growing stronger. She gripped the sink, her head bent forward. An image of David's body lying in the weeds swept through her mind. "No!" she said as the first tears burned her eyes. "No, damn it, no!"

She rode it out, her body trembling and her teeth clenched so hard her jaws ached. The storm of unbearable sadness passed, but it stayed flickering and rumbling on the horizon. Laura left the bathroom, walked through the untidy bedroom, through the den and to the kitchen. Her bare feet were cold on the floor. Her first stop, as usual, was the answering machine. No messages. She opened the refrigerator and drank orange juice straight from the carton. She took the array of vitamins the doctor had suggested for her, swallowing one after another the pills that might have choked a horse. Then she stood in the middle of the kitchen, blinking in the sunlight and trying to decide if she should have raisin bran or oatmeal.

First, call Kastle. She did. His secretary, who'd initially been sweetness and Georgia peaches but was now more crisp and lemony at Laura's sometimes-dozen calls a day, said Kastle was out of the office and wouldn't be back until after three. No, there was no progress. Yes, you'll be the first to know. Laura hung up. Raisin bran or oatmeal? It seemed a very difficult decision.

She had Wheat Chex. She ate standing up, and she spilled some milk on the floor and almost cried again, but she remembered the old saying so she let it go. She wiped the drops of milk away with her foot.

Her parents had gone home the previous morning. It was the beginning, Laura knew, of a cold war between her and her mother. Doug's mother had returned to Orlando two days previously. Doug had started back to work. Somebody's got to make some money, he'd told her. Anyway, there's no use just sitting around here waiting, is there?

Doug had said something the night before that had sent Laura into a rage. He'd looked at her, the *Wall Street Journal* on the sofa beside him, and he'd said, "If David's dead, it won't be the end of the world."

That remark had sliced through her heart like a burning blade. "Do you think he's dead?" she'd asked him savagely. "Is that what you think?"

"I'm not saying he's dead. I'm just saying that life goes on no matter what happens."

"My God. My God." Laura's hand had gone to her mouth, her stomach roiling with horror. "You *do* think he's dead, don't you? Oh Jesus, you do!"

Doug had stared at her with heavy-lidded eyes, and Laura had seen the truth in them. The subsequent storm had driven Doug out of the house, racing away in his Mercedes. Laura had called C. Jannsen's number. When a woman had answered, Laura had said bitterly, "He's on his way. You can have him, and I hope you enjoy what you get." She'd hung up, but not with a slam as she'd first intended. Doug wasn't worth the effort. Sometime before midnight she'd found herself sitting on the bed, cutting apart their wedding pictures with scissors. It came to her, as she'd sat with the shards of memories in her lap, that she was in real danger of losing her mind. Then she'd put all the pieces into a little pile atop the dresser and she'd taken two sleeping pills and searched for rest.

What to do? What to do? She wasn't ready for work yet. She could imagine herself trying to cover a social function and collapsing in the foie gras. She put on the coffeepot, and she wandered around the kitchen straightening things that were already straight. As she passed near the telephone, she thought of calling Neil Kastle again. Maybe there would be some news. She picked up the phone, put it down, picked it up once more, finally left it in a helter-skelter of indecision.

Straighten up in the den, she thought. Yes, it needed straightening.

Laura walked in and spent a few minutes going through magazines in the basket where they collected. She chose issues that were two or three months old and stacked them up for the trash. No, no; this one couldn't go. It had an article about breastfeeding in it. This one couldn't go, either; it had an article about how babies responded to music. She drifted away from the magazines to the bookshelves, and began to line the volumes up so that their spines were exactly even. The larger-sized books gave her a fit of consternation. And then she came to a volume that made her hand stop its relentless arranging.

Its title was *Burn This Book*.

Laura took the book down. Mark Treggs, the holdover hippie. No author's photo. Mountaintop Press, Chattanooga, Tennessee. A post office box. She skimmed through the book, searching for the part where Treggs had talked about the Weather Underground and the Storm Front. On page 72, she found it: "The Love Generation, bleeding from a thousand wounds inflicted by the militant counter-culture, may well have expired on the night of July 1, 1972, when police in Linden, New Jersey, cornered the terrorist Storm Fronters in a suburban tract house. Four Storm Fronters died in the firefight, one was captured alive but wounded, and four more escaped, including their main man 'Lord Jack' Gardiner. The pigs searched, but they could not find. Some say Canada, that saint of America's political fugitives, took them into her forests. You can hear it still today if you put your ear to the right track: the Storm Front's out there some-where. Maybe still licking their wounds, like old bears in a cave. Maybe muttering and dreaming, aging longhairs huddled over can-dles with their stashes of pot and acid. I knew one of the Storm

Fronters, a long time ago before the flames destroyed the flowers. She was a nice kid from Cedar Falls, Iowa. A farmer's daughter, can you dig it? To her I send a message: keep the faith, and love the one you're with."

Laura's gaze flickered back up the page. *I knew one of the Storm Fronters.*

Not Mary Terrell. She was born in Richmond. Who, then?

Somebody who might help the FBI find her baby?

Laura took the book to the telephone. She dialed Kastle's number in such a hurry that she messed up and had to redial. His secretary, the lemony bitch, answered after the second ring. No, Mrs. Clayborne, Mr. Kastle isn't in yet. I told you before, he won't be back until after three. No, I'm sorry, I don't have a number where he can be reached. Mrs. Clayborne, it's not doing anybody any good for you to keep calling. I'm terribly sorry about your situation, but everything possible is being done to find your—

Bullshit. Laura hung up.

She paced the kitchen, her heart pounding. Whom could she tell about this? Who could help her? She stopped at the telephone again, and this time she dialed Directory Assistance in Chattanooga.

The operator had no number for Mountaintop Press. There were two Treggses: Phillip and M.K. She scribbled down the latter number and called it, her stomach doing slow flip-flops.

Four rings. "Hello?" A woman's voice.

"Mark Treggs, please?"

"Mark's at work. Can I take a message?"

Laura swallowed, her throat dry. "Is this . . . the Mark Treggs who wrote the book?"

A pause. Then, cautiously: "Yes."

Thank God! she thought. Her hand was clenched around the receiver. "Are you his wife?"

"Who is this, please?"

"My name is Laura Clayborne. I'm calling from Atlanta. Is there a number where I can reach Mr. Treggs?"

Another pause. "No, I'm sorry."

"Please!" It came out too fast, too charged with emotion. "I've got to talk to him! Please tell me how I can find him!"

"There's no number," the woman said. "Laura Clayborne. I think I know that name. Are you a friend of Mark's?"

"I've never met him, but it's vitally important that I reach him. Please! Can't you help me?"

"He'll be home after five. Can I give him a message?"

Five o'clock seemed an eternity. In frustration, Laura said, "Thank you so much!" and this time she did slam the receiver down. She stood for a moment with her hands pressed against her face, trying to decide what to do. The image of David in the weeds came to her again, and she shook it off before it latched in her mind.

Chattanooga was about a two-hour drive from Atlanta, northwest along I-75. Laura looked at the clock. If she left now, she could be there around one. *I knew one of the Storm Fronters.* Treggs might know more about the Storm Front than he'd written in the book. A two-hour drive. She could make it in an hour and forty-five minutes.

Laura went into the bedroom, put on a pair of bluejeans that fit snugly around the puffiness she was still carrying, and she shrugged into a white blouse and a beige cable-knit sweater. It occurred to her that she might have to stay in Chattanooga overnight. She began to pack a suitcase, another pair of jeans and a crimson sweater, extra underwear and socks. She loaded up her toothpaste and toothbrush, decided to take her shampoo and her hair dryer. Money, she thought. Have to go by the bank and get a check cashed. Got my Visa, MasterCard, and American Express. Have to get the BMW's tank filled. Leave a note for Doug; no, forget that. Get the tires checked, too. It wouldn't be good to have a blowout, a woman alone in this hard old world.

She knew now that violence could strike from any direction, without warning, and leave tragedy in its wake. She walked to the dresser, opened the top drawer, and lifted up Doug's sweaters. She took the automatic pistol out, along with a box of ammunition. The shooting lessons be damned; if she had to use it, she'd learn fast.

Laura gave her hair a quick brushing. She forced herself to look at her face in the mirror. Her eyes had a glassy shine: either excitement or insanity, she couldn't decide which. But one thing she knew for sure: waiting in this house, day after day, for word about her baby would surely drive her over the edge. Mark Treggs might not know anything about the Storm Front. He might not have any information at all that could help her. But she was going to Chattanooga to find him, and nothing on earth was going to stop her.

She put on her black Reeboks, then deposited the automatic pistol and the box of ammunition in her suitcase, along with her hairbrush.

The pile of cut-up photographs caught her attention.

She swept them into a trash can with the edge of her hand. Then she picked up her suitcase, got her tan overcoat, and walked into the garage. The BMW's engine started, a throaty growl.

Laura drove away from the house on Moore's Mill Road, and she did not look back.

2.

The Pennywhistle Player

Chattanooga is a city that seems stopped in time, like a Rebel's rusted pocketwatch. The broad Tennessee River meanders around it, interstates pierce its heart, railroads connect the warehouses and factories with those in other places; the river, interstates, and railroads enter Chattanooga and leave it, but Chattanooga remains like a faded damsel waiting for some suitor long dead and buried. She turns her face away from the modern, and pines for what can never be again.

The huge mass of Lookout Mountain rises over Chattanooga, the faded damsel's dowager hump. It was Lookout Mountain that Laura saw before she saw the city. Its appearance, at first a looming purple shadow on the horizon, made Laura's foot heavier on the BMW's gas pedal. At eighteen minutes after one she pulled off the interstate at Germantown Road, found a pay phone with a phone book, and looked up M. K. Treggs. The address was 904 Hilliard Street. Laura bought a city map at a gas station, pinpointed Hilliard Street on it, and got the gas jockey to tell her the best way to get there. Then she was off again, driving in the bright afternoon sunlight toward the northeastern side of Chattanooga.

The address was a small woodframe house in a nest of similar houses across from a shopping center. It was painted pale blue, and the house's postage-stamp-size lawn had been turned into a rock garden with a pebbled walkway. The mailbox was one of those plastic jobs with redbirds on it. A rope and tire swing hung from a tree branch, and in the driveway was a white Yugo with rust splotches. Laura pulled her car in front of the house and got out. The chill breeze ruffled her hair, and made the six or seven wind chimes that hung from the front porch's rafters clang and bong and jingle and clink.

A dog next door began to bark furiously. Big brown dog behind a chain-link fence, she noted. She walked up onto the porch and rang the doorbell, surrounded by chimes.

The inner door opened, but the screen door stayed closed. A slender, petite woman with braided brown hair peered cautiously out. "Can I help you?"

"I'm Laura Clayborne. I called you from Atlanta."

The woman just stared at her.

"I called you at eleven," Laura went on. "I've come to talk to your husband."

"You're . . . the lady who called? You came from Atlanta?" She blinked, the information sinking in.

"That's right. I can't tell you how important it is that I see your husband."

"I know who you are." The woman nodded. "You're the one whose baby was taken. Mark and I talked about that. I knew I'd heard your name before!"

Laura stood there, waiting. Then the woman said, "Oh! Come on in!" She unlatched the screen door, and opened it wide to accept Laura.

In her college days Laura had been in many dorm rooms and hippie apartments. Her own apartment had been pretty much "hippified," or at least what passed for such at the University of Georgia. The house immediately took her back to those days. It was full of cheap apartment furniture, with crates serving as book and record cases, a big orange beanbag chair with *UT* emblazoned on it, and a beige sofa that looked as if it had been slept on for quite a number of years. Vases with dried flowers stood about, and on the walls were actual, genuine, real McCoy black light posters, one showing the astrological signs and the other depicting a three-masted ship against a full moon. A wood carving on one wall read LET IT BE. Laura was sure she smelled strawberry incense and lentils cooking. Fat, half-burned candles— those kinds with intricate wax designs and varicolored bands on them—were arranged on a countertop, next to books that included the works of Kahlil Gibran and Rod McKuen. Laura could look through a corridor and see a poster at the end of it: *War Is Not Healthy for Children and Other Living Things.*

The sensation of stepping back into time might have been complete for Laura except for some GoBots scattered on the floor and a Nintendo atop the television set. The woman with braided hair scooped up the GoBots. "Kids," she said with a toothy smile. "They leave stuff everywhere, don't they?"

Laura spotted a Barbie doll clad in a doll-size shimmery white gown, leaning against a record crate full of battered-looking album jackets. "You have two children?"

"Right on. Mark Junior's ten, and Becca's just turned eight. Sorry the place is a wreck. Getting 'em off to school some mornings's like a tornado passing through. Get you some tea? I've just made some Red Zinger."

It had been years since Laura had tasted Red Zinger tea. "That would be fine," she said, and she followed the woman into the cramped little kitchen. The refrigerator had peace signs painted all over it in vivid colors. The crayon drawings of children were taped up. *Love You, Mom* was printed on one of them. Laura looked quickly away from it, because a lump had risen into her throat.

"I'm Rose," the woman said. "Pleased to meet you." She offered her hand, and Laura shook it. Then Rose went about her task of getting cups and pouring the tea from a brown clay pot. "We've got raw sugar," she said, and Laura told her that would be fine, too. As Rose got their tea ready, Laura saw the woman had on Birkenstock sandals, staple hippie footwear. Rose Treggs wore faded jeans with patched knees and a bulky sea-green sweater that was a dozen rubs away from giving at the elbows. She was about five feet tall, and she moved with the quick, birdlike energy of petite people. In the kitchen's sunlight, Laura could see the hints of gray in Rose Treggs's hair. The woman had an attractive, open face and freckles across her nose and cheeks, but the lines around her mouth and at the corners of her dark blue eyes told a tale of a hard life. "Here you go," Rose said, giving Laura a rough clay cup with a hippie's long-jawed, bearded face molded into it. "You want lemon?"

"No, thanks." She sipped the tea. Few things in life remained the same, but Red Zinger persevered.

They sat in the living room, amid the relics of a bygone age. Looking around at it all, Laura imagined the voice of Bob Dylan singing "Blowin' in the Wind." She could feel Rose watching her, nervously waiting for her to speak. "I read your husband's book," Laura began.

"Which one? He's written three."

Burn This Book."

"Oh, right. That's sold the best. Almost four hundred copies."

"I reviewed it for the *Constitution.*" The review, however, had never been printed. "It was interesting."

"We've got our own publishing company," Rose said. "Mountain-top Press." She smiled and shrugged. "Well, it's just a typeset machine and some stuff in the basement, really. We sell mostly by mail order, to college bookstores. But that's how Benjamin Franklin started, huh?"

Laura leaned forward in her chair. "Rose? I have to talk to your husband. You understand what's happened to me, don't you?"

Rose nodded. "We saw it on the news and read about it, too. Blew our minds. But you don't look like your picture."

"My baby has been stolen from me," Laura said, holding the tears back by sheer willpower. "He was two days old. His name is David, and I . . . I wanted a child very badly." Careful, she thought. Her eyes were burning. "You know who took my baby, don't you?"

"Yeah. Mary Terror. We thought she was dead by now."

"Mary Terror," Laura repeated, her gaze fixed on Rose's face. "The FBI's looking for her. But they can't find her. It's been twelve days, and she's disappeared with my son. Do you have any idea how long twelve days can be?"

Rose didn't answer. She looked away from Laura because the woman's intense stare made her nervous.

"Every day can stretch and stretch until you feel as if it's never going to end," Laura continued. "You think the hours are stuck. And at night, when it's so quiet you can hear your heart beat . . . at night it's the worst. I've got an empty nursery in my house, and Mary Terrell has my son. I read your husband's book. I read about the Storm Front in it. He knows someone who was a member of the Storm Front, doesn't he?"

"That was a long time ago."

"I realize that. But anything he could tell me might help the FBI, Rose. *Anything.* As it is, they're spinning their wheels. I can't take many more days of waiting for a phone call to tell me if my David is alive or dead. Can you understand that?"

Rose released a long breath and nodded, her face downcast. "Yeah. When we heard about it, we had a long talk. We wondered how we'd feel if somebody took Mark Junior or Becca. It would be a heavy trip, that's for sure." She looked up. "Mark did know a woman who belonged to the Storm Front. But he didn't know Mary Terror. He doesn't know anything that would help you get your baby back."

"How can you be sure about that? Maybe your husband knows something that he doesn't think is important, but it could be of real value. I don't think I have to tell you how desperate I am. You're a mother. You know how you'd feel." She saw Rose frown, the lines deepening. "Please. I need to find your husband and ask him some questions. I won't take much of his time. Will you tell me where I can find him?"

Rose's teeth worked her lower lip. She swirled the Red Zinger around her teacup, and then she said, "Yeah. Okay. There's a phone number, but I didn't give it to you because they don't like to go out and track down the custodians. I mean, it's a big place."

"Where does your husband work?"

Rose told her where, and how to get there. Laura finished her tea, said thank you, and left the house. At the front door Rose wished her peace, and the chimes stirred in the chill breeze.

Rock City was perched atop Lookout Mountain. It was not a suburb of Chattanooga, but rather a tourist attraction of walkways winding between huge, wind-chiseled boulders, a waterfall plummeting from a sheer cliff, and rock gardens with benches for the weary. Signs with bearded elves pointed out the admission gate and the parking lot. On such a cold day, even with the sun shining, the lot was all but empty. Laura paid her money in a building where Indian arrowheads and Confederate caps were on sale, and she was told by the clerk that Mark Treggs was probably out sweeping the path near the Swinging Bridge. She started off, following the walkway over, around, and sometimes even through the center of gargantuan rocks, the denuded bones of Lookout Mountain. She easily got through a crevice called Fatman's Squeeze, and she realized she was losing the weight of pregnancy. The pathway took her up into the sunlight again, out of the freezing shadows of the stones, and she at last saw the Swinging Bridge ahead of her. There was no one on the path, though. She crossed the bridge, which indeed did creak and swing, a gorge full of rocks about sixty feet below. She continued along the path, her hands thrust into the pockets of her overcoat. She didn't see anyone else anywhere. One thing she noticed, though: the walkways couldn't have been cleaner. And then she came around a curve and she heard it: the high, birdlike notes of a pennywhistle.

Laura followed the music. In another moment she found him. He was sitting cross-legged atop a boulder, his rake and broom leaning against the stone, and he was playing a pennywhistle and staring toward a vast panorama of pine woods and blue sky.

"Mr. Treggs?" she said, standing at the boulder's base.

He kept playing. The music was slow and gentle, and sad in a way. A pennywhistle, Laura thought, was an instrument played in circuses by clowns with tears painted on their cheeks. "Mr. Treggs?" she repeated a little louder.

The music stopped. Mark Treggs took the pennywhistle from his mouth and looked down at her. He had a long dark-brown beard peppered with gray and his hair hung over his shoulders, a blue baseball cap on his head. Under thick, gray-flecked brows, his large, luminous hazel eyes peered at Laura from behind wire-framed granny glasses. "Yes?"

"My name is Laura Clayborne. I've come from Atlanta to find you."

Mark Treggs squinted, as if trying to get her into focus. "I don't . . . think I know . . ."

"Laura Clayborne," she said again. "Mary Terrell stole my baby twelve days ago."

His mouth opened, but he didn't say anything.

"I read *Burn This Book,*" she went on. "You talked about the Storm Front. You said you knew someone who belonged to it. I've come to ask you—"

"Oh," he said. It was a boyish voice that did not go with the gray. "Oh, wow."

"For help," Laura finished.

"I saw you on the tube! My old lady and I both saw you! We were talking about you just last night!" He scrambled down off the boulder with surefooted ease. He was wearing a brown uniform and a jacket with Rock City stenciled in red on one breast pocket and Mark on the other. Treggs stood about six three and was as skinny as a spider monkey, his face all beard, wild eyebrows, and goggly eyes behind the glasses. "Man, what a trip! I swear, we were talking about you!"

"I saw Rose. She told me where to find you." The cup, she thought. The face on it was his.

"You went to my *house?* Wow!"

"Mr. Treggs? Listen to me. I need your help. You know someone who belonged to the Storm Front. Is that right?"

His goofy smile began to fade. He blinked a few times, regaining his equilibrium. "Oh," he said. "That's why you're here?"

"Yes. I read your latest book."

"My book. Right." He nodded, and slid the pennywhistle into his back pocket. "Listen . . . excuse me, but I've got to get back to work." He retrieved the rake and broom. "I can't sit around too long. They get mad." He started to move away.

Laura followed him. "Wait a minute! Didn't you hear what I said?" She reached out, grasped his shoulder, and stopped his gawky, long-legged strides. "I'm asking you for your help!"

"I can't help you," he said flatly. "Sorry." Again he began striding away.

Laura kept pace, a surge of anger rising and whorls of red in her cheeks. "Mr. Treggs! Wait, please! Just give me one minute!"

He kept going, his speed picking up.

"Wait! Just hear me out!"

Faster still.

"I SAID WAIT, DAMN IT!" Laura shouted, and she grabbed Mark Treggs by the left arm, spun him around with all her strength, and slammed his back against a smooth boulder. He gave a little grunt, and the rake and broom slid from his hand. His eyes had grown larger, owlish, and frightened.

"Please," he said. "I can't stand violence."

"Neither can I! But by God my son was stolen from me by a

murderess, and you're going to tell me what I want to know!" She shook him. "Can you dig it, man?"

He didn't answer. Then, quietly: "Yeah, I can dig it."

"Good." Laura released him, but she blocked his way so he couldn't escape. "You knew a Storm Fronter. Who was it?"

Treggs looked around. "Okay, come on! Where're the pigs hiding? You brought 'em, didn't you?"

"No police. Nobody but me."

"Well, it doesn't matter anyhow." He shrugged. "I don't care if you're wired. So I was in a commune for a few months with Bedelia Morse. Didi to her friends. So what? I didn't hang out with the Storm Fronters, so you can put that in the pig pipe and let 'em smoke it."

"What happened to Bedelia Morse? Did she die at the shootout in New Jersey?"

"No, she got away. Listen, that's all I know. I was in a commune with Didi and about eight other people back in 'sixty-nine, before she got into the Storm Front. We were in South Carolina, and we broke up after four months because everybody got tired of getting rousted by the local pigs. End of story."

"Didn't you know her at Berkeley?"

"Uh-uh. She didn't go to Berkeley. She got hooked on the Storm Front when she went to New York. Listen, I didn't know anything else about her. Okay?"

"And you haven't heard from her since?"

"No way." Treggs bent his long body over and picked up the rake and broom. "You got your wire turned up loud enough for the pigs to hear? Read my lips: No way."

"What about Mary Terrell? Is there anything you can tell me about her?"

"Yeah." He took off his glasses, pulled a handkerchief from his shirt, and cleaned the lenses. "But you already know. She's crazy as hell. She won't give up to the pigs. They'll have to kill her."

"And she'll kill my son. Is that what you're saying?"

"I didn't say that." He put his glasses back on. "Listen, Mrs. Clayborne, I'm sorry about all this. Really I am. But I don't know anything else about the Storm Front that the pigs—I mean, that the police and FBI don't already know. I'm sorry you came all this way, but I can't help you."

Laura had an instant where she feared she might pass out. She'd built up her hopes—for what, she wasn't sure—and now this was nothing but a dead end.

"You don't look so good," Treggs said. "You want to sit down?" She nodded, and he took her by the arm and led her to a bench. "You want a Coke? I can get you one." She shook her head, fighting nausea. She realized that if she threw up, Treggs would have to clean up the mess. It might be worthwhile to do it, just for the hell of it. But she didn't, and she lifted her face to the breeze and felt the cold sweat begin to dry.

She said in a husky voice, "Is there anything else? Do you have any idea where Mary Terrell might be?"

"No. I don't know where Didi is, either. That was a long time ago." He sat down on the bench beside her, his long legs splayed out. He wore red Adidas sneakers with stars on them. "That commune," he mused. "Man, it seems like that was part of a different world. Well, it *was*, wasn't it?" He squinted in the sunlight, and watched a hawk circle above the mountain. "Long time gone," he said. "We had a nice life. Lived on a little farm, had a couple of cows and some chickens. We didn't bother anybody. All we wanted to do was find nirvana. Know what the pigs finally busted us for?" He waited for Laura to shake her head. "No business license. See, Didi made things. She was a potter, and she sold stuff in town. She was doing pretty good, too, then *bam:* no business license. Man, I don't see why we don't run out of trees, with all the paper you get choked with. I mean, how come we've still got forests, with all the paper that's been used in all of history? And think about wooden furniture, and houses, and everything else made of wood. How come we've still got forests?" He prodded her with a sharp elbow. "Huh?"

"I don't know. Maybe you should write a book about it."

"Yeah, maybe I will," he said. "But then that would be using more paper, wouldn't it? See? A vicious cycle."

They sat for a while in silence. The cold wind strengthened, and Laura heard the cry of a hawk on its current. Mark Treggs stood up. "You ought to see the rest of Rock City while you're here. It's nice. Peaceful, this time of year. You feel like you own the whole place."

"I don't feel much like sightseeing."

"No, I guess not. Well, I've got to get back to work. Can you find your way out?"

Laura nodded. Where was she going to go? And what was she going to do when she got there?

Treggs hesitated, holding the broom and rake. "Listen . . . for what it's worth, I'm really sorry about what's happened. I thought Mary Terrell was dead, buried in an unmarked grave somewhere. I guess you never know who's going to turn up, huh?"

"You never know," Laura agreed.

"Right. Well, you take care. Too bad you had to come all this way for nothing." He still lingered, throwing a skinny shadow at her feet. "I hope they find your baby," he said. "Peace." He made the sign, and then he turned and walked away.

She let him go. What was the point? At last, when she was sure she wasn't going to be sick, she stood up. What to do now? Go back to Atlanta. No, no. She didn't feel like making the drive this afternoon. Maybe she'd find a motel room, get herself a bottle of cheap red wine, and let it rip. Two bottles, maybe. What the hell?

She followed her shadow along the winding trail of Rock City; it was the thin, compressed shadow of a woman crushed between the past and the future, and every direction it pointed toward seemed hopeless.

3.

Eve of Destruction

Night had fallen. The boxes were alight. From their windows
came the glow of den lamps and televisions, small squares of
illumination that marched into the distance. There were thousands of
them in the darkness, thousands of lives going on about her as Mary
Terror guided the van between row after row of Linden's brick and
woodframe houses. Drummer, recently fed and changed, lay in his
new bassinet on the floorboard and sucked on a pacifier. The van's
heater had gotten cranky, wheezing with effort. Mary came to a
four-way intersection, slowed, and then drove on, deeper into the
heart of memory. The frigid wind swirled newspapers and

trash before the headlights, and two men in heavy coats and caps with earflaps crossed the street. Mary watched them move away, out of the lights. She kept going, looking for Carazella's grocery store. She thought she remembered it on the corner of Montgomery Avenue and Charles Street, but a topless bar called Nicky's stood there. She wound through the streets, searching for the past.

Mary Terror had changed. She had cropped her hair short, and dyed it light brown with reddish hints. She had dyed her eyebrows light brown as well, and dotted freckles over her nose and cheeks with an eyebrow pencil. She couldn't do much about her size but slump, but she was wearing new clothes: warmer duds—brown corduroy trousers, a blue flannel shirt, and a fleece-lined jacket. On her feet was a new pair of brown boots. A Hispanic man at a pawnshop in Washington's combat zone had given her twenty-five hundred dollars for her mother's seven-thousand-dollar ring, no questions asked. Since leaving her mother, Mary and Drummer had lived in a series of rooms that gave new meaning to the term "roach motel." One cold morning at the Sleep-Rite Inn near Wilmington, Delaware, Mary had awakened to find roaches scurrying across Drummer's face. She had plucked them off, one by one, and crushed them between her fingers. At the next place they'd stayed, Mary had had a bad feeling about the swarthy woman at the front desk. She didn't like the way the woman had looked at Drummer, as if some light switch were just about to click on in the woman's crack-fried brain. Mary had stayed there less than one hour, then had gotten Drummer out and hit the road again. The places they stayed took cash and didn't ask for identification, and most of the time the clientele were whores and johns, dopeheads and hustlers. At night Mary kept a chair against the door and her gun under her pillow, and she always made sure she knew the quickest way out.

A close call at the Omelet Shoppe outside Trenton, New Jersey, had given her pause for thought. Two pigs had come in while she was eating her pancakes—"griddle cakes," they called them up here—and Drummer was in his bassinet next to her. The pigs had sat down at the booth behind her, ordering up the Hungry Man Breakfasts. Drummer had started crying, a nettlesome sound, and he wouldn't be pacified. His crying had risen to a shriek, and finally one of the pigs looked over at Drummer and said, "Hey! You didn't get your mornin' java, or what?"

"She's always cranky in the morning," Mary had told the pig with a polite smile. How would he know whether Drummer was a boy or girl? She'd picked Drummer up and rocked him, cooing and clucking, and his crying had begun to ebb. Mary had been damp under her arms, her spine prickling with tension, and the little Magnum pistol in her new carry-all shoulder bag.

"Got a good set of lungs," the pig had said. "Oughta try out for the Met when she gets a little older, huh?"

"Maybe so," Mary had answered, and then the pig had turned away and that was all. Mary forced herself to finish her pancakes, but she couldn't taste them anymore. Then she stood up, paid her bill, and got Drummer out, and in the parking lot she'd spat on the pig car's windshield.

Where was Carazella's grocery store? The neighborhood had changed. "Been twenty years," she said to Drummer. "I guess everything changes, right?" She couldn't wait for Drummer to get older so he could carry on a conversation. Oh, the things she and Jack would teach him! He was going to be a walking fortress of militant politics and philosophy, and he wouldn't take shit from anybody on earth. She turned right onto Chambers Street. A flashing caution light was ahead, marking another intersection. Woodroan Avenue, she thought. Yes! That's where I turn left! In another moment she saw the sign, and there was the building on the corner that had been Carazella's. It was still a grocery store, but now it was called Lo Wah's. She drove on two more blocks, took a right on Elderman Street, and she stopped the van about halfway down the block.

There it was. They'd built the house back. It was gray, and in need of painting. Other houses were crowded in around it, the structures jammed together with little respect for space and privacy. She knew that behind the houses were tiny yards squared off with fences, and a warren of alleys for the garbagemen. Oh yes, she knew this neighborhood very, very well.

"This is it," she told Drummer in a reverential voice. "This is where your mama was born."

She remembered it: the first night of July 1972. The Storm Front was in that house, preparing its mission on the weeping lady. Gary Leister, a native New Yorker, had been renting the house under an alias. Lord Jack knew a dude in Bolivia who sent up cocaine in boxes of cigars, the smokes hollowed out and packed with blow. It was with two of these shipments that the Storm Front paid their black-market source in Newark for an assortment of automatic pistols, riot shotguns, hand grenades, plastic explosive, a dozen fresh sticks of dynamite, and a couple of Uzi submachine guns. The house, painted light green in those days, had been an arsenal from which the Storm Front stalked pigs, lawyers, and Manhattan businessmen whom they deemed cogs of the Mindfuck State. The Storm Fronters had kept themselves clean and quiet, holding down the volume of all music and cutting back on their pot smoking. The neighbors had thought that the kids who lived in the house at 1105 Elderman Street had been a strange mix of white, black, and Oriental, but this was the prime of "All in the Family" and the Archie Bunkers of the world groused in their armchairs but minded their own business. The Storm Fronters had made a point of being friendly to the neighbors, of helping the older residents paint their houses and wash their cars. Mary had even earned some extra cash by baby-sitting for an Italian couple a street over. CinCin Omara, a mathematics major at Berkeley, had tutored a neighborhood kid in algebra. Sancho Clemenza, a Chicano poet who spoke four languages, had been a clerk at Carazella's grocery. James Xavier Toombs, who had killed his first pig when he was sixteen years old, had been a short-order cook at the Majestic Diner on Woodroan Avenue. The Storm Fronters had blended into the neighborhood, had covered themselves over with the camouflage of the workaday world, and no one had ever guessed that they planned murders and bombings in midnight sessions that left them all flying high on their sweetest drug: rage.

And then, on the early evening of July 1, Janette Snowden and Edward Fordyce had gone out to get pizza and backed into a pig car on the way home.

"No sweat, no sweat," Edward had said as he and Janette had told the others after they'd gotten back with the cold pizzas. "Everything's cool."

"STUPID!" Lord Jack had shouted into Edward's gaunt, bearded face, coming up out of his chair like a panther. "Stupid as shit, man! Why the fuck didn't you look where you were going?"

"It's no problem!" Janette, tiny and feisty as a firecracker, was on her feet, too. "We screwed up, okay? We were talking and we screwed up. It was just a little dent, that's all."

"Yeah," Edward agreed. "Busted our taillight but didn't do shit to the pigs. They weren't supposed to be parked right on our ass."

"Edward?" It was CinCin's cool Oriental voice, her face like a carved yellow cameo framed with raven hair. "Did they ask to see your driver's license?"

"Yeah." A quick glance at Lord Jack. Mary sat in a rocking chair in the corner, her hands folded over the swelling of Jack's child in her belly. "But it was no sweat," Edward went on. The license was forged, as were all their licenses. Edward flipped his long brown ponytail back. "The pig even laughed about it, said he'd busted up his own car last week and his old lady was still giving him hell about it."

"Did the pigs follow you?" Akitta Washington asked. He was a barrel-chested black man who wore African beads and amulets around his neck, and he went to a window and peered out at the street.

"No. Hell, no. Why would they follow us?" There was a quaver in Edward's voice.

"Because," Mary said from her rocking chair, "some pigs have the sixth sense." She had golden blond hair that hung around her shoulders, her face high-cheekboned and serene: the face of an outlaw Madonna. "Some pigs can smell fear." She cocked her head to one side, her eyes cool and intense. "Do you think those pigs smelled any fear on you, Edward?"

"Get off his case!" Janette shouted. "The pigs didn't roust us, okay? They just ID'd Edward and let us go, that's it!"

Lord Jack began to pace the room: a bad sign. "Maybe it *is* okay," Didi Morse said, sitting on the floor cleaning a revolver with the same fingers that could shape raw clay into objects of earthen art. She was a lovely young woman with green eyes and braided hair as red as a battle flag, her bone structure Iowa solid. "Maybe it's no big deal."

Sancho grunted, smoking a joint. Gary Leister was already attacking one of the pizzas, and James Xavier Toombs sat with his pipe clenched between his teeth and a book of haiku in his lap, his face as emotionless as a black Buddha.

"I don't like it," Jack said. He went to the window, looked out, and paced again. "I don't like it." He continued to pace the room as some of the others began to feast on the pizzas. "Snowden?" he said at last. "Go upstairs and watch from the bedroom window."

"Why do I have to go? I always get the shit detail!"

"GO!" Jack roared. "And Edward, you get your ass upstairs and watch from the arsenal." It was the room where all their weapons and ammunition were hidden in the walls. "Move it, I said! Today, not next fucking week!"

They went. Jack's piercing blue gaze found CinCin. "Walk up to Carazella's and buy a paper," he told her. She left a slice of pizza half eaten and went without question, knowing he was telling her to go out and sniff the air for the stench of pigs. Then Jack walked over to Mary, and he placed his hand against her belly. She grasped his fingers and looked up into his fiery beauty, his long blond hair hanging around his shoulders and a hawk's feather dangling from a ring in his right earlobe. Mary started to say *I love you,* but she checked it. Lord Jack didn't believe in the word; what passed as love, he said, was a tool of the Mindfuck State. He believed in courage, truth, and loyalty, of brothers and sisters willing to lay down their lives for each other and the cause. One-to-one "love," he believed, came from the false world of button-down stiffs and their robotic, manicured prostitutes.

But she couldn't help it. She loved him, though she dared not say it. His wrath could strike like lightning and leave ashes in its wake.

Jack rubbed her belly, and he looked at Akitta. "Watch the backyard." Akitta nodded and went to do it. "Gary! You walk to the Laundromat and back. Take a couple of dollars and get some change in the machine." The Laundromat was two blocks away, in the opposite direction of Carazella's. Mary knew Jack was setting up a defensive perimeter. Gary walked out into the still, humid evening, and the smell of somebody's burgers on a grill drifted into the house. A dog barked in the distance, two more answering across the neighborhood.

Jack stood at the front window, working his knuckles. He said, "I don't hear Frodo."

James Xavier Toombs looked up from his haiku, his pipe in his mouth, and a small puff of blue smoke left his lips.

"Frodo." Jack's voice was low and hushed. "How come Frodo's not barking?"

Frodo was a stumpy little white mutt, the pet of the Giangello family two doors down the street. The Giangellos called him Caesar, but Jack had named him Frodo because of the dog's massive hairy paws. Frodo's bark was distinctive, a deep, throaty *woof* that started up with the regularity of a machine whenever any other dogs barked in the neighborhood. Jack looked at the other Storm Fronters. His tongue flicked out, lizardlike, to skim his lower lip. "Frodo's quiet," he said. "How come?"

No one spoke. There was electricity in the room, the pizzas

forgotten. Mary had stopped rocking, her hands gripped on the armrests. James Xavier Toombs returned the book of haiku to the well-stocked bookshelf. He removed a thick red volume titled *Democracy in Crisis*. He opened it and took his .45 automatic from the hollowed-out book. There was a crisp *click* as he checked the ammo clip. James Xavier Toombs, a man of few words, said, "Trouble."

Mary stood up, and the baby moved inside her as if it, too, were readying for action. "I'll go upstairs and keep watch," she said as she picked up a couple of slices of pizza and walked toward the stairs. Bedelia Morse took her revolver and went to the back to watch the northeastern corner of the house, Sancho took the southwestern corner, and Toombs and Lord Jack stayed in the front room. Mary checked on Edward and Janette; neither one had seen anything remotely suspicious. Then Mary settled herself in the small bedroom overlooking the street, and she sat in a chair near the window with the lights off. The lights were also off in the house directly across Elderman, but that was nothing unusual. The old couple who lived there, the Steinfelds, were in bed by seven o'clock, and it was after eight. Mr. Steinfeld had emphysema, and his wife suffered from a bad bladder and had to wear adult-sized diapers. Changing diapers was a task that would be in Mary's future. She figured it wouldn't be so bad once she got used to it. Besides, it would be Jack's child, and so perfect he'd probably pop out toilet trained. Right, she thought as she smiled faintly in the dark. Dream on.

CinCin returned with her newspaper. No pigs, she told Jack. Everything was quiet.

"Did you see anybody on the street?" he asked her, and when she said no he told her to go upstairs to the armory and get Edward and Janette to help her start loading up the guns and ammo. As a precaution, they were going to leave the house and go upstate for a few days.

Gary came back, a pocketful of change in his purple tie-dyed jeans. No problems, he said.

"Nothing different?" Jack prodded. "Nothing at all?"

Gary shrugged. "Panhandler was parked on the ground in front of the Laundromat, and he asked me for a hit on the way in. I gave him a quarter coming out."

"Had you ever seen the dude before?"

"Nope. It's no big deal, man. He was just a panhandler."

"You know the old lady who runs that place," Jack reminded him.

"You ever remember that stiff old bitch letting a panhandler set up shop in her front door?"

Gary thought about it. "No," he said. "I don't."

At nine forty-two, CinCin reported an unmarked, beat-up panel truck cruising slowly through the back alley. About half an hour later, Akitta thought he heard the metallic noise of a voice on a radio, but he wasn't sure where it was coming from. Toward eleven, Mary was still sitting in her chair in the dark when she thought she saw a movement in one of the black upstairs windows of the Steinfeld house. She leaned forward, her heart beating harder. Did something move over there, or not? She waited, watching, as the seconds ticked into minutes.

She saw it.

A tiny red circle, flaring in the dark and then ebbing again.

A cigarette, she thought. Somebody was smoking a cigarette.

In a house where an old man had emphysema, somebody was smoking.

Mary stood up. "Jack?" she called. Her voice trembled, and the sound shamed her. *"Jack?"*

A floodlight hit the house with such suddenness that it stole Mary's breath. She could feel its heat on her, and she dodged away from the window. A second floodlight came on, and a third, the first aimed from the Steinfeld house and the others from houses on either side of number 1105. "Shit!" she heard Edward cry out. There was the noise of somebody racing up the stairs, and other bodies flinging themselves to the floor. A few seconds later the lights in the house went out: one of the Storm Fronters had hit the fusebox.

The sound that Mary had dreaded for years finally came: the amplified voice of a pig through an electric bullhorn. "Attention, occupants of 1105 Elderman! This is the FBI! Come out into the light with your hands behind your heads! I repeat, come out into the light! If you follow my directions, nobody'll get hurt!"

Jack burst into the room, carrying a flashlight and an Uzi submachine gun. "Fuckers have ringed us! Must've cleared the fucking houses and we didn't even know it! Come on, load up!"

In the armory, guns were loaded and passed around by flashlight. Mary took an automatic and returned to the bedroom window. Janette joined her, carrying a shotgun and with three hand grenades clipped to her belt. The bullhorn squawked again: "We don't want bloodshed! Jack Gardiner, do you hear me?" The downstairs telephone began to ring; it ended when Jack ripped it off its wire. "Jack Gardiner! Give yourself and the others up! There's no point in getting anyone hurt!"

How they'd been nailed, Mary didn't know. She would find out, months later, that the pigs had evacuated the surrounding structures and been watching the house for five hours. The incident with the pig car had happened because the overeager Linden cop who'd been trailing Edward and Janette had wanted to see a Storm Fronter at close range. All Mary knew, as the floodlights blazed and her brothers and sisters crouched down and took aim, was that the eve of destruction had finally arrived.

James Xavier Toombs shot out the first floodlight. Gary hit the second, but before the third could be shot out the pigs switched on their auxiliary lights and opened fire on the green house.

Bullets tore through the walls, ricocheting off pipes and whining over their heads. "No surrender!" Lord Jack roared over the noise. "No surrender!" Akitta repeated. "No surrender!" CinCin Omara echoed. "No surrender!" Mary heard herself shout, and Janette's voice was lost in the hell of Storm Front guns bellowing their death cries. The pigs were firing, too, and in a matter of seconds every window in the green house was shattered, the air a razormist of flying glass. Janette's shotgun boomed, and Mary fired shot after shot at the window where she'd seen the glow of a pig's cigarette. In the scant lull between fusillades, Mary heard the crackle of radios and the shouts of pigs. Downstairs, someone was screaming: Gary Leister, shot through the chest and writhing in a pool of blood. Janette was pumping shells into the shotgun and blasting as fast as she could, the spent cartridges flying into the air. She stopped to pull a grenade from her belt, and she yanked its pin and stood up to toss it at the house across the street. The grenade bounced up under a car parked at the curb, and in the next second the vehicle was lifted up on a gout of fire and crashed over on its side, burning gasoline streaking across the pavement. By the flickering light, the pigshadows darted and ran. Mary shot at one of them, saw him stagger and fall onto the Steinfelds' front porch.

The next blast of pig bullets shook the green house on its foundations, blew a hole the size of a fist in the back of Sancho Clemenza's skull, and ripped away two of James Xavier Toombs's fingers. Mary heard Lord Jack shouting: "No surrender! No surrender!" One of the Storm Fronters threw a stick of dynamite with a sparking fuse, and the house next door exploded in a geyser of fire, wood, and glass. A vehicle of some kind was coming along the street: an armored car, Mary saw with a jolt of horror. The snout of a machine gun spat tracer bullets, and the slugs tore through the punctured walls like meteors. Two of those bullets hit Akitta Washington in the remains of the kitchen, and sprayed his blood across the refrigerator. Another stick of dynamite was thrown, destroying the Steinfeld house in a thunderclap. Flames leapt high, waves of black smoke rolling across the neighborhood. The armored car stopped, hunched on the street like a black beetle, fiery tracers spitting from its machine gun. Mary heard Janette sob, "The bastards! The bastards!" and Janette rose up in the flickering red light and yanked the pin from a second grenade. She threw her arm back to toss the grenade through the window, tears running down her face, and suddenly the room was full of flying wood splinters and ricocheting tracers and Janette Snowden was knocked backward. The grenade fell from her fingers, and Mary watched as if locked in a fever dream as the live grenade rolled across the blood-spattered floorboards.

Mary had a second or two in which her brain was seized up. Reach for the grenade, or get the fuck out? Janette's body was jittering on the floor. The grenade was still rolling.

Out.

The thought screamed. Mary stood up, crouched low, and ran for the door with cold sweat bursting from the pores of her flesh.

She heard the grenade thunk against the baseboard. In that instant she lifted her hands to shield her face, and she realized she should have shielded her unborn baby instead.

Surprisingly, she did not hear the grenade explode. She was aware only of a great heat lapping against her midsection, like the sun on a particularly fierce day. There was a feeling of lightness, of stepping outside her body and soaring upward. And then the sensation of gravity caught her again and wrenched her back to earth, and she opened her eyes in the upstairs hallway of the burning house, a hole in the bedroom's flaming wall and much of the ceiling collapsed and on fire. Somebody was trying to help her up. She saw a gaunt, bearded face and a ponytail. Edward. ". . . Up, get up!" he was saying, blood streaking his forehead and cheeks like war paint. She could barely hear him for the buzz in her ears. "Can you get up?"

"God," she said, and three seconds after that God answered by filling her body with pain. She began to cry, blood drooling from her mouth. She pressed her hands against the swell of her baby, and her fingers sank into a crimson swamp.

It was hatred that got her to her feet. Nothing but hatred that could make her grit her teeth and haul herself up as blood streamed down her thighs and dripped to the floor. "Hurt bad," she told Edward, but he was pulling her through the flames and she went with him, docile in her agony. Bullets were still ripping through the Swiss-cheese walls, smoke thick in the air. Mary had lost her gun. "Gun," she said. "Gun." Edward scooped up a revolver from the floor, near Gary Leister's outstretched hand, and she closed her fist on its warm grip. She stepped on something: the body of CinCin Omara, the cameo face unrecognizable as anything that had once been human. James Xavier Toombs lay on the floor, crouched and clutching at a stomach wound with his eight fingers. He looked at them with glazed eyes, and Mary thought she heard him gasp, "No surrender."

"Jack! Where's Jack?" she asked Edward, clinging to him.

He shook his head. "Gotta get out!" He picked up James Xavier Toombs's automatic. "Back door! You ready?"

She made a noise that meant yes, her mouth full of blood. Upstairs, some of the ammunition in the arsenal was starting to explode, the noise like Independence Day firecrackers. The back door was already hanging open. A dead pig lay on his back at the bottom of the steps. Jack had passed this way, Mary knew. Where was Didi? Still in the house? She had no time to think about anyone else. Smoke was billowing from the burning houses, cutting visibility to within a few yards. Mary could see the white tongues of flashlights licking at the smoke. "You with me?" Edward asked her, and she nodded.

They started across the back lawn, through the low-lying smoke. Gunshots were still popping, tracers flying through the haze. Edward scrabbled over a fence into the alley, and pulled Mary over. The pain made her think she was about to leave her guts behind, but she had no choice; she kept going, fighting back the darkness that tried to drag her down. Together they staggered along the alley. Blue lights were flashing, sirens awail. They went over another fence and crashed into garbage cans. Then they pressed up against the wall of a house, Mary shivering with pain and about to pass out. "Don't move. I'll be back," Edward promised, and he ran ahead to find a way through the pig blockade.

Mary sat with her legs outstretched. She released a moan, but she

clenched her teeth against a scream. Where was Jack? Alive or dead?
If he was dead, so was she. She leaned over and threw up, getting rid
of blood and pizza.

And then she heard a scraping noise, and she looked to her right at a
pair of shined black shoes.

"Mary Terrell," the man said.

She looked up at him. He wore a dark suit and a blue striped tie, his
chiseled face all but obscured by the smoke. There was a gleaming
silver badge on his lapel. He held a snub-nosed .38 in his right hand,
pointed somewhere between them.

"On your feet," the pig commanded.

"Fuck you," she said.

He reached for her arm, her hand sunken in the bloody mess of her
belly.

She let him grasp her with his slimy pig hand. And as she allowed
him to haul her up, incredible pain bringing tears to her eyes, she
lifted the revolver that had been hidden beside her and she shot him
in the face.

Mary saw his jaw explode. It was a wonderful sight. His gun went
off right in her ear, and the bullet whined about three inches from her
own face. His arm was out of control, the gun whipping around. More
bullets fired, one into the ground and two into the air. Mary shot him
again, this time in the throat. She saw the animal fear in his eyes, and
she heard him whine. Air and blood bubbled from his wound. He
staggered back, desperately trying to aim at her, but his fingers
twitched and lost the gun. The pig went down on his knees, and Mary
Terror stood over him and jammed the revolver's barrel against his
forehead. She pulled the trigger and saw him shudder as if stuck with
an electric prod. The gun clicked: no more bullets.

The pig's torn face wore a crooked, bleeding leer, one side of his jaw
hanging by tough red strands of muscle. She started to pick up his
gun, but the pain stopped her. She was too weak to even smash him in
the nose. She gathered bloody saliva in her mouth, and she spewed it
across his cheeks.

"Mary? I think I've found a—" Edward stopped. "Jesus!" he said,
looking at the man's ruined face. He lifted his gun and started to
squeeze the trigger.

"No," Mary told him. "No. Let him suffer."

Edward paused, then he lowered the gun.

"Suffer," Mary whispered, and she leaned forward and kissed the

pig's sweating forehead. He had thin brown hair, going bald. The pig made a gasping, clucking sound from his gaping throat. "Let's split!" Edward urged. Mary turned away from the pig, and she and Edward staggered off into the smoke, one of her hands pressed into her stomach as if to keep her insides from sliding out.

"Suffer," Mary Terror said, sitting in the olive-green van with Drummer. She rolled down her window and smelled the air. The reek of smoke and burning houses was all gone, but she remembered it. She and Edward had crawled past a parked pig car in the dense haze, a couple of pigs standing less than ten feet away and holding pump shotguns as they talked about kicking hippie ass. An abandoned concession stand four blocks north, at the edge of a weeded-up park, had a loose board. Mary and Edward had hidden there for over twenty-six hours, sleeping except when they had to kick the rats away from Mary's blood. Then Edward had gone out and found a pay phone, and he'd called some friends in Manhattan who owned a militant bookstore. Two hours after that, Mary awoke in an apartment listening to voices argue the fact that she was getting blood on everything and she couldn't stay there. Somebody came in with a medical bag, antiseptic, hypodermics, and shiny instruments. "Fucking mess," she heard him say as he removed the shrapnel and wood shards with forceps.

"My baby," Mary had whispered. "I'm going to have a baby."

"Yeah. Right. Eddie, give her another swig of the rum."

She drank the liquid fire. "Where's Jack? Tell Jack I'm going to have his baby."

Edward's voice: "Mary? Mary, listen to me. A friend of mine's going to take you on a trip. Take you to a house where you can rest. Is that all right?"

"Yes. I'm going to have a baby. Oh, I'm hurting. I'm hurting."

"You won't hurt long. Listen, Mary. You're going to stay at this house until you can get around, but you can't stay there very long. Only a week or so. Okay?"

"Underground railroad," she'd answered, her eyes closed. "I can dig it."

"I have to leave now. Can you hear me?"

"Hear you."

"I have to leave. My friend is going to take care of you. I've paid him some money. I've got to go right now. Okay?"

" 'Kay," she'd said. She had drifted to sleep, and that was the last time she'd seen Edward Fordyce.

Near Baltimore there was the gas station bathroom where Mary had delivered the dead infant girl from a belly held together with three hundred and sixty-two ragged stitches. There was a house in Bowens, Maryland, near the edge of Battle Creek Cypress Swamp, where Mary had lived for a week on lentil soup with a man and woman who never talked. At night the shrieks of small animals being devoured in the swamp sounded to her like crying babies.

The couple had let her read a *New York Times* story about the shootout. It was a difficult thing to read. Edward, Lord Jack, and Bedelia Morse had escaped. James Xavier Toombs had been captured, alive but badly wounded. He would never tell about the weeping lady, Mary knew. James Xavier Toombs had a hole inside himself, and he could retreat into it, close the lid, and recite haiku in his inner sanctum.

The worst night, though, was when she dreamed about herself giving a baby boy to Lord Jack. It was terrible, because when it was over she was alone again.

"I was born right there. See it?" Mary picked up Drummer's bassinet. But Drummer was asleep, his pink eyelids fluttering and the pacifier gripped in his mouth. She kissed his forehead, a gentler kiss than she'd once given a suffering pig, and she returned Drummer's bassinet to the floorboard.

There were ghosts at 1105 Elderman Street. She could hear them singing songs of love and revolution with voices that would be young forever. James Xavier Toombs had been killed in a riot at Attica; she wondered if his ghost had returned here, and joined those of the other sleeping children. Linden, New Jersey. July 1, 1972. As Cronkite would have said: *That was the way it was.*

She felt very old. Tomorrow she would feel young again. She drove back the sixteen miles to the McArdle Travel Inn outside Piscataway, and when she cried a little bit no one saw.

4.

A Crack in Clay

When the door opened, Laura thrust the half-killed bottle of sangria into Mark Treggs's face. "Here. I brought you a present."

He blinked, stunned, while behind him Rose stood up from the beanbag chair in which she'd been sitting, watching television. The two kids had been playing on the floor, the little girl with her Barbie and the boy with his GoBots; they stopped, too, and stared up at the visitor with wide eyes.

"Aren't you going to invite me in?" Laura asked, her breath smelling of sweet red wine.

"No. Please go away." He started to push the door shut.

Laura put her hand against it. "I don't know anybody here. It's a bitch drinking alone. Don't be rude, okay?"

"I don't have anything else to tell you."

"I know. I just want to be with somebody. Is that so bad?"

He looked at his wristwatch; Mickey Mouse was on the dial. "It's almost nine o'clock."

"Right. Time to do some serious drinking."

"If you don't leave," Treggs said, "I'm going to have to call the police."

"Would you really?" she asked him. A silence stretched, and Laura saw that he would not.

"Oh, let her in, Mark!" Rose stood behind him. "What's it going to hurt?"

"I think she's drunk."

"No, not yet." Laura smiled thinly. "I'm working on it. Come on, I won't stay long. I just need to talk to somebody, all right?"

Rose Treggs pushed her husband aside and opened the door to admit her. "We never closed our door in anybody's face, and we won't start now. Come on in, Laura."

Laura crossed the threshold with her bottle of wine. "Hi," she said to the kids, and the little boy said, "Hi" but the little girl just stared at her. "Close the door, Mark, you're letting the cold in!" Rose told him, and he muttered something deep in his beard and shut the door against the night.

"We figured you'd gone back to Atlanta," Rose said.

Laura eased down onto the sofa. Springs jabbed her butt. "Not much to go back to." She uncapped the sangria and drank from the bottle. The last time she'd drunk anything straight from a bottle, it was half-price beer back at the University of Georgia. "I thought I wanted to be alone. I guess I was wrong."

"Isn't anybody going to worry about you?"

"I left a message for my husband. He's o-u-t. Out." Laura took another swig. "Called Carol and told her where I was. Carol's my friend. Thank God for friends, huh?"

"Okay, rug rats," Treggs said to the children. "Time for bed." They instantly began to caterwaul a protest, but Treggs got them up and moving.

"Are you the lady whose baby got taken?" the little boy asked her.

"Yes, I am."

"Mark Junior!" the elder Mark said. "Come on, bedtime!"

"My dad thinks you're wearing a wire," the boy told her. "See my GoBot?" He held it up for her inspection, but his father grasped his arm and pulled him toward the hallway. "Nighty-night!" Mark Junior had time to say. A door slammed, rather hard.

"Bright child," Laura said to Rose. "I'm not, though. Wearing a wire, I mean. Why would I be?"

"Mark's a little suspicious of people. Goes back to his Berkeley days, I guess. You know, the pigs were putting wire mikes on kids posing as radicals and taping everything that was said at SDS meetings. The FBI got a lot of files on people that way." She shrugged. "I wasn't into politics that much. I mostly just, like, hung out and did macramé."

"I was into politics." Another sip of the red wine. Her tongue felt furry. "I thought we could change the world with flowers and candles. With *love*." She said it as if uncertain what it meant anymore. "That was pretty damned stupid, wasn't it?"

"It was where we were and what we were about," Rose said. "It was a good fight."

"We lost," Laura answered. "Read any newspaper, and you can see we lost. Damn . . . if all that energy couldn't change the world, nothing can."

"Right on, sad to say." Rose grasped the bottle of sangria, and Laura let her have it. "Ancient history doesn't go well with red wine. I'll make you some tea. Okay?"

"Yeah. Okay." Laura nodded, light-headed, and Rose walked into the kitchen.

After a while Mark Treggs came back into the front room. Laura was watching a movie on TV: *Barefoot in the Park,* with Robert Redford and Jane Fonda, pre-Hanoi. Treggs settled himself into a chair opposite her and crossed his long, gangly legs. "You ought to go home," he told her. "There's no point in your hanging around Chattanooga."

"I'll go in the morning. Soon as I get some rest." Which was going to be next to impossible, she knew. Every time she closed her eyes she thought she heard a baby crying and the wail of sirens.

"I can't help you. I wish I could, but I can't."

"I know. You've already told me that."

"I'm telling you again." He steepled his thin fingers together, and watched her with his owlish eyes. "If there was anything I could do for you, I would."

"Right."

"I mean it. I don't like not being able to help you. But look . . . all I am is a custodian who writes counterculture books that maybe a thousand people have read." Treggs kept his gaze on her face. "A wind-pisser, that's what I am."

"A *what?*"

"My father always said I was going to grow up to be a wind-pisser. Somebody who pisses into the wind. That's what I am, like it or not." His shoulders shrugged. "Maybe I've been pissing in the wind so long I like the way it feels. What I'm trying to say is that I've got a good little life—both of us do. We don't need much, and we don't want much. Just the freedom to speak and write, and up at Rock City I play my pennywhistle and meditate. Life is very good. You know why it's so good?" He waited for her to shake her head. "Because I have no expectations," he said. "My philosophy is: let it be. I bend with the breeze, but I do not break."

"Zen," Laura said.

"Yes. If you try to resist the breeze, you get a broken back. So I sit in the sun and play my music, and I write a few books on subjects that hardly anybody cares about anymore, and I watch my kids growing and I have peace."

"I wish to God I did," Laura said.

Rose came in from the kitchen. She offered Laura the clay mug with the image of her husband's face molded into it. "Red Zinger again," Rose said. "I hope that's o—"

"Not that mug!" Mark Treggs was on his feet as Laura's fingers closed around the handle. "Jesus, no!"

Laura blinked up at him as he reached out to take it away from her. Rose stepped back, out of her way. "It's got a crack in it, I mean!" Treggs said; a goofy smile slid across his mouth. "The bottom's leaking!"

Laura held on to it. "It was okay this afternoon."

His smile twitched. His eyes darted to Rose and then back to Laura again. "Can I have that mug, please?" he said. "I'll get you another one."

Laura looked at Treggs's face on the mug. It was wearing the same goofy smile. A hand-crafted mug, she thought. Made by someone who was an artist. She lifted the mug up, being careful not to spill any of the tea, and as she looked at the bottom for any trace of leakage she heard Treggs say in a tense voice, *"Give it to me."*

There was no crack on the bottom. The artist had signed it, though. There were two initials and a date: DD, '85.

DD. *Didi?*

As in *Bedelia?*

Didi made things, Treggs had said. *She was a potter, and she sold stuff in town.*

Laura felt her heart stutter. She avoided Treggs's stare, and she took a sip of the Red Zinger. Rose was standing a few feet from her husband, her expression saying she knew she'd screwed up. The moment hung as Redford and Fonda prattled on the TV and the chimes clinked outside. Laura drew a long breath. "Where is she?" she asked.

"I'd like you to leave now," Treggs said.

"Bedelia Morse. Didi. She made this mug, didn't she? In 1985? Where is she?" Her face felt hot, and her eyes locked on Treggs's face.

"I really don't know what you're talking about. I'm going to have to ask you to—"

"I'll pay you a thousand dollars to get me in contact with her," Laura said. "I swear to God, I'm not wired. I'm not working with the"—the word came out—"pigs. It's just me, alone. I don't care what she's done; all I care about is finding her, because she might help me find Mary Terrell and my baby. If I have to beg, then I'll beg: please tell me where she is."

"Look, I don't know what this is about. Like I told you before, I don't—"

"Mark?" Rose's voice was hushed.

He snapped a glance at her.

Rose stared at Laura, the corners of her mouth tight.

"Please," Laura said.

Rose spoke again, quietly, as if fearful of awakening the dead. "Michigan," she said. "Ann Arbor, Michigan."

The words were no sooner out of Rose's mouth than Treggs shouted, "Oh, Christ!" and his face mottled up with red. "Oh Christ almighty! Listen, you! I said I want you out of my house!"

"Ann Arbor," Laura repeated. She stood up, the mug still clenched in her hand. "What name does she use?"

"Don't you dig English?" Treggs demanded, flecks of spittle in his beard. He stalked to the door and opened it. A cold wind blew through. *"Out!"*

"Mark?" Rose said. "We have to help her."

He shook his head violently, his hair flying. "No! No way!"

"She's not working with the pigs, Mark. I believe her."

"Yeah, right! You want us both busted? Rose, the pigs could nail our asses to the wall!" His eyes, tormented behind his granny glasses, fixed on Laura. "I don't want any hassles," he said with a note of pleading. "Just leave. Okay?"

Laura stood where she was. Her light-headedness had fled, and her feet were rooted to the floor. "I'll pay you two thousand dollars to get me in contact with her," she told him. "The FBI doesn't have to know. It'll be between you and me. I swear to God, I won't breathe a word about where Bedelia Morse is. I don't care about what she's done, or what you've done to hide her. All I want is my son back. That's the most important thing in the world to me. Wouldn't you feel the same way if one of your children were missing?"

There was a long pause. The chimes jingled and rang. Laura waited, her nerves fraying more with each passing second.

At last Rose said, "Close the door, Mark."

He hesitated, a vein pulsing at his temple. The crimson had faded from his cheeks, his face gone chalky.

He closed the door, and when it clicked shut Laura saw him flinch.

"Aw, Jesus," Mark said softly. "Finish your tea."

He told Laura the story as she sat on the hard-springed sofa and tried very hard to keep herself from jumping out of her skin with anticipation. Mark had kept in contact with Bedelia Morse after the commune had broken up. He'd tried to talk her into getting away from the Storm Front, but she was "on fire," as he put it. Most of the time she was high on acid while she was with the Front, and she was always the type who needed to belong to some kind of group, whether it was a commune or a band of militant terrorists. About three months after the Storm Front was shot up in Linden, New Jersey, Mark had gotten a phone call from Didi. She'd wanted some money to change her face: a nose job and some work on her chin. Mark had sent her a "contribution to the cause." Over the years Didi had sent him and Rose all sorts of pottery: mugs, planters, and abstract sculptures. Mark had sold most of them, but some he'd kept, like the mug with his face on it. "The last time I talked to her was maybe five or six months ago," he said. "She was doing all right, selling her work in Ann Arbor. She was even teaching a couple of classes in pottery. I'll tell you something that I know for truth: Didi's okay. She's not who she used to be. She doesn't score acid anymore, and she'd be the last person on earth to snatch somebody's baby. I don't think she knows anything about Mary Terror other than what's been on the news."

"I'd like to find out for myself," Laura told him.

Mark sat for a moment with his hand cradling his chin, his eyes lost in thought. Then he looked at Rose, and she nodded. He stood up, went to the telephone, and opened a battered little book of phone numbers. Then he dialed and waited. "She's not home," he said after ten rings. "She lives in a house outside Ann Arbor." He checked his Mickey Mouse watch. "She doesn't usually keep late nights . . . or she didn't used to." He put the phone down, waited about fifteen minutes, and then tried the number again. "No answer," he reported.

"Are you sure she's still living there?"

"She was there back in September. She called to tell me about the classes she was teaching." Mark made himself a cup of tea as Rose and Laura talked, and then he tried the number a third time. Again no answer. "Bummer," Mark said. "She's not a night owl, that's for sure."

Toward midnight Mark dialed the number once more. It rang and rang, and went unanswered.

"Take me to her," Laura said.

"Uh-uh. No can do."

"Why not? If we left in the morning we could be back by Monday. We could take my car."

"To *Michigan?* Man, that's a long trip!"

Laura opened her purse and brought out her checkbook. Her hands were trembling. "I'll pay all expenses," she said. "And I'll write a check out to cash in the amount of three thousand dollars and give you the money as soon as we find Bedelia Morse."

"Three thousand dollars? Lady, are you rich or crazy?"

"I have money," Laura said. "Money's nothing. I want my son back."

"Yeah, I can see that. But I've . . . like . . . got a job to go to tomorrow."

"Call in sick. I don't think you're likely to make three thousand dollars over the weekend at Rock City, do you?"

Mark's fingers stroked his beard. He began to pace the room, stealing glances at both Laura and Rose. He stopped to dial the number once more. After a dozen rings, he said, "She must've gone somewhere. Like a trip or something. She could be gone all weekend."

"Three thousand dollars." Laura held up the check with *Cash* written on it. "Just take me to her house."

Rose cleared her throat and shifted in her seat. "That's a lot of heavy bread, Mark. We need some work on the car."

"Tell me about it." He continued his pacing, his face downcast. In another moment he stopped again. "No pigs? You swear to God, no pigs?"

"I swear."

Mark frowned, caught in a thicket of indecision. He looked at Rose for guidance, but all she could do was shrug her shoulders. It was up to him. "Let me think about it," he said to Laura. "Call me in the morning, about eight o'clock. If I can't reach Didi by then . . . I'll decide what to do."

Laura knew that was the best she could expect for now. It was almost twelve-thirty, and time to get some sleep if that was possible. She stood up, thanked Mark and Rose for their hospitality, and she took the check with her as she left. She walked out into the cold wind, her body bent against its force but her spine far from broken. Before she went to bed she would get down on her knees and pray. Those words to God—whether heard or unheard—were keeping her from losing her mind. She would pray that David would be safe for another night, and that her nightmare of sirens and snipers would not come true.

Laura got into the BMW and drove away.

The lights stayed on at the Treggs' house. Mark sat in a lotus position on the floor before the silent TV, his eyes closed, praying to his own deity.

5.

Reasonable

Saturday night, the seventeenth of February.

Tomorrow, the weeping lady. And Lord Jack, waiting for her and Drummer.

The baby was asleep, swaddled in his blanket on the other bed. The motel, in Secaucus, New Jersey, was called the Cameo Motor Lodge. It had a cramped little kitchenette and a view of a highway, and cracks riddled the ceiling from the vibrations of the trucks hauling freight in and out of New York City. Sometime before eleven, Mary

Terror licked a Smiley Face from her sheet of waxed paper, and she kissed Drummer on the cheek and sat in front of the TV.

A monster movie was on. Something about the dead struggling out of their graves to walk among the living. They came out dirty-faced and grinning, their mouths full of fangs and worms. Mary Terror understood their need; she knew the awful silence of the tomb and the smell of rot. She looked at the palms of her hands. They were wet. Scared, she thought. I'm scared about tomorrow. I've changed. Gotten older and heavier. What if he doesn't like the way I look? What if he thinks I'm still blond and lean and I'll see it in his face oh I will I'll see that he doesn't want me and I'll die. No, no. I'm bringing his son to him. Our son. I'm bringing him light in the dark, and he'll say Mary I love you I've always loved you and I've been waiting for you oh so long.

Everything will be cool, she thought. Tomorrow's the day. Two o'clock. Fourteen hours to go. She held her hands up and looked at them. She was trembling a little. I'm freaking, she thought. She saw the moisture on her palms begin to turn red, like blood seeping from her pores. Freaking. Sweating blood. No, no; it's the acid. Hang on, ride it out. A rider on the storm, oh yes . . .

Someone screamed. The sound jolted Mary. She saw a woman running on the TV, trying to get away from a shambling, half-decayed corpse. The woman, still screaming, stumbled and fell to the ground, and the monster in pursuit flailed on toward the screen.

The television screen cracked with a noise like a pistol going off, and in a shatter of glass the living corpse's head burst from the TV set. Mary watched in a trance of horror and fascination as the rotting thing began to winnow out of the television. Its shoulders jammed, but its body was all bones and sinew, and in another few seconds it pushed on through with a surge of frenetic strength.

The smell of grave dirt and mold was in the room. The living corpse stood up in front of Mary Terror. A few tendrils of long black hair hung from the shriveled skull, and Mary could see the almond-shaped eyes in a face as wrinkled as a dried apple. The mouth stretched open, a noise of whirring air came out that shaped words: "Hello, Mary."

She knew who this was, come to visit from the dead. "Hello, CinCin."

Cold fingers touched her shoulder. She looked to her left, and there stood another creature from the grave, wearing dirt-crusted African amulets. Akitta Washington had dissolved down to a skinny stick figure, and what remained of his once-ebony flesh was now a leprous gray. He held up two bony fingers. "Peace, sister."

"Peace, brother," she answered, and returned the sign.

A third figure was standing in a corner of the room, skeletal face cocked to one side. This person had been a petite woman in life, but in death she had bloated and burst and dark glistening things were leaking from the cavity where her insides used to be. "Mary," she said in an ancient voice. "You bitch, you."

"Hi, Janette," Mary replied. "You look like shit."

"Being dead doesn't do a whole lot for your looks," Janette agreed.

"Listen up!" Akitta said, and he came around the chair to stand beside CinCin. His legs were gray toothpicks, and where his sexual organs had been, small white worms feasted. "You're going there tomorrow. Going to be walking on a fine line, sister. You ever think that maybe the pigs planted that message in the *Stone?*"

"I thought about it. The pigs didn't know about the weeping lady. Nobody knew but us."

"Toombs knew," Janette said. "Who's to say he didn't tell the pigs?"

"Toombs wouldn't talk. Never."

"Easy to say, hard to know." CinCin spoke up now. "How can you be so sure it's a message from Lord Jack? The pigs might be behind it, Mary. When you go there tomorrow, you could be walking into a trap."

"I don't want to hear it!" Mary said. "I've got my baby now, and I'm taking him to Jack! Everything's going to be cool!"

Akitta bent his dead face toward her, his eyes as white as river stones. "You'd better watch your back, sister. You don't know for sure who sent that message. You sure as hell better watch your back."

"Yeah." Janette walked across the room to straighten a crooked picture on the wall. She left a dark trail on the brown carpet. "Pigs might be watching you right now, Mary. They might be setting up shop for you. Do you think you'd like prison?"

"No."

"Me neither. I'd rather be dead than in the slammer." She got the picture how she wanted it; Janette had always been tidy. "What are you going to do about the baby?"

"I'm going to give him to Jack."

"No, no," CinCin said. "What are you going to do about the baby if the pigs are waiting for you?"

"They won't be."

"Ah." CinCin gave a ghastly smile. "But let's say they will be, Mary. Let's say you fucked up somewhere, and the pigs squeak out of the woodwork tomorrow. You're going in loaded, aren't you?"

"Yes." She would be armed with the purse-size Magnum.

"So if the pigs are there waiting for you, and there's no way out, what are you going to do?"

"I . . . don't know . . . what—"

"Sure you do," Akitta said. "You're not going to let the pigs take you alive, are you? They'd throw you in a deep hole, Mary. They'd take the baby from you and give him to some piece of shit who doesn't deserve a child. You know her name: Laura."

"Yes. Laura." Mary nodded. She'd seen the newscasts and read about it in the paper. A picture of the woman had been in *Time* last week, next to an old snapshot of herself taken on a day the Storm Fronters played Frisbee at Berkeley.

"Drummer's your baby now," Janette said. "You're not going to give him up, are you?"

"No."

"So what are you going to do if the pigs are there?" CinCin repeated. "And there's no way out?"

"I'm . . . going to—"

"Shoot the baby first," CinCin told her. "Then take as many pigs with you as you can. Does that sound reasonable?"

"Yes," Mary agreed. "Reasonable."

"They've got all sorts of new weapons and shit now," Akitta said. "You'll have to kill the baby quick. No hesitation."

"No hesitation," Mary echoed.

"Then you can come join us." When Janette grinned, her dried-up husk of a face cracked at the jaw hinges. "We get high and party."

"I've got to find Jack." Mary could see her words in the air; they floated away from her, outlined in pale blue, like whorls of smoke. "Got to find Jack and give him our baby."

"We'll be with you," CinCin promised. "Brothers and sisters in spirit, like always."

"Like always," Mary said.

CinCin, Akitta, and Janette began to break apart. It was a silent breaking, a coming apart of the glue that held their bones together. Mary watched them fall to pieces with the same interest with which she might watch a mildly entertaining TV program. Out of their dissolving bodies came a gray mist shot through with streaks of blue, and this mist roiled toward Mary Terror. She felt it, cold on her lips and nostrils like San Francisco fog. It entered her through her nose and mouth, and froze her throat on its way down. She smelled a commingling of odors: strawberry incense, gravemold, and gunsmoke.

The television screen had healed itself. Another movie was on, this one a black-and-white film. *Plan Nine from Outer Space,* Tor and Vampira. Mary Terror closed her eyes and saw the weeping lady in her mind, torch uplifted over the dirty harbor. The lady had been weeping for a long time, her feet trapped in the concrete of the Mindfuck State, but she had never shown her tears before. The Storm Front had planned to show her tears to the world on that July Fourth in 1972. They had planned to kidnap five executives from Manhattan-based corporations and hold the weeping lady by force until the pigs could arrange television cameras for a live hookup, a million dollars in cash, and a jet plane to take them to Canada. It had never happened. The first of July had happened, but not the Fourth.

It was the eighteenth by now, Mary realized. Lord Jack would be waiting for her at two o'clock in the afternoon.

But if he *wasn't* there, what was she going to do?

Mary smiled grimly in her purple haze. That was CinCin talking. But what *if* the pigs are there?

Shoot the baby first. Then take as many pigs with you as you can. Reasonable.

Mary opened her eyes and stood up on mile-long legs. She was a walking heartbeat, the roar of blood through her veins like the noise of the freight-hauling trucks. She went into the room where Drummer was sleeping, and she sat on the bed and looked at him. She watched a frown pass over his face: a storm in babyland. Drummer sucked busily on the pacifier, and peace came to his face again. Lately he'd been waking up at three or four in the morning wanting to be fed. Mary was getting efficient at feeding him and changing his diapers. Motherhood suited her, she'd decided.

She could kill him if she had to. She knew she could. And then she would keep shooting until the pigs cut her down and she would join

Drummer and her brothers and sisters in a place where the love generation had never died.

Mary lay down on the bed beside Drummer, close enough to feel his heat. She loved him more than anything in the world, because he was hers.

If they had to leave this world together, so be it.

Karma. That was the way things worked.

Mary drifted off to sleep, the acid slowing her pulse. Her last thought was of Lord Jack, bright with beauty in the winter sun, as he accepted the gift she had brought him.

6.

A Real Popular Lady

Ten hours before Mary Terror's conversation with the dead, Laura rang the doorbell of a red brick house four miles west of Ann Arbor, Michigan. It was a sunny day, huge white clouds moving slowly across the sky, but the air was bitterly cold. Mark had his hands buried in his fleece-lined jacket, and puffs of breath plumed from his mouth. Laura and Mark had left Chattanooga on Friday morning, had driven to Dayton, Ohio, and spent Friday night there before continuing the rest of the way. They had driven through the sprawling University of Michigan, once a hotbed of student dissent in the late sixties and early seventies, and now better known for its Wolverines.

The door opened. An elderly man with a pleasant, leathery face and sun freckles on his scalp peered out. "Yes?"

"Hello." Laura offered a tight smile. "We're trying to find Diane Daniells. Do you know where she might be?"

He took a long look at her, another long look at Mark, and then he squinted toward the other side of the road, up at the stone cottage surrounded by oaks and elms at the end of a long dirt driveway. "Diane's not at home," he told her.

"We know. We were wondering if you had any idea where she is." This house and the one belonging to Diane Daniells—once known as Bedelia Morse—were the only ones on this stretch of road.

"Gone on a trip," he said. "Not sure where."

"When did she leave?" Mark asked.

"Oh, Thursday afternoon, I suppose it was. Said she was goin' north, if that's any help."

Laura had a knot in her throat, and she had to struggle to clear it. Being so close to where Bedelia Morse lived and being unable to find her was pure torture. "Did she say when she might be back?"

"Weekend trip, she said. You folks friends of Diane's?"

"I'm an old friend," Mark answered.

"Well, I'm sorry you missed her. If it's any help to you, I think she's gone birdin'."

"Birding?" Laura asked.

"Yep. Diane asked to borrow my binoculars. See, my wife and I are bird-watchers. We belong to the society." He scratched his chin. "Diane's a solitary kind of woman. Be a real good birder if she put her mind to it."

Laura nodded absently, turned, and looked at the stone cottage again. The mailbox had a peace sign painted on it. In front of the cottage stood an abstract clay sculpture, all sharp angles and edges.

"Diane's a real popular lady all of a sudden," the old man said.

"What?"

"Real popular," he repeated. "Diane usually don't have no visitors. She comes over and plays chess with me sometimes. Beats my socks off, too. Other fella was askin' about her yesterday."

"Other fellow?" Mark frowned. "Who?"

"Friend of hers," he said. "Fella with a bad throat. Had to plug a doohickey into his neck and talk through a speaker. Damnedest thing."

"Did Diane tell you who she might be going to visit?" Laura asked, getting the conversation back on track.

"Nope. Just said she was goin' away for the weekend. Headin' north, she said."

It was obvious the man didn't know anything else. "Thank you," Laura said, and the old man wished them a good day and closed his door.

On the walk back to Laura's BMW, Mark kicked a pinecone and said, "Sounds weird."

"What does?"

"About the guy with the bad throat. Sounds weird."

"Why? Maybe he's one of her pottery students."

"Maybe." Mark stood next to the car and listened to the wind roaming in the bare trees. "I've just got a funny feeling, that's all." He got into the car, and Laura slid behind the wheel. Their drive up from the South had been, for Laura, an education in radical philosophy and the teachings of Zen. Mark Treggs was a fount of knowledge about the militant struggles of the sixties, and they had gotten into a long discussion about the assassination of John F. Kennedy as the point when America had become poisoned. "So what do we do now?" he asked as Laura started the engine.

"I'm going to wait for Bedelia Morse to come home," she told him. "You've done your part. If you want, I'll buy you a plane ticket back to Chattanooga."

Mark deliberated as they drove back toward Ann Arbor. "Didi won't talk to you if I'm not there," he said. "She won't even let you in the door." He swept his long hair back over his shoulders and watched the countryside pass. "No, I'd better stick around," Mark decided. "I can get Rose to call in sick for me on Monday. No problem."

"I thought you'd be eager to get home."

"I am, but . . . I guess I'd like to see Didi. You know, for old times' sake."

There was something Laura had been meaning to ask, and now seemed the time. "In your book you dedicated a line to Didi: 'Keep the faith and love the one you're with.' Who were you talking about? Is she living with someone?"

"Yeah," Mark said. "Herself. I talked her out of slitting her wrists last summer." He glanced quickly at Laura and then away. "Didi's carrying a lot of heavy freight. She's not the same person she used to be. I guess the past eats at her."

Laura looked at her hands on the steering wheel and realized something that almost startled her. She was wearing no fingernail polish, and her nails were dirty. Her shower this morning had been a speed drill. The diamond of her engagement ring—a link to Doug—looked dull. Before this ordeal she'd been meticulous about her manicures and her ring cleaning. Such things now seemed incredibly pointless.

"A dude with a bad throat," Mark said quietly. "Asking for Didi. I don't know. That gives me the creeps."

"Why?"

"If he was one of her students, wouldn't he know she was going out of town for the weekend?"

"Not necessarily."

He grunted. "Maybe you're right. But it still sounds weird to me."

Laura said, "This okay?" and motioned to a Days Inn coming up on the left. Mark said it was fine with him, and she turned into the parking lot. The first thing she was going to do when she got to her room was call the FBI in Atlanta and check with Kastle, but she had no intention of betraying either Mark or Bedelia Morse. She knew she was going to be climbing the walls until she got a chance to talk to Didi face-to-face.

As Laura and Mark were checking into the Days Inn, the tall, gaunt man who had parked his dark blue Buick on a dirt road a half mile from Bedelia Morse's cottage walked back to his car through the woods, his boots crunching on dead leaves. He wore brown trousers and a gray parka with a hood: colors that helped camouflage him in the winter-gnawed forest. Around his neck was a Minolta camera with a zoom lens, and over his shoulder was a camouflage-mottled bag that held a small SuperSnooper listening dish, earphones, and a miniature tape recorder as well as a loaded .45 automatic. The man's face was hidden by the hood, but his breathing rattled.

When he reached his car, he unlocked the trunk and put the camera and shoulder bag into it, next to the black leather case that held a Valmet Hunter .308 rifle with a telescopic sight and a nine-round magazine.

His own house was about fifteen miles northwest, in a town called Hell.

He drove there, his black-gloved hands tight on the wheel and his grin demonic.

7.

The Devil of All Pigs

Behind Mary Terror was New York City. Above her was the gray sky, armored in clouds. Beneath her was the deck of the boat, ferrying a group of tourists across the wind-whipped water to what lay before her: the weeping lady on Liberty Island.

Mary stood within the glassed-in cabin, out of the wind, with Drummer in her arms. The weeping lady grew larger and larger, torch in one hand and book cradled against her breasts. The other passengers were mostly Japanese, and they took pictures like crazy. Mary rocked Drummer and cooed to him, and her heart slammed in her chest as the Circle Line boat neared its destination. In her large shoulder bag was her Magnum pistol, fully loaded. Mary licked her lips. She could see people walking around the base of the weeping lady, could see someone feeding sea gulls on the concrete dock where the boat would pull in. Mary looked at her wristwatch. It was about eight minutes before two o'clock. She realized how big Liberty Island was. Where was the contact supposed to be made? The message in the *Stone* hadn't said. A little burst of panic threatened her composure; what if she couldn't find Jack? What if he was waiting for her but she couldn't find him? Steady, she told herself. Trust in karma, and keep an eye on your back.

Drummer started to cry. "Shhh, shhh," she said softly, and she fed him his pacifier. There were dark circles under her eyes. Her sleep had been uneasy, and filled with phantoms: pigs with rifles and shotguns, converging on her from all sides. She had taken stock of the tourists waiting for the boat as she'd bought her ticket: none of them smelled like pigs, and none of them wore shined shoes. But out here in the open she didn't feel safe, and once she set foot on Liberty Island she would unzip her bag so she could get to her gun in a hurry.

The boat began to slow, the weeping lady gargantuan before her. Then the boat's crew threw out ropes, the craft sidled up against the dock, and a ramp was tied down. "Watch your step, watch your step!" one of the crewmen cautioned, and the tourists started getting off the boat with a chatter of excitement.

It was time. Mary waited for everyone else to get off, and then she unzipped the carryall and took Drummer across the ramp onto the concrete of Liberty Island.

Sea gulls screeched and spun in the eddies of cold air. Mary's eyes darted right and left: an elderly couple walked together near the railing; a heavyset woman herded two children along; three teenage boys in leather jackets jostled each other, their voices raucous; a man in a gray jogging outfit was sitting on a bench, staring blankly toward the city; another man, this one wearing a beige overcoat, was tossing peanuts to the sea gulls. He was wearing shined wingtips, and Mary walked quickly away from him, the back of her neck prickling.

A uniformed guide was gathering the Japanese group together. Mary passed him, striding along the walkway that went next to the water. Clumps of oil and dead fish floated in it, white bellies bloated. A woman was coming toward her, walking alone. She had long black hair that whipped in the wind, and she wore a red overcoat. When the woman was about six paces away, she suddenly stopped and smiled. "Hi there!" she said brightly.

Mary was about to answer, when a young dark-haired man passed her from behind. "Hi!" he answered the woman, and they linked arms. "You got away from me, didn't you?" he teased her. They turned away from Mary Terror, their bodies pressing against the railing, and Mary went on with Drummer.

She threaded her way through another clutch of Japanese tourists, cameras clicking up at the weeping lady. Her eye caught the glint of a badge, and she looked to her right. A pig in a dark blue uniform was strolling slowly along, about thirty feet from her. She veered away from him and walked to the railing, where she stood with Drummer and stared at the gray-hazed city. One hand rested on the lip of her bag, the Magnum within an instant's reach. She waited a few seconds and then turned away from the view, her heart pounding. The pig had walked on, beyond the Japanese tourists. She watched him go, the breath cold in her lungs. Not safe, she thought. Too open out here. It came to her like a blow: this wasn't the kind of place Lord Jack would have chosen for a meeting. There was no shelter here, no way out if a trap was sprung. She saw a black man in a Knicks jacket sitting on a bench, staring at her. She stared back long enough to make him look away, and then she started walking again. Mary didn't like it; this place was wrong, it wasn't Jack's style. When she glanced back, she saw the Knicks fan stand up and walk to the railing as if to keep her in sight.

Trap, she thought. An alarm began to scream inside her. The stench of pigs was in the air. The man who'd been feeding the sea gulls suddenly came into view, walking slowly beside the railing in his shined pig shoes, his hands deep in his overcoat pockets. She knew the look of a pig who was carrying firepower; the weight of a gun was in the bastard's walk. Tears of rage swelled in her eyes, and her mind shrieked the warning: *Trap! Trap! Trap!*

Mary began striding quickly away from the Knicks fan and the bastard with the shined shoes. Drummer made a little mewling sound around his pacifier, perhaps picking up some of Mary's tension. "Shhhh," she told him. Her voice quavered. "Mama's got her baby."

Her shoulders tensed. She was waiting for the noise of a whistle or the crackle of a radio: a signal for the enemy to move in on her. She knew what to do when that happened. First kill Drummer with a single shot to the head. Then keep firing at the mindfuckers until they took her down. Reasonable. She would not die without taking some of them with her, and damned if they'd get her alive.

Mary Terror suddenly stopped walking. A small gasp left her mouth.

There he was.

Right there. Ahead of her, leaning against the railing and looking out toward the Atlantic. His body was still slim and youthful, and his long blond hair hung around his shoulders in golden waves. He wore a battered leather jacket, faded jeans, and boots. He was smoking a cigarette, the smoke swirling back over his head in the wind.

Lord Jack. Right there, waiting for her and the baby.

She couldn't move. A tear—not of rage, but born of joy—streaked down her right cheek. There was a lump in her throat; how could she speak around it? She took a step toward him, her body tormented between frost and fire. He tapped ashes out on the railing and watched a sea gull wheel in the sky. Mary could see the fine etching of his nose and chin. He'd done away with his beard, but it was him. Oh dear God it was him, right there in front of her.

Mary walked to him, trembling. He was smaller than she remembered. Of course he was, because she was larger than she'd been. "Jack?" she said softly; it came out garbled. She took a breath and tried again, ready to see the flames in his eyes when he looked at her. *"Jack?"*

His head swiveled.

Lord Jack was a girl.

A teenager, maybe seventeen or eighteen. Her long blond hair danced in the wind, a tiny silver skeleton dangling from her right ear. She stared at Mary Terror with the cigarette gripped in her mouth, her eyes hard and wary. "Choo talkin' ta me?" she asked.

Mary stopped, her legs freezing up. She felt her face harden, felt her joy spin away from her like a sea gull on the wind. She made a noise, but she wasn't sure what she said; maybe it was a grunt of pain.

"Crazy fucka," the girl muttered, and she brushed past Mary Terror and stalked away.

It came. Close behind her. The voice.

"Mary."

Not a question. A knowing.

She turned, cradling Drummer with one arm and the other hand in her shoulder bag. Her fingers rested on the Magnum's grip.

"Mary," he said again, and he smiled with tears swamping his pale blue eyes.

It was the man who'd been feeding the gulls. He had short brown hair flecked with gray on the sides, and he wore tortoiseshell glasses. His face was bony, his chin too long, and his nose too large. Around his eyes were webbings of lines, and two deep lines bracketed his mouth. The wind caught the folds of his beige overcoat. Mary saw that he was wearing a black pin-striped suit, a white shirt, and a red tie with little white dots on it. She glanced down at his shined black wingtips, and her first impression was that the devil of all pigs had just spoken her name.

She didn't know his face. Didn't know his eyes. The pigs had sprung their trap. His hands were still in the pockets of his coat. She saw the uniformed pig walking toward them unhurriedly. The Knicks fan was lounging against the railing, staring at the gray water. It was time to play the game out, but on her terms. Mary drew the Magnum from her shoulder bag, her finger on the trigger, and she placed the barrel against Drummer's head. The baby shivered and blinked.

"*No!*" the stranger said. "Jesus, no!" He blinked, too, as surprised as Drummer. "I'm Edward," he said. "Edward Fordyce."

Liar! she thought. *Dirty fucking liar!* He didn't look at all like Edward! The pig was coming, approaching from behind the stranger. He was about ten or eleven paces away, and Mary's finger tightened on the trigger as she saw the noose falling.

"Put it away!" the man said urgently. "Mary, don't you know me?"

"Edward Fordyce had brown eyes." The trigger needed a quarter-ounce more pressure and the gun would go off.

"They're blue contacts," he said. "The glasses are fake."

The pig was almost upon them. In another moment he'd see the gun. Mary licked her lower lip. "Make me believe you."

"I got you out. Remember where we hid?" He frowned, his mind working furiously. "We kicked at rats all night," he said.

The rats. Oh yes, she remembered them, licking at her blood.

The pig was right behind Edward Fordyce. Edward was aware of him, too, and suddenly he turned toward the pig, keeping his body in front of Mary. "Cold out here, isn't it, Officer?"

"It's a bitch," the pig said. He had a square, wind-chapped face. "Snow in the air."

"We haven't had a lot of it yet, so we're due."

"You can have the white crap! Me, I wanna go south for the winter!"

Mary had no time to debate it any longer. She slid the gun into her shoulder bag, but she kept her hand on the grip.

The pig took a step to the side, and he looked at Drummer. "Your kid?" he asked Edward.

"Yeah. My son."

"Oughta get him out of this wind. Not good for a kid's lungs."

"We will, Officer. Thanks."

The pig nodded at Mary and walked on, and Edward Fordyce stared at her with his falsely colored eyes. "Where'd you see the message?"

Him. Not Lord Jack. Him. Mary felt a wave of dizziness swirl around her, and she had to lean against the railing for support. *"Rolling Stone,"* she managed to say.

"I put it all over the place: *Mother Jones,* the *Village Voice,* the *Times,* and a couple of dozen other papers. I wasn't sure anybody would see it."

"I saw it. I thought . . . somebody else had written it."

Edward glanced around. His eyes might be the wrong color, but they were as keen as a hawk's. "We'd better split. The boat's loading up. I'll carry the baby." He held out his arms.

"No," she said. "Drummer's mine."

He shrugged. "Okay. I've got to tell you, taking the kid out of that hospital was crazy." He saw her eyes blaze at the use of that word. "I mean . . . it wasn't too wise." She was a couple of inches taller than he, and maybe thirty pounds heavier. Her size, and the suggestion of brute strength in her hands and shoulders, frightened him. Her face had always had a dangerous, sullen quality about it, but now there was something savage in her face, too, like a lioness that had been squeezed into a cage and taunted by dumb keepers. "You've been all over the news," he said. "You drew a lot of attention to yourself."

"Maybe I did. That was my business."

This was no place to get into an argument. Edward turned his overcoat's collar up and watched the cop walking away; the pig was right, there was snow in the air. "You got a car?"

"A van."

"Where're you staying?"

"A motel in Secaucus. What about you?"

"I live in Queens," he told her. Now that she'd put that damned gun away, his nerves were starting to settle down, but he kept an eye on the cop. It had taken him a few minutes to recognize her after she'd stepped off the boat. She'd changed a lot, just as he knew he had, but realizing who she was had been a real shock. The FBI had to be hot on her trail, and even standing next to her made him feel like a target at a shooting gallery. "We'll go to your place," he decided. "We've got a lot to catch up on." He tried for a smile, but either he was too cold or too scared and his mouth wouldn't work.

"Wait a minute," she said as he started to walk toward the boat. He paused. Mary took a step toward him, and he felt dwarfed. "Edward, I don't take orders from anyone anymore." Her guts were twisted with disappointment. Lord Jack wasn't here, and it was going to take her a while to get over it. "I say we go to your place."

"Don't trust me, huh?"

"Trusting can get you killed. Your place or I'm gone."

He thought it over. There was a nettled scowl on his face, and by it Mary saw that he really was Edward Fordyce. It was the same scowl he'd worn when Jack Gardiner had jumped his case about backing into the pig car.

"Okay," he agreed. "My place."

He caved in too fast, Mary thought. Something about him put her on edge; his clothes and shoes were Mindfuck State goods, the uniform of the enemy. He bore careful watching.

"You lead," she said, and he started toward the boat with Mary a few paces behind, Drummer cradled against her and her hand still on the Magnum's grip.

In the Circle Line parking lot, when they were away from people, Mary slid the gun from her shoulder bag and put its barrel against the back of Edward's skull. "Stop," she commanded quietly. He did. "Lean against that car and spread your legs."

"Hey, come on, sister! What are you—"

"*Now,* Edward."

"Shit! Mary, you're pushing me!"

"Do tell," she said, and she shoved him hard against the car and spent a minute frisking him. No guns, no wire microphones, no tape recorders. She came up with his wallet, flipped it open, and checked his license. New York issued, under the name Edward Lambert. Address Apt. 5B, 723 Cooper Avenue, Queens. A picture of a young, smiling woman and a little boy who had his father's long chin. "Wife and kid?"

"Yeah. Divorced, if you want to know." He turned around, his face flamed with anger, and he snatched the wallet from her. "I live alone. I'm an accountant for a seafood company. I drive an 'eighty-five Toyota, I collect stamps, and I wipe my ass with Charmin. Anything else?"

"Yes." She put the Magnum's barrel against his stomach. "Are you going to fuck me over? I know there's a price on my head." It was twelve thousand dollars, put up by the Atlanta *Constitution* for her capture. "If you're thinking about it, let me tell you that you'll get the first bullet. Dig it?"

"Yeah." He nodded. "I dig it."

"Good." She believed him, and she put the gun away but she left the bag open. "Now we can be friends again, right?"

"Yeah." Said with a measure of new respect and maybe fear, too.

"I'll follow you. I'm in the van over there." She motioned to it. Edward started to walk to his red Toyota nearby, but Mary caught his arm. She felt a warm glow of nostalgia rise within her, and it helped to soothe the hurt that Jack wasn't here. "I love you, brother," she said, and she kissed his smooth-shaven cheek.

Edward Fordyce looked at her, puzzled and still angry about the frisk. She was off her rocker, that much was clear. Taking the baby had been insane, and put him in as much danger as she was in. He had a pang of wishing he'd never decided to write the message. But Mary was his sister in arms, they had lived and fought and bled together, and she was a link to a younger, more robust life. He said, "I love you, sister," and he returned the kiss. He smelled her body odor; she needed a bath.

He got into his Toyota, started the engine, and waited for her to get into the van with the baby. Drummer, she called him. Edward knew the kid's real name: David Clayborne. He'd followed the whole story in the news, but since that plane explosion over Japan the news hadn't given much coverage to Mary and the baby. He pulled out of the parking lot, glancing in the rearview mirror to make sure Mary—big old crazy Mary—was following. He hadn't expected to see Mary Terror step off that boat. Placing the message had been a shot in the dark, but he realized he'd hit a target far greater than he'd ever have hoped.

"Twelve thousand dollars?" he said as he merged into traffic heading for the Williamsburg Bridge. He glanced back; she was still with him, following closely. "Babycakes," he said, "you're going to make me a millionaire." He grinned, showing capped front teeth.

The Toyota and the van crossed the bridge, along with the flow of other cars, as small flakes of snow began to spin from the clouds.

V

The Killer Awoke

1.

Damaged Goods

I think we were followed," Mary said for the third time as she stood at the window of Edward Fordyce's one-bedroom apartment and looked down on Cooper Avenue. Snow flurries rushed past, shoved by the wind. A pile of trash bags on the street had burst open, and garbage and old papers fluttered along the sidewalk. Mary was feeding Drummer from a bottle of formula, the baby staring up at her with his blue eyes as he suckled on the nipple. She looked left and right along the dismal avenue. "It was a brown compact car. A Ford, I think."

"Your imagination," Edward answered from the kitchen, where he was fixing them canned chili. The building's radiators moaned and knocked. "Lots of cars in this city, so don't get paranoid."

"The driver had a chance to pass us a few times. He slowed down." The nipple popped out of Drummer's mouth, and Mary guided it back in. "I don't like it," she said, mostly to herself.

"Forget about it." Edward came into the front room, leaving the chili to bubble on the stove. He had taken off his overcoat and the jacket of his suit. He was wearing red suspenders—"braces," as he called them. "You want a drink? I've got Miller Lite and some wine."

"Wine," she said, still watching out the window for a brown compact Ford. She hadn't been able to get a good look at the driver. She remembered the Knicks fan: he'd come across on the boat with them, and so had the blond-haired girl in the leather jacket. A lot of people had come across too: a dozen Japanese tourists, an elderly couple, and about twenty others as well. Had one or more of them been a pig on her trail? There was another possibility: that someone had been following not her, but Edward. It wouldn't be the first time, would it?

He brought her a glass of red wine and set it on a table while she finished feeding Drummer. "So," Edward said, "you want to tell me why you took the baby?"

"No."

"Our conversation isn't going to get very far if you don't want to talk."

"I want to listen," she said. "I want you to tell me why you put the message in the papers."

Edward walked to another window and peered out. No brown compact Ford in sight, but Mary's insistence that they had been followed gave him the creeps. "I don't know. I guess I was curious."

"About what?"

"Oh . . . just to see if anybody would show up. Kind of like a class reunion, maybe." He turned away from the window and looked at her in the dank winter light. "It seems like a hundred years ago we went through all that."

"No, it was only yesterday," she said. Drummer had finished the formula, and she rested him against her shoulder and burped him, as her mother had demonstrated. Mary had already taken stock of Edward's apartment; he had some nice pieces of furniture that didn't go with the place, and he was dressed better than he lived. Her impression was that he'd had a lot of money at one time, but his money had run out. His Toyota puffed blue smoke from its tailpipe and it had a bashed left rear fender. His shined shoes, though, said he had once walked on expensive floors. "You're an accountant?" she asked. "How long?"

"Going on three years. It's an okay job. I can do it with my eyes closed." He shrugged, almost apologetically. "I got a business degree from NYU after I went underground."

"A business degree," she repeated. A faint smile stole across her face. "I knew it when I saw you. The Mindfuckers got you, didn't they?"

That familiar scowl creased his face again. "We were kids then. Naive and dumb in a lot of ways. We weren't living in reality."

"And now you are?"

"The reality," Edward said, "is that everybody has to work to live. There are no free tickets in this world. Don't you know that yet?"

"Has my brother turned into Big Brother?"

"No!" he answered, too loudly. "Hell, no! I'm just saying we thought everything was black and white back then! We thought we were right and everybody else was wrong. Well, we were fucked up. We didn't see the gray in the world." He grunted. "We didn't think we'd ever have to grow up. But you can't fight time, Mary. That's the one thing you can't put a bullet into or blow apart with a bomb. Things change, and you have to change with them. If you don't . . . well, look what happened to Abbie Hoffman."

"Abbie Hoffman was always true to a cause," Mary said. "He just got tired, that's all."

"Hoffman got busted selling *cocaine!*" he reminded her. "He went from being a revolutionary to being a drug salesman! What cause was he true to? Jesus, nobody cares who Abbie Hoffman was! You know what the true power of this world is? Money. Cash. If you've got it, you're somebody, and if you don't, you get swept away with the garbage!"

"I don't want to talk about this anymore," Mary said, rocking Drummer in her arms. "Sweet baby, such a sweet sweet baby."

"I need a beer." Edward went into the kitchen and opened the refrigerator. Mary kissed Drummer's forehead. He had an air about him; his diaper needed changing. She took him into the bedroom, laid him down on the bed next to her shoulder bag, and began the task. There was only one more diaper. She was going to have to go out and buy another box of Pampers. As she changed Drummer, she noticed a typewriter on a little desk in the room. The wastebasket had crumpled-up paper in it, squeezed like white fists. She took a wad of paper out and opened it. There were three lines on the paper: *My name is Edward Fordyce, and I am a killer. My killing was done in the name of freedom, a long time ago. I was a member of the Storm Front, and on the night of July first, 1972, I was reborn.*

Drummer began to cry, uncomfortable and sleepy.

Behind Mary, Edward said, "The publisher tells me I need a snappy opening paragraph. Something to hook a reader with real quick."

She looked up at him from the wrinkled paper. Drummer kept crying, the sound hurting her head.

Edward sipped his beer. His eyes seemed darker, his face tight with pressure. "They say they want a lot of blood in it. A lot of action. They say it could be a best seller."

Mary crumpled the paper again, into a hard little ball. Her fist clenched around it as Drummer cried on.

"Can't you get him quiet?" Edward asked.

The killer awoke. She felt it stir within her, like a heavy shadow. Edward was writing a book about the Storm Front. Writing a book to tell everything to the Mindfuck State. Going to spread the Front's blood, sweat, and tears out on the woodpulp pages to be licked by dumb jackals. *A reunion,* he'd said. *I guess I was curious.*

No, that wasn't why Edward Fordyce had put the message in the papers and magazines. "You wanted to find the others," she said, "so we could help you write your book."

"Background material. I want the book to be a history of the Storm Front, and there's a lot I don't know."

Mary's hand went into her bag. It came out with the Magnum, and she trained the gun on him, a stranger in enemy colors.

"Put that down, Mary. You don't want to shoot me."

"I'll blow your fucking head off!" she shouted. "No way are you making us whores! No way!"

"We were always whores. For the militant press and the rabble-rousers. We did what they dreamed of doing, and what did we get for it? You've turned into an animal, and I'm a forty-three-year-old failure." He swigged from the beer again, but his gaze stayed on her gun. "I was a stockbroker a few years ago," he said with a bitter smile. "Making a hundred K a year, living on the Upper East Side. A fast-tracker. Had a Mercedes, a wife, and a son. Then the bottom fell out of the market, and I watched everything go to pieces. It was like that night in Linden, but even worse because it was a house *I'd* built getting blown apart. Couldn't stop it. Couldn't. I spiraled down to where I am right now. So where do I go from here? Do I figure the books for Sea King the rest of my life and retire to an old folks' home in Jersey? Or do I take a gamble that a publisher might be interested in the Storm Front's story? It's past history, Mary. It's ancient and dusty . . . but blood and guts sells books, and you know we waded through the blood and guts together. So what's so wrong about it, Mary? You tell me."

She couldn't think. Drummer's crying was louder, more needful. Her brain was full of machinery that had lost its purpose. One squeeze of the trigger and he would be dusted. Everything was a lie; Lord Jack was not here, and he couldn't receive his son. This thing standing before her in Mindfuck State clothing vomited out bile and brimstone, but one fact remained: he had saved her life on a long-ago night of pain and fire.

That alone kept her from killing him.

"I've got an agent," Edward went on. "Big knocker in the business. He got me a contract on an outline. The manuscript's due at the end of August."

Mary kept the gun aimed at him as Drummer wailed.

"I don't want it to be just my story. I want it to be about all of us. Everybody who died and everybody who got away. Do you see?"

"I see a traitor," Mary said, "who deserves execution."

"Oh, crap! Forget the drama, Mary! This is the real dollars-and-cents world!" He slammed his bottle down atop a bureau, and beer sloshed out. "If we can make money off the hell we went through, why shouldn't we? I'd be willing to share the profits with you, no problem."

"Profits," she said, as if tasting something vile.

"Jesus! Can't you shut that kid up?" Edward walked toward Drummer. Mary stopped him by putting the Magnum against the side of his head and grabbing his red power tie at the knot. She wrenched at his tie, and Edward's face reddened. ". . . Choke . . ." he gasped. "Choking . . . me . . ."

Brrrring.

Telephone, Mary thought. Again: *Brrrring.*

"Door . . . buzzer," Edward managed to get out. "Downstairs. Somebody . . . wants in."

"Who're you expecting?"

"No-nobody. Mary, listen . . . you're choking me. Come on . . . stop it . . . okay?"

Brrrring.

She stared into his too-blue eyes and his mottled face. He was small, she decided. A small person who had given up and been seduced by the Mindfuck State. He was to be pitied. She didn't want to kill him, not yet. Drummer was crying and someone wanted in. She released Edward's tie, and he gasped in a shuddering breath followed by a coughing fit.

Mary pressed the pacifier into Drummer's mouth. His eyes were angry, and big wet tears had rolled down his cheeks. He looked the way she felt. She finished changing his diaper, the gun beside him on the bed.

In the front room, Edward gave a last ragged cough and pressed the intercom button. "Yeah?"

There was no answer.

"Anybody down there?"

Nothing.

He released the button. Neighborhood kids screwing around, he figured. About three seconds later: *Brrrring.*

He hit the button again. "Hey, listen up! You want to play, go play in the middle of the stre—"

"Edward Lambert?"

A woman's voice. Sounded nervous. "Yeah. Who is it?"

"Come downstairs."

"I don't have time for this, lady. What're you selling?"

"Damaged goods," she said. "Come downstairs." She clicked off.

"Who was that?" Mary stood in the bedroom's doorway, freshly diapered Drummer in her arms and the Magnum automatic in her right hand.

"Nobody." He shrugged. "Bag lady, probably. They're all over the place trying to get handouts."

Mary went to the window and looked out. The air was hazed with falling snow. And then she saw the figure standing down on the sidewalk, staring up at the apartment building. The wind had picked up, whipping at the figure's gray overcoat. There was a black cap on the person's head, and a long woolen muffler the same color around the neck.

Mary's eyes narrowed. She recognized the outfit. She'd seen this person before. Yes, she was sure of it. On the boat coming back from Liberty Island. This person had been standing at the stern, hands in pockets, next to the blond-haired girl in the leather jacket. As Mary watched, the figure began to walk slowly away from the building, bent against the wind. A few more steps, and a crosscurrent of winds snatched the cap and lifted it off the person's head.

A mane of red hair spilled down. A woman, Mary realized. The woman caught the cap before it could spin away, pushed her tresses up under it, and mashed it down again. Then she kept walking, shoulders slumped as if under a terrible burden.

Red hair, Mary thought. Red as a battle flag.

She had known another woman with hair that color.

"Oh my God," Mary whispered.

The red-haired woman turned a corner and went out of sight, snowflakes whirling behind her.

"Hold my baby," Mary told Edward, and she put Drummer in his arms before he could say no. She jammed the pistol down into the waistband of her jeans, under her baggy brown sweater, and she headed for the door.

"Where're you going? Mary! Where the hell are—"

She was already out the door and racing down the second-floor stairway. She ran out onto the street, into the cutting cold and snow. Then on to the corner where the red-haired woman had turned off Cooper Avenue, and Mary could see her about a block away. She was opening the driver's door of a brown compact Ford.

"Wait!" Mary shouted, but the wind was in her face and the woman couldn't hear. The Ford pulled out of its parking place and started coming toward Mary, who stepped into the street and walked forward to meet it. Flurries of snow swirled between them. Mary lifted her right hand and made a peace sign, and she strode toward the car as it came on.

She saw the woman's face through the windshield. Like Edward's, it was not a face she knew. And then the woman's eyes widened, her mouth opened in a cry Mary couldn't hear, and the Ford skidded to a stop on the gleaming pavement.

The woman got out, and the wind took her black cap, and the red tresses danced around her shoulders. Mary lowered her peace hand. Was this or was this not someone she knew? The hair was the same, yes, but the face was different. Bedelia Morse had been as lovely as a model, her nose small and graceful, her mouth and chin set with firm purpose. This woman had a crooked nose that looked as if it had been brutally broken and never properly set, her jowls were thick, and her chin had receded above a padding of flab. Deep lines flared out from the corners of her eyes and cut across her forehead. Mary could tell that the woman, who stood about five six, was heavy around the stomach and waist, a once-fine figure gone to seed. But the woman had green eyes: green as Irish moss. They were Didi's eyes, in a face that was almost toadish.

"Mary?" she said in Bedelia's voice grown husky and older. "Mary?"

"It's me," Mary answered, and Bedelia tried to speak again, but only a sob came out and it was tattered by the wind. Bedelia Morse rushed forward into Mary's arms, and they hugged each other with the pistol between them.

2.

The Idiot's Dream

On Monday morning between two and three, Laura Clayborne put on her heavy overcoat, got into her car in the Days Inn parking lot, started the engine, and drove west, heading for Didi Morse's cottage in the woods.

Sleep was impossible, the night full of phantoms. A crescent moon hung in the sky, the road empty before the BMW's headlights. Laura shivered, waiting for the heater to warm up. She and Mark had driven out to the cottage at ten o'clock, to see if Didi Morse had gotten home and was simply not answering her telephone, but the house had been dark. Laura wanted to drive, to have the sensation of at least going from one point to another. Her calls to Agent Kastle in Atlanta had told her how his investigation was going: Kastle, his secretary said, was out of the city and would get in touch with Laura whenever he returned. In other words: don't call us, we'll call you.

That wasn't good enough. Not good enough by a damned long shot.

Laura drove past the cottage. Still dark, no car in front. Wherever Didi was, her weekend trip had stretched out another day. Laura thought she might start chewing the walls of her motel room if she'd come all this way and couldn't find the woman. She'd stopped taking her sleeping pills because she didn't want her brain fogged with drugs. The downside of kicking the sleeping pills, though, was that she had maybe three or four hours of sleep a night and the other hours were haunted by visions of the madwoman on the balcony and the sniper with his rifle. Laura couldn't take looking at her face in a mirror; her eyes had seemingly sunken deeper, and there was a steely shine in them as if something hard and unknown were beginning to peer out.

About a mile west of the cottage, Laura turned around on a dirt road and headed back. Get something to eat, she thought. Find an all-night pancake house, maybe. Someplace with a lot of hot black coffee.

She slowed, nearing the cottage again. She glanced toward it as the BMW crept by. Dark, of course. Didi had gone birding, the old man had said. Borrowed his binoculars, and went bye-bye. Her hands tightened around the wheel. Didi Morse might be her only hope of finding David alive. David might be dead right now, torn apart like the dolls in the box they'd found in Mary Terrell's apartment. Dear God, Laura prayed, help me hold on to my sanity.

A light flashed.

A light.

In a window of Didi Morse's cottage.

Laura was past the house by a hundred yards before she could make her foot hit the brake. She slowed down gradually, not wanting the tires to shriek. Her heart was about to blow out of her chest. A light. Just a brief glimmer, maybe a second and then gone. It hadn't been a reflection of the moon, or of her headlights.

Someone was inside the house, prowling around in the dark.

Laura's first thought was to stop and call the police. No, no; she didn't want the police in this, not yet. She turned around again and drove past the house once more. This time no light shone. But she'd seen it; she knew she had. The real question was: what was she going to do about it?

She pulled the car off the road, stopped it on the brown-grassed shoulder, cut the headlights and the engine.

Her purse was on the seat beside her, but her pistol remained in her suitcase at the motel. She sat there, shivering as the warm air slipped away and the night came in. Who was inside Bedelia Morse's house? A burglar? Stealing what? Her pottery? Laura realized she could either sit there and thrash it around in her mind or walk back to the house. Courage was not a question here: it was a matter of desperation.

Laura got out, opened the trunk, and put her hand around the tire iron. Then she buttoned up her coat to the neck and began walking the couple of hundred yards back to the dirt driveway that curved up through the woods. No light shone in any of the cottage's windows. There was no other car anywhere in sight. Imagination or not? She tightened her grip around the tire iron and started up the driveway, the air's eighteen-degree temperature burning her nostrils and lungs.

The baby was crying again. The sound roused Mary from a dream of a castle on a cloud, and set her teeth on edge. It had been a good dream, and in it she'd been young and slim and her hair had been the color of the summer sun. It had been a dream that she hated leaving, but the baby was crying again. Babies were killers of dreams, she thought as she sat up in bed. Her dream had been to place the baby in Lord Jack's hands, and see him smile like a blaze of beauty. Lord Jack would love her again, and everything would be right with the world.

But Lord Jack wasn't here. He hadn't been at the weeping lady. Lord Jack wasn't coming for her. Not now. Not ever.

The baby was crying, a sound that razored her brain. She stood up, a well of despair, and she felt the old familiar rage begin to steam from the pores of her flesh.

"Hush," she said. "Drummer, hush." He wouldn't obey. His crying was going to wake the neighbors, and then the pigs might come calling. Why did the babies always try to betray her like this? Why did they take her love and twist it into hateful knots? What good was Drummer now if Lord Jack didn't want him? Drummer was a piece of crying flesh that had no purpose, no reason for being. She hated him at that moment because she realized what she'd done to bring him to Lord Jack. Now it was all over, and Lord Jack would never set eyes on the wailing rag.

"Won't you stop crying?" she asked Drummer as she sat on the narrow bed in the dark. She spoke in a quiet voice. Drummer gurgled and cried louder. "All right," Mary said, and she stood up. "All right, then. I'll make you stop."

She switched on the lights in the kitchenette. Then she turned on one of the stove's burners and swiveled its dial to high.

Laura walked slowly up the front steps of Bedelia Morse's house. A clay cat was crouched near the door, and dead leaves scuttled across the porch. Laura reached out and tried the doorknob, gently working it from side to side. Locked. She retreated from the door, went back down the stairs again and around to the rear of the house. Her fingers, clenched so hard on the tire iron, were stiffening up with the cold. There was a one-car garage and a larger stone outbuilding, its door sealed with a padlock and chain, where Laura assumed the pottery work was done. Strange clay sculptures stood amid the barren trees like alien plant life; Laura couldn't see them now, in the dark, but they'd been apparent when she and Mark had gone back there on their initial visit Saturday. All kinds of clay geegaws—bird feeders, mobiles, and other things not so readily identifiable—dangled on wires from the tree limbs. It was obvious that Bedelia Morse—or Diane Daniells, as she called herself now—had thrown herself heart and soul into the work she'd begun as a member of Mark's commune. Laura went to the back door, her shoes crunching on dead branches and leaves, and she tried this doorknob as well.

It turned easily. Laura's heart kicked again. She ran her hand over the door and found that one of its small rectangular panes of glass had been removed. Not broken, because there were no shards. Removed, as with a glass cutter.

She opened the door and stood on the threshold. Off in the woods somewhere, an owl spoke to the moon. The cold wind hissed through the trees and made the clay ornaments clink and clatter on their wires. She shivered involuntarily, and she stood in the doorway trying to see through the dark. Nothing in there but shapes upon shapes. She and Mark had looked through the door's panes on Saturday and seen a kitchen with a table and a single chair in the middle of the room. On

Saturday, the door had had all its panes of glass, and it had been securely locked.

Her heart pounding, Laura lifted the tire iron and walked into the house.

Mary picked up the baby. Her touch was rough. The infant's crying broke, faltered, and began to climb in volume again, a thin, high whine that Mary could not abide. "STOP IT!" she shouted into his reddened, squawling face. "STOP IT, YOU LITTLE SHIT!"

The baby cried on. Mary almost choked on a scream of rage. How could she have been so stupid to believe that Lord Jack had written the message? To believe that he wanted her and the baby after all these years? To believe that he *cared?* No one cared. No one. She had stolen this child and blown her disguise, had put herself in mortal danger from the pigs of the Mindfuck State . . . and all for Edward Fordyce's traitorous book about the Storm Front.

She would deal with Edward before she left. She would make herself put a bullet between his eyes and dump his body in a garbage can. But right now there was the baby, crying his head off. *Drummer,* she thought, and she sneered. "You want to cry?" She shook him. "You want to cry?" Shook him harder. His crying became a shriek. "Okay, I'll make you cry!"

She took him into the kitchenette, where the burner glowed fiercely red and its heat rose up in a shimmer. The baby was trembling, still wailing, legs trying to thrash. She didn't need the little bastard. Didn't need Lord Jack. Didn't need anyone. She would make Drummer stop crying, make him obey her, and then she'd leave what remained of him for the pigs and the woman named Laura Clayborne. Then she would go underground again, deep underground, where nothing and no one could touch her, and she would turn her back for the last time on the idiot's dream of love and hope.

"Cry!" she shouted. "Cry! Cry!"

And she grasped the back of the baby's head and pressed his face toward the red burner.

In the dark, Laura listened. The boom of her heart and the roar of her breathing got in the way. Get out, she told herself. You don't belong here. You're a long way from home, and you've gone too far. If a burglar was ransacking Bedelia Morse's house, that was his business. But she didn't leave, and her fingers groped for a light switch. Her hand hit something that jingled merrily and made her jump a foot in the air. Another damned pottery mobile. She was making more noise than a marching band.

In another moment she found a light switch, and she turned it on.

A warm breath washed against her neck.

She spun around, to the right, and looked into the face of the man who was standing there. She opened her mouth to scream. A black-gloved hand rose up, fast as a cobra's head, and clamped her mouth shut before the scream could get out.

The baby's face was almost on the burner. He was still wailing, stubbornly, and Mary braced for the scream of agony.

A scream came.

"NO!"

Someone grabbed her from behind, shoving her and the baby away from the hot burner. "No! Jesus, no!" A pair of hands winnowed in, trying to grasp Drummer. Mary slammed an elbow backward and heard a grunt of pain as it connected. A woman with red hair was fighting to take Drummer, and Mary didn't know her face. The woman was saying, "Mary, don't! Don't, please don't!" Her hands grasped at the baby again, and Mary shoved the red-haired stranger back hard against the wall. This was her baby, to do with as she pleased. She had risked her life to have this child, and no one would take him away from her. The woman was fighting her for Drummer once more, the red-glowing burner behind them and the baby wailing. "Listen to me! Listen!" the woman was pleading as she grabbed hold of Mary's shoulders and hung on. Mary looked at the woman's white throat, and she saw where she should punch into it to crush her windpipe. "Don't hurt the baby! Please don't!" the woman said, still hanging on. "Mary, look at me! It's Didi! It's Didi Morse!"

Didi Morse? Mary lifted her gaze from the vulnerable throat and stared into the woman's heavy-jowled, deeply lined face.

"No," Mary said over Drummer's crying. "No. Didi Morse was beautiful."

"I had surgery. Remember what I told you? I had the plastic surgeon do it. Don't hurt the baby, Mary. Don't hurt Drummer."

Plastic surgeon. Didi Morse, her face made ugly by a scalpel, silicone implants, and a hammer that had broken her nose. *I had it done when I went underground,* she'd told Mary and Edward. *A surgeon who did work on a lot of people who wanted to disappear.* Didi had actually paid to have herself made ugly, and the surgeon—who was part of the militant underground—had done the work in St. Louis. Didi Morse, still with green eyes and red hair but now drastically different. Pleading with her not to hurt Drummer.

"Hurt . . . Drummer?" Mary whispered. "Hurt my baby?" Tears came to her eyes. She heard Drummer crying, but the sound didn't razor her brain anymore; it was a cry of innocent need, and Mary pressed Drummer against her and sobbed as she realized what her rage had been guiding her toward. "Oh God, oh God, oh God," she moaned as the baby trembled in her arms. "I'm sick, Didi. I'm so sick."

Didi switched off the stove's burner. Her collarbone was still throbbing from the collision with Mary's elbow, and Mary had almost broken her back against the wall. She said, "Come on, let's sit down." She wanted to get Mary away from the stove. Her sight of the woman about to mash the infant's face down on that burner had been a horror beyond belief. She grasped Mary's arm with a careful touch. "Come on, sister."

Mary allowed herself to be steered out of the kitchenette. Tears were streaming down her face, her lungs ratcheted by sobbing. "I'm sick," she repeated. "Something's wrong with me, I get crazy. Oh God, I wouldn't hurt my sweet Drummer!" She hugged him close. His crying was starting to weaken. They were in Mary's room at the Cameo Motor Lodge. Didi and Mary had gone there after leaving Edward's at eight o'clock, and they'd shared a couple of bottles of wine and talked about the old days. Mary had folded down the sofa bed for Didi, and it was there that Didi had been sleeping when she'd heard Mary stalk out of the bedroom and go into the kitchenette. Then Mary had gone back for the crying baby, and the rest of what might have happened had been only narrowly averted.

Mary sat down in a chair and began to rock Drummer, the tears glistening on her face and her eyes red and swollen. Drummer was growing quiet, getting sleepy again. Didi sat on the rumpled sofa bed, her nerves still jangling.

"I love my baby," Mary said. "Can't you see I do?"

"Yes," Didi answered. But what she saw was an insane woman with a stolen infant in her arms.

"Mine," Mary whispered. She kissed his forehead and nuzzled his soft whorls of dark hair. "He's mine. All mine."

Sardonicus.

One side of the man's mouth was frozen open in a hideous rictus that showed teeth ground down to stubs. Like Sardonicus, Laura thought as the gloved hand clamped to her face. His cheek on the grinning side was caved in, his lower jaw crooked and jutting forward like a barracuda's underbite. He had black eyes, the one on the damaged hemisphere of his face sunken and glassy. A battlefield of scars streaked back from the corner of his grin across his collapsed cheek. In his throat there was a flesh-colored plug with a three-holed socket.

The sight was terrifying, but Laura had no time to be terrified. She struck out with the tire iron, the strength of desperation behind it, and hit him a glancing blow across the left shoulder. It was hard enough: the man staggered back, and he opened his ruined mouth and made a hissing sound of pain like a ruptured steam pipe.

At once he was on her again, reaching for her throat. Laura stepped back, giving herself room, and swung the tire iron once more. The man lifted his arm to ward off the blow; their forearms collided with a jolt that knocked numbness into Laura's hand, but it was the man who lost what he was holding. A small flashlight fell to the floor and rolled under the kitchen table.

He caught Laura's wrist, and they fought for the tire iron. The man was tall and sinewy, wearing a black outfit and a black woolen cap. His face was pallid, the color of the moon. He slammed Laura back against a counter, and pottery knickknacks clattered and fell. A knee came up, hitting Laura between the legs; the pain made her cry out, but she clenched her teeth and hung on to the tire iron. They careened across the kitchen, crashing into the table and throwing it over. The man grasped her chin with one hand and shoved her head back, trying to snap her neck. Laura clawed at his throat, digging furrows in his flesh. Her fingers found the plug, and she tore at it.

He retreated, clutching at his throat, the breath shrieking from his predator's grin. Laura advanced on him, her eyes wild. She lifted the tire iron for another blow, her intent to knock his brains out before he could kill her. He made a guttural growling sound that might have been rage, and he darted in before she could swing the tool. He trapped her arm, twisted his body, and lifted her off her feet, flinging her like a flour sack to the other side of the kitchen. She went down on her right shoulder, the air whooshing from her lungs as she slammed to the floor.

Time hitched and spun, knocked out of rhythm. Laura tasted blood. Pain throbbed through her shoulder, and her hand had lost the tire iron. When she could gather the strength to sit up, she found herself alone in Bedelia Morse's kitchen. The back door was wide open, dead leaves blowing in. Laura spat a red scrawl on the floor, and her tongue found the wound inside her cheek where her teeth had met. I'm all right, she thought. I'm all right. But she was starting to shake uncontrollably now that the man with the death's-head grin had gone, and fear and nausea hit her in tandem. She barely made it outside to throw up, next to one of the abstract sculptures. She heaved until nothing would come up, and then she sat on the ground away from her mess and breathed in lungfuls of frigid air. Between her thighs there was a pulse of pain. She felt warm wetness spreading there, and she realized with a flash of anger that the son of a bitch had torn her stitches open again.

She stood up and walked back into the kitchen. The flashlight was gone. Her tire iron remained. The urge to cry fell upon her, and she almost gave in to this brutal friend. But she couldn't trust herself to stop crying if she began, and so she stood with her hands pressed to her eyes until the urge passed. Shock lurked in the back of her mind, waiting its turn to creep over her. There was nothing to be done now but to go to her car and drive back to the Days Inn. Her right shoulder was going to be one black bruise tomorrow, and her back was aching where the man had driven her against the counter.

But she had not been killed. She had stood up against him, whoever he'd been, and she'd survived. Before all this had started, she would have crumpled into a heap and cried her heart out, but things were different now. Her heart was harder, her vision colder. Violence had suddenly and irrevocably become a part of her life.

She would have to tell Mark about this. The man with the plug in his throat, who'd been asking questions about Diane Daniells from the neighbor across the road. Who was he, and how did he fit into the puzzle?

Laura helped herself to a glass of water from the faucet, spitting blood into the sink. It was time to go. Time to leave the light and strike out into the darkness again. She retrieved the tire iron, and she waited for her trembling to subside. It wouldn't. She put out of her mind the image of the grinning man waiting for her out there somewhere. *Let it be,* she told herself. And then she switched off the light, closed the back door, and began walking the distance to her car. Nothing came after her, though she jumped at every sound, imagined or otherwise, and her fingers cramped around the tire iron.

Laura got into the BMW, turned on the ignition and the headlights.

That was when she saw it. Backwards letters, carved into her windshield by a glass cutter. Two words: **ƎMOH OƎ**

She sat there for a moment, stunned, looking at what she took to be a warning. *Go home.* Where was that? A house in Atlanta, shared by a stranger named Doug? A place where her parents lived, ready and eager to command her life?

Go home.

"Not without my son," Laura vowed, and she pulled the car off the shoulder and drove toward Ann Arbor.

3.

The Secret Thing

Sometimes," Mary said as Drummer slept in her arms, "I get crazy. I don't know why. My head hurts, and I can't think straight. Maybe everybody feels like that sometimes, huh?"

"Maybe," Didi admitted, but she didn't believe it.

"Yeah." She smiled at her sister in arms, the storm of madness passed for now. "I was so glad to see you, Didi. I can't tell you how much. I mean . . . you look so different and everything, but I've missed you. I've missed everybody. I think it was smart of you not to show up at the weeping lady. It could've been a trap, right?"

"Right." That was why Didi had gone to Liberty Island at noon, with the binoculars she'd borrowed from her neighbor Charles Brewer. She'd positioned herself on a vantage point where she could see the passengers getting off the boat, and she'd recognized Mary but not Edward Fordyce until he'd approached Mary. She'd followed them from Liberty Island, had seen them go into the apartment building, and had buzzed the apartment belonging to Edward Lambert. Her brown Ford was rented, and her real car—a gray Honda hatchback—was at the airport parking lot in Detroit. "What are you going to do from here?" Didi asked.

"I don't know. Make it to Canada, I guess. Go underground again. Except this time I'll have my baby."

They hadn't yet breached the difficult subject. Didi wanted to know: "Why'd you take him, Mary? Why didn't you just come up by yourself?"

"Because," Mary answered, "he's Jack's gift."

Didi shook her head, not understanding.

"I was bringing Drummer to Jack. When I saw the message, I thought it was from him. That's why I brought Drummer. For Jack. See?"

Didi did. She sighed softly, and averted her eyes from Mary Terror. Mary's insanity was as obvious as a scab; it was true that Mary was still cunning, in the way of a hunted animal, but the trial of the years—and her solitary confinement—had eaten her down to the desperate bones. "You brought the baby for Jack and he didn't show up." Now the display of rage made more sense to her, but its explanation was madness enough. "I'm sorry."

"I don't need him!" Mary snapped. "And don't you be sorry for me! No way! I'll be just fine now that I've got my baby!"

Didi nodded, thinking of the glowing burner. If she hadn't been here to stop it, the baby's face would have been scorched off his skull. One night—maybe not very far in the future—Mary would wake up in the throes of madness, and there would be no one to save the infant. Didi knew she'd done a lot of terrible things in her life. They were things that came back to her at night, bleeding and moaning. They haunted her dreams, and they had grinned and jabbered as she'd laid out the razor and soaked her wrists in hot water. She'd done terrible things, but she'd never hurt a baby. "Maybe you shouldn't take him with you," she said.

Her face like a block of stone, Mary stared at Didi.

"You can't move as fast with a baby," Didi went on. "He'll slow you down."

Mary was silent, rocking the sleeping child in her arms.

"You could leave him at a church. Leave a note saying who he is. They'd get him back to his mother."

"I *am* his mother," Mary said.

Dangerous ground, Didi thought. She was walking in a minefield. "You don't want Drummer to be hurt, do you? What'll happen if the police find you? Drummer might get hurt. Have you thought of that?"

"Sure. If the pigs find me, I shoot the baby first and I take as many of them with me as I can." She shrugged. "Reasonable."

Didi blinked, startled, and at that moment she saw the darkness of Mary Terror's soul.

"I can't let them take us alive," Mary said. Her smile returned. "We're together now. We'll die together, if that's how it has to be."

Didi looked at her hands clenched together in her lap. They were earth-mother hands, the palms broad and the fingers sturdy. She thought of bullets going into bodies, and one of her earth-mother hands on the gun. She thought of the newscasts on TV, the pictures of this child's mother leaving the hospital in Atlanta, her face tormented by worry, her body bent under a terrible weight. She thought of the secret thing, the thing she'd suspected for five years. Her life had been a twisted, treacherous road. She had destroyed her parents, driving her mother to drink and her father to a heart attack that had killed him in 1973. The farm was gone now, reclaimed by the bank. Her mother was in a sanitarium, babbling and wetting her bed. For Bedelia Morse the saying was viciously true: you can't go home again.

She had seen the message in January's issue of *Mother Jones*. At first she'd had no intention of going to the Statue of Liberty on the eighteenth of February, but the idea had kept gnawing at her. She wasn't sure exactly why she'd decided to go. Maybe it was pure curiosity, or maybe it was because the Storm Front had been her true family. She had bought a round-trip ticket on American Airlines, and left Detroit on Thursday night.

Her flight back to Detroit was at one-thirty in the afternoon. She hadn't planned on sleeping at Mary's motel, but it was cleaner than the hotel she was staying at on West 55th in Manhattan. She was glad now that she'd stayed with Mary, for the baby's sake. And much less glad that she'd seen the inner nature of Mary Terror, though the newscasts of the FBI agent being shotgunned had been a forewarning.

Didi turned the secret thing over and over in her mind, working it like a Rubik's Cube.

Mary saw Didi's vacant stare. "What're you thinking?"

"About Edward's book," Didi lied. At Mary's sarcastic insistence Edward had told her what he was writing. "I'm not sure Jack would like that."

"He'd want Edward executed," Mary said. "No pity for traitors. That's what he used to tell me."

Didi looked at the child in Mary's arms. An innocent, she thought. It was wrong for him to be there. Mary's arms were folded around him as if he were cradled by vipers. "You said . . . you wanted to give Jack the baby."

"I wanted to give him a gift. He always wanted a son. That's what I was carrying for him the night I got hurt." Was it true or not? She couldn't remember exactly.

"So you're going underground again?" *Click, click, click:* the mental Rubik's Cube at work.

"Tomorrow, after I take care of Edward. Then I'm heading for Canada. Me and Drummer."

She's going to kill Edward, Didi realized. And how long would it be before she had another fit and maimed or killed the baby? *Click, click:* more pieces, turning. Maybe Edward deserved to die. But he was a brother in arms, and didn't that count for something? The baby certainly did not deserve the fate ahead of him. *Click, click.* Didi stared at her earth-mother hands, and realized more human clay lay at her mercy. "Mary?" she said softly.

"What?"

"I—" She paused. The secret thing had been a secret so long, it was reluctant to be born. But two lives—Edward's and the infant's— hung on her decision. "I . . . think I might . . . know where Jack is," she said.

Mary sat without moving, her mouth partway open.

"I'm not sure. But I think Jack may be in California."

No response from Mary.

"Northern California," Didi continued. "A town named Freestone. It's about fifty miles north of San Francisco."

Mary moved: a shiver of excitement, as if all the blood had suddenly rushed back into her body. "That's near the house," she said. Her voice was tight and strained. "The Thunder House."

Didi had never been to the Thunder House, but she knew about it from the other Storm Fronters. The Thunder House was located above San Francisco, hidden somewhere in the woods that rimmed Drakes Bay. It was the birthplace of the Storm Front, where the first members had signed their names in blood on the pact of loyalty and dedication to the cause. Didi understood it had been a hunting lodge abandoned thirty or more years earlier, and its name came from the continual thunder of the waves on the jagged rocks of Drakes Bay. The Thunder House had been the Storm Front's first headquarters, their "think tank" from which all the West Coast terrorist missions had originated.

"Freestone," Mary repeated. "Freestone." Her eyes had lit up like spirit lamps. "Why do you think he's there?"

"I'm a member of the Sierra Club. Five years ago there was a story in the newsletter about a group of people who were suing the town of Freestone for dumping garbage near a bird sanctuary. There was a picture of them in the council meeting. I think one of those people might have been Jack Gardiner."

"You couldn't tell for sure?"

"No. Just the side of his face was in the picture. But I cut it out and kept it." She leaned forward. "Mary, I remember faces. My hands do, at least. Come to Ann Arbor and look at what I've done, and you tell me if it's him or not."

Mary was silent again, and Didi could see the wheels going around in her head.

"Don't kill Edward," Didi said. "Bring him with you. He'll want to find Jack, too, for his book. If Jack *is* in Freestone, you can take both Edward and the baby to him, and he can decide whether Edward should be executed or not." Buying time for Edward, she thought. And time for herself, to figure out how to get the child away from Mary.

"California. The land of milk and honey," Mary said. She nodded, her smile beatific. "Yes. That's where Jack would go." She hugged Drummer, waking the baby with a start. "Oh, sweet Drummer! My sweet baby!" Her voice rose on a giddy note. "We're going to find Jack! Going to find Jack and he'll love us both forever, yes he will!"

"My plane leaves at one-thirty," Didi told her. "I'll go on ahead. You and Edward can follow me."

"Yes. Follow you. That's what we'll do." Mary beamed like a schoolgirl, and the sight ripped at Didi's heart. Drummer began to cry. "He's happy, too!" Mary said. "Hear him?"

Didi couldn't bear to look at Mary's face anymore. There was something of death in it, something brutal and frightening in its maniacal joy. Was this the fruit of what we fought for? Didi asked herself. Not freedom from oppression, but madness in the night? "I'd better get back to my hotel," she said, and stood up from the sofa bed. "I'll leave you my phone number. When you get to Ann Arbor, call me and I'll give you directions to my house." She wrote the number on a piece of Cameo Motor Lodge stationery, and Mary tucked it into her shoulder bag along with Pampers, formula, and her Magnum pistol. At the door, Didi paused. The flurries had ceased, the air still and heavy with cold. Didi forced herself to look into the big woman's steely eyes. "You won't hurt the baby, will you?"

"*Hurt* Drummer?" She hugged him, and he made a little aggravated squalling sound at being so rudely awakened. "I wouldn't hurt Jack's child, not for anything in this world!"

"And you'll let Jack decide about Edward?"

"Didi," Mary said, "you worry too much. But that's part of why I love you." She kissed Didi's cheek, and Didi flinched as the hot mouth sealed against her flesh and then drew away. "You be careful," Mary instructed.

"You, too." Didi glanced at the infant again—the innocent in the arms of the damned—and she turned away and walked across the parking lot to her car.

Mary watched until Didi left, and then she closed the door. Behind it, she danced around the room with her baby, while God sang "Light My Fire" in her mind.

It was near the dawning of a brand-new day.

4.

Crossroads

J esus," Bedelia Morse said as she stood looking at her wrecked kitchen.

Afternoon sunlight slanted through the windows. The house was cold, and Didi saw the missing pane of glass in the back door. Dead leaves were scattered about, her antique kitchen table overthrown and two legs splintered. Someone had broken in, obviously, but the only sign of ransacking was in this room. Still, she hadn't checked the pottery workshop yet. She looked out a window, could see the padlock and chain were secure. She didn't have much of value; her stereo was still in the front room, and so was her little portable TV. She had no jewelry to speak of, just what she fashioned on the wheel. What, then, had the intruder been after?

Terror gripped her. She walked through a short hallway into her bedroom, where her unopened suitcase lay on the bed, and she opened the bottom drawer of her dresser. It was full of old belts, socks, and a couple of pairs of well-worn bell-bottom bluejeans. Her sigh of relief was explosive. Beneath the jeans was a photo album. Didi opened it. Inside were old, yellowed newspaper stories and grainy photographs, protected by cellophane. *Storm Front Shootout in N.J.,* said one of the headlines. *FBI Hunting Escaped Terrorists,* another trumpeted. *Storm Fronter Killed in Attica Riots,* a third headline said. There were pictures of all the Storm Front members: old photographs, snapped when they were young. The picture of herself showed her beautiful and lithe, waving at the camera from astride a horse. It had been taken by her father when she was sixteen. The picture of Mary Terrell, standing tall and blond and lovely in the summer sunlight, hurt her eyes to look at, because she now knew the reality.

Didi turned carefully to the back of the album. The last few stories had to do with Mary's kidnapping of David Clayborne. But before them was the article and black-and-white picture she'd clipped from the Sierra Club's newsletter five years earlier. *Citizen Group Saves Bird Sanctuary,* said the headline. The article was five paragraphs long, and the picture showed a woman standing at a podium before a council meeting. Behind her were seated several other people. One of them was a man whose head was turned to the right, as if talking to the woman beside him. Or avoiding the camera, Didi had thought when she'd first seen it. The lens had captured a portion of his profile—hairline, forehead, and nose. The names of the "Freestone Six," as they called themselves, were Jonelle Collins, Dean Walker, Karen Ott, Nick Hudley, and Keith and Sandy Cavanaugh. All of Freestone, California, the article said.

Didi had always had an eye for faces: the curve of a nose, the width of an eyebrow, the way hair fell across a forehead. It was detail that made up a face. Attention to detail was one of her strengths.

And she was almost certain that one of those men—Walker, Hudley, or Cavanaugh—used to be known as Jack Gardiner.

She put the album back in its place and closed the drawer. There was no evidence that the drawer had been tampered with or the album discovered. She went into the front room and circled the telephone. Call the police? Report a burglary? But what, if anything, had been taken? She roamed around the house, checking closets and drawers. A metal box that held two hundred dollars in ready cash hadn't been touched. Her clothes—Sears and Penney's ready-to-wear—all remained on their hangers. Nothing was missing; even the pane of glass that had been cut from the door was lying on the kitchen's countertop. She walked from room to room in the cottage, her Rubik's Cube clicking but no solution in sight.

The telephone rang, and Didi picked it up in the front room. "Hello?"

A pause. Then: *"Didi?"*

If her heart had been pounding before, now her stomach seemed to rise to her throat. "Who is this?"

"It's me. Mark Treggs."

"Mark?" It had been five or six months since they'd last spoken. She always called him, not the other way around. It was part of their understanding. But something was wrong; she could hear the tension thick in his voice, and she said quickly, "What is it?"

"Didi, I'm here. In Ann Arbor."

"Ann Arbor," she repeated, dazed. *Click, click, click.* "What're you doing here?"

"I've brought someone to see you." In his room at the Days Inn, Mark glanced at Laura, who stood nearby. "We've been waiting for you to get back from your trip."

"Mark, what's this all about?"

She's right on the edge, Mark thought. About to jump out of her skin. "Trust me, okay? I wouldn't do anything to hurt you. Do you believe that?"

"Somebody broke in. Trashed my kitchen. Jesus, I don't know what's going on!"

"Listen to me. Okay? Just settle down and listen. I wouldn't hurt you. We go back too far. I've brought someone who needs your help."

"Who? What are you talking about?"

Laura took a step forward and grasped the telephone before Mark could say anything else. "Bedelia?" she said, and she heard the other woman gasp at the unfamiliar voice speaking her name. "Don't hang up, please! Just give me a few minutes, that's all I'm asking."

Didi was silent, but her shock was palpable.

"My name is Laura Clayborne. Mark brought me here to see you."

Laura sensed Didi was about to slam down the phone, the hairs stirring on the back of her neck. "I'm not working with the police or the FBI," she said. "I swear to God I'm not. I'm trying to find my baby. Do you know that Mary Terrell stole my child?"

There was no answer. Laura feared she'd already lost Bedelia Morse, that the phone would crash down and she would be long gone by the time they drove to the house.

The silence stretched, and Laura felt her nerves stretch with it.

The kernel of a scream began to form, like a small dark seed, in Laura's mind. What she didn't know was that the same seed was growing in the mind of Bedelia Morse.

Finally, it came. Not a scream, but a word born from the seed: "Yes."

Thank God, Laura thought. She had squeezed her eyes shut, waiting for Didi to hang up. Now she opened them again. "Can I come talk to you?"

Another silence as Didi thought it over. "I can't help you," she said.

"Are you sure about that? Do you have any idea where Mary Terrell might have gone?"

"I can't help you," Didi repeated, but she didn't hang up.

"All I want is my baby back," Laura said. "I don't care where Mary Terrell goes, or what happens to her. I've got to have my child back. I don't even know if he's still alive or not, and it's tearing me to pieces. Please. I'm begging you: can't you help me at all?"

"Look, I don't know you," Didi replied. "You could be undercover FBI for all I know. I just got home from a trip, and somebody broke into my house while I was gone. Was it you?"

"No. But I saw the man who did." And her body remembered the scuffle, too. Her right shoulder was a mass of blue-green bruises under her white blouse and cable-knit sweater, and another line of bruises ran across her right hip beneath her jeans.

"The man." Didi's voice had sharpened. "What man?"

"Let me come see you. I'll tell you when I get there."

"I don't *know* you!" It was almost a shout of fear and frustration.

"You're going to," Laura answered firmly. "I'm giving the phone back to Mark now. He'll tell you I can be trusted." She handed the telephone to him, and the first thing he heard from Didi was an enraged "You *bastard!* You betrayed me, you bastard! I ought to *kill* you for this!"

"Kill me?" he asked quietly. "You don't really mean that, do you, Didi?"

She gave an anguished sob. "You bastard," she whispered. "You screwed me. I thought we were like a brother and sister."

"We are, and that won't change. But this woman needs help. She's clean. Let us come see you," Mark said. "I'm asking like a brother."

Laura walked away from him, opened the curtain, and looked outside at the cold blue sky. She could see her car in the parking lot, its windshield marked with the GO HOME warning. She waited in anguish, until Mark put down the receiver.

"She'll see us," he told her.

On the drive to Didi's house, Mark said, "Be cool. Don't go all to pieces or start begging. That won't help."

"Okay."

Mark touched the letters carved into the windshield. "Son of a bitch did a job on you, didn't he? I knew that guy sounded weird. Plug in his throat." He grunted. "I wonder what the hell he was after."

"I don't know, and I hope I never see him again."

Mark nodded. They were a couple of miles from the cottage. "Listen," he said, "there's something I've got to lay on you. I told you about Didi having plastic surgery, remember?"

"Yes."

"Didi used to be pretty. She's not anymore. She had the plastic surgeon make her ugly."

"Make her *ugly?* Why?"

"She wanted to change. Didn't want to be what she was before, I guess. So when you see her, be cool."

"I'll be cool," Laura said. "I'll be damned cool."

She slowed down and turned the BMW onto the house's dirt driveway. As Laura drove up to the cottage, she saw the front door open. A plump woman wearing a dark green sweater and khaki trousers came out. She had long red hair that fell in waves around her shoulders. Laura's palms were damp, her nerves raw. Be cool, she told herself. She stopped the car and switched off the engine. The moment had arrived.

Bedelia Morse stood in the doorway, watching, as Laura and Mark got out of the car and approached her. Laura saw the woman's toadish face and crooked nose, and she wondered what kind of plastic surgeon would have consented to do such work. And what private torment had made Bedelia Morse want to wear a face that had been sculpted into ugliness?

"You shit," Didi said to Mark, her voice cold, and she went inside without waiting for them.

In the cottage's tidy front room, Didi sat in a chair where she could look out a window at the road. She didn't offer seats to Laura or Mark; she kept her gaze on him because she recalled Laura's pain-stricken face from the newscasts and looking at her was difficult. "Hello, Didi," Mark said, trying for a smile. "It's been a long time."

"How much did she pay you?" Didi asked.

Mark's fragile smile evaporated.

"She *did* pay you, right? How many silver coins bought my head on a platter?"

Laura said, "Mark's been a friend to me. He—"

"He used to be *my* friend, too." Didi glanced quickly at Laura and then away. Laura Clayborne's eyes were deep sockets, and they burned with a terrible intensity. "You screwed me, Mark. You sold me, and she bought me. Right? Well, here I am." Didi forced her head to turn, and she stared at Laura. "Mrs. Clayborne, I've killed people. I walked into a diner with three other Storm Fronters and shot four policemen who were guilty of nothing but wearing blue uniforms and badges. I helped plant a pipe bomb that blinded a fifteen-year-old girl. I cheered when Jack Gardiner cut a policeman's throat, and I helped lift up the corpse so Akitta Washington and Mary Terrell could nail his hands to a rafter. I'm the woman mothers warn their children not to grow up to be." Didi offered a chilly smile, the shadows of bare tree branches slicing her face. "Welcome to my house."

"Mark didn't want to bring me. I kept at him until he did."

"Is that supposed to make me feel better? Or safer?" She placed her fingertips together. "Mrs. Clayborne, you don't know anything about the world I live in. I've killed people, yes; that's my crime. But no judge or jury had to give me a prison sentence. Every day of my life since 1972 I've been looking over my shoulder, scared to death of what might be coming up behind. I sleep maybe three hours a night, on good nights. Sometimes I open my eyes in the dark and I've jammed myself into a closet without knowing it. I walk down the street and think a dozen people see through this face to who I used to be. And with every breath I take I know that I stole the life from fellow human beings. Snuffed them out, and celebrated their murders with hits of acid by candlelight." She nodded, her green eyes hazy with pain. "I didn't need a prison cell. I carry one around with me. So if you're going to turn me over to the police, I'll tell you this: they can't do anything to me. I'm not here. I'm dead, and I've been dead for a very long time."

"I'm not going to turn you over to the police," Laura said. "I just want to ask you some questions about Mary Terrell."

"Mary Terror," Didi corrected her. "It was"—she'd almost said *crazy*—"stupid of her to take your baby. Stupid."

"The FBI lost her after she visited her mother in Richmond. Her mother told them she was headed for Canada. Do you have any idea where she might have gone?"

Here was the question, Didi thought. She stared at her hands.

Laura glanced at Mark for support, but he shrugged and sat down on the couch. "Anything you can tell me about Mary Terrell might be important," she told Didi. "Can you think of anybody she might have gotten in touch with? Anybody from the past?"

"The *past.*" Didi sneered it. "There's no such place. There's just a long damned road from there to here, and you die a little more with every mile."

"Did Mary Terrell have any friends outside the Storm Front?"

"No. The Storm Front was her life. We were her family." Didi drew a deep breath and looked out the window again, expecting a police car to pull up at any minute. If that happened, she wasn't going to fight. Her fighting days were over. She directed her attention to Laura again. "You said you saw the man who broke into my house."

Laura explained about the glint of the flashlight she'd seen that night. "I came in, turned on the lights in the kitchen, and there he was. His face—" She shuddered to remember it. "His face was screwed up. He was grinning; his face was scarred, and the grin was frozen on it. Dark eyes, either dark brown or black. And he had a thing in his throat like an electric socket. Right here." She showed Didi by placing her fingers against her own throat.

"The dude across the road saw him, too," Mark added. "Said the guy had to plug a speaker into his throat and talk through it."

"Wait." Didi's inner alarm had reached a shriek. "The man went to see Mr. Brewer?"

"That's right. He asked where you'd gone. Said he was a friend of yours."

"He asked for me by name? Diane Daniells?" She hadn't returned the binoculars to Charles Brewer yet, so she hadn't heard this. When

Mark nodded, Didi felt as if she'd taken a punch to the stomach. "My God," she said, and stood up. "My God. Somebody else knows. You bastard, somebody must've followed you!"

"Hold on a minute! Nobody followed us. Anyway, the dude was asking about you before we even got to Ann Arbor."

Didi felt her control slipping away. The man who'd broken in hadn't taken anything. He'd known her new name, and where she lived. Had asked Mr. Brewer where she'd gone. She sensed it like a noose tightening around her neck: someone else knew who she was.

"Please try to think," Laura plowed on. "Is there anyone Mary Terrell might have gone to for help?"

"No!" Didi's face contorted, her nerves about to snap. "I said I can't help you! Get out and leave me alone!"

"I wish I could," Laura said. "I wish Mary Terrell hadn't taken my baby. I wish I knew if my son was alive or dead. I can't leave you alone because you're my last hope."

Didi put her hands to her ears. "No! I don't want to hear it!"

She knows something, Laura thought. She walked to Didi, grasped her wrists, and pulled her hands away from her ears. "You *will* hear it!" Laura promised, her cheeks aflame with anger. "Listen to me! If there's anything you know about Mary Terrell—anything—you've got to tell me! She's out of her mind, do you realize that? She could kill my child at any time, if she hasn't already!"

Didi shook her head. The image of Mary pressing the baby's face toward the burner was too close. "Please, just leave me alone. All I want is to be left alone."

"And all I want is what's mine," Laura said, still grasping Didi's wrists. They stared at each other, inhabitants of different worlds on a collision course. "Won't you help me save my child's life?"

"I . . . can't . . ." Didi began, but her voice faltered. She looked at Mark and then back to Laura, and she knew that if she didn't help this woman, the ghosts that feasted on her soul would grow sharper teeth. But she and Mary were sisters in arms! The Storm Front had been their family! She couldn't betray Mary!

But the Mary Terrell Didi had known long ago was gone. In her place was a savage animal who knew no cause but murder. Sooner or later Mary Terror would snap, and this woman's baby would die screaming.

Didi said, "Please let me go." Laura hesitated a few seconds, and then she released Didi's wrists. Didi walked to the window, where she stood looking out at the cold world. *Click, click:* her Rubik's Cube was turning, but the answer was already in sight. "She . . . calls the baby Drummer," Didi said. Her heart hurt. In the electric silence that followed, Didi could hear Laura Clayborne breathing. "I saw Mary and your baby yesterday."

"Oh Jesus." It was Mark speaking in a low, stunned voice.

"He was all right," Didi went on. "She's taking good care of him. But . . ." She trailed off, unable to say it.

A hand like an iron pincer grasped her shoulder. Didi looked into Laura's face, and caught a glimpse of hellfire. "But *what?*" Laura demanded, barely able to speak.

"But . . . Mary's dangerous. Dangerous to herself, dangerous to your baby."

"What's that mean? *Tell* me!"

"Mary said . . . if the police find them . . . she'll kill the baby first"—Didi saw Laura wince as if she'd been struck—"and then she'll keep shooting until the police kill her. She's not going to give up. Never."

Tears stung Laura's eyes. They were tears of relief, at knowing David was still alive, and tears of horror at knowing that what Bedelia Morse said was true.

The rest of it had to be told. Didi steeled herself, and continued. "Mary's coming here. She and Edward Fordyce. He was part of the Storm Front, too. They're on the way now, from New York. They should get here sometime tomorrow."

"Whoa," Mark whispered, his eyes wide behind his glasses. "Far out."

Laura felt off balance, as if the room had suddenly begun to slowly spin around her. "Why are they coming here?"

It seemed to Didi that once unleashed, betrayal was like a swarm of locusts. It kept consuming until everything was gone. "I'll show you," she said, and she took her key chain from its wall peg beside the front door.

Laura and Mark followed Didi out behind the cottage, to the stone structure which was Didi's workshop. She unsnapped the padlock, drew out the chain, and opened the door. A thick, earthy aroma wafted from the chill darkness. Didi switched on the overhead lights, revealing a neatly swept workshop with two pottery wheels, shelves of glaze and paint, and various clay-shaping tools in their places on a pegboard. Another shelf held examples of Didi's labors in various stages of completion: graceful vases and planters, dishware, mugs, and ashtrays. On the floor beside one of the wheels was a huge urn, its surface patterned to resemble treebark. Didi paused to turn on a space heater, and she said, "This is what I sell. Back there is what I make for myself." She nodded toward a drawn curtain at the rear of the workshop.

Didi walked to the curtain and drew it open. The cubicle behind it was covered with another series of shelves, and on them were works far different from what Didi sold under the name of Diane Daniells.

Laura saw a pottery head: the face of a young woman with long, flowing hair, her mouth open in a scream and a dozen snakes bursting from the top of her skull. She didn't recognize the face, but Mark did. It was what Didi used to look like, before the butchery. Another face, this one of a man, was splitting open down the center, and a more fearsome, demonic visage was beginning to push through. There was a disembodied clay hand holding a perfectly formed clay revolver, the hand's fingernails transformed into grinning skulls. On the floor was a large work: a woman—again, as Mark saw, the image of the young Bedelia Morse—on her knees, her arms lifted upward in supplication and roaches scurrying from her mouth. Mounted on a wall were what appeared to be death masks: faces without expression, marked by stitches, zippers, or jagged scars. They looked to Laura like silent sufferers, saints of a hellish world, and she realized she was peering into the depths of Didi Morse's nightmares.

Didi picked up something that was wrapped in black plastic. She brought it out to one of the wheels, where she carefully set it down and began to remove the plastic. It took her a minute or two, her touch reverent. And when she was done she stepped back, allowing Laura and Mark a full view.

It was the life-size model of a man's head. The face was handsome and thoughtful, like that of a prince caught in repose. The clay hadn't been glazed or painted, and there was no color at all on the model, but Didi's fingers had rippled the scalp into curls of hair. The nose was an elegant curve, the forehead high and sloping, the thin-lipped and rather cruel mouth seemingly just about to open. The eyes held a regal incuriosity, as if they judged everyone else a step beneath him. It was the face, Laura thought, of a man who knew the taste of power.

Didi touched the wheel, and spun it around. The head slowly rotated. "I modeled this from part of a face I saw in a picture," she said. "I finished the part the picture showed, and then I did the rest of it. Do you know who that is?"

"No," Laura replied.

"His name is—was—Jack Gardiner. Lord Jack, we called him."

"The Storm Front's leader?"

"That's right. He was our father, our brother, our protector. And our Satan." The wheel was stopping. Didi spun it again. "The things we did for him . . . are unspeakable. He played our souls like violins, and made us obey like trained animals. But he was smart, and he had eyes that you thought could see every secret you ever tried to hide. Jack Gardiner made Mary Terrell pregnant. She was going to have the baby in July 1972. Then the world crashed in on us." Didi lifted her gaze to Laura. "Mary lost the baby. Delivered it dead in a gas station bathroom. So she's taking Drummer—your baby—to Lord Jack."

"What?" It was a gasp.

Didi told them about the message in *Mother Jones,* and that Mary had seen it in *Rolling Stone.* "She thought Jack was waiting for her. She took your baby to give him. But Edward Fordyce placed the message because he's trying to write a book about the Storm Front and he wanted to see who'd show up. So now Mary and Edward are on their way here." She had come to the secret thing again. Loyalty writhed within her, like a snake in hot ashes. But to whom was she being loyal? A dead ideal of freedom? An ideal that was never really true in the first place? She felt as if she'd been on a long, grueling journey, and she'd abruptly come to a crossroads of decision. One road led the way she'd been going: straight ahead, across a land of nightmares and old griefs come a-haunting. The new road faced a wilderness, and what lay beyond it no one could know.

Both roads were treacherous. Both roads glistened with blood, under a darkening sky. The question was: which road might lead to the saving of that infant's life?

Didi stared at the clay face of the man she had once adored, in her youth, and grown to hate in her ancient days. She decided on the road to take. "I . . . think Jack Gardiner is in California. That's where Mary and Edward'll be going after they leave here." The snake within her crunched itself into a tight coil, and expired with a final shudder in the embers. Didi almost cried, but she did not; yesterday was gone, and no tears could revive its clock of hours. "That's it," Didi said. "What now? Are you going to call the police?"

"No. I'm going to meet Mary when she gets here."

Mark's jaw would have dropped to the floor had it not been jointed to his face. "Uh-uh!" he said. "No way!"

"I'm not going to just let her breeze through here!" Laura snapped. "I don't want the police in this. If Mary Terror sees the police, my baby is as good as dead. So what choice do I have?"

"She'll kill you," Didi said. "She's packing at least two pistols, and maybe something else I haven't seen. She won't hesitate for a second before she blows you away."

"I'll have to take that chance."

"You won't *get* a chance. Don't you understand? You can't take her on!"

"You don't understand," Laura said firmly. "There's no other way."

Didi was about to protest again, but what could she say? The woman was right. She would be killed in a face-to-face encounter with Mary Terror, of that Didi had no doubt. But what other chance would she have? "You're crazy," Didi said.

"Yes, I am," Laura answered. "I wouldn't be standing here if I weren't. If I have to be as crazy as Mary Terror, then so be it."

"Sure." Mark grunted. "The only difference is, you've never killed anybody."

Laura ignored him, and kept her attention on Bedelia Morse. There was no retreating now, no calling for Doug to help her or the police to bring their eager snipers. Her mouth was dry at the prospect of impending violence, and the thought that the violence could easily catch David in its storm. "I've got to ask you for one more thing. That you'll let me know when Mary gets here."

"I don't want your blood on my walls."

"How about my child's blood on your hands? Do you want that?"

Didi drew a long breath and let it out. "No. I don't."

"Then you'll let me know?"

"I won't be able to stop her from killing you," Didi said.

"Okay. You won't have to cry at my funeral. Will you let me know?"

Didi hesitated. She had murdered people who didn't want to die. Now she was going to be helping murder someone who was begging for death. But once Mary left for California, any chance—however slim—of getting the baby back alive would be gone. Didi kept her gaze downcast, but she could feel the hot intensity of Laura's eyes on her. "They're supposed to call me when they get to Ann Arbor," she said at last. "I told Mary I'd give her directions to the house. God help me . . . but I'll call you when I hear from them."

"We're at the Days Inn. I'm in Room 119 and Mark's in Room 112. I'll be waiting by the phone."

"You mean waiting by your gravestone, don't you?"

"Maybe. But don't shovel the dirt on me yet."

Didi lifted her gaze and looked at Laura. She knew faces, and faces intrigued her. This woman's features said she'd lived a soft, pampered life, a life of comparative wealth and ease. But the pain she'd endured was showing, in the dark hollows under her eyes, the lines on her forehead, and at the corners of her grim-lipped mouth. There was something else in her face, too, something that was newly born: it might be called hope. Didi recognized Laura as a fighter, a survivor who wasn't afraid of overwhelming odds. That was how Didi herself used to be, a long time ago before the Storm Front had twisted and shaped her into a vessel of agony. Didi said, "I'll let you know." Four words: how easily a death warrant was signed.

They walked around the cottage to Laura's car, and Didi saw the *Go home* carved into the windshield's glass. She was going to take the binoculars back to Mr. Brewer, and get a full description of the man who'd been asking for her. That was the kind of thing that five years ago would have made her instantly pack a suitcase and hit the road. Now, though, she knew the truth: there was nowhere to hide forever, and old debts always came due.

Mark, muttering his discontent, got into the car. Before Laura did, she fixed Didi with a hard stare. "My son's name is David," she said. "Not Drummer." And then she got into the BMW, started the engine, and drove away, leaving Bedelia Morse standing alone in the lengthening shadows.

5.

Roadchart Through Hades

The telephone began to ring at three thirty-nine on Tuesday morning. A cold fist squeezed Didi's heart. She stood up from her chair, where she'd been sitting under a lamp reading a book on advanced pottery techniques, and she went to the phone. She picked it up on the third ring. "Hello?"

"We made it," Mary Terror said.

They'd probably left New York the morning before and had been driving all day and night, Didi figured. Mary was wasting no time in getting nearer to Jack. "Edward's with you?"

"Yeah. He's right here."

"Where are you?"

"A pay phone at a Shell station on—" Mary paused, and Didi heard Edward say "Huron Parkway" in the background. The sound of a baby crying came through the receiver. Mary said, "Rub behind his left ear, he likes that," instructions to Edward. Then she spoke into the phone again. "Huron Parkway."

Didi began to give Mary directions to her cottage. She could hear the nervousness in her voice, and she tried to speak slowly but it didn't help. "You all right?" Mary interrupted suddenly. *She knows,* Didi thought. But of course that couldn't be. "You woke me up," Didi said. "I had a bad dream."

The baby continued to cry, and Mary snapped, "Here, damn it! Give him to me and you take the phone!" When Edward was on the line, sounding exhausted, Didi repeated the directions. "Okay," he said through a yawn. "Turn right at the second light?"

"No. Right at the third light. Then right again at the second light and the road will veer to the left."

"Got it. I think. You ever try to drive a van with a kid screaming in your ear? And every time I tried to push it up past sixty-five Mary jumped my case. Jesus, I'm beat!"

"You can rest here," Didi told him.

"Let's go, let's go!" Mary said in the background. The child had stopped crying.

"Stone house on the right," Edward said. "See you soon."

"See you," Didi replied, and she hung up.

The silence shrieked.

Didi had given them the long route. They would be here in fifteen to twenty minutes if Edward didn't get them lost in his stuporous condition. Didi's hand hung over the telephone. The seconds were ticking past. The snake of loyalty had lifted its head from the ashes, and hissed a warning at her. This was the point of decision, and beyond it there was no turning back.

She sensed the ghosts gathering behind her. Sharpening their teeth on their wristbones, eager to gnaw into her skull. She had given her word. In a world of deceits, wasn't that the only true thing left?

Didi picked up the phone. She dialed the number she'd already looked up in the Yellow Pages, and she asked the clerk for Room 119.

Two rings. Then Laura's voice, instantly alert: "I'm ready."

Laura was still wearing her jeans and cable-knit sweater, and she'd slept for a few periods of about fifteen minutes each before the imagined sound of the phone had jarred her awake. She listened to what Didi had to tell her, then she hung up and went to the closet. From the top shelf she took the .32 Charter Arms automatic Doug had bought. She pushed a clip of seven bullets into its magazine and smacked it shut with her palm. It hurt her hand. She worked the safety back and forth, getting a feel for the loaded weapon. The gun was still oily-smelling, still evil in appearance; but now she needed its weight and power, and whether she had to use it or not, it was a worthy talisman. She slid it down into her purse. Then she put on her overcoat and buttoned it up against the cold. Nausea suddenly pulsed in her stomach. She rushed into the bathroom and waited, but nothing came up. Her face was hot, sparkles of sweat on her cheeks. Now would not be the time to faint. When she was reasonably certain she was neither going to throw up or pass out, she went back to the closet and put an additional clip of bullets into her purse, adding to the talisman's strength.

She was, as Stephen Stills had told the crowd at Woodstock, scared shitless.

Laura left her room, her purse over her shoulder. The chill air hit her, a welcoming blow. She walked to Mark's room, and she balled up her fist to knock on the door.

She stood there, fist balled up, and she thought of Rose Treggs and the two children. The wind moved around her; in it she imagined she heard the noise of chimes, calling Mark home. She had paid him his three thousand dollars. He had brought her to Bedelia Morse. Their agreement had been kept, and she would not take Mark any further into what lay ahead. She lowered her fist and opened it.

The world needed more writers who didn't give a damn about best seller lists, and who wrote with their heart's blood.

Laura silently wished him well. And then she turned away from Mark's door and walked to her car.

She drove away from the Days Inn and turned in the direction of Didi's house, her hands clenched hard on the wheel and the mice of fear scuttling in her belly.

Four miles west of Ann Arbor, Didi sat in her chair in the front room, the lamp's light glinting on the gray hairs amid the red. She was waiting for whom fate would bring first to her door. Her mind was resting, the Rubik's Cube finished. She had chosen her road, and the snake was dead.

She saw headlights through the trees.

Didi stood up on weightless legs. Her pulse had begun to knock, like Death's fist on a bolted door. The headlights came up the driveway, and behind their white cones was a battered olive-green van. It stopped near the front door with a little *skreek* of worn brakes. Didi felt her teeth digging into her lower lip. She went outside in her faded denims and her comfortable gray sweater with brown leather patches on the elbows. It was her working outfit; her jeans were blotched with paint, and flecks of clay clung to her sweater. She watched Mary get out of the van's passenger side, carrying the baby in a bassinet. Edward, a weary man, pulled himself from behind the wheel. "Found it!" Edward said. "I didn't do so badly, huh?"

"Come in," Didi offered, and she stepped back to let them enter. As Mary passed her, Didi smelled her unwashed, animalish odor. Edward staggered in, stripped off his down parka, and flopped onto the couch. "Man!" he said, his falsely blue eyes dazed. "My ass is *dead!*"

"I'll make some coffee," Didi said, and she walked back to the reassembled kitchen, where newspaper was taped up over the door's missing pane.

"Gotta change Drummer," Mary told her. She put the baby on the floor and lifted out the Magnum pistol from her shoulder bag, then retrieved a Handi Wipe and a Pampers diaper. The baby was restless, arms and legs in motion, face squalling up for a cry but no cry forthcoming.

"Cute little rug rat, isn't he?" Edward leaned back on the couch, kicked his shiny loafers off, and put his feet up. "I can say that now that he's not yelling in my ear."

"He's a good baby. Mama's good baby, yes he is."

Edward watched Mary change Drummer's diaper as Didi poured water into the Mr. Coffee machine. It was clear to him that Mary was nuts about the baby. When she'd called him yesterday morning at seven o'clock and told him they were driving to Ann Arbor, he'd said she had a screw loose. He wasn't planning on driving to Michigan in the company of a woman who had an FBI target painted on her back, no matter if she was a sister or not. But then she'd told him about Jack Gardiner, and that had put a new slant on his thinking. If it was true that Jack *was* in California, and Didi could lead them to him, his book on the Storm Front could have no better selling point than an interview with Lord Jack himself. Of course, he didn't know how Jack would feel about it, but Mary seemed to think it was a good idea.

She'd said she was wrong in jumping him about the book, that she'd let her first emotions get away from her. It would be good, she'd told him, to let the world know that the Storm Front still lived on. Edward was thinking more of *People* magazine coverage than making a political statement, but Mary had even promised to help him talk Jack into an interview. *If* Didi was right, and *if* Jack was in California. Two big ifs. But it was worth taking a few sick days off at Sea King to find out.

Mary took the soiled diaper into the kitchen, searching for a garbage can, and there she found Didi staring out a window toward the road. "What're you looking at?"

Didi kept herself from jumping by sheer willpower. "Nothing," she said. "I'm waiting for the coffee." She'd seen a car go slowly past and out of sight.

"Forget the coffee. I want to know about Jack." Mary stood beside Didi and glanced out the window. Nothing but dark. Still, Didi was nervous. It was in her voice, and Didi wasn't making eye contact. Mary's radar went up. "Show me," she said.

Didi left the coffee to brew, and she got the photo album from the bedroom. When she returned to the front room, Mary was sitting in a chair with the baby in her arms and Edward was still stretched out on the couch. The shoulder bag was beside Mary, the compact Magnum on top of the mélange of formula, Pampers, Handi Wipes, and baby toys. "Here it is." Didi showed the article and picture to Mary, and Edward struggled up from the couch to take a look.

"Right there." Didi touched the image of the man's face.

Mary studied the picture. "That's not Jack," Edward decided after a minute or two. "That guy's nose is too big."

"People's noses get larger as they age," Didi told him.

Edward looked again. He shook his head, partly disappointed and partly relieved that he didn't have to travel any farther with Mary Terror. "No. It's not Jack."

Didi turned the plastic-covered pages backward. Like a time machine, the dates on the articles regressed. She stopped at a photograph of a young, arrogantly smiling Jack Gardiner, resplendent in hippie robes and with long blond hair cascading around his shoulders. The article's headline said *Storm Front Leader Tops FBI Wanted List* and the date was July 7, 1972. "Then," Didi said, and she paged forward to the Sierra Club story, "and now. Can't you see the resemblance?"

Edward flipped ahead to the newer picture, then back to the old one again. Mary simply sat holding the baby, her eyes dark and unfathomable. "Okay, so he looks a little like Jack," Edward said. *"Maybe.* It's hard to tell." He looked closer. "No, I don't think so."

"Hold Drummer." Mary offered him to Edward, and Edward took the baby with a trace of a scowl. Then Mary held the photo album and began to turn back and forth between the two photographs. She stopped at an article on another page. "Shit," she said softly. "The son of a bitch lived."

"What?" Didi peered over her shoulder.

"The son-of-a-bitch pig I shot outside the house that night." Mary tapped the plastic sheet over the newspaper story, which had the headline *FBI Agent Survives Attack.* There was a picture of a man on a stretcher, an oxygen mask to his face, being loaded into an ambulance. "Remember him, Edward?"

Edward looked. "Oh, yeah. I thought you'd wasted him."

"So did I. A throat shot usually does it."

Didi felt frost in her veins. "A . . . throat shot?"

"Right. I hit him twice. Once in the face, once in the throat. I would've blown his fucking brains out, but I didn't have another bullet. Edward, it says his name was Earl Van Diver. Thirty-four years old, from Bridgewater, New Jersey. A wife and a daughter." She laughed quietly, a terrible laugh. "Get this: his daughter's name is Mary."

Didi was reading the story, too. She'd forgotten about clipping this from the Philadelphia newspaper several days after the shootout in Linden. She had saved everything she could find about the Storm Front: her own book of memories, like a roadchart through Hades. Earl Van Diver. Off the critical list, the story said. Severe facial and larynx damage.

Oh my God, Didi thought.

"I remember him," Mary said. "I bet he remembers me, too." She turned ahead to the Sierra Club newsletter's article and picture. She'd thought this would be easy, that she would recognize Jack at once, but this photo showed only a portion of a blond man's face. She read the men's names in the story: Dean Walker, Nick Hudley, Keith Cavanaugh. None of those held any significance for her, no magic weavings. Her heart had become leaden. Drummer started to give a mewling cry, and the sound made her head ache. "I can't tell," she said.

Didi took the album from her. Where were Laura and Mark? They should've been here by now! Her stomach was a solid knot of tension. "Come see what I've made," she offered. "Then tell me what you think."

In the workshop, with the overhead bulbs on, Mary circled the clay head that still sat on the pottery wheel. Didi laid the photo album down beside it, opened to the picture. The baby's crying had gotten louder, and Edward was doing his best to shush him. Mary stopped, staring at the face of Lord Jack.

"I made it from the picture," Didi said. A nervous quaver had crept into her voice again. "It looks like Jack. Older, I know. But I think it's him."

The lead had cracked and fallen away from Mary's heart. It had become a bird, flying toward the sun. It *was* Jack. Older, yes. But still handsome, still regal. She lifted the plastic sheet up from the photo album and took out the article and picture. Could it be? After all these years? Could it really be that Lord Jack was in Freestone, California, and this photographer had caught a slice of his face? She wanted to believe it in the most desperate way.

The baby's crying was strident, a demand for attention. Edward rocked him, but he wouldn't stop. Didi's nerves were about to shred. "Give him to me," she said, and Edward did. She rocked him, too, as Mary kept looking from the picture to the clay face again. The baby, bundled up in a downy white blanket, was warm in her arms, and she smelled the aromas of formula and pink baby flesh. "Shhhh," she said. "Shhhh." His blue eyes blinked up at her. "That's a good boy. David's a good ba—"

It was gone. Could not be recaptured. Gone through the air, and into Mary Terror's ears.

Though the workshop was chilly, Didi felt pinpricks of sweat rise on the back of her neck. Mary circled the clay head once more as she folded the newsletter's article into a little square. She put it into a pocket of her brown corduroys. When she looked up at Didi again, Mary was smiling thinly but her eyes were as dangerous as gun barrels. "My baby's name is Drummer. You knew that. Why did you call him David?"

There was nothing to be said. Mary came toward her with a smile like a razor. "Didi? Give Drummer back to me, please."

Standing outside the workshop's door, Laura heard Mary Terror step on a shard of clay that cracked beneath her shoe. Her heartbeat was thunderous, her face tight with fear. In her right hand was the Charter Arms automatic, its safety off. It was now or never, she thought. God help me. She stepped into the corridor of light that spilled from the doorway, and she aimed the gun at the hulking woman who had stolen her child. *"No,"* she heard herself rasp in a stranger's voice.

Mary saw her. It took maybe four seconds for the face to register. Mary's mind worked like a rat caught in a closing trap. She had left her shoulder bag and the Magnum in the house. Her Colt was up under the driver's seat in the van. But she still had two weapons.

Mary reached out with one arm, hooked Bedelia Morse's throat, and jerked her around between herself and Laura's pistol. Then she clamped her other hand firmly over the baby's mouth and nose, cutting off his air. The baby began struggling to breathe.

"Finger off the trigger," Mary commanded. "Point the gun down."

6.

Light Hurts

Laura didn't. Her hand trembled, and so did the gun. David's face was blotching with red, his hands clawing at the air.

"He'll smother in a few seconds. Then I'll come at you, and you don't know shit about killing anybody."

Rage thrashed within Laura. The woman's big hand was clenched tight over David's nostrils and mouth. Laura could see his eyes, wide with panic. Didi couldn't move, her own throat squeezed by Mary's other arm. Edward said, "Wait a minute. Wait," but who he was babbling to wasn't clear.

"Finger off the trigger," Mary repeated, her voice eerily calm. "Point the gun down."

Laura had no choice. She obeyed.

"Take the gun, Edward." He hesitated. *"Edward!"* Mary's voice snapped out like a whip. "Take the gun!"

He walked forward, grasped the automatic, and it was gone from Laura's hand. Their eyes met. "I'm sorry," he said. "I didn't know—"

"Shut up, Edward." Mary removed her hand from the baby's face. His mouth gasped, and then a shriek welled up out of it that almost destroyed the last of Laura's sanity. "Bring the gun to me," Mary said.

"Listen. We don't have to—"

"BRING IT TO ME!"

"Okay, okay!" He delivered the pistol to Mary's hand, and she placed the barrel against Didi's red-haired skull and took the child away from her with one arm. The shrieking went on as Mary backed away from Didi and turned the gun on Laura. "Who's with you?"

She almost said *the police.* No, no; Mary would kill David for sure. "No one."

"Liar! Are the pigs out there?"

"Would I be in here if they were?" Laura wasn't afraid anymore. Her fear had steamed away. There was no time to be scared, her mind occupied with trying to think of a way to get David.

Mary said, "Stand against the wall. Didi, you with her. Move, you bitch!"

Didi took her place beside Laura, her face downcast and tears on her cheeks. She was waiting for the execution bullet. Laura would not look away from Mary Terror. She stared at the woman, fixing the hard-jawed, brutal face forever in her mind.

"Edward, go to the house and get my bag and the bassinet. Take them to the van. We're clearing out." Edward did as he was told. The child continued to cry, but Mary's attention was riveted to the two women. "Damn you to hell," she said to Didi. "You betrayed me."

"Mary . . . please listen." Her voice was husky from the pressure of Mary's arm on her windpipe. "Let the baby go. He doesn't belong to—"

"He's mine! Mine and Jack's!" Splotches of red surfaced on Mary's cheeks, her eyes aflame. "I *trusted* you! You were my sister!"

"I'm not who I used to be. I want to help you, Mary. Please leave David here."

"HIS NAME IS DRUMMER!" Mary shouted. The gun remained steady, aimed somewhere between Laura and Didi.

"His name is David," Laura said. "David Clayborne. No matter what you call him, you know what his real name is."

Mary suddenly grinned. It was a savage grin, and she stalked across the workshop and stopped with the automatic almost touching the tip of Laura's nose. It took everything Laura had not to reach for David, but she kept her arms at her sides and her gaze locked with Mary's. "Brave," Mary said. "Brave piece of shit. I'm going to flush you. Flush you right down the dark hole. Think you'll like that?"

"I think . . . you're nothing but a lie. You've got a baby who's not yours. You're looking for a man who's forgotten about you." Laura saw Mary's hatred flare, like napalm bomb blasts. She kept going, deeper into the fire. "You don't stand for anything, and you don't believe in anything. And the worst lie is the one you tell yourself, that when you take David to Jack Gardiner, you'll be young again."

Mary could not stand Jack's name coming from this woman's mouth. In a blur of motion, she hit Laura across the face with the automatic's barrel. There was a crunching noise and Laura fell to her knees, her head throbbing with pain. Blood pattered to the floor from her nostrils, her nose almost broken. A blue-edged welt had appeared across her cheek. Laura made no sound, dark motes spinning before her eyes.

"Get her up," Mary told Didi. "We've got business to finish."

Mary herded them out of the workshop, Laura staggering and Didi holding her up. Edward was waiting at the van. She gave him the automatic and then took her Colt from under the driver's seat. "Walk into the woods," Mary said, cradling Drummer with one arm. "Away from the road. Go."

"Maybe you could just lock them up somewhere," Edward said as they walked. "You know? Lock them up and leave them."

Mary didn't answer. They walked on, through the oak and pine woods, leaves and sticks cracking underfoot. "You don't have to kill them," Edward tried again, his breath white in the frosty air. "Mary, do you hear me?"

She did, but did not answer. When they'd gotten about a hundred yards from the cottage, Mary said, "Stop." Her eyes were used to the dark now. She ripped Laura's purse off her shoulder, planning on searching it for cash and taking the credit cards. "Face me," she told the two women, and she stepped back a few paces.

"Please . . . don't do it," Didi begged.

Click. Mary had pulled the Colt's hammer back. The baby was silent, little plumes of white leaving his nostrils.

"Mary, don't," Edward said, standing beside her. "Don't, okay?"

"Any last words?" Mary asked.

Laura spoke, the side of her face swelling up. "Rot in hell."

"Good enough." Mary aimed the pistol at Laura's head, her finger on the trigger. Two squeezes, and there would be two less mindfuckers in the world.

She started to pull the trigger.

There was a shot: a quick *pop!* that echoed through the woods.

Edward staggered into her, hit her arm, and the Colt went off with a harsher *crack,* the bullet going into the trees over Laura's head. Something warm and wet had sprayed into Mary's face, all over her shoulder, and onto the baby. The white blanket was mottled with dark clots. She looked at Edward, and could tell that a sizable piece of his head was gone, steam swirling into the air from his oozing brains.

"Oh," Edward's mouth gasped, his face a blood mask. "Light hurts."

Another shot came. She saw the flare of fire off to her right in the woods. The bullet thunked into a treetrunk behind Mary and stung her scalp with pinebark. Edward was clinging to her arm. "Mama? Mama?" A sob left his dripping lips. "Eddie be good boy."

Mary shoved him aside. As she did, a third bullet exited Edward's chest in a hot spray, and she felt the slug pull at her sweater as it passed close to her back. Edward went down, gurgling like an overflowing drain. She dropped Laura's purse and squeezed off two shots toward the gun's flare, the Colt's noise making Drummer start screaming again. High-powered rifle, she thought. A pig gun. One sniper, at least. She turned away from Laura and Didi, and began racing back to the cottage with the baby trapped in her arm and Edward Fordyce's blood and brains on her face.

The rifle spoke again, clipping a branch less than six inches above Mary's head. She fired another shot, saw sparks fly as the bullet ricocheted off a rock. Then she was running for her life, slipping in the leaves and trailing the infant's scream behind her.

Someone shooting, Laura thought. Shooting at Mary Terror. David in her grasp. David in the path of the bullets. She, too, had seen the muzzle flash, saw it again as another bullet searched for Mary. Her gun. In Edward's hand. Laura took three strides forward and fell upon the twitching body, and she grasped the automatic and tore it free from Edward's fingers.

Then she stood up, aimed into the darkness where the sniper was, and pulled the trigger. The gun almost jumped out of her hand, its report cracking her eardrums. She kept shooting, a second bullet and a third, ripping the fabric of night. The other gun was silent. Over the buzz of pistol noise, Laura heard the roar of Mary Terror's van starting. "She's getting away!" Didi shouted. Car keys! Laura thought. She grasped her purse from the ground, and she began running toward the house.

Mary Terror threw the van into reverse and backed down the driveway, Drummer wailing in his bassinet on the floorboard. She saw it in her sideview mirror: a BMW parked on the road, blocking the driveway. She pressed her foot to the accelerator, and the van's rear end slammed against the BMW's passenger door, crumpling it in with a crash of metal and glass. The BMW trembled and groaned, but would not give way. Sweat was on her face, the taste of Edward's blood on her lips. She fought the gearshift into first, roared back up the driveway to try to knock the car aside again. The headlights caught Laura coming, gun in hand, followed by Bedelia Morse. No time to waste. Mary gritted her teeth, put the van into reverse again, and wheeled it off the driveway, knocking down thin pines and smashing one of Didi's abstract sculptures to rubble. The van scraped past the BMW's front fender, and Mary twisted the wheel to straighten the van out, hit the accelerator once more, and the van shot forward with a scream of rubber. She sped away, heading west.

Laura reached her car, saw the van's taillights in the distance—both the red lenses broken—before the vehicle took a curve and disappeared. She heard Didi breathing hard behind her, and she turned around and aimed the pistol into Didi's face. "Get in the car."

"What?"

"Get in the car!" She tried to open the rear door on the passenger side but the hinges were jammed. Laura grabbed Didi's arm and shoved her around to the other side, where she opened the driver's door. Didi balked, tried to fight free, but Laura put the gun's barrel up under Didi's jaw and all her resistance faded. When Didi was in, Laura slid under the wheel, fished her keys from her blood-spattered purse, and started the engine. Something rattled and skreeked under the hood, but the gauges showed no warning lights. Laura mashed down on the accelerator, and the battered car laid strips of rubber to match the van's.

The window on Didi's side was broken out, freezing wind shrieking into the car as the speedometer's needle passed sixty. Laura took the curve at sixty-five, skidding over into the left-hand lane. No taillights ahead, but another sharp curve lay in wait. Laura's foot didn't move toward the brake. She battled the car around the curve, went off onto the shoulder and almost into the woods before she got the car back up onto the road again. Laura glanced at the speedometer: the needle was moving past seventy. Didi was jammed back into her seat, her red hair flying in the wind, her face strained with terror in the dashboard's green glow.

A third curve almost threw the BMW into the trees, but Laura held tight to the shuddering steering wheel. Then there was a long straightaway ahead, and two white lights on it. Laura wiped her bleeding nose with her forearm and let the car wind up, the engine roaring and the speedometer showing eighty. But the van was going fast, too, black smoke billowing from its crumpled exhaust pipe. On both sides of the road the barren trees swept past in a dark blur. Laura got up close enough to read the numbers on the Georgia tag, and then the taillights flashed; Mary was cutting her speed, going into another wicked right-hand curve. Laura had to hit the brakes, too, and she faded back as the tires bit into the curve, wrenched them right, left, and then led them into another straightaway. Now Mary was standing on the accelerator, the van shooting forward with a fishtailing slipslide that made the breath freeze in Laura's lungs. If the van went off the road, David could be killed. She realized she couldn't ram the van, force it off onto the shoulder, or fire a bullet at a tire. Any of those things might cause Mary Terror to lose control of the wheel. A bullet aimed at a tire might go through the van's body, or hit the gas tank. David would die in the flaming wreckage as surely as by one of Mary Terror's bullets. Laura cut her speed, began to let the van pull away. The speedometer's needle dropped: through seventy-five . . . seventy . . . sixty-five . . . sixty. Mary kept the speed up at seventy and the van was moving away, dark smoke billowing behind. Laura saw a sign on the right: I-94, 6 MI.

The highway west, she thought.

The automatic's barrel pressed against Laura's right temple.

Didi had picked the gun up from beside her. "Stop the car," Didi said.

Laura kept driving, the speed now at a constant sixty.

"Stop the car!" Didi repeated. "I'm getting out!"

Laura didn't answer, her attention focused on the road and the van ahead. Mary Terror would take the interstate because it was the fastest route to California.

"I SAID STOP THE CAR!" Didi shouted over the wind's racket.

"No," Laura said.

Didi sat there, stunned and helpless with the gun in her hand.

Laura's nostrils were jamming up with blood. She blew her nose into her hand, enduring a savage pain that shot through her cheekbones, and then she wiped the scarlet mess onto her jeans. "I'm not going to lose Mary."

Didi's emotions ripped like a ragged flag. "I'LL KILL YOU IF YOU DON'T STOP THE CAR!" she screamed. "I'LL BLOW YOUR DAMNED BRAINS OUT!"

Laura didn't let up on the pedal. "You're not a killer anymore," she said without even glancing in Didi's direction. "That's all over. Besides, do you want to go back to your house and try to explain to the police why Edward Fordyce is lying dead in the woods?"

"Stop the car, I said." Didi's voice was weaker.

"Where are you going to go if I do?"

"I'll find somewhere! Don't you worry about me!"

Laura's head was pounding fiercely, the blood beginning to thicken in her nostrils. She had to breathe through her mouth to get any air. Bitch knocked the shit out of me, she thought. "I need you," she said.

"I've already ruined my life for you!"

"Then you don't have anything else to lose. I need you to help me get my baby back. I'm going to keep following Mary Terror all the way to California. All the way to hell if I have to."

"You're crazy! She'll kill the kid before she'll let you take him!"

"We'll see about that," Laura said.

Didi was about to demand to be let out again when a pair of headlights blazed in the rearview mirror. Didi looked back, saw a car gaining fast on them. "Christ!" she said. "I think it's the cops!" She lowered the gun from Laura's temple.

Laura watched the car coming. The damned thing was absolutely flying, doing over eighty. No siren or blue lights yet, but Laura's heart had jammed in her throat. She didn't know what to do: hit the accelerator or the brakes? And then the car was upon them, its headlights glowing like white suns in the rearview mirror. Laura jinked the BMW to the right as the car veered alongside them and screamed past. It was a big, dark blue or black Buick, maybe six or seven years old but immaculate, and the winds of its passage almost whirled the BMW off the road. The Buick tore on, swerved into the lane ahead of Laura, and kept going. It had a Michigan tag and a sticker that said WHEN GUNS ARE OUTLAWED, ONLY OUTLAWS WILL HAVE GUNS on the rear bumper.

In the van, Mary Terror saw the new arrival coming. Drummer was still crying, his bassinet having overturned on one of the curves. Pigs, she thought. Here come the fucking pigs. Edward's blood was sticky on her face, bits of his skull and brains spattered on her clothes. She cocked her Colt and rolled down her window, and she eased up on the accelerator as the big car left its lane and started to pull around her.

"Come on," she said into the wind. "Come on, little piggie!"

The car pulled up alongside her and hung there, both of them doing about seventy on the backwoods road. Mary saw no police or FBI markings, and she couldn't see the driver's face either. But suddenly the car whipped to the right, and there was a crash of metal as it slammed against the van. The wheel shuddered. Mary shouted a curse and the van veered toward the right shoulder. She fought its weight, the dark woods reaching out to embrace her and Drummer. Mary got the van back up onto the road again, and again the big car slammed into her side, trying to butt her off the pavement like an enraged bull. The car hit her a third time, and sparks flew into the air as pieces of metal ground together. The van was shoved sideways, the wheel trying to tear itself out of Mary's grip. She looked to her left, saw the passenger's window going down, a smooth electric slide. The car pulled up, its driver almost even with her. There was a loud *crack,* a flare of fire, and something metal clattered in the back of the van.

Bullet, Mary realized. Handgun. Son of a bitch was shooting at her.

It dawned on her, quite suddenly, that whoever was in the big Buick was the bastard who'd killed Edward. This wasn't exactly pig procedure. The fucker was trying to kill her, that much was certain.

She hit the accelerator again, whipping past a sign that read I-94, 2 MI. The Buick stayed abreast. Another *crack* and fire flare, and she heard the whine of the slug ricocheting inside the van. The Buick remained with her, touching eighty miles an hour. Mary held on to the wheel with one hand and fired a shot at the car. The bullet didn't hit, but the Buick backed off a few yards. Then it lunged forward and crashed into the van's side again, shoving the van toward the shoulder. Mary fired once more, trying to hit the Buick's engine. The van's tires slipped on loose gravel, the vehicle's rear end fishtailing. Two seconds passed in which Mary thought the van was going over, but then the tires found pavement again and the scream died behind Mary's teeth. The Buick, its right side battered and scraped, started to pull up even with her. Mary's foot was already on the floor, the van at the limit of its power. The Buick was coming, its long, scarred snout easing up. Mary dropped the Colt, reached into her shoulder bag, and brought out the Compact Magnum.

Before she could get off a shot, the BMW that had come up from behind veered into the left lane and slammed into the Buick's rear fender. The collision jarred the finger that was squeezing a pistol's trigger, and the bullet whacked into the van's side seven inches behind Mary Terror's skull.

Mary fired downward with the Magnum, the noise explosive and the kick thrumming through her forearm and shoulder. The Buick's right front tire popped, and as the driver stomped on the brake Laura jerked the BMW's wheel to the right and cleared the Buick by half a foot, pulling her front fender right up behind the speeding van. The Buick, its tire shredding to pieces, went across the left lane and down a knoll into a copse of trees and bushes.

"Back off! Back off!" Didi was shouting, and Laura hit her brakes just as Mary did the same. Fenders clanged together like swords. Laura veered to the left, saw the interstate's ramp just ahead. And then Mary Terror was swinging the van up onto it, black smoke gouting from the exhaust. I-94 WEST, the sign said. Mary swerved off the ramp onto the highway, reached down, and righted Drummer's bassinet. He was still wailing, but he would have to cry himself out. She glanced into the rearview mirror, saw the BMW about fifty yards behind, cutting its speed. She cut hers, too, down to about sixty. Whoever was in the Buick would have to change the tire, and by that time she'd be long gone.

But Laura Clayborne was in the car behind her. Maybe Bedelia was with her. Traitor, she thought. A bullet wasn't enough for her; she should be slit open and gutted for the crows, like the lowest kind of roadkill.

The BMW kept its distance. Mary returned the Magnum to her

shoulder bag. She was trembling, but she'd shake it off soon enough. At this time of the morning the interstate was almost empty, just a few trucks hauling freight. Mary began to relax, but her gaze kept ticking to the BMW's headlights. Should've blown out the tires when I had the chance, she thought. Why didn't the bitch bring the pigs with her? Why had she come alone? Stupid, that's why. Stupid and weak.

"What are you going to do?" she asked the headlights. "Follow me to California?" She laughed: a harsh, nervous bark.

"Earl Van Diver is his name," Didi was saying to Laura. "An FBI agent. Mary shot him in the throat in 1972, at the shootout in Linden. I think he found out who I am, but he doesn't want me." She nodded toward the van. "He wants Mary."

Laura had turned the heat up to high, but the BMW's interior was still uncomfortably cold, the wind shrieking in around them. There was nothing else left to do. Nothing except to keep that van with the broken taillights in sight. Sooner or later Mary would have to stop to get gas. She would get sleepy, hungry, and thirsty. She would have to pull off, sooner or later. And when that happened . . . what then?

Laura checked her own gas gauge. A little less than half a tank. If she had to stop first, Mary would pull on out of sight. She might turn off the interstate, try to hide until she was sure Laura couldn't find her again. But Mary was interested in only one direction, and one destination. Between here and there was over two thousand miles, and who knew what might happen in that terrible distance?

"I want out," Didi said. "I'm not going with you."

Laura was silent, her nose clogged with dried blood and her injured cheek turning blue-black.

"I swear to God!" Didi told her. "I'm not going with you!"

Laura didn't answer. She had watched a human being be murdered this morning. His blood was all over her purse, and the smell of death was in the car. She felt the horror of what she'd seen start to consume her mind, take her away from the task she had set for herself, and she did the only thing she could: she just stopped thinking about Edward Fordyce, and thrust the memory of his writhing body back to a place from where it couldn't easily be summoned. She had to think about one thing and one thing only: David, in the van fifty or sixty yards ahead. Mary Terror at the wheel. Armed and dangerous. Two thousand miles between her and a man who might or might not be Jack Gardiner.

"I want out! First gas station!"

They passed one in a few minutes. It was all lit up.

The van kept going, its speed constant at sixty-five.

Didi was quiet. She put her hands to her ears, to shut out the wind's scream.

You'll stop somewhere, Laura thought. *Maybe ten miles. Maybe fifty. But you'll stop, and when you do I'll be right there behind you.*

She glanced at the automatic lying on the seat where Didi had put it down. The grip had a dried smear of scarlet on it. Then she returned her attention to the broken taillights, and she brushed aside the nagging question of how she could possibly get David away from Mary Terror without the woman putting a bullet through his head.

Laura almost cried, but she held back the tears. Her face felt like leather stretched over hot iron. Tears wouldn't help the pain, and they wouldn't help get David back alive. She didn't need her eyes swollen up, that was for sure.

"You're crazy," Didi said. A last shot: "Going to get us both killed and the baby, too."

There was no reply from Laura, but the comment had worked itself in like a thorn. Laura concentrated on keeping a steady fifty yards or so behind the van. No need to spook Mary. Just make her feel nice and comfortable up there in her van with her two guns and the child she called Drummer.

He was going to grow up as David. Laura vowed it, over her dead body.

The van and the BMW, both dented and battered from their first encounter, headed west on the quiet interstate. Mary Terror checked her gas gauge and kept glancing back at Laura's car, marking its position. As Drummer's crying dwindled, Mary began to sing "Light My Fire" in a low, wandering voice.

Follow me, she was thinking. Her gaze ticked to the BMW's headlights again. *That's right. Follow me so I can kill you.*

The van and the car passed on. Back at the entrance ramp about thirty minutes later, Earl Van Diver tightened the last lug nut and released the air from the inflatable jack. He was wearing a black woolen cap and a jump suit in camouflage green and brown, his pallid, bony face scratched by foliage. He returned his tools to their proper niches in his trunk, where the sniper's rifle and boxes of ammunition were stored along with his SuperSnooper listening dish and tape recorder. He removed a palm-size black box from the trunk, which he mounted with adhesive pads on the underside of the dashboard. Then he plugged a connection into the cigarette lighter, started the engine, and turned a switch on the black box. A little blue light pulsed, but no numerals showed up yet on the display. On his rear windshield was an antenna that resembled that of a cellular phone, but was for a different purpose. Van Diver made another connection, the antenna's jack into the black box. Still no numerals. That was all right. The magnetic homing device he'd planted in the right front wheel well of Mary Terror's van wouldn't pick up on the display until he was within about four miles. It had been a precaution, for such a case as this.

Beneath his seat was a hiding place where his Browning automatic pistol could slide in and out. It would be used well before he was finished with Mary Terror.

And if the other two women got in the way, they were dead meat, too.

Earl Van Diver backed the Buick up the embankment to the road and then drove onto the interstate's ramp. West to California, he thought. Looking for Jack Gardiner. It was all on the tape, their voices caught by the SuperSnooper dish and the wireless amplification bug he'd planted inside a pottery vase in Bedelia Morse's front room. Going to California, the land of nuts and fruits.

It was a good place to kill a nightmare.

The Buick's speed hung between seventy and seventy-five, the pavement singing beneath the new tire. Van Diver, an executioner on a mission long awaited, hurtled toward his target.

VI
On the Storm

1.

Happy Herman's

The sun was coming up, into a pewter sky. The warning light on the BMW's gas gauge had begun blinking. Laura tried not to pay any attention to it—tried to will it begone—but the light kept snagging her eye.

"Low on gas," Didi said over the wind's scream.

The heater was purring merrily, warming their feet and legs while they froze from the waist up. The positive side of this, though, was that neither Laura nor Didi could be lulled to sleep with the cold and the wind singing them a banshee symphony. Didi kept her hands in her pockets, but every so often Laura had to unclench one hand from the steering wheel, flex the blood back into it, put it back where it was and do the same to the other. Ahead of them, between fifty and sixty yards away, was the olive-green van, its left side scraped to the bare metal and the rear looking like a sledgehammer had been taken to it. Traffic had picked up on the interstate: more trucks, zooming past in defiance of the legal limit. Twenty minutes or so before, Laura had seen a patrol car speed past on the other side of the median, blue lights flashing. She wondered if the sight had given Mary Terror as much of a start as it had herself. Beyond Mary's van, the sky was still dark and ominous, as if night refused to recede from the shore of dawn.

"Gas is almost gone," Didi said. "Hear me?"

"I hear you."

"Well, what're you going to do? Wait until we have to push the damned thing?"

Laura didn't answer. She really didn't know what she was going to do; this was a wing-it-by-the-seat situation. If she pulled into a gas station first, then Mary Terror might turn off I-94 at the nearest exit. If she waited much longer, the gas would give out and they'd be coasting. There was something darkly comedic about this, like a twisted Lucy and Ethel on the trail of a celebrity when Ricky went to Hollywood. *Don Juan,* she thought. Wasn't that the movie Ricky visited Hollywood to film? Or was it *Casanova?* No, *Don Juan.* She was almost sure of it. That was the first sign of old age: forgetting details. Who was it that Lucy had gotten a booth next to at the Brown Derby? William Holden? Hadn't she spilled soup on his head? Or was it a salad instead of s—

The blare of an air horn behind her almost lifted Laura out of her seat and caused Didi to yelp like a dog. She jerked the wheel to the right, back into the lane she'd drifted out of, and the huge truck that was looming on her tail roared past like a snorting dinosaur.

"Screw you!" Didi shouted, and shot the truck's driver a bird.

Laura's heart began to pound.

Mary Terror was cutting her speed, and easing over toward an exit ramp that was about a quarter mile ahead.

Laura blinked, wasn't sure if she was walking on the paths of La-La Land again or not.

In the sky was an apparition. A symbol of high karma, as Mark Treggs might have said. Up on stilts on the roadside was a gigantic yellow Smiley Face, and a sign that said HAPPY HERMAN'S! GAS! FOOD! GROCERIES! NEXT EXIT!

Oh yes, Laura thought. That was where Mary Terror was going. Maybe she needed gas. Maybe she needed something to keep her awake. In any case, Happy Herman's Smiley Face was a beacon, drawing Mary Terror off the interstate like a hippie to a be-in.

"Where's she going?" Didi said excitedly. "She's getting off!"

"I know." Laura moved into the right lane. The exit ramp was coming up. Mary Terror took it, committing the van to a long curve to the right, and Laura cut the BMW's speed as she followed.

Happy Herman's was on the left. It was a yellow cinderblock combination grocery store, burger joint, and gas station, with full-serve and self-serve pumps. Big yellow Smiley Faces were painted on the windows. A couple of trucks were at the diesel pumps, and a station wagon with an Ohio tag was being fueled with self-serve premium unleaded. Mary Terror slid the van under a yellow plastic awning. As her front tires went over a rubber hose across the concrete, a shrill bell rang. She stopped at the full-serve pumps, her gas port lined up with the regular leaded hose. Then she sat there and watched in the sideview mirror as the BMW came in and went to the self-serve pumps thirty feet away. Laura Clayborne got out, the injured side of her face bruised and swollen and her hair windblown. Was there a gun in her hand? Mary saw the woman start to walk toward the van, and then a man's wrinkled face appeared at the window. He tapped on the glass, and Mary quickly glanced in the rearview mirror at her own face to make sure she'd gotten all of Edward's blood off with her saliva and fingernails. Some blood remained at her hairline, but it would have to do. She cranked the window down. "Fill 'er up?" the man asked. He wore a yellow, grease-stained Happy Herman cap and he was chewing vigorously on a toothpick.

Mary nodded. The man moved away from the window, and Mary stared at Laura, who stood less than ten feet away. Her hands were empty; no gun. Behind her, Didi was fueling up the BMW. Laura took two steps closer, and stopped when Mary rested her arm on the window frame, the baby's blood-spattered white blanket over her hand and about three inches of the Colt's barrel showing.

The sight of the bloody white blanket transfixed Laura. She couldn't take her eyes off it, and she felt a hot surge of sickness rising in her throat. And then Mary's other arm came into view and there was David, alive and sucking on a pacifier. The Colt's barrel moved a few inches, taking aim in the direction of the baby's skull.

The gas pump's motor was humming, the numbers clicking higher.

Mary sensed the Happy Herman attendant returning before he got there. She slid her arm down beside her, the gun resting against her thigh. He peered in at her, his eye catching for a second or two on the baby. "Somebody don't like you," he told Mary.

"What?"

He dug at a molar with the toothpick. "Got bullet holes in your van. Somebody don't like you."

"I bought it at a government auction," she said, her expression blank. "It used to belong to a drug dealer."

The man stared at her, his toothpick working. "Oh," he said. Then he sprayed the windshield with cleaning fluid and started to wash it with a squeegee as the gas kept flowing into the tank.

Laura Clayborne was no longer there.

She stood in the dank women's room, where there were no Smiley Faces and the only thing yellow was the toilet water. She glanced in the mirror and saw a fright mask. Then she hurriedly soaked paper towels in water from the sink and cleaned her blood-clogged nostrils. Touching her face sent electric jolts of pain through her cheekbones, but she had no time to be gentle. Her vision was hazed by tears when she finished. She crumpled the bloody towels, dropped them into the wastebasket, and then she relieved the pressure on her bladder. There was a dribble of blood between her legs, too, the stitches popped by Earl Van Diver's knee. When she was done, Laura went out into the cold again, and she saw Mary Terror carrying David into the grocery store, the shoulder bag over her arm and probably both guns in it.

The attendant had finished pumping the gas into the van. Laura walked to it and opened the driver's door. Mary Terror's smell, a heavy, animalish odor, lingered within. No keys in the ignition, of course. Laura reached under the dashboard and gripped a handful of wires. One good yank, and . . . and what? she asked herself. The situation wouldn't change. Maybe the van wouldn't start, but Mary would still have David, still have her guns, and still kill him as soon as the police arrived. What was the point of disabling the van if David would die as the result?

She released the wires. "Damn it," she said quietly. She'd only waste her strength shouting.

She looked behind the van's front seats. In the back were suitcases and a couple of large paper sacks. Laura reached over and searched in them, finding such items as potato chip bags, cartons of doughnuts and cookies, a box of Pampers, and some baby formula as well as paper cups and a half-full plastic bottle of Pepsi. Traveling food, she thought. Groceries that Mary and Edward Fordyce had bought for their trip. Also amid the clutter in the van's rear was a pillow and a blanket. She took the blanket and one of the sacks containing junk food, the cups, and the Pepsi. She left the diapers and the formula where they were. Something else caught her attention: a pacifier on the passenger seat. She picked it up, intending to keep it. It had her baby's saliva on it, and his aroma. But no, no: if David had no pacifier to ease his crying, the crying might snap Mary Terror's nerves, and then . . .

Laura put the pacifier down. It might have been the hardest thing she'd ever had to do.

Laura carried the booty to her car. And that was when she realized the gas portal was closed, the pump shut off, and Bedelia Morse was gone.

In the store, as Mary Terror paid for her gas, a box of No-Doz tablets, a jug of pure water, and a package of trash bags, she watched Laura raiding her van. Won't touch the engine or the tires, she thought. Bitch knows what would happen if she did.

"Is that all?" the woman behind the register asked.

"Yeah, I think—" She stopped. Beside the register was a glass bowl. On the glass bowl was written in black Magic Marker *Don't Worry! Be Happy!* In the bowl were hundreds of little yellow Smiley Face pins. She wouldn't have stopped at Happy Herman's but for the sign, and the feeling that she was invincible under its power. It had proved her right. Laura Clayborne couldn't touch her. "How much are those?"

"Quarter apiece."

"I'll take one," Mary said. "And one for my baby." She pinned one on the light blue sweater she'd bought Drummer in New Jersey, and then she pinned the other on her own sweater, next to what she realized looked like dried oatmeal but were flecks of Edward's brain.

"Somebody get hurt?" the woman asked when the bill had been paid. She was looking distastefully at the splotches of crimson on the blanket nestled around Drummer.

"Nosebleed." The answer came fast and smooth. "I always get them in cold weather."

She nodded, putting Mary's purchases into a sack. "Me, my ankles swell up. Look like a couple a' treetrunks walkin' around the house. They're swole up on me right now."

"Sorry," Mary said.

"Means a storm on the way," the woman told her. "Weatherman says all hell's 'bout to break loose out west."

"I believe it. Have a nice day." Mary took the sack under one arm, cradling Drummer with the other, and she walked out of the store toward her van. She had to pee, but she didn't want to let the van out of her sight so she'd have to hold it until she was desperate. She put Drummer's bassinet on the passenger-side floorboard, and then she made a quick check of what Laura had taken. A sack of groceries and the blanket. No big deal, Mary decided as she put the new supplies and her shoulder bag in the back of the van. She took the Colt out of the bag and put it under the driver's seat. Then she popped the No-Doz open, swallowed two tablets with a drink of the bottled water, and slid behind the wheel. She put the key into the ignition, the engine starting with a throaty roar.

Then she looked over at the BMW, and Laura Clayborne standing beside it, staring at her.

She didn't like the woman's face. *You're nothing but a lie,* she remembered it saying.

Mary reached under her seat, gripped the Colt, and withdrew it. She cocked the pistol as she brought it up, and she aimed the barrel with a steady hand at Laura's heart.

Laura saw the gun's dull gleam. She inhaled a sharp breath that made the cold sting her nostrils. There was no time to move, and her body tensed for the shot.

The baby began to cry, wanting to be fed.

Mary caught sight of a car in the sideview mirror, pulling up to the pumps behind her. It wasn't just any car; it belonged to the Michigan highway patrol. She lowered the Colt, easing the hammer back into place. Then, without another glance at Laura, she drove away from the pumps and turned back onto the road that led to I-94's westbound lanes.

Laura was looking frantically for Didi. The woman wasn't anywhere in sight. She's left me, Laura thought. Gone back to the gray world of false faces and names. She couldn't wait any longer, Mary Terror was getting away. She got into the car, started the engine, and was about to pull away when a woman shouted, "Hey! Hey, you! Stop!"

The cashier had come outside and was hollering at her. The state trooper, a burly block of a man with a Smokey the Bear hat, devoted his full attention to the BMW. "You ain't paid for your gas!" the cashier shouted.

Oh shit, Laura thought. She put on the parking brake again and reached for her purse from the backseat, where she'd left it. Only her purse wasn't there. From the corner of her eye she saw the trooper walking toward her, and the cashier was coming, too, indignant that she'd had to venture out into the cold. The trooper was almost to the car, and Laura realized with a start that the Charter Arms automatic was lying within sight on the floorboard. Where was the damned purse? All her money, her credit cards, her driver's license: gone.

Didi's work, she thought.

Laura just had time to slide the automatic up under the seat when the trooper looked in, hard-eyed under the Smokey the Bear rim. "Believe you owe some money," he said in a voice like a shovel digging gravel. "How much, Annie?"

"Fourteen dollars, sixty-two cents!" the cashier said. "Tryin' to skip on me, Frank!"

"That so, lady?"

"No! I've—" Claw your way cut, she thought. Mary Terror was getting farther away! "I've got a friend around here somewhere. She took my purse."

"Not much of a friend, then, huh? I guess that means you don't have a license, either."

"It's in my purse."

"I suspected so." The trooper looked at the windshield, and Laura knew he was taking in the *Go home* carved there. Then he looked at her bruised cheek again, and after a few seconds of deliberation he said, "I believe you'd better step out of the car."

There was no point in pleading. The trooper retreated a couple of paces, and his hand touched his hip near the big pearl-handled pistol in his black holster. My God! Laura thought. He thinks I might be *dangerous!* Laura cut the BMW's engine, opened the door, and got out.

"Walk to my car, please," the trooper said, a clipped command.

He would ask for her name next, Laura figured as she walked. He paused to take a look at her tag, memorizing the numbers, and then he followed behind her. "Georgia," he said. "You're a long way from home, aren't you?"

Laura didn't answer. "What's your name?" he asked.

If she made up a name, he'd know soon enough. One call on his radio to check the tag would tell him. Damn it to hell! Mary was getting away!

"Your *name,* please?"

There was no use in resisting. She said, "Laur—"

"What's going on, sis?"

The voice made Laura stop in her tracks. She looked to her left, at Didi Morse standing there with the purse over her shoulder and a bag with grease stains on it in her hand. "Any trouble?" Didi asked innocently.

The trooper gave her his hard glare. "Do you know this woman?"

"Sure. She's my sister. What's the problem?"

"Tryin' to steal fourteen dollars and sixty-two cents worth of gas, that's what!" the cashier replied, her swollen ankles aching in the bitter cold and the breath pluming from her mouth.

"Oh, here's the money. I went over there and bought us some breakfast." Didi nodded toward the burger-joint section of Happy Herman's, which had a sign announcing their trucker's breakfast special of sausage and biscuits. She took the wallet out, counted a ten, four ones, two quarters, and two dimes. "You can keep the change," she said as she offered the cashier her money.

"Listen, I'm sorry." The woman brought up a nervous smile. "I saw her startin' to drive away, and I thought . . . well, it happens sometimes." She took the cash.

"Oh, she was probably just moving the car. I had to go to the bathroom, and I guess she was coming to pick me up."

"Sorry," the cashier said. "Frank, I feel like a real dumb-ass. You folks take it easy, now, and watch the weather." She began walking back to the grocery store, shivering in the frigid wind.

"You ready to hit the road?" Didi asked Laura brightly. "I got us some coffee and chow."

Laura saw the shine of fear deep down in Didi's eyes. *You wanted to run, didn't you?* Laura thought. "I'm ready," she said tersely.

"Hold on a minute." The trooper planted himself between them and the car. "Lady, it might not be any of my business, but you look like somebody gave you a hell of a knock."

A silence stretched. Then Didi filled it. "Somebody did. Her husband, if you want to know."

"Her husband? He did *that?*"

"My sister and her husband were visiting me from Georgia. He went crazy and punched her last night, and we're on the way to our mother's house in Illinois. Bastard took a hammer to her new car, broke the window out and cut up the windshield, too."

"Jesus." The hardness had vanished from the trooper's eyes. "Some men can really be shits, if you'll pardon my French. Maybe you ought to get to a doctor."

"Our father's a doctor. In Joliet."

If she weren't about to jump out of her skin, Laura might have smiled. Didi was good at this; she'd had a lot of practice.

"Mind if we go now?" Didi asked.

The trooper scratched his jaw, and stared at the darkness in the west. Then he said, "All men ain't sonsabitches. Lemme give you a hand." He walked to his car, opened the trunk, and brought out a tarpaulin of clear blue plastic. "Go in there and get some duct tape," he told Didi, and he motioned toward the grocery store. "It'll be back on the hardwares shelf. Tell Annie to put it on Frank's tab."

Didi gave Laura the breakfast bag and strode quickly away. Laura was fighting a scream; with every second, Mary Terror was getting farther away. Frank produced a penknife and began to cut out a fair-sized square of blue plastic. When Didi returned with the silver duct tape, Frank said, "Long way to Joliet from here. You ladies need to keep warm," and he opened the BMW's door, slid across the driver's seat under which the automatic pistol rested, and taped the plastic up over the window frame. He did a thorough job of it, adding strip after strip of the silver tape in a webbing pattern that fixed the plastic securely in place. Laura drank her coffee black and paced nervously as Frank finished the job, Didi looking on with interest. Then Frank came back out of the car, the duct tape reduced to about half its previous size. "There you go," he said. "Hope everything works out all right for you."

"We hope so, too," Didi answered. She got into the car, and Laura was never so thankful in her life to get behind a steering wheel.

"Drive carefully!" Frank cautioned. He waved as the patched-up BMW pulled away, and he watched as it sped up and swerved onto I-94 West. Funny, he thought. The lady from Georgia had said her "friend" had her purse. Why hadn't she said "sister"? Well, sisters could be friends, couldn't they? Still . . . it made him wonder. Was it worth a call in to get a vehicle ID or not? Should've checked her driver's license, he decided. He'd always been a sucker for a hard-luck story. Well, let them go. He was supposed to be looking for speeders, not giving grief to battered wives. He turned his back to the west, and went to get himself a cup of coffee.

"Fifteen minutes on us," Laura said as the speedometer's needle climbed past seventy. "That's what she's got."

"Thirteen minutes," Didi corrected Laura, and she began to tear into a sausage and biscuit.

The BMW reached eighty. Laura was even passing the massive trucks. The wind flapped the plastic a little, but Frank had done a good job and the duct tape held. "Better hold it back," Didi said. "Getting stopped for a ticket won't help."

Laura kept her speed where it was, on the high side of eighty. The car shuddered, its aerodynamics spoiled by the caved-in passenger door. Laura's gaze searched for an olive-green van in the gloomy light. "Why didn't you leave me?"

"I did."

"You came back. Why?"

"I saw him rousting you. I had your purse. I knew it was about to be over for you."

"So? Why didn't you just let him arrest me and you take off?"

Didi chewed on the tough sausage. She washed it down with a sip of hot coffee. "Where was I going to go?" she asked quietly.

The question lingered. To it there was no answer.

The BMW sped on, toward the steel-gray West while the sun rose in the East like a burning angel.

2.

The Terrible Truth

Laura had to cut her speed down to sixty-five again when she saw another state trooper car heading east. After almost half an hour, there was still no sign of Mary Terror's van. "She's turned off," Laura said. She heard the desperation rising in her voice. "She took an exit."

"Maybe she did. Maybe she didn't."

"Wouldn't *you?*" Laura asked.

Didi thought about it. "I'd turn off and find a place to wait for a while, until you had time to pass me," she said. "Then I could get back on the highway whenever I pleased."

"Do you think that's what she's done?"

Didi looked ahead. The traffic had picked up, but there was no sign of an olive-green van with broken taillights. They had passed the exits to Kalamazoo a few miles before. If Mary Terror had turned off at any one of those, they'd never find her again. "Yes, I think so," Didi answered.

"Damn it!" Laura slammed the wheel with her fist. "I knew we'd lose her if we couldn't keep her in sight! Now what the hell are we going to do?"

"I don't know. You're driving."

Laura kept going. There was a long curve ahead. Maybe on the other side of it they'd catch sight of the van. The speed was creeping up again, and she forced herself to ease off. "I didn't say thank you, did I?"

"For what?"

"You know for what. For coming back with my purse."

"No, I don't guess you did." Didi picked at one of her short, square fingernails, her fingers as sturdy as tools.

"I'm saying it. Thank you." She glanced quickly at Didi and then fixed her attention on the highway once more. Behind them, the sun glowed orange through chinks in interlocked clouds the color of bruises, and ahead the sky was a dark mask. "And thank you for helping me with this, too. You didn't have to call me when Mary was on the way."

"I almost didn't." She looked at her hands. They had never been pretty, like Laura's hands were. They had never been soft, never unworked. "Maybe I got tired of being loyal to a dead cause. Maybe there never was a cause to be loyal to. The Storm Front." She grunted, a note of sarcasm. "We were children with guns, smoking dope and getting high and thinking we could change the world. No, not even that, really. Maybe we just liked the power of setting off bombs and pulling triggers. Damn." She shook her head, her eyes hazed with memory. "That was a crazy world, back then."

"It's still crazy," Laura said.

"No, now it's insane. There's a difference. But we helped it get from there to here. We grew up to be the people we said we hated. Talk-talk-talkin' 'bout our generation," Didi said in a soft, singsong voice.

They rounded the bend. No van in sight. Maybe on the next stretch of road they'd see her. "What are you going to do now?" Laura asked. "You can't go back to Ann Arbor."

"Nope. Damn, I had a good setup, too. A good house, a great workshop. I was doing all right. Listen, don't get me started or I might curse you out for this." She checked her wristwatch, an old Timex. It was a little after seven. "Somebody'll find Edward. I hope it's not Mr. Brewer. He always wanted to set me up with his grandson." She sighed heavily. "Edward. The past caught up with him, didn't it? And it caught up with me, too. You know, you had a hell of a nerve tracking me down like you did. I can't believe you talked Mark into helping you. Mark's a rock." Didi put her hand against the piece of plastic tarp and felt it flutter. The heater was keeping the car's interior toasty now that the wind was blocked off. "Thanks for not bringing Mark to the house," she said. "That wasn't the place for him."

"I didn't want him getting hurt."

Didi turned her head to stare at Laura. "You've got balls, don't you? Walking in there with Mary like you did. I swear to God, I thought we were both finished."

"I wasn't thinking about anything but getting my son back. That's all I care about."

"What happens if you can't get him back? Would you have another baby?"

Laura didn't answer for a moment. The car's tires sang on the pavement, and a truck hauling lumber moved into her lane. "My husband . . . and I are through. I know that for sure. I don't know if I'd want to live in Atlanta anymore. I just don't know about a lot of things. I guess I'll cross those bridges when I—"

"Slow down," Didi interrupted, leaning forward in her seat. She was looking at something ahead, revealed when the lumber truck had changed lanes. "There! See it?"

There was no van. Laura said, "See what?"

"The car there. The Buick."

Laura did see it, then. A dark blue Buick, its right side scraped to the metal and its rear fender bashed in. Earl Van Diver's car.

"Slow down," Didi cautioned. "Don't let him see us. Bastard might try to run us off the road."

"He's after Mary. He doesn't want us." Even so, Laura cut her speed and lagged a hundred yards behind the Buick and off to the right.

"I don't trust anybody who fires a bullet close enough for me to hear. Some FBI agent, huh? He didn't care if he hit David or not."

And that was the terrible truth of it, Laura thought. Earl Van Diver was hunting Mary, not to arrest her for her crimes, but to execute her. Whether he killed David or not made no difference to him. His bullets were meant for Mary, but as long as Mary had David, one of those bullets might rip through him just as easily as through her. Laura stayed far behind the Buick, and after a couple of miles she watched it pull over toward an exit ramp on the right.

"Getting off," Didi said. "Good riddance."

Laura eased the BMW over, following Van Diver toward the ramp. "What the hell are you doing?" Didi demanded. "You're not getting off, are you?"

"That's just what I'm doing."

"Why? We could still catch up with Mary!"

"And we still can," Laura said. "But I don't want that bastard catching up with her first. If he stops at a gas station, we're going to take his keys."

"Yeah, right! *You* take his keys! Damn it, you're asking to get shot!"

"We'll see," Laura said, and she turned onto the ramp in the wake of Van Diver's car.

In the Buick, Earl Van Diver was watching the monitor under his dashboard. A little red light was flashing, indicating a magnetic fix. The liquid crystal display read SSW 208 2.3: compass heading, bearing, miles between the main unit and the homer. As he came off the ramp's curve, he saw the display change to SW 196 2.2. He followed the road that led south from I-94, passing a sign that said LAWTON, 3 MI.

"He's not stopping for gas," Didi said. Van Diver had gone straight past a Shell station on one side of the road and an Exxon on the other. "He's taking the scenic route."

"Why'd he get off, then? If he's so hell-bent on catching Mary, why'd he get off?" She kept a car and a pickup truck between them as she followed. They'd gone maybe two miles when Laura saw a blue building with a garish orange roof off to the left. INTERNATIONAL HOUSE OF PANCAKES, its sign announced. The Buick's brake lights flashed, the turn indicator went on, and Van Diver made the turn into the IHOP's parking lot.

Van Diver's savage grin twitched. The olive-green van, its left side battered and scraped, was sitting in the parking lot between a junker

Olds and a Michigan Power panel truck. Van Diver swung the Buick into a parking space up close to the building, where he could watch the exit. He cut the engine and unplugged the monitor, which read NNE 017 0.01.

Close enough, he thought.

Van Diver put on his black gloves, his fingers long and spidery. Then he slid the Browning automatic from beneath his seat, clicked the safety off, and held it against his right thigh. He waited, his dark eyes on the IHOP's door. It opened in a few seconds, and two men in blue parkas and caps came out, their breath frosty in the morning air. They walked toward the Michigan Power panel truck. Come on, come on! he thought. He'd figured he could be patient after all these years. But his patience had run out, and that was why he'd hurried the first shot that had hit Edward Fordyce instead of Mary Terror's skull.

The skin prickled on the back of his neck. Van Diver sensed movement behind him and to his left. His head swiveled in that direction, his hand coming up with the Browning in it and his heart hammering.

He looked into the snout of a pistol pressed against the window's glass, and behind it stood the woman he'd first seen on the newscasts from Atlanta and later had met in Bedelia Morse's kitchen.

She wasn't a killer. She was a social columnist for the Atlanta *Constitution,* and she was married to a stockbroker. She had, up until the kidnapping of her baby, never felt the agony of heartrending pain. She had never suffered. All these things Earl Van Diver knew, and weighed in the balance as he prepared to bring his gun up and fire through the window at her. His shot would be faster and more deadly because she didn't have the courage to kill a man in cold blood.

But he didn't do it. He didn't, because of what he saw in Laura Clayborne's bruised face. Not hopelessness, not pleading, not weakness. He saw desperation and rage there, emotions he knew all too well. He might get off the first shot, but she would certainly deliver the second. Bedelia Morse suddenly reached past Laura and opened the door before Van Diver could hit the lock. "Put the gun down," Laura said. Her voice was tight and strained. Could she shoot him if she had to? She didn't know, and she hoped to God she wouldn't have to find out. Van Diver just sat there, grinning at her with his frozen face, his eyes dark and alert as a rattlesnake's. "Put it down!" Laura repeated. "On the floor!"

"Take the clip out first," Didi added.

"Yeah. Like she said."

Van Diver looked at the automatic in Laura's hand. He saw it shake a little, her finger on the trigger. When Van Diver moved, both women flinched. He popped the bullet clip out of his Browning, held it in his palm, and put the gun on the floorboard. "Take your keys and get out of the car," Didi told him, and he obeyed.

Laura glanced over at Mary Terror's van and then back to Van Diver. "How'd you know she was here?"

Van Diver remained silent, just staring at her with his fathomless eyes. He'd taken off his woolen cap, and his scalp was bald except for a few long strands of gray hair pressed down on the skin, a fringe of gray-and-brown hair around his head. He was slim and wiry, standing about five ten, by no means a large man. But Laura knew his strength from painful experience. Earl Van Diver was a taut package of muscle and bone powered by hatred.

"What's the antenna for?" Didi asked. She had already checked out the Buick's interior. "There's no car phone."

No answer. "The bastard can't talk without his throat plug," Didi realized. "Where's your plug, shitface? You can point, can't you?" No reaction. Didi said, "Give me your gun," and took it from Laura. She stepped forward and jammed the pistol up against Earl Van Diver's testicles, and she looked him right in his cold eyes. "Came to Ann Arbor to find me, didn't you? What were you doing? Staking out my house?" She shoved the gun's barrel a little harder. "How'd you find me?" Van Diver's face was a motionless mask, but a twisted vein at his left temple was beating fast and hard. Didi saw a garbage dumpster back toward the rear of the IHOP, where a patch of woods sloped down to a drainage ditch. "We're not going to get anything out of him. He's nothing but an"—she pressed her face closer to his—"old fucked-up pig." The *pig* sprayed bits of spittle onto Van Diver's cheeks, and his eyes blinked. "Let's walk." She pushed him toward the dumpster, the gun moving to jam against his back.

"What are you going to do?" Laura asked nervously.

"You don't want him following Mary, do you? We're going to take him into the woods and shoot him. A bullet in one of his knees ought to take care of the problem. He won't get too far crawling."

"No! I don't want that!"

"*I* want it," Didi said, shoving Van Diver forward. "Son of a bitch killed Edward. Almost killed us and the baby, too. Move, you bastard!"

"No, Didi! We can't do it!"

"You won't have to. I'm paying Edward's debt, that's all. I said *move*, you fucking pig!" She punched him hard in the small of the back with the gun's barrel, and he grunted and staggered forward a few paces.

Earl Van Diver lifted his hands. Then he pointed to his throat and moved his finger toward the Buick's trunk.

"Now he wants to talk," Didi said. Under her clothes she had broken out in a cold sweat. She would have shot him if she'd had to, but the idea of violence made her stomach clench. "Open it," she told him. "Real slow." She kept the gun against his back as he unlocked the trunk. Laura and Didi saw the listening dish, the tape recorder, and the sniper's rifle. Van Diver opened a small gray plastic case and took out a cord with a plug on one end and a miniature speaker on the other. He slid the plug's prongs into his throat socket with practiced ease, and then he clicked a switch on the back of the speaker and adjusted a volume control. He lifted the speaker up before Didi's face.

His mouth moved, the veins standing out in his throat. "The last person who called me a pig," the metallic voice rasped, "fell down a flight of stairs and broke his neck. You knew him by one of his names: Raymond Fletcher."

The name stunned her for a few seconds. Dr. Raymond Fletcher had done the plastic surgery on her face.

"Walk to the car." Didi slammed the Buick's trunk shut and shoved Van Diver toward the BMW. When Van Diver was in the backseat with Didi beside him, the gun trained on him, and Laura sitting behind the wheel, Didi said, "Okay, I want to hear it. How'd you find me?"

Van Diver watched the IHOP's door, but his voice filtered through the speaker in his hand. "A policeman friend of mine was working undercover on Fletcher in Miami, trying to catch him doing surgery on people who wanted to disappear. Fletcher called himself Raymond Barnes, and he was working on a lot of Mafia and federal-case clients. My friend was a computer hacker. He cracked Barnes's computer files and dug around in them. Everything was in code, and it took maybe five months to figure it out. Barnes kept all his case records, back to when he'd first started in 'seventy. Your name came up, and the work you'd had done in St. Louis. That's when I got involved. Unofficially." His black eyes fixed on Didi. "By the time I got to Miami, my friend was found floating in Biscayne Bay with his face blowtorched. So I went to visit the good doctor, and we went to his office to have a nice long talk."

"He didn't know where I was!" Didi said. "I'd moved three times since I had my face changed!"

"You came to Barnes with a letter of recommendation from an ex-Weatherman named Stewart McGalvin. Stewart lived in Philadelphia. He taught classes in pottery. It's amazing what surgical instruments can do, isn't it?"

Didi swallowed thickly. "What happened to Stewart?"

"Oh," the voice from the speaker said, "he drowned himself in the bathtub. He was the tight-lipped type. His wife . . . well, she must've shot herself in the head when she found him."

"You *son of a bitch!*" Didi shouted, and she pressed the gun's barrel against his throat socket.

"Careful," the speaker's voice cautioned. "I'm sensitive there."

"You killed my friends! I ought to blow your damned head off!"

"You won't," Van Diver said calmly. "Maybe you could cripple me, but you don't have any killing left in you, Bedelia. How did you put it? 'I didn't need a prison cell. I carry one around with me.' I got into your house to plant a microphone bug. I've been watching your house for almost four years, Bedelia. I even moved from New Jersey to be close to you."

"How'd you find me if Stewart didn't tell you anything?"

"His wife remembered you. You'd sent her a set of plates. Nice work. She mailed you a check for six cups to go with them. She had the canceled check, made out to Diane Daniells. The First Bank of Ann Arbor's stamp was on the back, and your signature. When I saw you for the first time, Bedelia, I wanted to sing. Do you understand how a person can love someone and hate them at the same time?"

"No."

"I can. See, you were always a rung on the ladder. That's all. You were a hope—however slim—to find Mary Terror. I watched you come and go, I checked your mailbox, I camped in the woods outside your house. And when you went on your trip, I knew something important was going on. You'd never left Ann Arbor before. Mary was in the news. I knew. I *knew.*" The voice through the speaker was terrible, and bright tears glistened in Earl Van Diver's eyes. "This is what my life is about, Bedelia," he said. "Executing Mary Terror."

Laura had been listening with fascinated horror, and at that moment she saw the object of Van Diver's attention emerge from the IHOP with David's bassinet in her arms.

"Mary," Van Diver's voice whispered. A tear streaked down his cheek, over the gnarled scar tissue of his mouth. "There you are."

Mary had just finished her meal of pancakes, eggs, hash browns, and two cups of black coffee. She'd fed Drummer, and changed his diaper in the bathroom. Drummer was content now, sucking on his pacifier, a little bundle of warmth. "Good baby," Mary said. "You're a good baby boy, aren't—" And then she looked up and saw the BMW sitting there in the parking lot, not far from her van, and her legs seized up. She saw Laura Clayborne at the wheel, Didi sitting in the back with a man she didn't recognize. "Goddamn it!" she snarled. How the hell had they found her? She held Drummer with one arm, and her other hand snaked into her shoulder bag and touched the Colt, the Compact Magnum automatic farther down amid the baby things. Blow out the tires! she thought, enraged. Shoot that bitch in the face, and kill Didi, too! She took a couple of strides toward the BMW, but then she stopped. The sounds of the shots would bring other people out of the IHOP. Somebody would get her tag number. No, she couldn't open fire here. It would be stupid, when she knew at last where Lord Jack was waiting. Smiling thinly, she walked to the BMW and Laura Clayborne got out.

They stood about twenty feet apart, like two wary animals, as the wind swirled around them and sliced to their bones. Laura's gaze found a Smiley Face button on Mary's sweater, pinned over the heart.

Mary brought the Colt out and rested it against Drummer's side, because she saw that Didi was holding a gun. "You must have good radar," she said to Laura.

"I'll follow you all the way to California if I have to."

"You *will* have to." She looked at the *Go home* scratched on the windshield. "Somebody gave you some good advice. You ought to go home before you get hurt."

Laura saw the woman's bloodshot eyes, her face lined and weary. "You can't keep driving without sleep. Sooner or later you'll nod off behind the wheel."

Mary had been planning on finding a motel to crash in when she reached Illinois. The No-Doz and coffee had charged her up, but she knew she was going to need rest in a few hours. "I've gone two days straight without sleep before, when I—"

"Was young?" Laura interrupted. "You can't make it all the way to California."

"You can't follow me all the way, either."

"I've got a co-pilot."

"I've got a pretty little baby boy." Mary's smile tightened. "You'd better pray I don't run off the road."

Laura took another step closer. Mary's eyes narrowed, but she didn't retreat. "You understand this," Laura said, her voice husky with rage. "If you hurt my baby, I'll kill you. If it's the last thing I do on this earth, I'll kill you."

Nothing was going to be gained standing in this parking lot wasting time, Mary thought. She had to get back on the interstate and head west again. Later on she'd figure out a way to shake her trackers. She began to back toward the van, the Colt still resting against Drummer's side and the baby's cheeks flushed with the sharp cold.

"Mary?"

It was a man's voice. The man in the backseat of Laura's car. But there was something strange and metallic about it: the voice of a steel-throated robot.

She saw the man staring at her, his face carved into a pallid, scarred grin and his eyes the color of midnight. "Mary?" the robot voice spoke again. "You made me suffer."

Mary stopped her retreat.

"You made me suffer. Do you remember, Mary? That night in Linden?"

The voice—almost disembodied, and made directionless by the swirl and sweep of the wind—caused the rise of chill bumps on the back of Mary Terror's neck.

"I killed Edward," he said. "I was aiming at you. I got excited after all these years. But I'll get you, Mary." The volume suddenly cranked up to a soulless shout: "I'LL GET YOU, MARY!"

She backed quickly to her van as Laura got behind the BMW's wheel. Mary put Drummer down and started the engine. The BMW's engine roared to life an instant later. Then Mary backed out of the parking slot, the black coffee sloshing in her belly, and she wheeled the van in the direction of I-94 West. Laura said to Didi, "Take his keys and get him out of here."

Didi worked the Buick's keys from Van Diver's fist, the automatic jammed against his side. "You'll never take her without me," Van Diver said. "She'll kill both of you before the day's over."

"Get him out!"

"You put me out," he said, "and the first thing I'll do is call the Michigan highway patrol. Then the FBI. They'll set a roadblock for her before she makes the Illinois line. You think Mary's going to give your baby up without a fight?"

Laura reached back, grabbed the cord, and yanked the speaker's plug from Van Diver's throat. *"Out!"* she told him.

"He can still write," Didi realized. "We'd have to break the bastard's fingers."

There was no time for further argument. Laura let off the parking brake and drove after Mary Terror. Van Diver made a gasping noise, but his attempt to tell Laura about the magnetic homer and the receiver unit in his car was stillborn. Laura stepped hard on the accelerator, leaving the IHOP behind and racing after the van. Didi kept the pistol pressed into Van Diver's side. That was all right with him. Sooner or later she'd have to relax. Both these women had soft white throats, and he had hands and teeth.

Nothing and no one was going to stop him from killing Mary Terror. If he had to dispose of these women to take control of the car, so be it. He had no code now but vengeance, and whoever wandered in the path of its fire would be reduced to ashes.

Laura saw the van ahead, slowing for its turn onto I-94 West. She followed it, and in another moment she veered into the lane behind Mary and let the speed wind up to sixty-five. The car and the van stayed about fifty yards apart, the highway getting crowded with morning traffic. In the van, Mary looked at the BMW's bashed front fender in her sideview mirror. The memory of that metallic voice still chilled her. *You made me suffer,* it had said. *That night in Linden.*

Do you remember, Mary?

She did remember. A bullet tearing a pig's cheek, and a second bullet mangling his throat.

Suffer.

This was far out, she thought. Groovy weirdness. She recalled reading about the pig in Didi's photo album, but she couldn't remember his name. Didn't matter, though. He was as crazy as Laura if he thought he could stop her. She was trekking to California with

Drummer, and no one was going to get in her way and live. She'd watch her speed and be a good girl for the highway patrol piggies, and she'd figure out how to take care once and for all of Laura Clayhead, Benedict Bedelia, and the sufferer.

She went on, arrowing along the gray highway toward the promised land, with the BMW in dogged pursuit.

3.

Good Boys

South of Chicago's sprawl, I-94 became I-80, but the highway still aimed across the flatlands of Illinois. Mary had to pull into another gas station near Joliet, and Laura—who'd gone the last ten miles with her fuel warning light on—pulled in after her and filled up the tank while Didi held the gun on Earl Van Diver. "I need to use the bathroom," Van Diver said through his speaker, and Didi said, "Sure. Go ahead," and handed him one of the paper cups.

Laura got into the backseat with Van Diver while Didi relieved herself in the bathroom, and then Didi took the wheel. Within fifteen minutes the car and the van were back on the highway again, both keeping a steady sixty-five and fifty yards apart. Van Diver closed his eyes and slept, a soft, groaning noise coming from his mouth every so often, and Laura had a chance to relax, if only in body and not in mind. The miles reeled off and the exits went past, and Didi felt the car shudder as the winds hit them in hard crosscurrents.

At two o'clock in the afternoon, with Moline, Illinois, twenty miles ahead, the sky was the color of wet cotton, and wandering shards of yellowish light speared through holes in the clouds. Mary Terror, her system raw with caffeine, nevertheless felt the weariness starting to overtake her. Drummer was tired and hungry, too, and kept crying with a high, thin wail that she couldn't block out. She gauged the BMW behind her, and watched the Geneseo exit coming up. It was time to make the move, she decided. She kept in the left lane, making no indication that she had her eye on the exit. When it was almost too late to turn, she stepped on the brake, veered the van across two lanes in front of a Millbrook bread truck whose driver pounded his horn and displayed his command of expletives, and then Mary was speeding up the exit ramp and the BMW had flashed past.

Didi shouted, "Oh, shit!" and hit the brake pedal. Laura, roused from an uneasy sleep in which snipers on rooftops took aim at Mary Terror and David on a balcony, saw Didi struggling with the wheel, the van no longer in front of them, and instantly realized what had happened. Van Diver's eyes came open, his senses as alert as those of a predatory animal, and he looked back and saw the van turning to the right off the exit ramp. "SHE'S GETTING AWAY!" the metallic voice roared, the speaker at top volume.

"No, she's not!" Didi fought the car across the lanes, the tires shrieking and other cars blowing their horns and dodging around her. Didi got the BMW into the emergency lane, put it into reverse, and started backing toward the Geneseo exit. In another moment she was speeding up the ramp, and at the intersection she took a hard right that threw Van Diver into Laura and crushed Laura against the door. Then she was racing north along a county highway that cut across flat, winter-browned fields, a few clusters of tract housing on either side and a factory in the distance, its chimneys spouting gray smoke above the horizon. Didi passed a Subaru, almost blowing it off the road, and she saw the van about a half mile ahead. She kept giving the engine gas, the distance rapidly closing.

Mary saw the BMW approaching. The van didn't have enough power, there was no way to outrace the car, and there was nowhere to hide on this straight, flat road. Drummer was crying steadily, and rage flew up inside Mary like sparks swirling from a bonfire. "SHUT UP! SHUT UP!" she screamed at the baby, but he wouldn't be quiet. She saw a sign on the left: *Wentzel Brothers Lumber.* A red arrow pointed along a narrower road, and the lumberyard stood surrounded by brown fields. "Okay, come on!" Mary shouted, and as she took the turn she lifted the Colt out of her shoulder bag and laid it on the passenger seat.

She went between a pair of open iron gates that had a sign saying WARNING! GUARD DOGS! The lumberyard was maybe four or five acres across, a maze of timber stacked anywhere from six to ten feet high. There was a trailer, before which was parked a pickup truck, a forklift, and a brown Oldsmobile Cutlass with rust-eaten sides. Mary turned the van deeper into the maze, her tires throwing up dust from the unpaved surface. She pulled up alongside a long, green-painted cinderblock building with high, dirty windows, and she got out, holding Drummer's bassinet and the Colt revolver. She searched for a good killing ground, the dust roiling around her and the crying baby. As soon as she stepped around behind the building, she was met with a fusillade of barking as loud as howitzer shells. Within a dogpen topped by a green plastic canopy were two stocky, muscular pit bulls, one dark brown and the other splotched with white and gray. They threw themselves against the pen's wire mesh, their white fangs bared and their bodies trembling with fury. Beyond the dogpen were more stacks of lumber, piles of tarpaulins, and other odds and ends.

"Jesus H. Christ!" a man bellowed, coming from around a pile of timber. "What the hell's goin' on with you boys?" He was big-bellied and wore overalls and a red plaid jacket, and he stopped next to the cage when he saw Mary's gun.

Mary shot him, as much of an involuntary reaction as the pounding of her heart. The bullet hit him like a punch to the chest, and he went down on his butt on the ground, the color leaching from his face.

The noise of the shot and the violence of the man's fall sent the pit bulls into paroxysms of rage. They ran back and forth in the pen, colliding with each other then caroming off, their barking savage and their beady eyes on Mary and the infant.

Didi hit the brake as she saw the van, and the BMW skidded to a stop. Laura was out first. She could hear the hoarse, rapid barking of dogs, and she started running toward the sound with the automatic gripped in her hand.

Didi and Van Diver got out, and Van Diver did not fail to notice the keys left in the ignition. Behind the cinderblock building, Laura found the dogpen and the man lying on his back on the ground, blood on his chest just below his collarbone. He was breathing harshly, his eyes glassy with shock. The pit bulls raged behind the wire mesh, running back and forth over their territory, and Laura saw the beef bones of past meals scattered about on the ground. Laura carefully walked on between the high stacks of lumber, her gaze searching for Mary. She stopped abruptly, listening. The dogs were barking loudly, but had she heard the sound of David's crying? She went on, wary step after wary step, her knuckles white around the gun's grip and her heavy coat blowing around her.

Back near the car, Van Diver hesitated and let Didi walk on. Mary Terror's van was parked next to the building, and Bedelia Morse was between Van Diver and the van. She carried no weapon, but she'd been a blood-spilling member of the Storm Front. It would take a quick snap of her neck, he thought, to send her to her reward, and then he could plan on getting the gun away from Laura. He made up his mind: three seconds of judge, jury, and executioner.

He strode toward Didi, the speaker dangling from its plug in his throat, and he reached out for her.

He grabbed a handful of her hair. She said, "Wha—" and then he was twining his other arm around her throat from behind. Instantly, Didi started fighting to get away, her head thrashing before he could tighten his arm.

Mary Terror stepped out from the opposite end of the building with Drummer's bassinet held by one arm. She fired twice, a bullet for each of them.

The first shot shattered Earl Van Diver's right shoulder in a burst of flesh, bone, and blood. The twisting of Didi's head saved her from having her brains blown out. She was aware of a *zip* and a wasp's sting, but did not yet know that a chunk of her right ear was gone. Didi screamed, Van Diver fell to his knees, and Laura heard the shots and the scream and raced back between the lumber stacks the way she'd come.

Didi ran for cover. Mary shouted, "TRAITOR!" as she fired a third time. The bullet thunked into a pile of lumber and sent jagged splinters flying, but then Didi flung herself to the ground and scrambled into the maze of corridors between the lumber stacks.

Mary aimed her gun at the man on his knees. He was clutching his ruined shoulder, his face glistening with pain sweat. His speaker had been pulled out of his throat and lay beside him. He was grinning at Mary, an unearthly grin. She walked toward him, and saw steam rising from the man's face and bald scalp in the frigid air. Mary stopped. *Suffer,* she thought. "Oh, yeah," she said. "I remember." She pulled the hammer back, to blow his grin to pieces.

"Don't do it!" Laura said. She stood in the shelter of Mary's van, her gun trained on the big woman. "Put it down!"

Mary smiled, her eyes dark with hatred. She turned the Colt's barrel on the baby's head. "You put it down," she said. "At your feet. Right now."

And behind the building, the Wentzel brother who'd been shot in the chest was sitting up, his mouth gasping. The pit bulls were going crazy, smelling carnage. He held something in a bloody hand. It was a key ring he'd taken from his pocket, and a small key was ready to be used. "Good boys," he managed to say. "Somebody did your daddy real good." He pushed the key into the dogpen's lock. "Gonna chew up their asses, ain't you, boys?" The lock clicked open. He pulled against the dogpen's door. It swung open. "CHEW 'EM UP!" he commanded, and the pit bulls snarled and shivered with excitement as they boiled out of the cage. The brown one raced on, but the mottled dog paused to lick his master's chest for a few seconds before he, too, went hunting for meat.

"Down," Mary repeated. "Do it."

Laura didn't. "You won't hurt him. What would Jack say?"

"You won't shoot *me.* You might hit the baby." In five seconds, Mary decided, she would lunge to her knees—a movement that would take Laura by surprise—and fire the remaining bullets. She counted: one . . . two . . . three . . .

She heard a savage snarling, and she saw Laura's face contort with horror.

Something hit Mary's right side like a miniature freight train, its power knocking Drummer loose from her grip. As Mary fell, so did the baby's bassinet. It hit the ground alongside her and Drummer spilled out, his face red and his mouth open in a silent, indignant yell.

Something took hold of Mary's right forearm. It tightened like an iron vise, and Mary screamed with pain as her fingers spasmed open and the Colt dropped. Then she saw the brown pit bull's jaws clenched to her arm, its eyes staring into hers with murderous intent, and the beast suddenly shook its head back and forth with a violence that almost snapped her arm at the elbow. Mary clawed at the dog's eyes, its teeth ripping down through her brown sweater into the flesh and pain streaking up her shoulder.

Laura got her legs thawed and ran for her baby. Mary screamed in agony as the dog tore at her arm, her other hand trying to reach the Colt. And then Laura saw the gray and white pit bull race out from beside the building. It made a course change that froze Laura's heart.

It was going after David.

She dared not shoot, terrified of hitting the child. The pit bull was almost upon him, its jaws opening to ravage the precious flesh, and Laura heard herself shout "NO!" in a voice so powerful it made the animal's head tick toward her, its eyes aflame with bloodfever.

She took two more running strides and kicked the dog in the ribs as hard as she could, staggering it away from David. The pit bull whirled in a mad circle, snapping at the air, and then it went for the baby again, darting in so fast Laura had no time to aim a second kick. Its teeth snapped shut, snagging the baby's white blanket which was splotched with Edward Fordyce's dried blood. And then the pit bull shivered lustily and began to drag David through the sawdust on his back, the blanket tangled around his body.

Mary dug her fingers into the brown pit bull's eyes. The beast made a half groan, half howl and shook its head violently, its teeth tearing down through her flesh. It pulled against her arm with a terrible force, the shoulder muscles shrieking. The arm was about to be broken. Mary reached for her Colt, but her fingers lost it as the pit bull jerked her again and fresh agony filled her up. Then she went mad herself, punching at the animal's skull as it tried to drag her. The pit bull released her, backed off, and sprang again, its white fangs bared. Its jaws clamped on her right thigh, the teeth working through her corduroy jeans into the meat of her leg with crushing pressure.

Laura threw herself at the dog that was dragging David. She grabbed around its muscular throat and hung on. The pit bull let go of David's blanket and went for her face, its body quivering with power and its teeth snapping at her cheek with the sound of a bear trap springing. She shielded her face with her left hand. The jaws found it, and clenched shut.

She heard a sound like sticks cracking. A terrifying bolt of electric agony speared up through her wrist and forearm. Broke my hand! she realized as she kept fighting to pull the dog away from her baby. Bastard broke my hand! The pit bull savagely twisted her hand, more pain ripping through her fingers and wrist. She could feel the teeth grinding on the bones. She thought she screamed, but she wasn't sure. Her brain felt like a fever blister about to burst. She pressed the automatic's barrel against the pit bull's side and squeezed the trigger twice.

The dog shuddered with the shots, but it did not let go. And now it was trying to drag her, blood streaming from its side and foaming from its mouth. Its claws dug into the sawdust. Laura's wrist was about to snap. She fired again, into the side of the pit bull's blocky head, and the dog's lower jaw exploded in a spray of bone chips and blood.

Mary was fighting her own battle ten feet away. She slammed her knee into the brown pit bull's skull with everything she had behind it. Then a second and third time, as the dog's teeth kept tearing her thigh open. She got a finger hooked into one of the eyes and yanked it out like a white grape, and at last the pit bull grunted and released her thigh. It danced with pain, shaking its one-eyed head back and forth and snapping at the air. Mary crawled for the Colt, tried to latch her fingers around it, but they were spasming out of control, the nerves and muscles of her injured arm rioting. She looked up as the pit bull charged at her again, and she cried out and shielded her face with her arms.

It hit her shoulder with a bone-bruising blow, knocked Mary aside, and fell with a pain-maddened snarl upon Laura.

The dying dog was still hanging on to Laura's left hand. The one-eyed beast fastened its teeth on the overcoat sleeve of her right arm and began to tear at it. She couldn't get her gun angled to shoot it. She kicked and screamed, the one-eyed dog working on her right arm and the other animal still trying to crunch her hand with its ruined jaws.

Mary scrambled to the wailing baby, scooped him up with her left arm, and struggled to her feet. Blood streamed from her gnawed thigh, her jeans leg drenched. The two dogs had Laura between them, the woman trying to wrench loose. Mary saw the Colt on the ground. Her right hand was still convulsing, drops of blood falling from her fingertips. Panic flared within her. She was hurt badly, near passing out. If she fell and the dogs turned on her and Drummer . . .

She left the gun and hobbled toward the van, ignoring the man she'd shot. As Mary transferred Drummer to her right arm and used her left hand to open the driver's door, Didi came at her with a two-by-four she'd plucked off a lumber pile. Mary saw the blow coming and dodged it, the wood whacking against the van's side. And then Mary stepped in and drove a knee up into Didi's stomach, and Didi cried out and doubled over. Mary brought her left arm down across Didi's back, the blow whooshing the air from Didi's lungs and dropping her to her knees.

Didi groaned, her battle-flag-red hair hanging over her face in defeat. Mary could see how gray it was. Didi looked up at her, eyes watery with pain. It was the face of an old woman, tortured by the things that were.

"Go on," Didi said. "Kill me."

Laura kicked the dying pit bull away from her broken hand, and the animal staggered in dazed circles. The other dog still had hold of her ragged coat sleeve, its fangs starting to reach the flesh. She couldn't get a shot at it, unless . . .

She dropped the gun and wrenched her arm out of the overcoat, the dog's teeth snapping shut in its wake. Then she picked up the automatic, jammed the barrel right up under the pit bull's throat, and squeezed the trigger.

Mary Terror flinched at the sound of the shot. Blood was running down her leg in hot rivulets. Before her, Didi kneeled with sawdust in her hair, and Didi saw the raw fear in Mary's eyes. Mary's right hand was still spasming, torn muscles twitching in the forearm wound. Drummer was screaming in her ear, the world starting to turn gray. Mary got into the van with Drummer and slammed the door. She backed away from the building's side, intending to crush Didi beneath the wheels, but Didi had shaken the cobwebs loose and crawled to the safety of the lumber stacks. Mary got the van turned around and sped toward the gates, the tires throwing dust.

Five seconds later, Didi heard another car door open and close. She emerged from her hiding place as the BMW's engine started. Earl Van Diver was behind the wheel, his face a grinning, terrible rictus. As Van Diver twisted the wheel with his shattered shoulder, Didi saw his mouth open in a soundless scream. The BMW tore away, in pursuit of Mary Terror. Its right front tire went over the speaker and crushed it to bits.

Didi stood up. She saw the mottled pit bull lying on the ground. Laura was on her knees, her right arm free of the tattered coat sleeve, and the brown pit bull faced her six feet away. Didi picked up the two-by-four, her ear stinging, and walked toward the animal.

Before she got there, the pit bull groaned deep in its blasted-open throat and collapsed, its eyes fixed on the woman who'd delivered the bullet.

Tears of pain glistened on Laura's cheeks, but her face was shocked clean of all emotion. She looked at the bluish-red lump of her left hand. There were only three fingers and a thumb on it. The little finger was gone, torn off at the knuckle. Her hand made her think of a fresh steak, tenderized by a butcher's mallet.

"Oh my God," Didi said. Blood was dripping from her right ear like a chain of rubies. "Your . . . hand . . ."

Laura had gone deathly pale. She blinked, staring at Didi, and then she keeled over onto her side.

Laura's purse was in the car, Didi realized. Her money, credit cards . . . everything was gone. It was over, and Mary had won.

"Help me! Somebody!" The voice was coming from over near the dogpen. "I'm dyin' over here!"

Didi left Laura and went back to where the big-bellied man lay against the dogpen. He was a mess, but Didi saw that the blood wasn't spewing out so no arteries had been hit. He looked at her blearily, trying to focus. "Who're *you?*"

"Nobody," she said.

"You gonna kill me?"

She shook her head.

"Listen . . . listen . . . call an ambulance. Okay? Phone's in the office. Locked up." He offered her the bloody key ring. "Call an ambulance. Goddamn Kenny took off early. Oh, I'm hurtin'. Do it, okay?"

Didi accepted the key ring. One of the keys, she saw, was for a General Motors car. "The Olds is yours?"

"Yeah. Yeah. The Cutlass. Call an ambulance, I'm bleedin' to death."

She didn't think so. She knew a dying man when she saw one. This guy had a broken collarbone and maybe a punctured lung, but he was breathing all right. Still, she'd have to call the ambulance. "You just be quiet and don't move."

"What am I gonna do? A fuckin' polka?"

Didi hurried back to Laura, who was sitting up again. "Can you walk?"

"I think . . . I'm going to pass out."

"I've found us a car," Didi said.

Laura looked up at her friend, her eyes swollen and her broken hand throbbing almost beyond endurance. She wanted to lie on the ground, curl up, and cry in the cold. But she could not, because Mary Terror still had her baby, and Mary Terror was on her way to California. Laura had something left; she pulled it from a deep, unknown place, the same place where people gritted their teeth and fought uphill against the iron-spiked wheels of life. She had to keep going. There was no quitting, no surrender.

Laura lifted her right hand, and Didi helped her stand. Then Didi picked up the automatic, and she and Laura walked together past the dead dogs.

In the trailer, Didi called 911 and told the operator there'd been a shooting, that an ambulance was needed at the Wentzel Brothers Lumberyard near Geneseo. The operator said an ambulance would be there in eight to ten minutes, and for her to stay on the line. Didi hung up. A small metal box atop the office's desk caught her attention, and she spent forty seconds finding the right key to unlock it. Inside were a few checks clipped to copies of receipts, and a bank deposit envelope that held seventy-one dollars and thirty-five cents. She took the money.

Didi got behind the wheel of the Cutlass, with Laura lying semiconscious amid burger wrappers and crumpled beer cans in the backseat. A pair of large red plastic dice hung from the rearview mirror, and there was a Playboy bunny decal stuck prominently on the rear windshield. The Olds chugged, refusing to start as she turned the key. Didi thought she could hear a siren, getting closer. The Olds chugged again as Didi pumped the accelerator. And then the car shuddered, and with a cannon's *boom* black smoke blew from the tailpipe. Didi checked the gas gauge, seeing that its needle stood at a quarter of a tank.

The Cutlass creaked and groaned like a frigate in a tempest as Didi backed up, wrestled the grimy wheel, and drove toward the gates. She could feel the tires wanting to slew off to the right, and she decided it was best she hadn't looked to see how much tread they still wore. Then they were through the gates and heading back to the interstate, the Cutlass slowly but steadily gaining speed and making a racket like bricks in a cement mixer. An ambulance appeared ahead of them, approaching across the flat fields. It passed them, its siren yowling, on the way to save a Wentzel.

The two women went on, and only when they were five or six miles farther west along I-80 did Didi give one gasping, terrible sob and wipe her eyes with her dirty sleeve.

4.

White Tide

Across the Mississippi River, where I-80 shot straight and true toward Iowa City, Earl Van Diver was gaining on the woman who had savaged his life.

The van was going almost eighty, the BMW pushing past eighty-five. Van Diver gripped the wheel with his one good hand, the other hand cold and dead at the end of his torn-open shoulder. Blood was streaked over the seats, spattered across the instrument panel, soaked into the carpet beneath him. He was filling up with winter, his vision turning gray. It was getting more difficult to hold the wheel steady, the wind and his own weakness conspiring against him. Cars veered out of the paths of the two vehicles, a wake of horns echoing behind Van Diver. He glanced at the speedometer, saw the needle vibrating at eighty-seven. Mary had kept the van's speed up over eighty since they'd left the Geneseo exit, swinging back and forth from lane to lane to keep cars between them. Now, though, it was clear from the blue coughs of burning oil coming from the tailpipe that the van's engine was worn out, and she couldn't maintain that speed. Good, he thought as he felt the cold creeping through his cheeks. Good. He wasn't going to let her get away. Oh, no; not this time.

He felt no remorse for leaving Laura and Bedelia. The opportunity to take the car was there. Mary could not be allowed to roam free. She was an animal, and must be put to death like a rabid dog drooling foam. Put to death and death and death.

About the baby he had no emotion. The baby was there. Babies had died before; there were always babies. What was the death of a single baby if an animal like Mary Terror could be ground under? He knew he could never have made Laura Clayborne understand his life's purpose. How could she understand that every time he looked into a mirror he saw the face of Mary Terror? How could she understand the nightmare rages that had driven his wife and daughter away from him? How could she understand that the name *Mary* drove him crazy with hatred, and that his daughter's name had made him look at her with hatred, too. Laura Clayborne had lost a baby; he had lost himself, down into a dark hole of torment so horrible that it began to—dear God—make him dream of fucking Mary with the barrel of his gun, ah yes ah yes sweet sweet Mary you bitch you soul-sucking bitch, and in the mornings he would wake up wet and sated for a time.

But not for very long.

You're mine, Van Diver thought, his black eyes glazed and shiny.

Two more feet, and the BMW's front fender smashed into the van's rear with a jolt that cracked the stubs of his teeth together. He pushed the van toward the right, trying to force it off the highway, and tires shrieked in a burn of rubber as Mary fought the van back to the left again. A station wagon was in front of her, a Garfield stuck with suction cups to the rear windshield. Mary grazed the station wagon as it careened aside, scraping off a sheet of sparks. Then she was past it, veering around a tractor-trailer truck and back into the left lane. She looked up into the rearview mirror at the BMW's battered snout, and she saw the man's grinning, terrible face above the wheel. Little pig wants to play, she thought, and she stomped on the brake.

The BMW crashed into the back of the van, the hood crumpling and pieces of glass and metal flying up. Van Diver was lifted off his seat, his body thrown forward to strain the limits of his seat belt and his chin slamming against the steering wheel. His entire body tensed for the rest of the wreck, but Mary's foot was planted on the accelerator again and the van was pulling away with a backfire of burning oil, the BMW still traveling seventy miles an hour. Van Diver trembled, his muscles shocked from the impact and his trousers wet between his legs. He backed off from the van, swung into the right lane, and was looking at the back of a school bus about thirty yards away. A twist of the wheel and an inner scream, and he missed the school bus by a foot and a half. Then he powered the BMW forward again, red lights pulsing on the dashboard and a whip of smoke starting to flail back from the crumpled hood.

Mary saw him coming. Drummer was on the passenger-side floorboard on his stomach, his hands clasping and opening. Mary stomped the brake again and braced for the jolt. Once more the BMW collided into the back of the van, further smashing the hood and throwing its driver forward in the second before Mary hit the accelerator. The gap between them widened, Mary's backbone aching from the force of the collision, and her teeth clenched together. Her gnawed thigh was wet with blood, her right forearm ripped open, and red muscle tissue spasmed in the fissure. The wounds were numb and cold, but black motes spun before her eyes. Oily sweat had risen on her cheeks and forehead, and she could feel the clammy fingers of shock trying to drag her under. If she gave in to it, she was finished.

The BMW was coming up fast again. Mary started to hit the brake, but the car suddenly swerved around her into the right lane, on Drummer's side. The van shuddered and moaned as the BMW smashed into it, the impact rolling Drummer across the floorboard like a limp rag and almost knocking the wheel from Mary's white-knuckled grip. She fought back, slamming the van into the BMW. Like two enraged beasts, the car and the van crashed back and forth along the interstate at almost eighty miles an hour. Streamers of smoke were whirling from the BMW's wrecked hood, a shriek of scraping metal coming from the engine. Van Diver saw the temperature gauge's needle shoot up past the warning line, the car beginning to shimmy out of control. Blue light winked in the rearview mirror, and both Van Diver and Mary saw the trooper car roaring after them.

Mary took the Compact Magnum from her bag, the pain waking up with a ferocious bite in her forearm.

Still Van Diver rammed the BMW against the van's side, Mary's left tires going onto the grassy median. She felt true fear clutch her throat; ahead of her in her lane was what looked like a tanker truck of some kind. Van Diver hit her again, keeping her from moving over. The trooper car was speeding up onto Van Diver's rear, lights flashing and siren awail. Ahead of Mary, the tanker truck—painted with brown and white blotches like a cow's hide and with the pink-painted udders of hose nozzles underneath—was trying to get over into the right lane. She saw the red sign stenciled on its side: SUNNYDALE FARMS DAIRY.

Mary let go of the wheel, the van beginning to slide over onto the median, and she strained toward the passenger door with her foot pressed on the accelerator. She put the gun against the glass, aimed downward at the BMW, and pulled the trigger, her face contorted with the strain.

The driver's window exploded in on Van Diver, glass blasting his face. He was blinded with blood, and as he opened his mouth to give a soundless scream he heard the ghost voices and static of a highway patrol radio sparking from the metal in his jaw. Something—another bullet, hot as a shock—tore into his right knee and seized up the muscles. He wrenched the wheel to the right, trying to get away from the van, and as he felt the car violently fishtail into a skid and the tanker loom in his windshield he heard a single, awful voice from the phantom radio say, "Oh Jesus."

At the same instant as Earl Van Diver skidded into the dairy tanker at seventy-eight miles per hour, Mary Terror was throwing her weight against the wheel, forcing the van onto the median. The back end of the tanker was right there in front of her. Going to hit! she screamed inwardly, bracing for the impact. Going to hit!

The van cleared a collision by less than half a foot, grass and clumps of dirt flying up behind the rear wheels. As the BMW hit the tanker broadside, it folded up like an accordion being squeezed. In the rending of metal and smashing of glass, red flames shot high, followed by an explosion of white, frothy milk as the tanker's storage compartment ripped open at the seams. The milk flooded forth, a white tide surging through the air, and it deluged the highway patrol car as the trooper tried to make the right shoulder. The tires lost their purchase, the patrol car turned sideways and flipped over as it left the interstate, crashing through the guardrail and turning over twice more before it came to rest, upside down and smoking, in the brown dirt of a bean field.

Mary Terror was already swerving into the left lane on the other side of the wreck, which had taken about four seconds from the BMW's impact to the overturning of the trooper's car. She glanced in the sideview mirror, the air behind her hazed with smoke and burning milk, the tanker on its side and the truck's driver struggling out from behind the wheel. Of the BMW, nothing could be seen but a scorched tire rolling westward for ten yards before it went off onto the median.

Both the lanes behind her were blocked by fire and tangled metal. Mary picked Drummer up by the back of his jump suit. He was crying, the tears streaming down his face. His nose and his left cheek had been scraped raw, little drops of blood trickling from his nostrils. Mary licked the blood away and held him against her as he cried. "Shhhhh," she said. "Shhhhhh. Mama's got her baby now. Everything's cool."

But it wasn't. A second highway patrol car, lights flashing, passed her going east toward the wreck. It was time to get off I-80 for a while, and find a place to rest. She was near exhaustion, her eyes heavy-lidded, the smell of her own blood making her sick. It was time to find a hole to hide in.

She took the next exit. A sign stood at a crossroads on the flat land, pointing one way to Plain View and another to Maysville. Farm-houses stood about, smoke rising from chimneys, acres of fields going on toward the far horizon. Mary kept driving, drowsy with loss of blood. On the other side of Plain View's two streets and meager gathering of buildings, she pulled off onto a dirt road that twisted into an orchard of denuded apple trees. She cut the engine, and there she sat with Drummer cradled against her.

Her vision was fading, the world closing in on her. She was afraid of falling asleep because she might not awaken. She felt a pressure on her index finger; Drummer had grasped it, was holding it tightly. Dark-ness pulled at her, a seductive current. She folded her arms around the baby in a coil of protection. Sleep for just a little while, she thought. Maybe an hour or two, and then get back onto the interstate west. Just an hour or two, and she'd be all right.

Mary's eyes closed. The baby's fingers played with her Smiley Face button. Mary dreamed of Lord Jack sitting in a sunlit room talking to God about why he drowned in a bathtub in Paris.

On the interstate twelve miles west, Didi joined the backup of cars and trucks stopped by the wreckage. Laura was unconscious in the backseat, but every so often she gave a muffled, gasping moan that tore at Didi's heart. The troopers and firemen were out in force, guiding the traffic onto the tire-scarred median around the wreck. A news-team van was there, minicams at work, and a helicopter buzzed overhead. "What happened?" Didi asked a fireman as she approached the wreckage at a crawl, and the man said, "Milk truck and car hit. Smokey went off the road, too."

"You're sure it was a car? It wasn't a van?"

"Car," he said. "Truck driver says some damn yuppie plowed right into him, must've been goin' eighty."

"A yuppie?"

"Yeah. One of them yuppie cars. Come on, I think you can get past now." He waved her on through.

Didi negotiated the median. A wrecker was in the midst of the scorched metal, trying to pull part of a car free. The firemen were hosing down the pavement, and the air smelled of hot iron and clabbered milk.

She passed a tire lying in the brown grass. On its dented wheel cover was a circle cut into blue and white triangles, and the scarred letters BMW.

Didi looked away from it as if the sight had stung her. Then the Cutlass picked up speed and left the dead behind.

5.

Doctor Didi

The darkness came.

The wind blew cold across the plains, and flurries of snow spat from the clouds. At the Liberty Motor Lodge six miles east of Iowa City, Laura lay in bed in Room 10 and alternately shivered and sweated beneath the sheet and coarse blanket. The TV was on, tuned to a family sitcom. Laura couldn't focus on it, but she liked the sound of the voices. On the bedside table was the debris of her dinner: two plastic McDonald's burger containers, an empty french fries pack, and a half-finished Coke. A plastic bag full of crushed ice lay at her side, useful when the pain in her hand got to be excruciating and she needed to numb it. Laura stared fixedly at the TV set, waiting for Didi to come back. Didi had been gone thirty minutes, hunting for a drugstore. They had agreed on what needed to be done, and she knew what was ahead for her.

Every so often she chewed her lower lip. It had gotten raw, but she kept chewing it. She could hear the whine of the wind outside, and once in a while she imagined she heard the sound of a baby crying in it. She had gotten up once to look outside, but the effort had so drained her that she couldn't force herself to get up again. So she listened to the wind and the crying baby and she knew she was very, very close to the edge and it would not take much for her to open that door and go wandering in the hungry dark.

They had lost Mary Terror and David. That much was certain. Exactly how Van Diver had crashed into the milk tanker, Laura didn't know, but Mary and David were gone. But Mary had been badly hurt, too, losing a lot of blood. She'd been weary—maybe even more weary than Laura—and she couldn't have gotten very far. Where would she have stopped? Surely not a motel; not with blood all over her and her leg chewed up. Would she have just found a place to pull the van over and spend the night? No, because she'd have to run the engine all night or she and David would freeze to death. So that left one other possibility: that Mary had invited herself into somebody's house. It wouldn't be hard for her to do, not with the farmhouses spread hundreds of acres apart. How far west had Mary gotten before she'd decided to leave the interstate? Was she ahead of them, or behind them? It was impossible to know, but Laura did know one vital thing: Mary Terror's destination. Wherever Mary was, however long she rested and let her wounds heal, she would sooner or later be back on the highway with David, heading for Freestone, California, and the memory of a lost hero.

And that, too, was Laura's destination, even if she had to get there on her hands and knees. Minus one finger, with scar tissue toughening her heart. She was going to get David back, or die trying.

When Laura heard the key slide into the door's lock, she thought she might be sick. But her food stayed down, and Didi came in with snowflakes in her red hair and a sack in her arms.

"Got the stuff," Didi said as she closed the door against the cold and double-latched it. She had found not a drugstore but a K-Mart, and she'd bought them both gloves, woolen socks, fresh underwear, toothpaste, and toothbrushes as well as the other necessities. As Didi put the sack down, Laura realized Didi had gained about twenty pounds since she'd left the motel. Didi pulled off her sweater and revealed the weight gain: there were two more thick sweaters underneath the first one.

"My God," Laura rasped. "You shoplifted."

"I had to do it," Didi said as she peeled another layer off. "We've only got about thirty-five dollars left." She smiled, the lines deepening around her eyes. "Shoplifting isn't what it used to be. They watch you like a hawk."

"So how'd you do it without getting caught?"

"You give a kid in a Quiet Riot jacket a buck to knock over a display of skiwear, and then you come out of the dressing room, put your head down, and walk. It helps to be buying other items, too. That way you don't go out past the guard, and those cashiers don't give a crap." She threw one of the sweaters on the bed beside Laura, who picked it up with her right hand.

"Inferior quality," Laura decided. It was dark gray, banded with green stripes the color of puke. Didi's new sweater was yellow with cardinals on the front. "Did prisoners sew these?"

"Beggars can't be choosers. Neither can shoplifters." But the fact was that she *had* been careful to choose the bulkiest knits she could find. The cold of Nebraska and Wyoming would make Iowa's weather seem balmy. Didi continued to take items out of the sack. At last she came to the wooden tongue depressors, the gauze bandages, a small pair of scissors, a box of wide Band-Aids, and a bottle of iodine and a bottle of hydrogen peroxide. Didi swallowed hard, getting herself ready for what had to be done. This was going to be like trying to build a house with thumbtacks, but it was the best they could do. She looked at Laura and offered another smile, the woman's face bleached with pain. "Doctor Didi's come to call," Didi said, and then she looked away before her smile cracked and betrayed her.

"Do your ear first."

"What? That scratch? Just got skin, that's all." Her wounded ear, hidden beneath her hair, had crusted over. It hurt like hell, but Laura needed the attention. "Oh, I got this, too." She took a bottle of Extra-Strength Excedrin from her pocket and set it aside. "Courtesy of my fast hands." She wished it were industrial strength, because before this night was over they were both going to need some heavy drugs. "Sorry I couldn't get you any liquor."

"That's all right. I'll survive."

"Yeah, I believe you will." Didi went to the bathroom, wet a washrag, and brought it out for Laura. When the pain got really bad, Laura was going to need something to chew on. "You ready?"

"Ready."

Didi got the tongue depressors out. A little wider than Popsicle sticks, they were. "Okay," she said. "Let's take a look." She peeled the covers back from Laura's hand.

Laura watched Didi's face. She thought that Didi did a very good job of not flinching at the sight. Laura knew it was hideous. The mangled hand—hamburger hand, she thought—was burning hot, and every so often it throbbed with a pain so intense it sucked away Laura's breath. The stub of the little finger was still drooling some watery blood, which had soaked into a towel underneath her hand and onto the sheet. The three other fingers and thumb were curved into claws.

"What'll my manicurist say?" Laura asked.

"You should've soaked in Palmolive."

Laura laughed, but it had a nervous edge. Didi sighed, wishing to God there was someone else who could do this. It could've been worse, though. The dogs could've gotten to Laura's throat, or torn up her legs, or chewed into her other arm. Or killed the baby. Didi looked at the wedding band and engagement ring on the swollen finger. There was no way short of cutting them to get them off.

"The diamond," Laura said. "Can you work it out of the setting?"

"I don't know." She touched the upraised diamond and found it was already loose, two of its six prongs broken.

"Try. I'll hang on."

"Why do you want the diamond out?"

"We've got only thirty-five dollars left," Laura reminded her. "Have we got anything else to pawn but my diamond?"

They did not. Didi grasped Laura's bruised wrist as gently as she could and went to work with the scissors, trying to pry the diamond out. Laura was braced for agony, but none came. "That finger's dead," she said. In a few minutes Didi had managed to loosen a third prong. The diamond jiggled around, but it still didn't have quite enough room to be popped out. The fourth prong was tougher. "Hurry, okay?" Laura asked in a faint voice. After two or three more minutes, Didi got the fourth prong bent enough to slide a tip of the scissors blade under the diamond and lever it out. It popped free, and Didi held it in her palm. "Nice rock. What'd your husband pay for it?"

"Three thousand dollars." Sweat sparkled on Laura's face. "That was eight years ago."

"Maybe we can get five hundred for it. An honest pawnbroker's not going to touch an unmounted diamond without ownership papers." She wrapped the diamond up in a Band-Aid and put it into her pocket. "Okay. Ready for the big job?"

"Yes. Let's get it over with."

Didi began by washing the hand with hydrogen peroxide. Bloody foam hissed up from the bite wounds, and Laura moaned and chewed on the washrag. Didi had to repeat the task twice more, until all the grit was washed away. Laura's eyes were squeezed shut, tears trickling from the corners. Didi reached for the iodine. "Well," she said, "this ought to sting just a little." Laura pushed the rag between her teeth again, and Didi began the awful work.

There was a pain that Laura would always remember. She had been nine years old. She'd been riding her bike, flying hell-for-leather on a country road, when the tires had slipped out from under her on loose gravel. There had been bloody holes in her knees, her arms were raw, her elbows bleeding, her chin gashed. And the worst of it was that she'd been two miles from home. There was no one to hear her cry. No one to help her. So she got up, remounted that traitorous bike, and started pedaling again, because it was the only way. "Laura!" she remembered her mother screaming. "You've crippled yourself!"

No, the injury hadn't been crippling. She had grown scabs and scars, but on that day she had begun to grow up.

This pain also taught a hard lesson. It was like sticking her hand into hot charcoals, dousing it with salty water, and then back into the coals again. She shivered, the sweat rising in beads from her pores. It was a mercy that ten seconds after Didi began the task, Laura lost consciousness. When she awakened, Didi had finished the application of disinfectant and was completing the splint on Laura's ring finger, pulling it out straight and bandaging one of the sticks along Laura's palm and finger. Then it was the middle finger's turn.

When Didi touched it, Laura winced. "Sorry," Didi said. "There's no other way."

She began to pull the finger out straight, and Laura screamed behind the washrag.

Again Laura passed out, which was a blessing because Didi could do the work quickly, getting the splint into place and securing it with Band-Aids. She had just finished the index finger when Laura's eyelids fluttered. Laura spat the rag out, her face yellowish-white. "Sick," she gasped, and Didi rushed to get a trash can up to Laura's mouth.

The ordeal wasn't yet over. Didi splinted the thumb, another exercise in torment, and wrapped the hand with gauze bandages, the pressure again making Laura groan and sweat. "You don't want to go through life with a claw, do you?" Didi asked as she cut the gauze and began a new layer. Laura breathed like a slow bellows, her eyes vacant and clouded with pain. "Almost got it wrapped up," Didi said. "That's supposed to be funny." It wasn't, really. In the morning the bandages would have to be changed, the wounds cleansed again, and they both knew it.

"Lucy," Laura whispered as Didi finished the wrapping.

"What? Lucy who?"

"Lucy and Ethel." She swallowed, her throat parched. "When they were . . . wrapping the candies . . . and the candies started coming faster and faster off the conveyor belt. Did you see that one?"

"Oh, yeah! It's a scream!"

"Good show," Laura said. Her hand was a seething mass of fire and anguish, but the healing process had begun. "They don't . . . make 'em like that anymore."

"I liked the one where Lucy was in Las Vegas and she had to walk down a staircase with that big headdress on. Remember? And the one where she puts too much yeast in the bread and it shoots out of the oven like a freight train. Those were great." She cut the gauze and taped it down with a couple of Band-Aids. "It always killed me when Lucy tried to get a part in one of Ricky's shows, and he blew up at her in Spanish." Didi rested Laura's bandaged hand against the ice pack. "I watched those with my mom and dad. We had a TV with a round screen, and the damned thing was always shorting out. I remember my dad on his knees trying to fix the set, and he said, 'Didi, the guy who can figure out how to keep these things working is going to make a lot of money.'"

"Why?" Laura asked weakly.

"Why what?"

"Why did you join the Storm Front?"

Didi rolled the remainder of the gauze up and closed the box of

Band-Aids. She put the scissors and the other items atop the room's cheap dresser. Beyond the window, Didi could hear the high waspish whine of the freezing wind. "What do you expect me to say?" Didi finally asked when she saw Laura still watching her. "That I was a bad kid? That I pulled the legs off grasshoppers and beat kittens with baseball bats? No, I didn't grow up like that. I was president of the home economics club in high school, and I made the honor roll every semester. I played piano for the youth choir at my church." She shrugged. "I wasn't a monster. The only thing was, I didn't know what was growing inside me."

"What was that?"

"A yearning," Didi said. "To be different. To know things. To go places my folks only read about. See, you take Lucy: if you only watched shows like that on TV, night after night, soon you'd start thinking that's all the world had to offer. My folks were afraid of real life. They didn't want me out in it. They said I was going to make a fine wife for some local boy, that I'd live maybe three or four miles from their front door and raise a houseful of kids and we'd all get together for pot roast on Sundays." Didi opened the curtains and looked out the window. Snowflakes spun before the light; the cars in the parking lot were frosted over. "They were amazed when I said I wanted to go to college. When I said I wanted to go to college out of Iowa, it was the first day of a long cold war. They couldn't understand why I didn't want to stay put. I was a fool, they said. I was breaking their hearts. Well, I didn't understand this then, but they needed me between them or they wouldn't have any common ground. They didn't want me to grow up, and when I did . . . they didn't know me anymore. They didn't want to." She let the curtains fall. "So I guess part of why I left home was to find out what my folks were so afraid of."

"Did you?"

"Yes, I did. Like any generation, they were terrified of the future. Terrified of being insignificant and forgotten." She nodded. "It's a deep terror, Laura. Sometimes I feel it. I never got married—oh, bourgeois disease!—and I never had a child. My time for that is over. When I die, no one's going to cry at my funeral. No one's going to know my story. I'll lie under weeds near a road where strangers pass, and no one will remember the sound of my voice, the color of my hair, or what I gave a damn about. That's why I've stayed with you, Laura. Do you understand?"

"No."

"I want you to get your baby back," Didi said, "because I'm never going to have a child of my own. And if I can help you find David . . . that's kind of like he's mine, too, isn't it?"

"Yes," Laura answered. She could feel herself drifting away from the world, on waves of raw pain. It was going to be a long, terrible night. "Kind of."

"It's good enough for me." Didi got Laura a cup of water and gave her two aspirin. The fever sweat glistened on Laura's face again, and she groaned as her hand pulsed with white-hot agony. Didi drew a chair up beside the bed and sat there as Laura fought the pain as best she could. What was going to happen tomorrow, Didi didn't know. It depended on Laura: if she was well enough to travel, they ought to be heading west again as soon as possible. Didi got up after a while, and took the plastic bag out to the ice maker for a refill. While she was there, she found a newspaper vending machine, and used her last change to buy an Iowa City *Journal*. Back in the warm room, the smells of iodine and sickness thick in the air, Didi got Laura's hand situated on the ice pack and then sat down to read.

She found the story of the crash on I-80 on page three. The body, a male, remained unidentified. "Not much left to work from," the coroner had remarked. Except that the car, a late-model BMW, had a Georgia license plate. Didi realized that by now the tracing of the tag would be done and the FBI would know whose car it was. The police-beat reporters would smell a new scent on an old story, and pretty soon Laura's picture would start showing up in the papers again. And Mary Terror's picture, too. The death of Earl Van Diver might well make Mary and the baby front-page news once more.

Didi looked at Laura, who had fallen into an exhausted sleep. Any picture of the old Laura that appeared in a newspaper wouldn't resemble the woman who lay there, her face pinched with anguish and tough with determination. But if Mary and the baby were back prominently in the news, that meant more of a chance for someone to recognize her. And more of a chance that some Smokey with a macho complex might spot her, do something stupid, and get David killed.

She turned on the TV, keeping the volume low, and she watched the ten o'clock Iowa City newscast. Coverage of the wreck was there as well, and an interview with the milk tanker driver, a fat-cheeked man with a bloody bandage on his forehead and a glazed stare that said he'd had a peek into his own grave. "I seen this van and the other car comin' and the highway patrol right behind 'em," the driver explained in a quavering voice. "Maybe doin' eighty, all three of 'em. The van was flyin' up on my tail and I tried to get over in the right lane and then wham the car hit my tanker and it was all she wrote." The newscaster said the highway patrol and state police were searching for a dark green van with a Georgia license plate.

As Didi listened to the rest of the news, she picked up a notepad with Liberty Motor Lodge and a cracked bell printed across the top. With a motel pencil she wrote *Mary Terror.* Then *Freestone,* and three names she had memorized long ago: *Nick Hudley, Keith Cavanaugh, Dean Walker.* Beneath the third name she drew a circle, put two dots in it for eyes and the arc of a mouth: a Smiley Face, like the button she'd seen on Mary's sweater there at the lumberyard.

The troopers would be on the sniff for Mary's van. They'd be out in droves tomorrow. But they might also be looking for a stolen Oldsmobile Cutlass with a Playboy bunny decal on the rear windshield. It wouldn't hurt to scrape that damned thing off, do away with the hanging dice, and, while she was out in the cold dark, swap license plates with one of the other cars parked outside. How many people looked at their plates, especially on a frigid gray morning? The scissor blades might work to loosen screws as well as the prongs of an engagement ring. If not, then not.

Didi tore off the notepad's page, folded it, and put it into her pocket along with the diamond. She destroyed the next two pages, getting rid of the indentations. She put on her second sweater and her gloves, checked again on Laura's hand—blood coming up through the gauze, but there was nothing more to be done but freeze it with ice—and then Didi went outside to do things that told her she still had the instincts of a Storm Fronter.

6.

Sanctuary of Wishes

Pigs were searching for a dark green van with a Georgia license plate?

Good, Mary thought. She was half dozing, her feet up on the Barcalounger and the TV on before her in the cozy little den. By the time the pigs found the van in Rocky Road's barn, she'd be long gone with Drummer.

Her stomach was full. Two ham sandwiches, a big bowl of potato salad, a cup of hot vegetable soup, a can of applesauce, and most of a bag of Oreo cookies. She had fed Drummer his formula—warmed on the stove, which he appreciated—burped him, changed his diaper, and put him to sleep. He'd gone out like a light, in the bed shared by Rocky Road and Cherry Vanilla.

Mary watched the TV through eyelids at half mast. Pigs were searching, the newscaster had said on the ten o'clock news from Iowa City, sixteen miles west of the farmhouse she'd invited herself to visit. Baskin was the name on the mailbox. Mary used to buy ice cream at Baskin-Robbins in Atlanta. Her favorite flavor was Rocky Road. He'd looked like Rocky Road, dark-haired and chunky, enough of a roll of flab around his belly to make him soft and slow and oh-so-easy. His wife was blond and petite, with rosy cheeks. Cherry Vanilla, she was. The fourteen-year-old boy was dark-haired like his father, but more wiry: Fudge Ripple, she figured he'd be if he were a flavor.

There were family pictures on the paneled walls. Smiling faces, all. They no longer smiled. In the garage were two vehicles: a brown pickup truck with a University of Iowa sticker on the rear bumper, and a dark blue Jeep Cherokee. The Cherokee was roomy and had almost a full tank of gas. All she'd have to do is move her suitcases, the baby supplies, and her Doors records from the van, and she'd be ready to roll. An added prize had been finding Rocky Road's gun cabinet. He had three rifles and a Smith & Wesson .38 revolver, with plenty of ammunition for all of them. The revolver would join her own Magnum when she packed the Cherokee.

Mary had taken a shower. Had washed her hair and scrubbed her face, and carefully cleaned her wounds with a solution of rubbing alcohol and warm soapy water that had left her gasping with pain on the bathroom floor. Her forearm wound looked the nastiest, with its raw red edges and its glint of bone down in the crusted matter, and her fingers from time to time would convulse as if she were clawing the air. But it was her torn thigh that kept oozing blood and hurting like a barefoot walk on razor blades. Her knee had turned purple and had swollen up, too, and the bruises advanced all the way to her hip. Mary had packed cotton against the wounds, put bandages from the medicine cabinet on top of those, and bound her forearm and thigh with strips of torn sheets. Then she'd put on one of Rocky Road's woolen bathrobes, gotten herself a Bud from the refrigerator, and eased herself into the Barcalounger to wait out the night.

The newscast's weather segment came on. A woman with blond hair sculpted into a spray-frozen helmet stood in front of a map and pointed to a storm system growing up in northwest Canada. Should be hitting the Iowa City–Cedar Rapids area in thirty-six to forty-eight hours, she said. Good news for the ski resorts, she said, and bad news for travelers.

Mary reached over beside her chair and picked up the road atlas she'd found in Fudge Ripple's room, there on his desk next to his geography homework papers. It was opened to the map of the United States, showing the major interstate highways. I-80 would be the most direct route to San Francisco and Freestone, taking her through Iowa, Nebraska, curving up into Wyoming and down again into Utah, through Nevada and finally into northern California. If she kept her speed at sixty-five and the weather wasn't too bad, she could make Freestone in another couple of days. When she left here depended on how she felt in the morning, but she wasn't planning on spending another night in a dead man's house. The telephone had rung five times since she'd herded them into the barn at six o'clock, and that made her nervous. Rocky Road might be the mayor or the preacher around here, or Cherry Vanilla might be the belle of the farm-life social set. You never knew. So it was best to clear out as soon as her bones could take the highway again.

She was weary, and she ached. Growing old, she thought. Giving in to pain and getting weak.

Ten years ago she could have strangled Bedelia Morse with one hand. Should've beat her to death with a piece of wood, she thought. Or shot her with the Magnum and then run the van over the other bitch. But things had been moving so fast, and she'd known she was torn up and she was deep-down scared she was going to pass out before she and Drummer could get away. She'd figured the pit bulls were going to finish Laura Clayborne off, but now she was wishing she'd been certain.

I panicked, she thought. *I panicked and left them both alive.*

But their car was gone. The dogs had done a number on Laura, at least as bad as the damage done to herself. Should have killed her, Mary fretted. Should have run over her with the van before I left. No, no; Laura Clayborne was finished. If she was still alive, she was gasping in a hospital bed somewhere. *Suffer,* she thought. *I hope you suffer good and long for trying to steal my baby.*

But she was growing old. She knew it. Growing old, getting panicked, and leaving loose strings.

Mary slowly and painfully got out of the lounger and limped back to check on Drummer. He was sleeping soundly on the bed, cuddled up in a clean blue blanket, the pacifier clenched in his mouth, and his cherub face scraped from friction with the floorboard. She stood there, watching him sleep, and she could feel fresh blood oozing down her thigh but she didn't mind. He was a beautiful boy. An angel, sent from heaven as a gift for Jack. He was so very beautiful, and he was hers.

"I love you," Mary whispered in the quiet.

Jack was going to love him, too. She knew he would.

Mary picked up her bloody jeans from the floor and reached into a pocket. She brought out the clipping from the Sierra Club newsletter, now stained with spots of gore. Then she limped back to the den, and the telephone there. She found a phone book, got the area code she needed, and dialed directory assistance in northern California. "Freestone," she told the operator. "I'd like the number of Keith Cavanaugh." She had to spell the last name.

It was rattled off by one of those computer voices that sound human. Mary wrote the number down on a sheet of yellow notepad paper. Then Mary dialed directory assistance a second time. "Freestone. I'd like the number of Nick Hudley."

It joined the first phone number on the sheet. A third call: "Freestone. Dean Walker."

"The number you have requested is not available at this time," the computer voice said.

Mary hung up, and put a question mark beside Dean Walker's name. An unlisted number? Did the man not have a phone? She sat in a chair next to the phone, her leg really hurting again. She stared at Keith Cavanaugh's number. Did she dare to dial it? What would happen if she recognized Jack's voice? Or what if she dialed both numbers and neither voice was Jack's? Then that would leave Dean Walker, wouldn't it? She picked up the receiver again; her fingers did their clutching dance, and she had to put the phone down for a minute until the spasms had ceased.

Then she dialed the area code and the number of Keith Cavanaugh.

One ring. Two. Three. Mary's throat had dried up. Her heart was pounding. What would she say? What *could* she say? Four rings. Five. And on and on, without an answer.

She hung up. It was a little after nine o'clock in Freestone. Not too late to be calling, after all these years. She dialed Nick Hudley's number.

After four rings, Mary heard the phone click as it was being picked up. Her stomach had knotted with tension.

"Hello?" A woman's voice. Hard to say how old.

"Hi. Is Nick Hudley there, please?"

"No, I'm sorry. Nick's at the council meeting. Can I take a message?"

"Um . . ." She was thinking furiously. "I'm a friend of Nick's," she said. "I haven't seen him for a long time."

"Really? What's your name?"

"Robin Baskin," she said.

"Do you want Nick to call you back?"

"Oh, no . . . that's all right. Listen, I'm trying to find the number of another friend of mine in Freestone. Do you know a man named Dean Walker?"

"Dean? Sure, everybody knows Dean. I don't have his home number, but you can reach him at Dean Walker Foreign Cars. Do you want that number?"

"Yes," Mary said. "Please."

The woman went away from the phone. When she returned, she said, "Okay, Robin, here it is." Mary wrote down the telephone number and the address of Dean Walker Foreign Cars. "I don't think they're open this late, though. Are you calling from the Freestone area?"

"No, it's long distance." She cleared her throat. "Are you Nick's wife?"

"Yes, I am. Can I give Nick your number? Council meeting's usually over before ten."

"Oh, that's all right," Mary said. "I'm on my way there. I'll just wait and surprise him. One more thing . . . see, I used to live in Freestone, a long time ago, and I've lost touch with people. Do you know Keith Cavanaugh?"

"Keith and Sandy. Yes, I do."

"I tried to call Keith, but nobody's home. I just wanted to make sure he still lived there."

"Oh, yes. Their house is just down the road."

"Good. I'd like to go by and see him, too."

"Uh . . . may I tell my husband you called, Robin?"

"Sure," Mary said. "Tell him I'll be there in a couple of days."

"All right." The woman's voice was beginning to sound a little puzzled. "Have we ever met?"

"No, I don't think so. Thanks for your help." She hung up, and then she dialed Cavanaugh's number once more. Again there was no answer. Mary stood up, her thigh swollen and hot, and she limped to the Barcalounger and her can of beer. Two days and she'd be in Freestone. Two days, and she'd find Lord Jack again. It was a thought to dream on.

Mary fell asleep, with the lights on and the TV going and the wind shrilling outside. In her sanctuary of wishes, she walked with Lord Jack across a wide, grassy hillside. The ocean was spread out in a tapestry of blue and green before them, and the thunder of waves echoed from the rocks. She was young and fresh, with her whole life before her, and when she smiled there was no hardness in her eyes. Jack, wearing tie-dyed robes, held Drummer in his arms, and his blond hair flowed down around his shoulders and back like spun gold. Mary saw a house in the distance, a beautiful two-story house with rock chimneys and moss growing where the Pacific spray had touched. She knew that house, and where it stood. The Thunder House was where the Storm Front had begun, in its ritual of candles and blood oaths. It was where she had first been loved by Lord Jack, and where she had given her heart to him forever.

It was the only house she'd ever called home.

Lord Jack hugged their baby close, and he put an arm around the tall, slim girl at his side. They walked together through flowers, the air damp and salty with ocean mist, a lavender fog creeping across Drakes Bay. "I love you," she heard Jack say close in her ear. "I've always loved you. Can you dig it?"

Mary smiled and said she could. An iridescent tear rolled down her cheek.

They went on toward the Thunder House with Drummer between them and the promise of a new beginning ahead.

And in the Barcalounger, Mary slept heavily in an exhaustion of blood loss and weary flesh, her mouth partway open and a long silver thread of saliva drooling over her chin. The bandages on her thigh and forearm were splotched with red. Outside, snow flurries spun from the sky and frosted the barren fields, and the temperature fell below fifteen degrees.

She was a long way from the land of her dreams.

Ten miles west of where Mary rested, Laura moaned in a fever sweat. Didi roused herself from a cramped sleep in the chair to check on Laura, and then she closed her eyes again because there was nothing she could do to ease the other woman's pain, both physical and mental. The scissor blades had proved worthless for the task of removing screws from license plates, but Didi had gone through an assortment of junk in the Cutlass's trunk and found a screwdriver that would work. The Cutlass now bore a Nebraska tag, its Playboy decal had been scraped away, and the red plastic dice trashed.

Sleep took the sufferers, and for a little while shielded them from hurt. But midnight had passed and a cold dawn was coming, storm clouds already sliding down from Canada in the iron dark. The baby woke up with a start, his blue eyes searching and his mouth working the pacifier. He saw strange shapes and unknown colors, and he heard the shrill and bump of muffled sounds: the threshold of a mysterious, frightening world. In a few minutes his heavy eyelids closed. He drifted off to sleep again, innocent of sin, and his hands clutched for a mother who was not there.

VII
Funeral Pyre

1.

The Power of Love

H orn blowing.

Mary's eyes opened, the lids gummy and swollen.

Horn blowing outside. Outside the house.

Her heart kicked. She sat up in the Barcalounger, and every joint in her body seemed to scream in unison. A gasp of pain came from Mary's lips. Horn blowing outside, in the gray gloom of a winter morning. She'd gone to sleep with the TV going and the lights on; a man with a crew cut was talking about soybean production on the tube. When she tried to stand up, the jolt of agony that shot through her thigh took her breath. The bandages were crusted with dark blood, the smell of copper rank in the room. Her forearm wound pulsed with heat, but it was numb and so was her right hand. She stood up from the chair with an effort that made the air hiss between her teeth, and she hobbled to a window where she could see the front of the house.

A thin layer of snow had fallen during the night, and covered the fields. Out on the white-dusted road, about sixty yards from the farmhouse, sat a school bus with CEDAR COUNTY SCHOOLS on its side. Come to pick up Fudge Ripple, Mary knew. Except the boy wasn't ready for school. He was fast asleep, under the hay. The school bus sat there for fifteen seconds more, and then the driver gave a last frustrated honk on the horn and the bus pulled away, heading to the next house down the road.

Mary found a clock. It was seven thirty-four. She felt weak, light-headed, and nausea throbbed in her stomach. She staggered into a bathroom and leaned over the toilet, and she retched a few times but nothing much came up. She looked at herself in the mirror: her eyes sunken in swollen folds, her flesh as gray as the dawn. Death, she thought. That's what I look like. Her leg was hurting with a vengeance, and she searched through a closet in the bathroom until she found a bottle of Excedrin. She took three of them, crunching them between her teeth and washing them down with a handful of water from the tap.

She longed to rest today. Longed to go back to sleep here in this warm house, but it was time to get out. The school bus driver would wonder why Fudge Ripple hadn't come out this morning when all the lights were on in the house. He'd tell somebody about it, and they'd wonder, too. Routines were the vital fabric of the Mindfuck State; when a routine was disrupted, like a missed stitch, all the little ants got stirred up. It was time to get out.

Drummer began to cry; Mary recognized it as his hungry cry, pitched a tone or two lower and less intense than his frightened cry. It was more of a nasal buzzing with a few pauses for the summoning of breath. She'd have to feed him and change his diaper before they left. A sense of urgency got her moving. First she changed her bandages, wincing as she peeled away the crusty cotton. She repacked the wounds and wrapped them tightly with fresh strips of torn sheet. Then she popped open her suitcase, put on fresh underwear, and got a pair of flannel socks from Rocky Road's dresser. Her jeans were too constrictive at the thighs for her swollen leg, so she pulled on a pair of looser denims—again, courtesy of her departed host—and cinched them tight with one of her belts. She put on a gray workshirt, a maroon sweater she'd had since 1981, and she pinned the Smiley Face button on the front. Her scuffed boots went on last. In Rocky Road's closet hung a tempting assortment of heavy coats and parkas. She took a brown corduroy coat with a fleece-lined collar off its hanger and laid it aside for later, and chose a green goosedown parka to zip Drummer up in as a makeshift bassinet. A pair of man-sized leather gloves were also set aside for later.

As Mary fed Drummer, she continually squeezed a tennis ball in her right hand to warm up the sinews. Her strength in that hand was about a third of what it normally was, her fingers cold and numb. Nerve damage, she thought. She could feel the twitching of the ravaged muscles down in the forearm wound; the damned dog had come close to gnawing an artery open, and if that had happened, she'd be dead by now. The thigh wound was the real bitch, though. It needed fifty or sixty stitches and a hell of a lot better antiseptic than what she'd found in Rocky Road's bathroom. But just as long as it stayed crusted over, she could make herself keep going.

The telephone rang as she was changing Drummer's diaper. It stopped after twelve rings, was quiet for five minutes, and then rang eight more times.

"Somebody's curious," she told Drummer as she swabbed him clean with a Handi Wipe. "Somebody wants to know why the boy didn't come out to the school bus, or why Rocky Road's not clocked in at work yet. Yes somebody does, yes him does!"

She started moving a little faster.

The telephone rang again at eight-forty as Mary was loading up the Cherokee in the garage. It went silent, and Mary continued the task. She loaded her suitcase and a garbage bag full of food from the kitchen: the rest of the sliced ham, a pack of bologna, a loaf of wheat bread, a jug of orange juice and a few apples, a box of oat bran cereal and a big bag of Fritos corn chips. She found a bottle each of mineral supplement tablets and vitamins that might've choked a horse. She swallowed two of both. When she was packed and ready to take Drummer out, she paused for a minute to make herself a bowl of Wheat Chex and drink down a Coke.

She was standing in the kitchen, finishing the cereal, when she glanced through a window and saw a pig car coming slowly up the drive.

It pulled up in front of the house, and a pig wearing a dark blue parka got out. The car had CEDAR COUNTY SHERIFF'S DEPARTMENT on its side. By the time the pig—who was maybe in his early twenties, just a kid—reached the front door and rang the buzzer, Mary had loaded one of the remaining rifles from the gun cabinet.

She stood around a corner from the door, waiting. The pig rang the buzzer again, then knocked with a gloved fist. "Hey, Mitch!" he called, his breath showing in the frosty air. "Where you at, boy?"

Go away, Mary thought. Her leg had started hurting her again, a deep biting ache.

"Mitch? You to home?"

The pig backed away from the door. He stood looking around for a minute, his hands on his hips, and then Mary watched him start to walk to the right. She went to another window, where she could track him. He walked to the back door and peered in, his breath fogging the glass. He knocked again, harder. "Emma? Anybody?"

Nobody here you want to meet, she thought.

The pig tried the back door's knob. Worked it left and right. Then she watched him turn his head and look toward the barn.

He called "Mitch?" and then he began walking away from the house, his boots crunching in the icy snow on his way to where the bodies and the van were.

Mary stood at the back door, the rifle in her hands. She decided to let him find Mitch and Emma.

The pig opened the barn's door and walked inside.

She waited, her eyes glittering with a kind of lust.

It didn't take long. The pig came running out. He staggered, stopped, bent over, and threw up onto the snow. Then he started running again, his long legs pumping and his face ghastly.

Mary unlocked the door and stepped out into the chill. The pig saw her, came to a skidding halt, and started reaching for his pistol. The holster's flap was snapped down, and as the pig's gloved fingers fumbled to unsnap it, Mary Terror flexed her numb hand, took aim, and shot him in the stomach at a range of thirty feet. He was knocked backward to the ground, the breath bursting white from his mouth and nostrils. As the pig rolled over and tried to struggle to his knees, Mary fired a second shot that took away a chunk of his left shoulder in a mist of steamy blood. The third bullet got him in the lower back as he was crawling across the crimson snow.

He jerked a few times, like a fish on a hook. And then he lay still, facedown, his arms splayed out in an attitude of crucifixion.

Mary breathed deeply of the cold air, savoring its sting in her lungs. Then she went back into the kitchen, set the rifle down, and finished the last two spoonfuls of Wheat Chex. She drank the milk, and followed it with the final swig of Coke. She limped to the bedroom, where she put on the corduroy coat and the gloves, then picked up Drummer in the folds of the goosedown parka. "Pretty boy, yes you are!" she said as she carried him to the kitchen. "Mama's pretty little boy!" She kissed his cheek, a surge of love rising within her like a glowing radiance. She looked out the back door again, verifying that the pig had not moved. Then she put Drummer into the Cherokee, cranked open the garage door, and slid behind the wheel.

She pulled out of the garage, past the pig car and down the driveway. Then she turned right on the road that led back to I-80 and the route west. Her shoulder bag was on the floorboard, full of Pampers and formula and holding her Magnum and the new Smith & Wesson revolver to replace the lost Colt. She felt so much better this morning. Still weak, yes, but so much better. It must be the vitamins, she decided. Got some iron in her blood, and that made all the difference.

Or maybe it was the power of love, she thought as she glanced on the seat beside her at her beautiful baby.

The list of names and phone numbers was in her pocket, along with the bloodstained Sierra Club newsletter article. To the west the sky was a dark purple haze, the land white as a peace dove.

It was a morning rich with love.

The Cherokee went on, aimed toward California, freighted with firepower and madness.

2.

Strip Naked

Checkout time was noon. At ten thirty-six the rust-eaten Cutlass with a Nebraska tag pulled out of the Liberty Motor Lodge's parking lot. The red-haired woman behind the wheel turned right, onto the ramp that merged into the westbound lanes of I-80. The Cutlass's passenger, a pallid woman with a bandaged hand and hellfire in her eyes, wore a dark gray sweater banded with green stripes. She kept an ice pack pressed against her left hand, and she chewed on her raw and swollen lower lip.

The miles clicked off. Snow flurries spun from the gloom, the headlights of cars on and their wipers going. The Cutlass's wipers shrieked with a noise like a banshee party, and the car's engine chugged like a boiler with spark plugs. In Des Moines, eighty miles farther west, Didi and Laura stopped at a Wendy's and got the works: burgers, fries, salad bar, and coffee. As Laura ate with no thought of manners and an eye on the clock, Didi went to the pay phone and looked up pawnbrokers in the Yellow Pages. She tore the page out, rejoined Laura, and they finished their food.

The clerk at Honest Joe's, on McKinley Avenue, examined the diamond through his loupe and asked to see some identification. They took the stone back and went on. The female clerk at Rossi's Pawn on 9th Street wouldn't talk to them without seeing proof of ownership. At the dismal, aptly named Junk 'n Stuff Pawnshop on Army Post Road, a man who made Laura think of John Carradine's head stuck on Dom DeLuise's body looked at the diamond and laughed like a chain saw. "Get real! It's paste, lady!"

"Thank you." Laura picked up the diamond and Didi followed her toward the door.

"Hey, hey, hey! Don't go away mad! Hold up a sec!"

Laura paused. The fat man with the thin, wrinkled prune of a face motioned her back with a ring-studded paw. "Come on, let's dicker a little bit."

"I don't have time for that."

"What, you're in a hurry?" He frowned, looking at her bandaged hand. "I think you're bleedin', lady."

Spots of red had seeped through the bandages. Laura said, "I cut myself." She drew up her spine straight and tall and walked back to the counter. "My husband paid over three thousand dollars for this diamond eight years ago. I've got the certification. I know it's not paste, so don't give me that crap."

"Yeah?" He grinned. No horse had bigger or yellower teeth. "So let's see the certification, then."

Laura didn't move. She didn't speak either.

"Uh-huh. So let's see a driver's license."

"My purse was stolen," Laura said.

"Oh, yeah!" He nodded, drumming his fingers on the countertop. "Where'd you steal the rock from, ladies?"

"Let's go," Didi urged.

"You're undercover cops, right?" the man asked. "Tryin' to sting my ass?" He snorted. "Yeah, I can smell cops a mile off! Comin' in here with a phony southern accent! You people won't stop roustin' me, will you?"

"Let's *go.*" Didi grasped Laura's arm.

She almost turned away. Almost. But her hand was killing her and they were down to the last of their cash, a gloomier day she'd never seen, and Mary Terror was out there somewhere with David. She felt her frayed temper snap, and the next thing she felt was her hand reaching up under her sweater. She grasped the handle of the automatic in the waistband of her jeans, and she brought the gun up and pointed it at the man's horse teeth.

"I'll take a thousand dollars for my diamond," Laura said. "No dickering."

The man's grin hung by a lip.

"Oh God!" Didi wailed. "Don't kill him like you did that other one, Bonnie! Don't blow the brains out of his head!"

The man trembled and lifted his arms. He had on cuff links that looked like little gold nuggets.

"Open the cash register," Laura told him. "You just bought a diamond."

He hustled to obey, and when the register was open he started counting out the cash. "Bonnie gets crazy sometimes," Didi said as she went to the front door and turned over the WE'RE OPEN sign to SORRY WE'RE CLOSED. There was nobody on the street anywhere, the wind and the snow keeping saner people indoors. "She shot a guy through the head in Nebraska yesterday. Trigger crazy is what she is."

"You want big bills?" the man gasped. "You want hundreds?"

"Whatever," Didi answered. "Come on, hurry it up!"

"I've only . . . I've only got . . . got six hundred dollars in the register. Got some more in the safe. Back there." He nodded toward a door with an OFFICE sign on it.

"Six hundred's enough," Didi said. "Take the money, Bonnie. Got to get us to Michigan, doesn't it?" She took the automatic from Laura as Didi pocketed the cash. "Anybody else in here?"

"Wanda Jane's in the back. She's the bookkeeper."

"Okay, go on through that door real nice and slow."

The man started to walk, but Laura said, "Wait. Take the diamond. You bought it." Didi flashed her a glance of disapproval, and the scared clerk just stood there not knowing what to do. "Take it," Laura said, and at last he did.

In the office, a wizened woman with butch-cut gray hair was smoking a cigarette, sitting in a smoke haze and talking on the telephone as she watched a soap opera on a portable TV. Didi didn't have to speak; the man's face and the pistol did all the talking. Wanda Jane croaked, "Jumpin' Jesus! Hal, I think we're bein'—" Didi put her hand down on the phone's prongs, cutting the connection.

"Wanda Jane, you keep your mouth shut," Didi ordered. "You two strip naked."

"The *hell* I will!" Wanda Jane thundered, her face reddening to the roots of her hair.

"They've already killed somebody!" the clerk said. "They're both crazy!" He was already unbuttoning his shirt. When he unbuckled his belt, his huge paunch flopped out like the nose of the Goodyear blimp.

Didi hurried them up. In a couple of minutes they were both nude and lying on their bellies on the concrete floor, and an uglier two moons Laura had never been so unfortunate to see. Didi tore the phone out of the wall and scooped their clothes up. "You lie here for ten minutes. Bobby's watching the front door. If you come out before ten minutes are up, you're dead meat, because Bobby's even crazier than Bonnie. Hear me?"

Wanda Jane grunted like a bullfrog. The man with horse teeth gripped his new diamond in his fist and bleated, "Yeah, we hear you! Just don't kill us, okay?"

"See you next time we come through," Didi promised, and she pushed Laura out of the office in front of her.

Outside, Didi dumped the clothes in a trash can. Then she and Laura ran to the Cutlass, which was parked down the street a few doors from the pawnshop, and Didi took the wheel again. In five minutes they were heading back toward I-80, and in ten minutes they were on their way west again, six hundred dollars richer and minus a diamond that had become to Laura only a dead weight.

Didi kept checking the rearview mirror. No flashing lights, no sirens. Yet. The speedometer's needle showed a little over sixty, and Didi left it there. "From shoplifting to armed robbery in less than a day," Didi said, and she couldn't hold back a wicked grin. "You're a natural."

"A natural what?"

"Outlaw."

"I didn't steal anything. I left him the diamond."

"That's right, you did. But didn't it feel good, making him look at that gun and bust a gut?"

Laura watched the wipers fight the spits of snow. It *had* been thrilling, in a way. It had been so alien to her normal sense of propriety that it had seemed like someone else holding the gun, wearing her skin, and speaking in her voice. She wondered what Doug might think of it, or her mother and father. One thing she realized was true, and it filled her with gritty pride: she might not be an outlaw, but she *was* a survivor. " 'Strip naked,' " she said, and she gave a hard note of laughter. "How'd you think of that?"

"Just buying time. I couldn't think of any other way to keep them in that office for a while."

"Why'd you keep calling me Bonnie? And you said we were on our way to Michigan?"

Didi shrugged. "Pigs'll be looking for two women on their way to Michigan. One of them has a southern accent and is named Bonnie. They may be traveling with a male accomplice named Bobby. Anyway, the pigs'll look in the opposite direction from where we're going. They won't know what to make of somebody trading a three-thousand-dollar diamond for six hundred bucks at gunpoint." She smiled faintly. "Did you hear what I said? 'Pigs.' I haven't said that and meant it in a long time." Her laughter bubbled up, too. "Did you see Wanda Jane's face when I told them to strip? I thought she was going to drop a fig!"

"And when that guy's belly came out I thought it was going to flop right to the floor! I thought Des Moines was about to have an earthquake!"

"Guy needed a girdle! Hell, he couldn't find a girdle *big* enough!"

They were both laughing, the laughter taking some of the edge off what they'd just done. As Laura laughed, she forgot for a precious moment the pain in her hand and in her heart, and that was mercy indeed.

"He needed a whale girdle!" Didi went on. "And did you see the butts on those two!"

"Butt and Jeff!" Laura said, tears in her eyes.

"The Honeymooners!"

"Two moons over Des Moines!"

"I swear to God, I've seen bowls of Jell-O with better—" *Muscle tone,* she was about to say, but she did not because of the flashing blue light that had suddenly appeared in the rear windshield. The scream of a siren came into the car, and the hair stood up on the back of Laura's neck.

"Christ!" Didi shouted as she jerked the Cutlass over into the right lane. The patrol car was roaring up in the left lane, and Didi's heart hammered as she waited for it to swerve on their tail. But it kept going, sweeping past them in a siren blare and dazzling blue lights, and it sped away into the murk of swirling sleet and snow.

Neither woman could speak. Didi's hands had clamped into claws around the steering wheel, her eyes wide with shock, and Laura sat there with her stomach cramping and her bandaged hand pressed against her chest.

Four miles farther west, they passed a car that had skidded off the highway into the guardrail. The patrol car was parked nearby, the Smokey talking to a young man in a sweatshirt with SKI WYOMING across the front. Traffic had slowed, the afternoon had darkened to a plum violet, and the pavement glistened. Didi touched her window. "Getting colder," she said. The Cutlass was a laboring, gas-guzzling beast, but its heater was first rate. She cut their speed back to fifty-five, grainy snow flying before the headlights.

"I can drive if you want to take a nap," Laura offered.

"No, I'm fine. Let your hand rest. How're you doing?"

"Okay. Hurting some."

"If you want to stop somewhere, let me know."

Laura shook her head. "No. I want to keep going."

"Six hundred dollars would buy us airline tickets," Didi said. "We could catch a flight to San Francisco from Omaha and rent a car to Freestone."

"We couldn't rent a car without a driver's license. Anyway, we'd have to give up the gun to board a plane."

Didi drove on a few more miles before she spoke again, bringing up a subject that had been needling her since the incident at the lumberyard. "What good is a gun going to be, anyway? I mean . . . how are you going to get David back, Laura? Mary's not going to give him up. She'll die first. Even with a gun, how're you going to get David back alive?" She emphasized the last word.

"I don't know," Laura answered.

"If Mary finds Jack Gardiner . . . well, who knows what she'll do? Who knows what *he'll* do? If she shows up at his door after all these years, he might flip out." She glanced quickly at the other woman and then away, because the pain had crept back onto Laura's face and latched there in the lines. "Jack was a dangerous man. He could talk other people into doing his killing for him, but he did his share of murders, too. He was the mind behind the Storm Front. The whole thing was his idea."

"And you really think that's him? In Freestone?"

"I think that's him in the photo, yeah. Whether he's in Freestone now or not, I don't know. But when Mary gets to him with David as some kind of a . . . love offering, God only knows how he'll react."

"So we've got to find Jack Gardiner first," Laura said.

"There's no telling how far Mary is ahead of us. She'll get to Freestone before us if we don't go by plane."

"She can't be that far ahead. She's hurt, too, maybe worse than I am. The weather's going to slow her down. If she gets off the interstate, it'll just slow her down more."

"Okay," Didi said. "Even if we do find Jack first, what then?"

"We wait for Mary. She'll give the baby to Jack. That's why she's going to Freestone." Laura gently touched her bandaged hand. It was hot enough to sizzle, and throbbed with a deep, agonizing pulse. She would have to stand the pain, because she had no choice. "When my baby is out of Mary's hands . . . that's why I might need the gun."

"You're not a killer. You're tough as old leather, yeah. But not a killer."

"I'll need the gun to hold Mary for the police," Laura told her.

There was a long silence. The Cutlass's tires hummed. "I don't think Jack would like that," Didi said. "Whatever identity he's built for himself, he's not going to let you call the police on Mary. And once you get David back . . . I'm not sure I can let you do that either."

"I understand," Laura said. She'd already thought about this, and her thoughts had led her to this destination. "I was hoping we could work something out."

"Right. Like a presidential pardon?"

"More like a plane ticket to either Canada or Mexico."

"Oh boy!" Didi smiled bitterly. "Nothing like starting life over in a foreign country with zilch money and a K-Mart sweater!"

"I could send you some money to help you get settled."

"I'm an *American!* Get it? I live in *America!*"

Laura didn't know what else to say. There *was* nothing else, really. Didi had started her journey to this point a long time ago, when she'd cast her lot with Jack Gardiner and the Storm Front. "Damn," Didi said quietly. She was thinking of a future in which the fear of someone coming up behind her suffocated the days and haunted the nights, and everywhere she walked she carried a target on her back. But there were a lot of islands in the waterways of Canada, she thought. A lot of places where the mail came in by seaplane and your closest neighbor lived ten miles away. "Would you buy me a kiln?" she asked. "For my pottery?"

"Yes."

"That's important to me, to do my pottery. Canada's a pretty country. It would be inspiring, wouldn't it?" Didi nodded, answering her own query. "I could be an expatriate. That sounds better than exile, don't you think?"

Laura agreed that it did.

The Cutlass passed from Iowa into Nebraska, following I-80 as it snaked around Omaha and on across the flat, white-frosted plains. Laura closed her eyes and rested as best she could, with the wipers scraping across the windshield and the tires a dull roar.

Thursday's child, she thought.

Thursday's child has far to go.

She remembered one of the nurses saying that, at David's birth.

And she hadn't thought of this before, but it came to her between the scrape and the roar: she'd been born on a Thursday, too.

Far to go, she thought. She'd come a long way, but the most dangerous distance still lay ahead. Somewhere on that dark horizon, Mary Terror was traveling with David, getting closer to California with the passing of every mile. Behind Laura's eyes, she saw David lying in a pool of blood, his skull shattered by a bullet, and she shoved the image away before it took root. Far to go. Far to go. Into the golden West, dark as a tomb.

3.

He Knows

Three hours ahead of the Cutlass, the snow was whirling before Mary's headlights. It was coming down fast and heavy now from the solid night, a blowing snow that the wipers were straining to clear. Every so often a gust of wind would broadside the Cherokee and the wheel would shudder in Mary's hands. She could feel the tires wanting to slew on the slick interstate, and around her the other traffic—which had thinned out dramatically since nightfall—had slowed to half the posted speed.

"We're going to be fine," she told Drummer. "Don't you worry,

Mama'll take care of her sweet baby." But the truth was that the ants of fear were crawling under her skin, and she'd passed two pileups since she'd left a McDonald's in North Platte, Nebraska, twenty minutes before. This kind of driving shredded the nerves and shot the eyes, but the interstate was still clear and Mary didn't want to stop until she had to. Drummer had been fed and changed at the McDonald's, and he was getting sleepy. Mary's injured leg was numb from driving, but the pain in her forearm wound woke up occasionally and bit her hard and deep just to let her know who was really in charge. She felt feverish, too, her face moist and swollen with heat. She had to go on, as far as she could tonight, before her suffering body gave out on her.

"Let's sing," Mary said. "'Age of Aquarius,'" she decided. "The Fifth Dimension, remember?" But of course Drummer did not. She began to sing the song, in a voice that might have been pleasant in her youth, but was now harsh and incapable of carrying a tune. "'If You're Going to San Francisco,'" she said: another song title, but she couldn't recall the artist's name. She began to sing that, too, but she knew only the part about going to San Francisco with flowers in your hair, so she sang that over and over a few times and then let it go.

The snow blew against the windshield and the Cherokee trembled. The flakes hit the glass and stuck there, large and intricate like Swiss lace, for a few seconds before the wipers could plow them aside and the next ones came.

"'Hot Fun in the Summertime,'" Mary said. "Sly and the Family Stone." Except she didn't know the words to it, all she could do was hum the tune. "'Marrakesh Express.' Crosby, Stills, and Nash." She knew almost all of that one; it had been one of Lord Jack's favorites.

"'Light My Fire,'" the man in the backseat said in a voice like velvet and leather.

Mary looked into the rearview mirror and saw his face and part of her own. Her skin was glistening with fever sweat. His was white, like carved ice.

"'Light My Fire,'" God repeated. His dark hair was a thick mane, his face sculpted with shadows. "Sing it with me."

She was shivering. The heater was blasting, she was full of heat, but she was shivering. God looked just like he did when she'd seen him up close in Hollywood. She smelled the phantom aromas of pot and strawberry incense, the combination like an exotic and lost perfume.

He began to sing, there in the back of the Cherokee, as the snow flailed down and Mary Terror gripped the wheel.

She listened to his half moan, half snarl, and after a while she joined him. They sang "Light My Fire" together, his voice tough and vibrant, hers searching for the lost chord. And they were on the part about setting the night on fire when Mary saw red flames erupt in the windshield. Not flames, no: brake lights. A truck, its driver stomping on the brakes just in front of her.

She wrenched the wheel to the right and felt the tires defy her. The Cherokee was sliding into the rear of a tractor-trailer rig. She made a choked noise as God sang on. And then the Cherokee lurched as the tires found traction; the vehicle went off onto the right shoulder and missed slamming into the truck by about two feet. Maybe she had screamed; she didn't know, but Drummer was awake and crying shrilly.

Mary put the emergency brake on, picked up Drummer, and hugged him against her. The song had stopped. God was no longer in the backseat; he had abandoned her. The truck was moving on, and a hundred yards ahead blue lights spun and figures stood in the sweeping snow. It was another wreck, two cars jammed together like mating roaches. "It's all right," Mary said as she rocked the child. "It's all right, shhhhhh." He wouldn't stop, and now he was wailing and hiccuping at the same time. "Shhhhh, shhhhhh," she whispered. She was burning up, her leg was hurting again, and her nerves were raw. He kept crying, his face squeezed with anger. "SHUT UP!" Mary shouted. "SHUT UP, I SAID!" She shook him, trying to rattle his crybox loose. His breath snagged on a series of hiccups, his mouth open but nothing coming out. Mary felt a jolt of panic, and she pressed Drummer against her shoulder and thumped his back. "Breathe!" she said. "Breathe! Breathe, damn you!"

He shuddered, pulling the air into his lungs, and then he let out a holler that said he was through taking shit.

"Oh, I love you, I love you so much!" Mary told him as she rocked him and tried to quiet him down. What if he'd strangled to death just then? What if he hadn't been able to breathe and he'd died right here? What good would a lump of dead baby be for Jack? "Oh Mama loves her baby, her sweet sweet Drummer, yes she does," Mary crooned, and after a few minutes Drummer's tantrum subsided and his crying ceased. "Good baby. Good baby Drummer." She found the pacifier he'd spat out and stuck it back in his mouth. Then she laid him on the floorboard again, snuggled deep in a dead man's parka, and she got out of the Cherokee and stood in the falling snow trying to cool her fever.

She limped away a distance, picked up a handful of snow, and rubbed it over her face. The air was wet and heavy, the snowflakes whirling down from a heaven as dark as stone. She stood watching other cars, vans, and trucks go past, heading west. The cold made her head clear and sharpened her senses. She could go on. She had to go on.

Jack was waiting for her, and when they were joined again life would be incense and peppermints.

Back behind the wheel, Mary repeated the three names over and over again as the night went on and the miles clicked away. "Hudley . . . Cavanaugh . . . Walker . . . Hudley . . ."

"Cavanaugh . . . Walker," God said, returned to the Cherokee's backseat.

He came and went, at his whim. There were no chains on God. Sometimes Mary looked back at him and thought he favored Jack, other times she thought there had never been another face like his and there never would be again. "Do you remember me?" she asked him. "I saw you once." But he didn't answer, and when she glanced in the rearview mirror again the backseat was empty.

The snow was getting heavier, the wind rocking the Cherokee like a cradle. The land changed from flat to rolling, a preview of Wyoming. Mary stopped at a gas station near Kimball, twenty-five miles east of the Wyoming state line, and she filled the Cherokee's tank and bought a pack of glazed doughnuts and black coffee in a plastic cup. The brassy-haired woman behind the counter told her she ought to get off the interstate, that the weather was going to get worse before it got better, and there was a Holiday Inn a couple of miles north. Mary thanked her for the advice, paid what she owed, and pulled out.

She crossed the Wyoming line, and the land began to rise toward the Rocky Mountains. The lights of Cheyenne emerged from the snow-torn dark, then disappeared in Mary's rearview mirror as she drove on. The wind's force had increased, shrieking around the Cherokee and shaking it like an infant with a rattle. The wiper blades were losing their combat with the snow, the headlights showing cones of whirling white. Fever sweat glistened on Mary's face, and from the backseat the voice of God urged her on. Forty miles past Cheyenne, Laramie went past like a white dream, and the Cherokee's tires began to slip as I-80 rose on its rugged ascent between mountain ranges.

Another twenty miles beyond Laramie, into the teeth of the wind, and Mary suddenly realized there were no more vehicles coming from the west. She was alone on the highway. An abandoned tractor-trailer truck, its emergency lights flashing, came out of the snow on her right, its back freighted with frost. The highway's ascent was steeper now, the Cherokee's engine lugging. She felt the wheels slide on patches of ice, the wind savage as it howled across the mountain peaks. The wiper blades were getting loaded down, the windshield as white as a cataract. She had to fight the wheel from side to side as the wind beat at the Cherokee, and she passed two more abandoned cars that had slammed together and skidded off onto the median. Yellow emergency lights were flashing ahead of her again, and in another moment she could make out the big blinking sign that stood on the interstate: STOP ROAD CLOSED. A highway patrol car was parked nearby, its lights spinning in the murk of snowflakes. As Mary slowed the Cherokee, two troopers in heavy overcoats began to wave red flashlights at her, flagging her down. She stopped, rolled her window down, and the cold that swept in iced her lungs and overpowered the heater in four seconds. Both the troopers wore ski masks and caps with earflaps, and the one who stepped up to her window to speak to her shouted, "Can't go any farther, ma'am! I-80's closed between here and Creston!"

"I have to get through!" Her lips were already freezing, the air's temperature fallen below zero and snowflakes clinging to her eyebrows.

"No, ma'am! Not tonight! Highway's iced up over the mountains!" He aimed his flashlight to Mary's right. "You'll have to pull off here!"

She looked where the light was pointed, and saw a sign that said EXIT 272. Below the exit number were MCFADDEN and ROCK RIVER. A snowplow was shoving a mound of white off the exit road.

"The Silver Cloud Inn's about two miles toward McFadden!" the trooper went on. "That's where we're sending everybody!"

"I can't stop! I've got to keep going!"

"We've had three fatalities on that stretch of highway since this storm started, ma'am, and it's not going to get any better before daylight! You're not in a big enough hurry to get yourself killed!"

Mary looked at Drummer, swaddled in the parka. Again the

question came to her: what good would a lump of dead baby be for Jack? Her leg was hurting her, she was tired and it had been a long day. It was time to rest until the storm had passed. "All right!" she told the trooper. "I'll pull off!"

"Just follow the signs!" he said, and he waved her toward the exit with his flashlight.

Mary trailed the snowplow for a few hundred yards and then eased the Cherokee around it. Her headlights caught a sign that said SILVER CLOUD INN NEXT LEFT. SEE THE WORLD-FAMOUS DINOSAUR GARDENS! She took the left turn when it came, and had to fight the Cherokee uphill on a curving road bordered with dense, snow-weighted woods. The tires moaned as they lost their grip, and the Cherokee skidded violently to the right and careened off the guardrail before rubber found pavement again. Mary kept pushing the Cherokee onward, and around the next curve she saw abandoned cars on the sides of the road. Maybe a hundred yards farther, and the Cherokee's tires lost their purchase again, this time swinging the vehicle toward the left and slamming into a four-foot-high snowbank. The engine rattled and died with an exhausted moan, and the wind's shriek reigned over all. Mary started the engine again, backed away from the snowbank, and tried to force the Cherokee on, but the tires slipped and slid and she realized the rest of the way would have to be on foot. She turned onto the left shoulder, cut the engine, and pulled up the emergency brake. Then she buttoned up her corduroy coat to her neck, zipped Drummer securely in the parka, and put her bag with its cache of baby supplies and guns over her shoulder. She picked Drummer up, opened her door, and stepped out into the storm.

The cold overpowered her fever as it had the Cherokee's heater. It was a solid thing, hard as iron, and it locked around her and turned every movement into an agony of slow motion. But the wind was fast and loud, and the snow-covered trees thrashed in white torment. She limped along the left lane, her arms folded around the infant and snow slashing into her face like bits of razor blade. She felt wet heat on her thigh wound: new blood oozing up through the broken crust, like lava seething from a volcanic core.

The road leveled off. The woods gave way to mounds of blowing snow, and Mary could see the yellow lights of a long, ranch-house-type building ahead. Something gargantuan was suddenly towering above Mary and the baby, its reptilian head agrin with jagged teeth. Another massive form with armor plates on its back stood nearby, the snow up to its snout. The world-famous Dinosaur Gardens, Mary realized as she limped between the concrete monsters. A third huge beast reared up from the snow on her left, an alligator's head on a hippo's body. On her right what looked like a tank with glass eyes and concrete horns stood as if about to charge the rearing statue. Between her and the Silver Cloud Inn was a prehistoric landscape, dozens of dinosaurs frozen on the snowfield. She limped onward, carrying her own history. Around her stood fourteen-foot-tall thunder lizards and meat eaters, their sculpted heads white with snow and bearded with icicles, snow wedged into the cracks of their skins. The wind roared like a great monstrous voice, a memory of dinosaur song, and it almost knocked Mary to her knees amid the beasts.

Headlights hit her. An enclosed vehicle on treads was coming toward her, snow whirling up in its wake. When it reached her, a man in a cowboy hat and a long brown coat got out and grasped her shoulder, guiding her around to the passenger side. "Anybody else behind you?" he shouted into her ear, and she shook her head.

When they were inside the snow buggy, the heater on full blast, the man picked up a CB radio's microphone and said, "Found the new arrivals, Jody. Takin' 'em in."

"That's a big ten-four," a man's voice answered through crackling static. Mary figured it was one of the pigs down on I-80. Then the cowboy turned the buggy around and started driving toward the inn, and he said, "Get you good and warm in just a few minutes, ma'am."

The Silver Cloud Inn was made of bleached stones and had a huge pair of antlers over the front door. The cowboy pulled the buggy up to the steps, and Mary got out with Drummer pressed against her. Then the cowboy came around and started to take her shoulder bag, but Mary pulled back and said, "I've got it," and he opened the inn's door for her. Inside, there was a large lobby with oak beams and a stone fireplace that a car could have parked in. The fire was popping sparks, the lobby sweet with the smell of woodsmoke and delicious warmth. Twenty or more people of all ages and descriptions were on cots or in sleeping bags around the fireplace, and another dozen or so were talking or playing cards. Their attention was drawn to Mary and the baby for a few seconds, and then they went back to what they were doing.

"Lord, what a night! Storm's a screamer, for sure!" The cowboy took off his hat, revealing thinning white hair and a braided ponytail with a band around it made of multicolored Indian beads. He had a grizzled, heavily lined face and bright blue eyes beneath white brows. "Rachel, let's get this lady some hot coffee!"

A gray-haired, plump Indian woman in a red sweater and bluejeans began to draw coffee from a metal dispenser into a plastic cup. On the table beside the coffeemaker were a few sandwiches, some cheese, fruit, and slices of poundcake. "Name's Sam Jiles," the cowboy said. "Welcome to the Silver Cloud Inn. I'm sorry you couldn't see it on a better day."

"That's all right. I'm glad to be here."

"Rooms were all gone around seven o'clock. Cots ran out around nine, but we might have a sleepin' bag left. You travelin' alone with your baby?"

"Yes. Going to California." She felt him waiting for more. "To meet my husband," she added.

"Bad night to be on the road, I swanee." Jiles walked to the registration desk, where another CB radio was set up. "Excuse me just a minute." He picked up the mike. "Silver Cloud to Big Smokey, come on back, Smokey." The static crackled and hissed, and the pig's voice answered, "Big Smokey. You got an ear, Silver Cloud."

Rachel brought Mary the coffee, and she looked at Drummer in the parka's folds. "Oh, that's a new one!" she said, her eyes large and dark brown. "Boy or girl?"

"Boy."

"What's his name?"

"Brought 'em in real fine, Jody," Sam Jiles was saying over the radio. "You fellas want me to bring you down some eats?"

"I hear you talkin', Sam. We're stuck here till I-80's open."

"Okay, bring you down some grub and coffee pronto."

"Does he have a name yet?"

Mary blinked, looking into the Indian woman's eyes. What was going through her head was the thought that she was trapped with strangers at her back and two pigs guarding the only way out. "David," she said, and the name was foul in her mouth, but Drummer was his real and secret name, not to be shared with everyone.

"That's a nice, strong name. I'm Rachel Jiles."

"I'm . . . Mary Brown." It had come from the color of the woman's eyes.

"We have some food left." Rachel motioned toward the table. "Ham and cheese sandwiches. Some beef stew there, too." She nodded at bowls and a clay pot. "Help yourself."

"Thanks, I will." Mary limped over to the table, and Rachel stayed with her.

"Did you hurt your leg?" Rachel asked.

"No, it's an old injury. Broken ankle didn't heal right." Drummer began to cry at that moment, as if shouting to the world that Mary Terror was lying. She rocked him and cooed to him, but his crying soared up and up with increasing power. Rachel suddenly held out her stocky arms and said, "I've had three boys. Maybe I can try it?"

What would it hurt? Besides, the pain in Mary's leg was so bad it was sapping her strength. She handed Drummer over and fed herself while Rachel rocked him and sang softly in a language Mary didn't understand. Drummer's crying began to quiet, his head cocked to one side as if listening to the woman's singing. In about two minutes he had ceased crying altogether, and Rachel sang and smiled, her round face almost radiant with care for a stranger's child.

Sam Jiles made food packages for the two troopers, loading up sandwiches, fruit, and cake into two sacks and adding cups and a thermos of coffee. He asked one of the men to go with him in the tracked snow buggy, and he kissed Rachel on the cheek and said he'd be back quicker than a skillet sizzles grease. Then he and his companion left the Silver Cloud, a gust of freezing wind and snow coming through the front door with their departure.

Rachel seemed to enjoy cradling Drummer, so Mary let her hold the baby while she ate and drank her fill. She limped over to the fireplace to warm herself, threading a path through the other people, and she took off her gloves and offered her palms to the flames. Her fever had returned, throbbing with a hot pulse at her temples, and she couldn't stay near the fire very long. She glanced at the faces around her, judging them: predominant in the mix were middle-aged people, but there was a couple who might have been in their sixties and two young couples who had the tanned, fit look of ardent skiers. She moved away from the hearth, back toward where Rachel stood with Drummer, and that was when she felt someone watching her.

Mary looked to her right, and found a young man sitting against the wall, his legs crossed beneath him. He had a thin, hawk-nosed face and sandy-brown hair that spilled down over his shoulders, and he wore black horn-rimmed glasses, faded jeans with patches on the

knees, and a dark blue turtleneck sweater. Beside him was a battered
army jacket and a rolled-up sleeping bag. He was watching her
intently with deep-socketed eyes the color of ashes. His stare didn't
waver as she returned it, and then he frowned slightly and began to
examine his fingernails.

She didn't like him. He made her nervous. She went back to Rachel
and took her child. Rachel said, "He's sure a good baby! All three of
my boys used to holler like screech owls when they were as little as
him. How old is he?"

"He was born on . . ." She didn't know the exact date. "The third
of February," she said, which was when she'd taken him from the
hospital.

"Do you have any other children?"

"No, just Drum—" Mary smiled. "Just David." Her gaze skittered
back to the young man. He was staring at her again. She felt fever
sweat on her cheeks. What was that fucking hippie looking at?

"I'll see if I can find a sleeping bag for you," Rachel said. "We
always keep a supply on hand for the campers." She went off across
the lobby and through another door, and Mary found a place to sit on
the floor away from everyone else.

She kissed Drummer's forehead and crooned softly to him. His
skin was cool against her lips. "Going to California, yes we are. Going
to California, Mama and her sweet baby." She realized with a start
that there were two spots of blood, each about the size of a quarter, on
the thigh of her jeans. The blood was seeping up through her
makeshift bandage. She set Drummer aside, took off her coat, and
laid it across her lap.

She looked up, and saw the hippie watching her.

Mary pulled her shoulder bag, with its small Magnum automatic
and the .38 from Rocky Road's gun cabinet, against her side.

"He knows."

The voice sent chill bumps shivering up her spine. It had been
spoken from her left, and close to her ear. She turned her head. God
was there, hunkered down beside her, his glacial face gaunt and his
eyes dark with truth. He wore skin-tight black velvet and a gold chain
with a crucifix on it. On his head was a floppy-brimmed black hat
with a snakeskin band. It was the same outfit he'd worn when she'd
seen him up close in Hollywood. Except for one thing: God wore a
yellow Smiley Face button on his lapel. "He knows," the cruel mouth
repeated in a whisper.

Mary Terror stared at the young hippie. He was looking at his fingernails again; he darted a glance at her, then shifted his position and studied the fire.

Or pretended to.

"Road's closed," God said. "Pigs at the roadblock. Your leg's busted open again. And that fucker knows. What'cha gonna do, Mary?"

She didn't answer. She couldn't.

She leaned her back against the wall and closed her eyes. She could feel him watching, but every time she opened her eyes she couldn't catch him at it. Rachel returned with a tattered but usable sleeping bag, and Mary spread it out like a mattress and laid on top of it instead of confining herself inside. She kept the shoulder bag's strap around her arm, its top zippered shut, and Drummer alternately drowsed and fretted beside her.

"He knows," she heard God whisper in her ear as she drifted toward sleep. His voice pulled her away from rest. She felt swollen with damp, pulsing heat, her thigh and forearm wounds heavy with crusted blood under the bandages. A firm touch to her thigh made searing pain travel from her hip to her knee, and the blood spots were growing.

"What'cha gonna do, Mary?" God asked, and she thought he might have laughed a little.

"Damn you," she rasped, and she pulled Drummer closer. It was the two of them against a hateful world.

The exhaustion won over pain and fear, at least for a while. Mary slept, Drummer sucked busily on his pacifier, and the young hippie scratched his chin and watched the woman and her infant.

4.

Thunder Lizards

Two o'clock passed, and the Cutlass kept going into the white whirlwinds.

Didi was at the wheel, her face a bleached mask of tension. The Cutlass, traveling at thirty miles an hour, was alone on I-80. Laura had driven for several hours back in Nebraska, between Lincoln and North Platte, and she'd gotten good at guiding the car with one hand and an elbow. The snowstorm's intensity had strengthened near North Platte, the wind broadsiding the car like a bull's charge, and Laura had pulled over to let somebody with two hands drive. The last tractor-trailer truck they'd seen had been turning off at Laramie, ten miles behind them, and the snowswept highway was climbing steadily toward the Rocky Mountains.

"Should've stopped at Laramie," Didi said. This had been her refrain ever since they'd left its lights. "We can't keep going in this." The wiper in front of her face shrieked with effort as it plowed the snow away, while the wiper on Laura's side had ground to a halt just east of Cheyenne. "Should've stopped at Laramie, like I wanted to."

"She didn't," Laura said.

"How do you know? She might be back in Nebraska, sleeping in a warm Holiday Inn!"

"She'll go as far as she can. She'll go until she can't drive anymore. I would."

"Mary might be crazy, but she's not a fool! She's not going to get herself and David killed out here! Look! Even the trucks can't make it in this!" Didi dared to unhinge the fingers of her right hand from the wheel and point to the tractor-trailer rig that was abandoned on the shoulder, its emergency lights flashing. Then she gripped the wheel hard again, because a gust of wind slapped the Cutlass and fishtailed it into the left lane. Didi let off on the accelerator and fought the car straight again, her heart pounding and a coil of fear deep in her belly. "Jesus, what a mess!"

The snowfall, made up of flakes the size of half dollars, was spinning into their headlights on almost a horizontal plane. Laura was scared, too, and every time the tires slipped and slid she felt her heart rise to her throat and lodge there like a peach pit, but the violence of the wind was keeping the snow from piling up on the pavement. Patches of ice glistened on the highway like silver lakes, but the road itself was clear. She scanned the snowy darkness, her broken hand mercifully numb. Where are you? she thought. In front of us, or behind? Mary wouldn't have turned off I-80 for a secondary route because the road atlas they'd gotten at their last gas-and-food stop showed no other way west across the state but I-80's broad blue line. Somewhere on the highway, probably in Utah by now, Mary Terror was cleaving the night with David at her side. An overnight stop in Laramie would only increase the distance between Laura and Mary by at least four hours. No, Mary was on her way to find Jack. The storm might slow her down to a crawl, but she wasn't going to stop unless she was forced to, either by hunger or weariness.

Laura had her own cure for the latter. She swallowed another Black Cat tablet—"the truck driver's friend," the man behind the counter at the Shell station had said when they'd asked for something strong—and followed it with a sip of cold coffee. And then Didi shouted "Christ!" and the Cutlass swerved to the right as its tires hit an ice patch, and the last of the coffee went all over Laura's lap.

The car skidded out of control as Didi tried to muscle the wheel back toward the center line. It slammed into the guardrail, the right-side headlight exploding. The Cutlass scraped along the rail, sparks flying back with the snowflakes, and then the car shuddered as the tires gripped gravel and responded to Didi's hands. The Cutlass swerved away from the guardrail and onto the highway again, casting a single beam of light before it.

"Should've stopped at Laramie." Didi's voice was as tight as her face, a pulse beating quickly at her temple. She had cut the speed to just under thirty. "No way we can keep going in this!"

The highway was getting steeper, the Cutlass's engine rattling with the strain. They passed two more abandoned cars, almost completely shrouded in white, and after another minute Didi said, "Something in front of us."

Laura could see flashing yellow lights. Didi began to slow down. A blinking sign emerged from the blowing snow: STOP ROAD CLOSED. A highway patrol car was there, too, its blue lights going around. Didi eased the Cutlass to a halt, and a bundled-up state trooper holding a flashlight with a red lens cap walked around to the passenger side and motioned for Didi to lower her window.

Mary's eyes opened. She heard the shrilling of the wind outside and the crackle of burning wood in the fireplace. Beads of sweat shivered on her skin.

The young hippie was sitting cross-legged five feet from her, his chin supported by his palms and his elbows on his knees.

Mary sucked in her breath and sat up. She looked at Drummer, who was in baby dreamland, his eyes moving behind the thin pink lids and the pacifier gripped in his mouth. She wiped her cheeks with the back of her hand, her coat over her thighs and hips to hide the bloodstains. "What is it?" she asked, her brain still fogged with fever and her voice thick.

"Sorry," the hippie said. "Didn't mean to wake you." He had a Yankee accent, a voice like a reedy flute.

"What is it?" she asked again, rubbing the sleep from her eyes. Her bones throbbed like bad teeth, and her thigh felt sticky-wet. She looked around. Most of the people in the lobby were asleep, but a few were still playing cards. Rachel Jiles was sleeping in a chair, and her cowboy husband was talking on the CB radio. Mary returned her attention to the young hippie, who was maybe twenty-three or twenty-four. "You woke me up."

"I went to the bathroom," he said as if this were important news. "When I came back, I couldn't sleep." He stared at her, with his spooky, ashy eyes. "I swear I know you from somewhere."

Mary heard the ringing of alarm bells. She slipped the shoulder bag's strap off her arm. "I don't think so."

"When you came in with your baby . . . I thought I recognized you, but I couldn't figure it out. Real weird seeing somebody you think you know but you can't figure out from where. Know what I mean?"

"I've never seen you before." She glanced at Sam Jiles. He was putting on his coat, then his gloves and hat.

"You ever been to Sioux Falls, South Dakota?"

"No." She watched Sam Jiles awaken his wife with a gentle nudge, and he said something to her that got her on her feet. "Never."

"I'm a reporter on the paper there. I write a music column." He leaned forward and held out his hand. "My name's Austin Peevey."

Mary ignored the hand. "You shouldn't sneak up on people. It's not cool." The front door opened and closed: the cowboy had gone out into the storm. Rachel Jiles lifted the coffee dispenser's lid and peered inside, then left the lobby area.

Austin Peevey withdrew his hand. He was smiling with his thin-lipped mouth, a little tuft of sandy hairs on the point of his chin. "Are you somebody famous?" he asked.

"No."

"I swear your face is familiar. See, I've got like tons of old records and tapes. I'm into, like, sixties stuff. I was trying to figure out if I'd seen your face on a record jacket . . . you know, like Smith or Blue Cheer or some old band like that. It's right here"—he tapped his skull—"but I can't see it."

"I'm nobody." Mary summoned up a yawn and delivered it into his face. "How about leaving me alone now."

He stayed where he was, ignoring what she'd said as she'd ignored his hand. "I'm going to Salt Lake City for a record collectors' convention. It's my vacation. Thought I'd drive it and see the sights, but I didn't count on getting stuck in a snowstorm."

"Look, I'm real tired. Okay?"

"Oh, sure." The leather of his brown boots squeaked as he stood up. "I've seen you before, though. Somewhere. You ever go to record conventions?"

"No."

Rachel Jiles had returned with a pitcher of water, which she poured into the coffeemaker. Then she unscrewed a jar of Maxwell House and sifted coffee into the filter. It clicked in Mary's head that new arrivals were coming from the interstate.

Still Austin Peevey wouldn't leave her alone. "What's your name?"

"Listen, I don't know you and you don't know me. Let's keep it that way."

"Mary?" Now Rachel was walking over, and Mary felt rage gnawing at her insides. "You want a cup of fresh coffee?"

"No. I'm trying to rest."

"Oh, I'm sorry." She cast her voice into a whisper. "I see David's out like a light."

"Cute kid," Peevey said. "My dad's name is David."

Her patience reached its end. "Let me get some goddamned sleep!" she shouted, and both Rachel and the young hippie drew back. The force of Mary's voice woke Drummer up with a start, his pacifier popped from his mouth, and a wail blossomed. "Oh, shit!" Mary's face contorted with anger. "Look what you've done!"

"Hey, hey!" Peevey lifted his hands to show his palms. "I was only trying to be friendly."

"Fuck it! Move on, man!" Mary picked up Drummer and started desperately trying to rock him back to sleep.

"Oh!" Rachel winced as Peevey turned and began to walk away. "Mary, such terrible language!"

Peevey took another step and stopped.

Mary felt her heart slam. She knew. Whether the kid had suddenly put together the names *Mary* and *David*, whether her description in a newspaper story had become clear in his mind, or whether the word *terrible* had translated into Terrell or Terror, it was impossible to say. But Austin Peevey stood very still, his back to her.

God spoke next, right in her ear: "He's tagged you."

Peevey started turning toward her again. Mary zipped open the shoulder bag and slid her hand down amid the Pampers, her fingers closing on the Magnum's grip. Peevey's face had gone chalky, his eyes wide behind his horn-rims. "You're . . ." he said, but he couldn't get it out. "You're . . . you're the woman who stole—"

Mary pulled the automatic out of her bag, and Rachel Jiles gave a shocked gasp.

"—the baby," Peevey finished, taking a backward stagger as the gun pointed up at him.

Mary hooked the bag's strap over her shoulder again and stood up with the crying baby held in her other arm. As she did, such fierce pain ripped through her thigh that it robbed her breath for a few seconds and left her dizzy. Oily sweat clung to her face, a damp bloodstain in a large crescent on her jeans. "Stand back," she told them, and they obeyed.

The front door opened.

The cowboy entered first, snow caught on the brim of his hat and on his shoulders. Behind him were two women shivering in thick sweaters, their faces reddened by the cold.

"—get these big 'uns in February," Jiles was saying. "The skiers like 'em when they're over and done with."

Laura heard a baby crying. She knew that sound, and her gaze tracked it like a hawk on the wing. The broad-shouldered woman holding the infant stood twenty-five feet away.

Her eyes locked with Mary's. Time slowed to a nightmare crawl, and she heard Didi say, "Oh . . . my . . . God . . ."

Mary Terror was frozen. It was a majesty of bad karma, a weird acid trip bursting its paisley seams. There they were, the two women Mary despised most on earth, and if she had not felt such overwhelming, white-hot hatred she might have laughed at the twisted joke. But there was no time for laughter, and no time for freaking out. She turned the pistol on Laura.

The Indian woman let loose a shriek and attacked Mary, grabbing at the hand that held the gun. The Magnum went off an instant after Laura and Didi had flung themselves to the oak-planked floor, and a hole the size of Sam Jiles's fist punched through the door in a spray of splinters. The cowboy scrambled behind the registration desk, as Mary and Rachel fought for the gun. Laura reached beneath her double sweaters for her own automatic in the waistband of her jeans, but as she tried to yank it out, something snagged in the folds.

The sleepers were awake. "She's got a gun!" somebody shouted, as if the sound of a Magnum going off could be mistaken for a kernel of corn popping.

Mary held on to Drummer with one arm and clenched the gun in her other hand as Rachel Jiles tried to force her fingers open. Her husband came up from behind the registration desk, his hat off, his blue eyes wild, and an ax handle in a two-handed grip. Mary kicked the Indian woman in the shin as hard as she could with her left foot, and Rachel let go and staggered back, her eyes squeezed shut. Mary saw Laura struggling to pull a gun from her waistband, Didi crawling for cover behind a big urn full of dried wildflowers. She was aware of Sam Jiles swinging the ax handle at her like a baseball bat, and she fired a shot at Laura without aiming as the cowboy released his grip and the ax handle came spinning at her.

The bullet tugged at Laura's K-Mart sweater, passing across her right side like a burning kiss and then slamming into the wall. A heartbeat after that, the ax handle thunked into Mary Terror's left shoulder, about three inches from Drummer's skull, and knocked her to the floor. She held on to Drummer, but her hand lost the gun. It skidded over beside Rachel Jiles, who had gone down and was gripping her splintered shin.

The cowboy came over the registration desk, and Mary grabbed the ax handle. He got a kick in at her, hitting her shoulder near where the first blow had been, and the air hissed between her clenched teeth. Pain shivered through her, and then it was her turn: she swung at one of the man's knees with the ax handle, striking it with a noise like a grapefruit bursting open. As Jiles cried out and limped backward, Mary came up off the floor in a surge of desperate power. She swung at him again, this time hitting him on the collarbone and reeling him against the registration desk.

Laura wrenched the automatic free. She saw the fury in Mary's eyes, like that of an animal who has heard the noise of a cage springing shut. Didi was scrambling across the floor after the fallen Magnum. Laura saw Mary look from one to the other, trying to decide whom to attack. And then the big woman suddenly wheeled around, took two long strides, and smashed the ax handle down upon the CB radio, turning technology to junk in an eye blink. The communication to the pigs taken care of, Mary turned again, her teeth gritted in her sweating face, and hurled the ax handle at Laura.

As it came flying at her, Laura shielded her head and curled her body up into a ball. The ax handle hit the floor beside her and skidded past.

"Stop!" Didi shouted, aiming the gun at Mary's legs.

Mary ran. Not toward the front door, but the way Rachel had left the lobby to get water for the coffee. She grunted with pain as she dragged her bad leg behind her, and she burst through a pair of double doors into a long hallway with more doors on both sides. People were coming out, alerted by the noise. As Mary half ran, half limped and Drummer wailed in her grip she rummaged in her shoulder bag until her hand found the .38 revolver. The sight of the gun cleared the hallway of human obstruction, and Mary kept going with tears of torment clouding her eyes.

In the lobby, Didi was helping Laura to her feet and some of the others were going to the aid of Sam and Rachel Jiles. "Call the troopers, call the troopers," Jiles was saying as he clutched his broken collarbone, but the CB radio was way past saving. "This way!" Didi pulled at Laura, and Laura followed her into the corridor Mary had taken.

"She's bleeding!" Didi said, pointing to drops of scarlet on the floor. She and Laura were about halfway down the corridor, a few people nervously peering from their doorways, when both heard David crying. The sound stalled them, and suddenly Mary Terror leaned out from around a curve in the hallway and an overhead light glinted off the revolver in her hand. Two bullets fired, one hitting the wall to Laura's left and the second putting a hole through a door next to Didi and spraying the side of her face with splinters. Didi fired back, the slug smashing the glass of a fire alarm at the hallway's curve and setting off the siren. Then Mary was gone, and Didi saw a green sign overhead: EXIT.

"Don't shoot at her!" Laura shouted. "You might hit David!"

"I hit what I was aiming at! If we don't shoot back, she'll just stay in one place and take us to pieces!"

Didi crouched along the wall, watching for Mary to reappear around the curve. But on the other side the corridor was empty, and there was a safety door with a glass inset and snow whirling beyond in the exterior floodlights. Blood spattered the floor.

Mary was out in the storm.

Didi went out first, expecting a bullet and throwing herself on her stomach into the snow. No bullet came. Laura emerged cautiously through the door into the freezing wind, the automatic clenched in her fist. The snow aged them within seconds, turning their hair white as grannies.

Didi's eyes narrowed. "There," she said, and she pointed straight ahead.

Laura saw the figure, just at the edge of the light, limping frantically through the blowing snow toward the monsters of the Dinosaur Gardens.

Amid the prehistoric beasts, in the swamp of snow, Mary trudged on. She had left her gloves and the warm, fleece-lined coat behind. Drummer was zipped up in his parka, but the wind was tearing through her sweater. Her hair was white, her face tight with cold. Her thigh wound had split open, and she could feel the hot rivulets of blood oozing down her leg and into her boot. The crust of her forearm wound had also opened again, the bandage wet and red drops falling from her fingertips. But the cold had chilled her fever and frozen the beads of sweat on her face, and she felt that God was somewhere very close, watching her with his lizard eyes. She was not afraid. She had lived through worse injuries, both to the body and the spirit, and she would live through this. Drummer's crying came to her, a high note tattered by the wind. She zipped up his face as best she could without smothering him, and she concentrated on keeping her balance because it seemed that all the world was in tumultuous motion. It seemed the dinosaurs were roaring—the cries of the doomed— and Mary lifted her head toward the iron sky and roared with them.

But she had to keep going. Had to. Jack was waiting for her. Ahead, at the end of the road. In sunny, warm California. Jack, with his face a blaze of beauty and his hair more golden than the sun.

She could not cry. Oh no. The cold would freeze her eyelids shut if she did. So she blocked out the pain and thought of the distance between herself and the Cherokee on the mountain road. Two hundred yards? Three hundred? The monsters towered over her, grinning. They knew the secrets of life and death, she thought. They were crazy, just like her.

She looked back, could make out the two figures advancing on her against the lights from the Silver Cloud Inn. Laura Clayhead and Benedict Bedelia. They wanted to play some more. They wanted to be taught a lesson in the survival of the fittest.

Mary crouched down against a dinosaur's curved tail, the beast twelve feet tall, and she positioned herself so she was shielded from most of the wind and she could watch them coming. They would be on her in a couple of minutes. They were walking fast, those two, on healthy legs. Come on, she thought. Come to Mama. She cocked the revolver, propping her arm up on the monster's tail, and she took careful aim. Her damned hand was jittering again, the nerves all screwed up. But the figures were good targets against the lights. Let them get closer, she decided. She wanted to be able to tell Clayhead from Benedict. Let them get real close.

"Where'd she go?" Laura shouted to Didi, but Didi shook her head. They went on twenty more yards, the cold gnawing at them and the wind shrieking around the dinosaurs. Mary was lost from sight, but her ragged trail through the snow was clear enough. Didi leaned her head close to Laura's and shouted, "Her car's got to be parked on the road down there! That's where she's going!" She thought of the blood in the corridor. "She could be hurt pretty badly, though! She could have fallen and passed out!"

"Okay! Let's go!"

Didi caught her arm. "One other thing! She could be waiting for us in there!" She nodded toward the monsters of the Dinosaur Gardens. "Watch your ass!"

They went on, following Mary Terror's tracks through mounds of snow as high as their knees. The brutal wind howled into their faces and stung them with bits of ice. They passed between dinosaurs, snow caught on the curves of the mountainous spines and foot-long icicles hanging from the jaws like vampire fangs. It had occurred to Didi that she didn't know how many bullets remained in the Magnum automatic. Two had been fired in the inn; the gun probably held four or five if the magazine had been full. But shooting at Mary would be playing Russian roulette with David, a fact that Laura already feared. Even a shot at Mary's legs might go wild and hit him. If I were Mary, Didi thought, I'd find a place to set up an ambush. We've got the inn's lights behind us and the wind in our faces. But there was no choice but to follow the trail, and both Didi and Laura saw black spots of blood on the snow.

The furrow Mary had left behind her curved toward a tableau of dinosaurs frozen in an attitude of combat, fangs bared and claws swiping the air. The road wasn't too far beyond it. There was no sign of Mary but the trail, and snow was already blowing over it. Didi didn't like the looks of the dinosaur tableau; Mary could be hiding behind any one of the statues. She stopped, and grabbed Laura's shoulder to stop her, too. "I don't want to go through here!" she said. "Go around it!"

Laura nodded and started walking to the right of the monsters, heading for the road. Didi was two paces behind, her shoulders hunched against the wind and her body starting to shiver uncontrollably. Ice chips struck her cheeks, and she turned her head slightly to the left to protect her eyes.

That was when she saw the figure stand up from behind the tail of one of the thunder lizards, about a dozen feet away.

The big woman's face was ghastly white, snowflakes snagged in her hair. Didi could see the shine of the Silver Cloud Inn's lights in her eyes, a glint of light leaping like an electric spark from the yellow Smiley Face button on her sweater. Mary held a bundle in the crook of her left arm, her right arm outstretched and the revolver at the end of it. The gun was pointed at Laura, who hadn't yet seen the danger.

Didi had an instant of gut-wrenching terror, and she realized exactly how Mary had earned her name. Mary's expression was a white blank, without triumph or anger: just the sure knowledge of who held the upper hand.

Didi's shout would be lost in the wind. There was no time for anything else. She threw herself at Laura, hitting her with a solid shoulderblock, and at the same instant she heard Mary's gun go off: *crackcrack.*

Laura went down on her stomach into the snow. Didi felt the bite of a bullet at her throat, and something hit her in the chest like the kick of a mule. The pain choked her, her finger spasming on the Magnum's trigger and the bullet going up into the sky. Then Laura had twisted her body, and as Mary fired again, snow kicked up where she'd been a second before. Laura saw the woman standing there, behind the dinosaur's tail, and she had an instant to make her decision. She took aim and pulled the automatic's trigger.

The bullet hit its mark: not Mary Terror, but the larger target of the dinosaur's gray-scaled hip. Chips of concrete flew up, and Mary dodged behind the monster's body. Laura got up and threw herself against the shelter of a stegosaurus's concrete-plated back. She looked at Didi, who lay on her side. Darkness was spreading around her. Laura started to crawl back to her friend, but she was stopped short when a bullet hit one of the dinosaur's spine plates next to her head and ricocheted off with a scream.

On her knees, Mary fumbled in her shoulder bag for the box of .38 shells she'd taken from the dead man's gun cabinet. Her fingers were stiffening up and slick with icy blood. She got two more bullets into the revolver and lost two into the snow. But she was freezing, her strength going fast, and she knew she couldn't stay out in this cold much longer. Benedict Bedelia was down, the other bitch behind cover. Getting to the Cherokee was going to be tough, but it had to be done. There was no other way out.

It was time to get moving, before her legs were useless. She fired another shot at Laura, the bullet knocking a second chunk off the stegosaurus's hide, and then she stood up with Drummer and began to struggle toward the road again.

Laura peered out from her refuge and saw Mary limping through the snow. "Stop!" she shouted. "STOP!" The wind took her voice, and she stepped out from cover and aimed her pistol at the other woman's back.

She had a vision of the bullet passing through Mary's body and ripping into David. She lifted her gun and fired it into the air. "STOP!" she screamed, her throat raw. Mary didn't look back; she kept going with a crippled but determined stride through the white drifts.

Laura started after her. Three strides and she stopped, the gun hanging at her side. She looked at Didi, lying in a black pool. Then at Mary again, the figure drawing steadily away. Back to Didi, steam swirling up from the blood.

She turned toward Didi, walked to her side, and knelt down.

Didi's eyes were open. A creeper of blood spilled from her mouth, her face plastered with snow. She was still breathing, but it was a terrible sound. Laura looked at Mary, limping away with Drummer in her arms, about to leave the Dinosaur Gardens and reach the road.

One of Didi's hands rose up like a dying bird, and clutched the front of Laura's shoplifted sweater.

Didi's mouth moved. A soft groan emerged, taken quickly by the wind. Laura saw Didi's other hand twitch, the fingers grasping at the pocket of her jeans. There was a message in Didi's pain-shocked eyes, something she wanted Laura to understand. Didi's fingers kept clawing at the pocket with fading strength.

The pocket. Something in Didi's pocket.

Laura carefully worked her hand into it. She found the car keys and a folded piece of paper, and she brought them out together. Unfolding the paper, she made out the cracked bell of the Liberty Motor Lodge. The distant lights of the Silver Cloud Inn helped her see the names of the three men written on it, above a Smiley Face.

Didi pulled her close, and Laura bent her head down.

"Remember," Didi whispered. "He's . . . mine, too."

Didi's hand let go of the sweater.

Laura knelt in the snow, beside her sister. At last she lifted her head, and looked toward the road.

Mary Terror was gone.

Perhaps two minutes passed. Laura realized Didi was no longer breathing. Her eyes were filling up with snow, and Laura closed them. It wasn't a hard thing to do.

Somewhere the bells of freedom were ringing.

Laura put the piece of paper into her pocket and stood up, the gun and keys in her hand. Streaks of ice were on her face, but her heart was an inferno. She began to trudge away from the dead woman, after the walking dead who had her baby. The wind hit her, tried to knock her legs out from under her, spat snow in her face, and wrenched her hair.

She walked faster, pushing through the snow like a hard-eyed engine. In another moment she roused up everything within her that could still pump out heat and she began to run. The snow grabbed at her ankles, tripped her up, and sent her sprawling. Pain tore through her broken hand, the bandages dangling down. Laura got up again, fresh tears on her face. There was no one left to hear her crying. Her companion now was agony.

She kept going, plowing the snow aside, her body shivering and her jeans and sweater and face wet, her hair white beyond her years, and the beginnings of new lines at the corners of her eyes.

She kept going because there was no going back.

Laura left the snowfield and the Dinosaur Gardens, where the prehistoric creatures were frozen for all time, and she started down the road to the car that would now carry a solitary traveler.

5.

Fight the Furies

In the warmth of the Cherokee, Mary's bladder let go.

The wet heat soaked into the seat beneath her hips and thighs. All she could think of was another song from the memory vault: "MacArthur Park," and all that sweet green icing flowing down. She was backing the Cherokee down the mountain road, the tires skidding left and right. The feeling was returning to her hands now, the prickling of a thousand hot needles. Her face felt as if several layers of flesh had been flayed off, and the blood on her jeans had frozen into a shine. Her right hand was streaked with crimson, the fingers twitching their nerve-damage dance. Drummer was still crying, but she let him sing; he was alive, and he was hers.

The Cherokee's rear end bashed into one of the abandoned cars on the roadside. She got the vehicle straightened out again, and in another moment metal shrieked as the Cherokee skidded over to the right and grazed a station wagon. Then she had reached the bottom of the road, and she turned the Cherokee toward I-80, the heater buzzing but the cold still latched deep in her lungs. She found a sign that pointed to I-80 West, and she turned onto the entrance ramp, the snow swirling like underwater silt before her lights. Blocking her way was another big flashing sign: STOP ROAD CLOSED. But there was no pig car this time, and Mary plowed the Cherokee through the snow on the right shoulder and got back on the ramp.

It made a long, snow-slick curve onto I-80 that Mary took at a crawl. And then she was on the interstate, the pig car at the McFadden exit a quarter mile behind her. She slowly let the speed wind up to forty miles an hour, the highway ascending under her wheels. Snow was still coming down hard, the wind a fierce beast. She was on her way across the Rockies.

Less than ten minutes after Mary had turned onto I-80, a rust-eaten Cutlass with one eye made the ramp's curve and came after her.

The icy tears were thawing on Laura's face. She was wired, her pulse racing. One hand was clenched firmly on the wheel, the elbow of her other arm helping steer. The single working wiper was making a shrill whining noise as it pushed the snow away, and Laura feared the wiper motor might be about to burn out. The Cutlass was climbing, the highway ahead waxy with ice. She kept her speed between thirty and thirty-five, and she prayed to God that Mary was still alert enough not to go off the road. Mary was badly hurt and half frozen, just like her. Under the bandages, Laura's mangled hand was a swollen blaze. Her body had reached and passed its threshold of pain, and now she was going on sheer willpower and Black Cats. She was still going because tears wouldn't get David back, and neither would she get her son by crawling into a corner and surrendering. She had come too far now to give up. She'd left her friend behind, in the snow. Mary Terror had another sin to pay for.

The wind thrashed at the Cutlass, and the car's frame moaned like a human voice. Laura stared straight ahead, unblinking, into the storm.

She was looking for red taillights, but there was nothing but snow and darkness beyond. The highway was curving to the right, still ascending. The tires slid over a sheet of ice and Laura's heart stuttered, but then the tires gripped pavement again. The wiper motor's whine had gotten louder, and that frightened Laura more than the ice. If the wiper failed, she was finished until the storm ended. Now the road began to descend and curve to the left, and Laura had to ease on the brake. The tires slipped once more, the Cutlass sliding over almost to the median's ice-crusted guardrail before she regained control. Sheets of snow that looked solid were flailing at the windshield, and again the highway climbed. A gust of wind hit the Cutlass like a punch from the left, the wheel shivering in her grip.

She had to go on even if she was making only ten miles an hour. She had to go on until the wiper motor burned out and the snow closed in. The only thing in her life that mattered worth a damn anymore was holding her son in her arms, and she would fight the furies every mile of the way if that's what had to be done.

Ahead, Mary had slowed the Cherokee. The road had leveled off, and snowdrifts four and five feet high stood on this section of I-80. The winds were beating at the Cherokee from both sides, their noise like banshee wails. Mary threaded a path between the drifts, her tires spinning on ice and then catching again. The Cherokee suddenly got away from her and fishtailed, and she fought the wheel, but there was nothing she could do. The entire vehicle made a slow spin and crunched into a snowdrift. She powered the Cherokee through it, the engine straining. Thirty more yards, and the drifts were all around her, some of them sculpted to eight feet high. She kept going, trying to find a path through them, but she had to stop again because the snowdrifts were up to the hood and would not be bullied.

She looked in the rearview mirror. Darkness upon darkness. Where was the bitch? Still back at the Silver Cloud Inn? Or on the highway? The bitch was a fighter, but she wasn't crazy enough to try to cross the Rockies in a blizzard. No, that kind of insanity was Mary's domain.

She wasn't going anywhere for a while. There was plenty of gas in the tank. The heater was all right. In a couple of hours dawn would break. Maybe in the light she could find a way out of this.

Mary pulled up the emergency brake, then switched off the headlights and the wipers. Within seconds the windshield was covered over. She let the engine idle, and she picked up Drummer. He was through crying, but now he was making mewling hungry noises. She reached for her bag and the baby's formula. The acidic smell of urine drifted to her: Drummer had joined her in wetting himself. Hell of a place to change a diaper, she thought, but she was a mother now, and such things had to be done. She glanced in the rearview mirror again. Still nothing. The bitch had stayed at the Silver Cloud with Benedict Bedelia. The shots would've hit Laura Clayhead if Didi hadn't gotten in the way. They'd been good shots, the both of them. She didn't know exactly where Didi had been hit, but she didn't think Didi was going to be chasing anybody for a while.

Two miles behind the Cherokee, Laura heard a grinding noise. It went on for ten seconds, and then the wiper stopped. Snow blanked the windshield. "Damn it!" Laura shouted as she eased pressure on the brake. The car began to skid, first to the left and then back to the right, turning and sliding sideways along I-80. Laura's nerves were screaming, but all she could do was brace herself for a collision. At last the Cutlass straightened out, began to respond to the brake, and rolled to a slippery halt.

Her traveling was over until the snow stopped. There was nothing to do but pull up the emergency brake and turn off the headlight. The heater was rattling, but it was pumping out warm air. There was a little more than a half tank of gas. She could survive for a few hours.

In the darkness Laura forced herself to breathe slowly and deeply, trying to calm down. Mary might get away from her, but she knew Mary's destination. Mary wasn't going to be driving very fast or far in this storm. She might even pull off I-80 and try to sleep. The important thing was to get to Freestone before Mary and find Jack Gardiner, if indeed he was one of the three men on Didi's list.

The wind shrieked like discordant violin notes around the Cutlass. Laura leaned her head back and closed her eyes. The image of Didi's face came to her: not the face of the woman who lay dying in the snow, but her face as she worked carefully on the splints for Laura's hand. She saw Didi in the pottery workshop, showing the items that had been created from a tormented mind. And then she saw Didi's face as the woman might have looked when she was much younger, a teenager in a black-and-white high school yearbook picture, something from the late sixties. Didi was smiling, her hair sprayed and flipped up on the ends and her face freckled and healthy-looking with a little farmgirl chub in her cheeks. Her eyes were clear, and they gazed toward the future from a place where murder and terror did not live.

The picture began to fade.

Laura let it go, and she slept in the arms of the storm.

The tasks of a mother done, Mary put Drummer on the passenger seat and zipped up the parka around him again. For a few minutes she brooded on the distance she had yet to go—two hundred miles across Utah, then into Nevada for more than three hundred miles, passing through Reno into California, down to Sacramento, and then through the Napa Valley toward Oakland and San Francisco. Have to buy more diapers and formula for Drummer. Have to get some pain pills and something to keep me awake. She still had plenty of money from her mother's ring and forty-seven dollars and some change she'd taken from Rocky Road's house. She would have to change her jeans before she went into a store, and getting her swollen thigh into fresh denim was going to be a job. She had another pair of gloves somewhere in her belongings, so she could hide her bloodied hand. How long would it be before the pigs got on her case? Not very long, she figured. Have to haul ass when she got over the mountains, maybe find a place to lay low until the heat passed.

She couldn't deal with these things right now. Her fever had returned, her body a raw pulse, and she realized she was fading fast. She found the baby's face in the dark, kissed his forehead, and then reclined the driver's seat back. She closed her eyes and listened to the wind. God's voice was in it, singing "Love Her Madly" to her.

Mary heard only the first verse, and then she was asleep.

6.

A Harley Man

*T*ap tap.

"Lady?"

Tap tap. "Lady, you okay?"

Laura woke up, the effort as tough as swimming through glue. She got her eyes open, and she saw the man in a hooded brown parka beside her window.

"You okay?" he asked again, his face long-jawed and ruddy in the cold.

Laura nodded. The movement made the muscles of her neck and shoulders awaken and rage.

"Got some coffee." The man was holding a thermos. He lifted it in invitation.

Laura rolled her window down. She realized suddenly that the wind had died. A few small snowflakes were still falling. The gray sky was streaked with pearly light, and by its somber glow Laura could see the huge white mountain ranges that marched along I-80. The man poured some coffee into the thermos's cup, gave it to her, and she downed it gratefully. In another life she might have wished for Jamaican Blue Mountain; now any pot-boiled brew was delicious if it got her engine running.

"What're you doin' out here?" he asked. "The road's still closed."

"Took a wrong turn, I guess." Her voice was a froggish croak.

"Lucky you didn't wind up askin' directions from St. Peter. It was a damned mess between here and Rock Springs. Drifts higher'n my head and wide as a house."

Was a mess, he'd said. The noise of machinery came to her. "My wipers are out," she said. "Could you clear my windshield off?"

"Reckon I can." He started raking the snow away with a leather-gloved hand. The powder was almost five inches thick, the last inch iced to the glass. The man dug deep, got his fingers hooked, and wrenched upward, and the plate of ice cracked like a pistol shot and slid away. The windshield on her side was clear, and through it she could see a yellow snowplow at work forty yards ahead, smoke chugging from its exhaust pipe. Another plow was shoving snow aside over on the interstate's eastbound lanes, and a third plow sat without a driver twenty feet from the Cutlass. Laura realized she must've been dead to the world not to have heard that thing approaching. Behind the plows were two large highway department trucks, their crews shoveling cinders onto the patches of ice. Gears clicked and meshed in her brain. "You came from Rock Springs?"

"My men got on at Table Rock, but the drifts are broke up from here on. Hell of a mess, I'm tellin' ya."

The snowplows had come from the west. The way to California was open.

"Thank you." She returned the cup to him. The Cutlass's engine was still idling, the gas tank down almost to the *E*. She figured by the amount of daylight that she'd been asleep at least four hours. She released the emergency brake.

"Hey, you'd better find a place to pull off!" the plow's driver cautioned. "It's still mighty dangerous. Nobody ever tell you about snow chains?"

"I'll make it. Where's the nearest gas station?"

"Rawlins. That's ten miles or so. I swear, you're about the second luckiest woman in this world!"

"The *second* luckiest?"

"Yeah. At least you don't have a little baby that could've frozen to death."

Laura stared up at him.

"Woman and her baby caught in the drifts couple of miles ahead," he told her, taking her silence for curiosity. "Worked herself in good and tight. She didn't have no snow chains neither."

"She was in a van?"

"Pardon?"

"A green van? Is that what she was in?"

"Nope. One of them Jeep wagons. Comanche or Geronimo or somethin'."

"What color?"

"Dark blue, I reckon." He frowned. "How come you're askin'?"

"I know her," Laura said. A thought occurred to her. "Did you give her coffee, too?"

"Yup. Drunk it like a horse."

Laura smiled grimly. They had drunk from the same bitter cup. "How long ago was that?"

"Thirty, forty minutes, I reckon. She a friend of yours?"

"No."

"Well, she asked where the nearest gas station was, too. Rawlins, I said. I tell you, travelin' with a little bitty baby in a blizzard without snow chains . . . that woman must be crazy!"

Laura put the car into drive. "Thanks again. You take care."

"That's my middle name!" he said, and he stepped back from the window.

She started off, guarding her speed. The tires crunched over cinders. Snow chains or not, she was going to make it to Rawlins. She skidded in a couple of places, the highway climbing and then descending across the mountains, but she took it slow and easy and watched the quivering needle of her fuel gauge. Somewhere along the line Mary Terror had ditched her van; that much was clear. Where Mary had gotten the new vehicle, Laura didn't know, but she guessed more blood was on Mary's hands.

The same hands that held the fate of David.

She turned into the gas station at Rawlins, filled the tank, and scraped the rest of the snow off the windshield. She relieved herself in the bathroom, swallowed another Black Cat tablet—its caffeine equivalent to four cups of strong black coffee—and she bought some junk food guaranteed to make her blood sugar soar. The gas station's small grocery also sold gauze bandages, and she bought some to rewrap her hand with. Another bottle of Extra-Strength Excedrin and half a dozen canned Cokes, and she was ready to go. She asked the teenage girl behind the counter about seeing a big woman with a baby, traveling in a dark blue Jeep wagon.

"Yes, ma'am, I seen her," the girl answered. She would be pretty when she got her acne under control, Laura thought. "She was in here 'bout thirty minutes ago. Cute little ol' baby. He was raisin' a ruckus, and she bought him some diapers and a new passy."

"Was she hurt?" Laura asked. The girl stared blankly at her. "Bleeding," Laura said. "Did you see any blood on her?"

"No, ma'am," the girl said in a wary voice. Laura could not know that Mary had awakened, seen the plows coming in the early light, and had removed her bloodstained trousers, blotting up the leakage with the last Pampers and struggling into a fresh pair of jeans from her suitcase.

Laura paid what she owed and went on. She figured she was thirty to forty minutes behind Mary Terror. The snowplows and cinder trucks were out on I-80 like a small army. Except for some flurries, the snowfall had ceased and it was all over but the cleaning up. She began to see more cars on the interstate as she crossed the Continental Divide west of Creston, the mountains looming around her in a rugged white panorama and the sky chalky gray. The highway began its long, slow descent toward Utah. When she passed Rock Springs, she saw state troopers waving tractor-trailer rigs back onto I-80 from a crowded truck stop. The interstate was officially open again, the Rockies stood swathed in the clouds behind her, and she gradually increased her speed to fifty-five, then to sixty, then to sixty-five.

She crossed the Utah state line and immediately saw a sign that said Salt Lake City was fifty-eight miles ahead. She looked for a dark blue Jeep wagon, spotted a vehicle that fit the description, but when she got up beside it she saw a Utah tag and a white-haired man at the wheel. The interstate took her into Salt Lake City, where she made a gas stop, then curved along the gray shore of the Great Salt Lake, straightened out, and shot her toward the sandy desert wastes. As Laura ate her lunch of two Snickers bars and a Coke, the clouds opened and the sun glared through. Patches of blue appeared in the sky, and little whirlwinds kicked up puffs of dust from the winter desert.

She passed Wendover, Utah, at two o'clock, and a big green sign with a roulette wheel on it welcomed her to Nevada. Desert land, jagged peaks, and scrub brush bordered I-80 all the way to the horizon. The carcasses of road kill were being plucked at by vultures with wingspans like Stealth bombers. Laura passed signs advertising "giant flea" markets, chicken ranches, Harrah's Auto Museum in Reno, and a rodeo in Winnemucca. Several times she looked to her right, expecting to see Didi sitting on the seat beside her. If Didi was there, she was a quiet ghost. The tires hummed and the engine racketed, dark blooms of burning oil drifting out behind. Laura kept watching for Mary's Jeep wagon; she saw a number of them, but none were the right color. On the long straight highway, cars were passing her doing eighty and ninety miles an hour. She got into the windbreak of a tractor-trailer truck and let the speed wind up to seventy-five. Nevada became a progression of signs, the names of desert towns blowing past: Oasis . . . Wells . . . Metropolis . . . Deeth, the second *e* of which someone had altered with spray paint to spell *Death*.

She was truly alone now, journeying into frightful country.

At the end of the road was Freestone, fifty miles north of San Francisco. What was she going to do when she found Jack Gardiner? What would she do if none of those three men *was* Jack Gardiner? What kind of man would he be now? Would he shun Mary Terror or embrace her? Surely he'd read about her in the papers or seen the story on TV. What if—and this thought sickened her—he was still a killer at heart, and he took David as an offering and he and Mary fled together? What if . . . what if . . . what if. Those questions were unanswerable. All she knew for sure was that this road led to Freestone, and Mary was on it.

The Cutlass shuddered.

She smelled something burning. She looked at the dashboard and saw the temperature gauge's needle almost off the dial. Oh Jesus! she thought as panic chewed at her. "Don't quit on me!" she shouted, looking for an exit. There wasn't one in sight, and Deeth was two miles behind. The Cutlass's engine was rumbling like a concrete mixer. "Don't quit on me!" she repeated, her foot pressed down on the gas pedal. And then the hood burst upward, steam spewed out with a train-whistle shriek, and she knew the radiator was finished. The car, like her own body, had been pushed past its threshold of pain. The only difference was, she was stronger. "Keep going! Keep going!" she shouted, tears of frustration in her eyes. The Cutlass had given up. Its speed was falling, whips of steam flailing back from the overflowing radiator. The truck in front of her kept going; the world was short of shining knights. "Oh Christ!" Laura yelled. "Damn it to hell! Damn it!" But cursing would produce no cure. She guided the wounded car over off the interstate, and it rolled to a stop in gravel next to a vulture-picked jackrabbit.

Laura sat there as the radiator bubbled and moaned. She could feel Mary moving farther away from her with every passing second. She balled up her fist and slammed the wheel, and then she got out to survey the carnage. Whoever said the desert was hot had never visited it in February, because the chill pierced her bones. But the radiator was a little spout of hell, rusty water flooding out and the engine ticking like a time bomb. Laura looked right and left, saw desolation on both sides. A car flashed past, then another a few seconds later. She needed help, and fast. A third car was coming, and Laura lifted her right arm to flag it down. The car left grit stinging her face. Then the interstate was empty, just her, the busted Cutlass, and a jackrabbit chewed down to the rib cage and ears.

Deeth was too far to walk. What the next exit was, and where a service station might be, she had no idea. Mary was on her way to Freestone, and Laura wasn't going to wait here all day for a Samaritan. She walked out into the interstate and faced east.

Maybe a minute passed. And then sunlight glinted off glass and metal. The car—a station wagon, it looked to be—was coming fast. She put her hand up under her double sweaters and touched the automatic's grip. If the car didn't start to slow down in five seconds, she was going to pull the gun and do a Dirty Harry. "Stop," she whispered, the wind raw in her face. "Stop. Stop." Her hand tightened on the grip. *"Stop, damn it!"*

The station wagon began to slow down. There was a man at the wheel, a woman on the passenger side. They both looked less than eager to be helpful, and Laura saw a child's face peering up over the front seat. The man was driving as if he still hadn't decided whether to lend a hand or not, and the woman was jabbering at him. Probably think I look like a hard case, Laura thought. It occurred to her that they would be correct.

The man made his decision. He pulled the station wagon over behind the Cutlass and rolled down his window.

Their names were Joe and Cathy Sheffield, from Orem, Utah, on their way to visit her parents in Sacramento with their six-year-old son Gary. All this Laura learned on the way to the next exit, which was a place called Halleck four miles up the highway. She told them her name was Bedelia Morse, and she was trying to get to San Francisco to find an old friend. It seemed right. Gary asked why her hand was all bandaged up and why there was a boo-boo on the side of her face. She said she'd had a bad fall at home. She didn't answer when he asked where her home was. Then, after another minute or two, Gary asked her with all innocence if she ever took a bath, and Cathy shushed him and laughed nervously but Laura said it was okay, she'd been on the road a long time.

Joe took the Halleck exit. It wasn't much of a town, just a few cinderblock buildings, some weatherbeaten houses, a diner made from an old train car, and a stucco post office with an American flag snapping in the wind. But one of the cinderblock buildings bore a crudely painted sign that identified it as Marco's Garage, with a row of gas pumps out front and a couple of cars sitting around that looked as if they'd been stripped by pack rats. Behind the garage was a dump of old car hulks and a mound of bald tires. There was a bright orange towtruck, though, and Joe Sheffield pulled his station wagon up beside it.

A man emerged from inside one of the two garage bays. He was short and stocky as a fireplug, and he wore grease-stained overalls and a T-shirt, his muscular arms covered with tattoos from wrists to shoulders. His hands were black with grime. He was also slick bald, and had on yellow-tinted goggles.

"Well!" Joe said cheerfully. "Here's somebody!"

Laura had a moment of knowing what she should do. She should pull her gun, order the Sheffields out of the station wagon, and leave them there while she sped on after Mary. Marco's Garage was an armpit, and getting her car fixed here was going to be a trial by frustration. She should pull the gun and take the station wagon, and she should do it right now.

But the moment passed. They were good people. There was no need to mark their lives with the barrel of a gun even though she never would dream of using it as anything but a bluff. Some hard case, she thought.

"Thanks for the lift," she told them, and got out.

The station wagon pulled away. Gary waved at her through the rear window. And then Laura turned to face the bald-headed grease monkey who stood about three inches shorter than her and stared up at her through his yellow goggles like a bullfrog.

"You fix cars?" she asked stupidly.

"Naw." He laughed like a snort. "I *eat* 'em!"

"My car's broken down a couple of miles from Deeth. Can you tow it here?"

"How come you didn't go to Deeth, then?"

"I was heading west. I came here. Can you tow it?" She realized the tattoos on the man's arms were interlocked figures of naked women.

"Busy right now. Got a car in both bays and two waitin'."

"Okay. When can you tow it?"

"An hour, give or take."

Laura shook her head. "No. I can't wait that long."

"Sorry, but that's the breaks. See, I'm all alone here. I'm Marco, like the sign says."

"I want you to go get my car right now."

He frowned, deep lines furrowing across his broad forehead. "Got wax in your ears, babe? I said I—"

Laura had the gun in her hand. She placed it against his bald skull. "What did you say?"

Marco swallowed, his Adam's apple bulging. "I . . . said . . . I'm ready when you are, babe."

"Don't call me *babe.*"

"Okay," he said. "Whatever you say, chief."

On the subject of baths, Marco had a lot to learn. Laura knew she didn't smell like roses, but Marco exuded an odor of stale sweat and dirty underwear that made one wish for a whiff of Limburger cheese. At the Cutlass, Marco peered into the radiator and whistled. "Hey, chief! You ever heard of puttin' coolant in this thing? You got enough rust in here to sink a battleship!"

"Can you fix it?"

"You can shoot it and put it out of its misery." He looked at the gun Laura held by her side. "Why don't you put that away now, Annie Oakley? Have I got a target on my ass?"

"I have to get back on the road. Can you fix it or not?" The towtruck was starting to look attractive, but trying to steer that damned thing with one hand and an elbow would be beastly.

"You want honest or bullshit?" he asked her. "Bullshit says yeah, sure, no sweat. Honest says you'll need a new radiator, bottom line. Got some rotten hoses in there and belts that are about to go. Oil lines look like a rat's been chewin' on 'em. You still with me?"

"Yes."

"Major labor," he went on, and he scratched his pate with black fingers. "Have to find a radiator that'll fit this clunker. Probably have to drive to the parts shop in Elko to get one. We're talkin' two big bills, and I'm not gonna be able to even get started good before closin' time."

"I can spend four hundred dollars," Laura said. In her pocket was five hundred and thirty-four dollars, what remained of the cash from her engagement diamond. "Can I buy a used car around here anywhere?"

"Yeah, I can find you somethin'." He cocked his head at her, his hands on his bulbous hips. "It'll have an engine, but it might not have a floorboard in it. Four bills ain't gonna buy you much, unless . . ." He grinned, showing a silver tooth. "You got somethin' to trade?"

She pretended not to have heard that, because he was real close to becoming a soprano. She needed his hands, not his dubious equipment. "How about *your* car, then?"

"Sorry, chief. I'm a Harley man."

"I'll pay you four hundred and fifty dollars to fix my car," she said. "Except I want you to keep working on it until it's finished."

The lines furrowed deep again. "What's the rush? You kill somebody?"

"No. I'm in a hurry to get where I'm going."

He prodded at the right front tire with a boot that had been scrubbed with steel wool. "Let's see your money," he said.

Laura returned the pistol to her waistband, reached into her pocket, and showed him the cash. "Can you do it in three hours?"

Marco paused, thinking about it. He looked up at the sun in the cloud-dappled sky, back to the radiator, and sucked air across his lower lip. "I can put a radiator in and do a patch job. Got a retarded kid who helps me sometimes, if he ain't readin' his Batman funnies. Have to close down the pumps and shut up shop except for the one job. Elko's about twenty miles there and back. Four hours, minimum."

It was approaching three o'clock. That would get her out of there by seven. San Francisco was still over five hundred miles away, and Freestone another fifty miles north, according to the maps. If she drove all night she could make Freestone before dawn. But when would Mary get there? Sometime after midnight if she kept going straight through. Laura felt tears pressing to burst free. God had turned a blind eye. Mary was going to get to Freestone at least four hours before she would.

"That's the best I can do, chief," Marco said. "Honest."

Laura drew a deep breath. They were wasting time talking. "Get it done," she said.

7.

Little Black Snakes

How many nights?" the desk clerk asked, glasses perched on the end of his nose.

"Just one," she said.

He gave her a piece of paper on which to fill out her name and address. She put down *Mrs. Jack Morrison, 1972 Linden Avenue, Richmond, Virginia.* Across the top of the paper was Lux-More Motel, Santa Rosa, California.

"Sweet little baby, yes she is!" The clerk reached over the registration desk to tickle Drummer under the chin. Drummer didn't like it; he was tired and hungry, and he squirmed restlessly in Mary's arms.

"My son," Mary said. She drew away, and the clerk offered a chilly smile and got her room key. "I'll need a wake-up call," she decided. "Five o'clock."

"Five o'clock. Wake-up call for Room Twenty-six. Got it, Mrs.—" He checked the paper. "Mrs. Morrison." He pushed his glasses off his nose. "Ah . . . cash in advance, please."

Mary paid him the thirty dollars. She left the motel office, limping into the cool, damp air of northern California. It was just after two-thirty in the morning. Mist drifted around the halogen lights on I-101, which cut through Santa Rosa and headed north toward the redwood ranges. A fifth of a mile from the Lux-More, County Highway 116 cut across the verdant, rolling hills toward the Pacific Ocean, and eleven miles away down that road was the town of Freestone.

She got into the Cherokee, drove it along the motel lot to Room 26, and parked it in the designated space. She was too weary to care if the night clerk noticed that a woman who said she was from Virginia had an Iowa tag. The revolver in the bag over her shoulder, she unlocked the door of Room 26 and took Drummer in, then closed the door and bolted it.

She was trembling.

She laid Drummer down on the single bed. The curtains were decorated with faded blue roses, and stains marred the gray carpet. A red sticker on the television set cautioned that the X-rated closed-circuit channel should be viewed only by mature adults. The bathroom had a shower and a tub and two cigarette butts floating in the toilet. She didn't look at herself in the mirror. That chore would be for later. She sat down on the bed, and springs groaned. The ceiling was riddled with earthquake cracks. That was California for you, she mused. Thirty dollars for a ten-dollar room.

God, her body hurt. Her mind was tired; it craved a blank slate. But there was still much to be done before she could sleep.

She lay on her back next to Drummer, and stared up at the cracks. There was a design to them if you really noticed. Like Chinese quill strokes. Shouldn't have spent that hour in Berkeley, she thought. That was dumb, walking the streets. She'd planned only on driving through, but there was something so ripe, so haunting about Berkeley that she couldn't leave it without seeing the old places. The Golden Sun coffee shop, where she had first met Jack, the Truck On Down head shop, where she and the other Storm Fronters bought their roach clips and bong pipes, Cody's Bookstore, where political discussions of the Mindfuck State had made Lord Jack rage with care for the downtrodden masses, the Mad Italian pizzeria, where CinCin Omara used to be the night manager and slip her brothers and sisters free pizzas: all those were still there, aged maybe, wearing new paint, but still there, a vision of the world that used to be.

A young world, Mary thought. A world full of brave dreamers. Where were they now?

She'd have to get up in a minute. Have to take a hot shower, wash her hair, and squeeze the watery yellow pus from her oozing thigh wound. Have to get herself ready for Jack.

But she was so tired, and all she wanted to do was crash. It wouldn't be right to let Jack see her like this, grimy with road dirt, her teeth unbrushed and her armpits foul. That was why she'd stopped at the 7 Eleven just before the Oakland Bay Bridge; there was a sack in the Cherokee that she had to go get.

Drummer began to cry louder. Hungry cry. With an effort she roused herself, got his formula ready, and stuck the bottle's nipple into his mouth. As he sucked on it, he stared at her with eyes that were every bit as blue as Jack's. Karma, she thought. Jack was going to look at Drummer and see himself.

"You're scared."

God was standing in the corner, next to a lamp with a crooked shade. "You're scared shitless, Mary my girl. Aren't you?"

"No," she answered, and the lie made God grin. Two heartbeats and he was gone. "I'm not scared!" Mary said stridently. She concentrated on feeding her baby. Her stomach was a tight bag of nerves. Her right hand twitched around the baby's bottle.

The thought crept in again, as it had several times today, like a little black snake at a picnic: what if Jack weren't one of those three men?

"He is, though," she said to Drummer. His eyes were searching the room, his mouth clamped tightly on the nipple. "It's him in the picture. Didi knew it was him." She frowned. Her head hurt when Didi's face came to mind; it was like holding a metal photograph with saw-toothed edges. And another little black snake crawled into her realm of summer: where was the bitch?

The bitch knew all about Lord Jack and Freestone. Benedict Bedelia had told her. So where was the bitch right now, as the clock ticked toward three?

When she found Jack, they would go away somewhere safe. A place where they could have a farm, maybe grow some weed on an acre or two, kick back in the lamplight and look at the stars. It would be a mellow place, that farm where the three of them would live in a triad of love and harmony.

She wanted that so very very badly.

Mary finished feeding Drummer. She burped him, and his eyelids were getting heavy. Hers were, too. She lay with Drummer in the crook of her arm, and she could feel his heart: *drum* . . . *drum* . . . *drum*ming. Have to get up and bathe, she thought. Wash my hair. Decide what to wear. All those things, the heavy details of life.

She closed her eyes.

Jack was walking toward her, wearing a white robe. His golden hair hung over his shoulders, his eyes blue and clear, his face bearded and chiseled. God was at his side, in black leather. Mary could smell the sea and the aroma of pines. The light streamed through bay windows behind Jack. She knew where they were: the Thunder House, on Drakes Bay about forty miles from the Lux-More. The beautiful chapel of love, the place of the Storm Front's birth. Jack walked across the pinewood floor, his feet in Birkenstock sandals. He was smiling, his face alight with joy, and he reached out to take his gift.

"She's scared shitless," she heard God, that demon, say.

Jack's arms accepted Drummer. He opened his mouth, and the shrill ring of a telephone came out of it.

Mary sat up. Drummer was wailing.

She blinked, her brain sluggish in its turn toward thinking. Phone ringing. Phone. Right there, next to the bed. She picked up the receiver. "Yeah?"

"It's five o'clock, Mrs. Morrison."

"Okay. Thanks." The clerk hung up. Mary Terror's heart began to hammer.

The day had come.

Her clothes were damp, her fever sweat returned with a vengeance. She let Drummer cry himself out, and she left the room and got her suitcase and the 7 Eleven sack from the Cherokee. The sky was still black, tendrils of mist drifting across the parking lot. Morning stars glittered up above; it was going to be a sunny, California-groovy day. In the bathroom of number 26, Mary stripped her clothes off. Her breasts sagged, there were bruises on her knees and mottling her arms. Her thigh wound was a dark, festered crust, yellow pus glistening in the dried blood. The bite on her forearm was less severe but just as ugly. When she touched her thigh to try to squeeze out some of the infection, the pain brought fresh blisters of sweat up on her cheeks and forehead. She turned on the shower's taps, mixing the water's temperature to lukewarm, and she stepped into the shower with a new cake of soap she'd bought that smelled of strawberries.

Her shampoo, also purchased at the 7 Eleven, left her hair with the aroma of wildflowers. She'd seen an ad for it on TV, young girls with white teeth and shiny tresses. The water and suds washed the grime off her body, but Mary left her wounds alone. She had no electric dryer, so she toweled her hair and ran a comb through it. She swabbed under her arms with Secret roll-on, and taped her wounds with wide bandages. Then she dressed in a clean pair of bluejeans—painfully tight on her swollen leg, but it couldn't be helped—and a pale blue blouse with red stripes. She shrugged into a black pullover sweater that had a mothball smell in it, but it made her look not so heavy. She put on clean socks and her boots. Then she reached down to the bottom of the sack and brought out the vials of makeup.

Mary began to fix her face. It had been a while since she'd done this, and her right hand began to spasm, so she had to use the left, awkwardly. As she worked, she watched herself in the mirror. Her features were strong, and it wasn't hard to see the young girl who used to live in that face. She wished her hair were long and blond again instead of reddish-brown and cropped short. She recalled that he liked to curl her hair around his fingers. There were dark hollows, purple as bruises, beneath her eyes. Put a little more makeup on them. Now they weren't so bad. A touch of rouge on the cheeks, just a touch to give her face some color. Yes, that's good. Blue eyeshadow on the puffy lids. No, too much. She rubbed some of it off. The final touch was a light sheen of rose-colored lipstick. There. All done.

Twenty years fell away. She looked at her face in the mirror, and she saw the chick Lord Jack loved. He would love her twice as much now, when she brought him their son.

Mary was afraid. Seeing him, after all this time . . . the thought made her stomach churn, and she feared she might throw up in her terror, but she hung on and the sickness passed. She brushed her teeth twice, and gargled with Scope.

It was nearing six o'clock. It was time to go to Freestone and find her future.

Mary pinned the Smiley Face button, her talisman, on the front of her sweater. Then she took her suitcase out to the Cherokee, the sky just beginning to turn a whiter shade of pale. She went back for Drummer, pushed the new pacifier into his mouth, and hugged him close. Her heart was the drummer now, pounding in her chest. "I love you," she whispered to him. "Mama loves her baby." She left the key in the room and closed the door, and then she limped to the Cherokee with Drummer in her arms.

Mary started the engine in the silence of the dawn.

Seventeen minutes before Mary Terror turned the key, a Cutlass with a new radiator had roared past the community of Navato, thirty miles south of the Lux-More Motel. Laura was speeding north on I-101 at seventy miles an hour. The green hills of Marin County rose before the highway in the faint violet light, hundreds of houses nestled in their folds, houseboats on the calm water of San Pablo Bay, peace in the misty air.

There was no peace within Laura. The flesh of her face was drawn tight, her eyes glassy and sunken in her skull. The fingers of her right hand had cramped into a claw on the wheel, her body numbed by its all-night ordeal. She had slept for two hours in the office of Marco's Garage, and popped the last Black Cat between Sacramento and Vallejo. Electricity had surged through her when she'd seen a sign pointing the route to Santa Rosa. Just to the west of Santa Rosa was Mary's destination, and hers as well. The miles were ticking off, one after the other, the highway almost deserted. God help her if a trooper got on her tail; she wasn't slowing down now, not even for Jesus or the saints. Sacramento had been her last gas stop, and she'd been flying ever since.

So close, so close! God, what if Mary's already found him! she thought. Mary must've gotten there hours before! Oh God, I've got to hurry! She glanced at the speedometer, the needle nosing toward eighty and the car starting to vibrate. "Take it easy on 'er," Marco had urged before Laura had pulled out of the garage near seven-thirty. "Once a clunker, always a clunker! You go easy on the gas and maybe you'll get where you're goin'!"

She'd left him four hundred and fifty dollars richer. Mickey, the retarded kid who liked Batman, had waved at her and hollered, "Come back soon!"

SANTA ROSA, a sign said. 14 MI.

The Cutlass hurtled on as the orange ball of the sun began to rise.

WELCOME TO FREESTONE, THE HAPPY VALLEY TOWN.

Mary drove past the sign. Orange light streaked the windows of small businesses on the main thoroughfare. Grassy hills rose around the town, which had not yet awakened. It was a small place, a collection of tidy streets and buildings, a flashing caution light, a park with a bandshell. The speed limit was posted at fifteen miles an hour. Two dogs halted their sniffing on the sidewalk, and one of them began to bark noisily at Mary as she eased past. Just beyond the caution light there was a gas station—still closed, at this hour—with a pay phone out front. She pulled into the station, got out of the Cherokee, and checked the phone book.

Cavanaugh, Keith and Sandy. 502 Muir Road.

Hudley, N. 1219 Overhill Road.

No home-number listing for Dean Walker, but she had the address of his auto dealership Hudley's wife had given her. *Dean Walker Foreign Cars. 677 Meacham Street.* Was there a map of Freestone in the phone book? No, there was not. She looked around for a street marker, and found one on the corner under the caution light. The street she stood on was Parkway, the cross street McGill.

Mary tore out the listings for Cavanaugh and Hudley, and returned to the Cherokee. "Going to find him!" she said to Drummer. "Yes, we are!" She got back on Parkway, and continued slowly in the direction she'd been going. "He might be married," she told Drummer, and she checked her lipstick in the rearview mirror. "But that's all right. See, it's a disguise. You have to do some things you don't like to fit in. Like at the Burger King where I used to work. 'Thank you ma'am.' 'Yes sir, would you like fries with that sir?' Those kind of things. If he got married, it's so he can hide better. But nobody knows him like I do. He might be living with a woman, but he doesn't love her. He's using her to play a role. See?"

Oh, the things she and Jack would teach their son about life and the world would be miraculous!

The next cross street was Meacham.

One block to the right, beside a Crocker Bank, was a brick building with a fenced-in lot that held a couple of Jaguars, a black Porsche, an assortment of BMWs, and various other imports. A sign with blue lettering said DEAN WALKER FOREIGN CARS.

Mary pulled up to the front of the building. It was dark, nobody at work yet. She took the revolver from her shoulder bag, got out, and limped to the building's plate glass window. On the glass-fronted door was a sign that told her the place opened at ten and closed at five. She decided that today it would open three hours and thirty-eight minutes early.

She smashed the door glass with the revolver handle. An alarm screamed, but she'd been prepared for that because she'd already seen the electric contact wires. She reached in, found the lock and twisted it, and then she pushed through the door. In the small showroom stood a red Mercedes. There was a couch with a coffee table where car magazines and brochures were stacked. On either side of a water cooler were two doors with nameplates. One said JERRY BURNES and the other said DEAN WALKER. His office was locked. The alarm was going to wake this sleeping town up, so she had to hurry. She was looking for something to batter the door open with when she saw a framed color photograph on the wall, above a row of shining brass plaques. Two men stood in the photograph, smiling broadly at the camera, the larger man with his arm over the smaller one's shoulder. The caption read: "Freestone Businessman of the Year Dean Walker, right, with Civitan President Lyndon Lee."

Dean Walker was big and fleshy and had a slick salesman's smile. He wore a diamond pinky ring and a power tie. He was black.

One down.

Mary limped back to the Cherokee, its engine still running. Dogs were barking, it seemed, all over town. She drove away from the car dealership, passing a garbage truck that had pulled over to the curb, two men getting out. She turned to the left at the next cross street, which was named Eastview. She went through a stop sign on the following street—Orion—but she hit the brake when she saw the next street marker coming up: Overhill Road.

Which way? She turned to the right. In another minute she saw she'd made the wrong choice, because there was a dead end sign and a stream that ran through a patch of woods. She turned the Cherokee around again, heading west.

She left the business section of Freestone and entered a residential area, small brick houses with neatly manicured lawns and flower boxes. She slowed down, looking for addresses: 1013 . . . 1015 . . . 1017. She was going in the right direction. The next block started with 1111. And then there it stood, in the golden early sunlight: the brick house with a mailbox that had 1219 Overhill on it.

She turned into the short driveway. Under the carport's canopy were two cars, a small Toyota and a midsize Ford, both with California plates. The house was similar to all the others in the neighborhood, except for a birdbath and a wooden bench in the front yard. "Trying to fit in," she told Drummer as she cut the engine. "Playing the suburban role. That's how it's done." She started to get out, but raw fear gripped her. She checked her makeup in the mirror again. She was sweating, and that fact dismayed her. The house awaited, all quiet.

Mary eased out of the Cherokee and limped toward the white front door, leaving Drummer and her gun behind. She could hear the faint, distant shrill of the dealership's alarm, and dogs barking. A couple of birds fluttered around the birdbath. Before she got to the door, her heart was beating so hard and her stomach was so fluttery she thought she might have to stagger to the ornamental bushes and retch. But she forced herself on, and she took a deep breath and pressed the buzzer.

She waited. Cold sweat slicked her palms. She was shaking like a girl on her first date. She pressed the buzzer again, miserable in her impatience. Oh God, let it be him, she thought. Let it be . . . let it be . . . let it—

Footsteps.

A latch was slipped back.

She saw the doorknob start to turn.

Oh God . . . let it be him . . .

The door opened, and a man with sleep-swollen eyes peered around its edge.

"Yes?" he asked.

She couldn't speak. He was a rugged-looking, handsome man, but he had a froth of curly white hair and he was probably in his mid-sixties. "Can I help you, miss?" Irritation had sharpened his voice.

"Uh . . . uh . . ." Her brainwheels were jammed. "Uh . . . are you . . . Nick Hudley?"

"Yes." His brown eyes narrowed, and she saw them tick toward the Smiley Face button.

"I'm . . . lost," Mary said. "I'm looking for Muir Road."

"That way." He motioned to his right, farther along Overhill, with an uptilting of his chin. "Do I know you?"

"No." She turned away, began hurrying to the Cherokee.

"Hey!" Hudley called, coming out. He wore pajamas and a green robe with sailboats on it. "Hey, how do you know my name?"

Mary slid behind the wheel, closed the door, and backed onto Overhill Road. Nick Hudley was standing in his yard, and two birds were fighting for dominion in the birdbath. Dogs howled, finding the alarm's note. Mary drove on, following her star.

A quarter of a mile from Hudley's house, Muir Road branched to the right. Mary took the curve. Marching toward the hazy ocean were green hills dotted with redwood houses spaced far apart and set back from the winding road. Mary looked for names or numbers on the mailboxes. She came around a long curve where pampas grass grew wild, and she saw the name on a box that had a blue whale painted on it: *Cavanaugh.*

A crushed-gravel driveway led twenty yards uphill to a redwood house with a balcony looking toward the Pacific. In front of the house was a copper-colored pickup truck. Mary guided the Cherokee up behind the truck and stopped. Drummer had started bawling, upset about something. She looked at the house, her hands clenched on the wheel. She would not know for sure until she knocked at the door. But if he answered, she wanted him to see their son. She put the bag over her shoulder, picked up Drummer, and got out.

It was a pretty, well-kept house. A lot of labor had gone into it. A sundial stood on a pedestal in the yard, and red flowers that looked like shaving brushes grew in beds around it. The air was chilly, a breeze blowing from the distant sea, but the sun warmed Mary's face and its heat calmed Drummer's crying. She saw a sign painted on the driver's door of the pickup: YE OLDE HERITAGE, INC. Below that, in script, were the Cavanaughs' names and the telephone number.

Mary held the baby tightly, like a dream she feared losing, and she climbed the redwood steps to the front door.

There was a brass door knocker in the shape of an ancient, bearded face. Mary used her fist.

Her guts pulsed with tension, the muscles like iron bands across the back of her neck. Sweat sparkled on her cheeks, and she stared fixedly at the doorknob as Drummer's hand found her Smiley Face button and plucked at it.

Before she could knock again, she heard the door being unlocked.

It opened, so fast the movement made her jump.

"Hi!" A slim, attractive woman with long, light brown hair and hazel eyes stood there. She smiled, lines bracketing her mouth. "We've been looking for you! Come on in!"

"I'm . . . here to . . ."

"Right, it's ready. Come in." She moved back from the doorway, and Mary Terror stepped across the threshold. The woman closed the door and motioned Mary into a large den that had a vaulted ceiling, a rock fireplace, and a grandfather clock. "Here it is." The woman, who wore a pink sweatsuit and pale blue jogging shoes, unzipped a satchel that was sitting on the den's beige sofa. Inside was something in a lustrous wooden frame. "We wanted you to see it before we wrapped it," the woman explained.

It was a coat of arms, two stone towers on either side of what resembled a half horse, half lion against a field of flames. Across the bottom, in the same ornate handwriting as was on the pickup truck's door, was scrolled a name: Michelhof.

"The colors came out very well, don't you think?" the woman asked.

She didn't know what to say. Obviously the woman—Sandy Cavanaugh, Mary presumed—had been expecting someone to come pick up the coat of arms that morning. "Yes," Mary decided. "They did."

"Oh, I'm glad you're pleased! Of course, the family history's included in the information packet." She turned the frame around to show an envelope taped to the back, and Mary caught the glint of her wedding and engagement rings. "Your brother's going to love this, Mrs. Hunter."

"I'm sure he will."

"I'll get it wrapped for you." She returned the coat of arms to the satchel and zipped it up. "You know, I have to say I expected an older woman. You sounded older on the phone."

"Did I?"

"Uh-huh." The woman looked at Drummer. "What a precious baby! How old?"

"Almost a month."

"How many children do you have?"

"Just him," Mary said, and smiled thinly.

"My husband's a fool for babies. Well, if you'll make out the check to Ye Olde Heritage, Inc., I'll go downstairs and get this wrapped. Okay?"

"Okay," Mary said.

Sandy Cavanaugh left the den. Mary heard a door open momentarily, and the woman's voice: "Mrs. Hunter's brought her baby. Go say hello while I wrap this."

A man cleared his throat. "Is it all right?"

"Yes, she likes it."

"That's good," he said. There was the noise of footsteps descending stairs. Mary felt dizzy, and she placed a hand against the wall in case her knees buckled. A TV set was on somewhere at the back of the house, showing cartoons from the sound of it. Mary limped toward the foyer. Before she could get there, a man suddenly walked around the corner into the room and stopped just short of running into her.

"Hi, Mrs. Hunter," he said, summoning a smile. He offered his hand. "I'm Keith Cava—"

His smile cracked.

8.

Castle on a Cloud

Under the blue morning sky, an alarm was shrieking in Freestone.

Laura followed the noise. She turned the Cutlass onto a street named Meacham, and found a green and gray police car parked in front of a brick building whose sign brought a gasp from her. A garbage truck was nearby, two men talking to a policeman. One of them pointed along Meacham, in the opposite direction. There were a few other onlookers: a trim elderly couple in sweatsuits, a teenaged girl wearing an MTV jacket, and a young man who wore a Day-Glo orange jersey and skin-tight black bicyclist shorts, his bike leaning on its kickstand as he talked to the girl. Laura could see that the front door of Dean Walker's foreign car dealership had been shattered, and a second policeman was walking around inside.

Laura stopped the car across the street, got out, and walked to the group of bystanders. "What's going on?" she asked the young man, the alarm echoing across town.

"Somebody broke in," he answered. "Just happened about ten minutes ago."

She nodded, and then she drew the piece of Liberty Motor Lodge notepad paper from her pocket. "Do you know where I can find these men?" She showed him the three names, and the teenage girl looked too.

"This is Mr. Walker's place," the young man reminded her.

"I know that. Can you tell me where he lives?"

"He's got the biggest house on Nautica Point," the girl said, and she pushed her long, lank hair away from her face. "That's where."

"What about the other two?"

"I know Keith. He lives on Muir Road." The young man pointed toward the northwest. "It's over that way, maybe five miles."

"Addresses," Laura urged. "Do you know the addresses?"

They shook their heads. The elderly couple were looking at her, so she moved to them. "I'm trying to find these three men!" she told them. "Can you help me?"

The man peered at the list, looked at her bandaged hand and then into her face. "And who might you be?"

"My name's Laura Clayborne. Please . . . it's very important that I find these men."

"Is that so? Why?"

She was about to burst into tears. "Would you at least tell me how to get to Muir Road and Nautica Point?"

"Are you from around here?" the man inquired.

"Tommy doesn't know how to be nice to strangers!" the elderly woman spoke up. "Dear, Muir Road's off Overhill. The second street that way is Overhill." She jabbed a finger toward it. "Turn left and keep going about three miles. Muir Road goes off to the right, you can't miss it." The alarm suddenly ceased, dogs barking in its wake. "Nautica Point is back the other way, off McGill. Turn right at the caution light and you go eight or nine miles." She grasped Laura's hand and angled it so she could look at the piece of paper. "Oh, Nick's a town councilman! He lives on Overhill. It's a house with a birdbath in front."

"Thank you," Laura said. "Thank you so much!" She turned away and ran to the Cutlass, and she heard the elderly man say, "Why didn't you just tell her where we live so she can go rob *us,* too?"

Laura backed up to Parkway and drove toward Overhill. Nick Hudley's house seemed to be the nearest. She picked up speed, looking for a dark blue Jeep wagon, the automatic pistol on the floorboard under her seat.

Keith Cavanaugh's mouth worked. Nothing came out.

Mary Terror could find no words either. The baby gurgled happily. Shock settled between them like a purple haze.

The man who stood before Mary did not wear white robes. He was dressed in a plaid shirt with a button-down collar, a charcoal gray sweater with a little red polo player on the breast, and khaki pants. On his feet were scuffed loafers instead of Birkenstocks. His hair was more gray than golden, and it didn't flow down to his shoulders. There wasn't enough of it to cover his scalp. His face—ah, there was the treachery of time—was still Lord Jack's, but grown softer, shaved beardless, loose at the jowls. A padding of fat encircled his waist, a little mound of it bulging his sweater at the belly.

But his eyes . . . those blue-crystal, cunning, beautiful eyes . . .

Lord Jack was still behind them, deep in that man who called himself Keith Cavanaugh and made coats of arms in lustrous frames.

"Jesus," he whispered, his face bleached of blood.

"Jack?" Mary took a step forward. He retreated two. There were tears in her eyes, her flesh and soul fevered. "I brought you . . ." She lifted Drummer toward him, like a holy offering. "I brought you our son."

His back met the wall, his mouth opening in a stunned gasp.

"Take him," Mary said. "Take him. He belongs to us now."

The telephone rang. From downstairs, the woman who did not know her husband's true name called, "Jenny, would you get that?"

"Okay!" the voice of a little girl replied. The phone stopped ringing. The noise of TV cartoons went on.

"Take him," Mary urged. Tears streaked down her cheeks, ruining her makeup.

"Daddy, it's Mrs. Hunter!" the little girl said. "She can't come until this afternoon!"

Three heartbeats passed. Then, from downstairs: *"Keith?"*

"Take him," Mary whispered. "Take him. Take *me,* Jack. Please . . ." A sob welled up like a groan, because she could see that her one true love, her savior, her reason for living and the man who had caressed her in her dreams and beckoned her across three thousand miles, had wet his pants. "We're together now," she said. "Like we used to be, only more groovy because we've got Drummer. He's ours, Jack. I took him for *us."*

He slid away from her, stumbled in his retreat, and almost went down. Mary limped after him, through the foyer and toward a hallway. "I did it all for us, Jack. See? I did it so we can be together like we used to—"

"You're crazy," he said, his voice strangled. "Oh my God . . . you . . . stole that baby . . . for *me?"*

"For you." Her heart was growing wings again. "Because I love you sooooo much."

"No. No." He shook his head. Jack had seen the story on the newscasts and in the papers, had followed its progress until more important matters had pushed it from the lead position. He had seen all the old pictures of the Storm Front, all the faces young in their years and ancient in their passions. He had relived those days a thousand times, and now the past had come through his door carrying a kidnapped infant. "Oh God, no! You were always dumb, Mary . . . but I didn't know you were out of your mind!"

Always dumb, he'd said. *Out of your mind.*

"I . . . did it all for us . . ."

"GET AWAY FROM ME!" he shouted. Red flared in his pudgy cheeks. "GET AWAY FROM ME, GODDAMN YOU!"

Sandy Cavanaugh came through a doorway and stopped when she saw the big woman holding her baby out to Keith. He looked at her and yelled, "Get out! Get Jenny and get out! She's crazy!" A pretty girl maybe ten or eleven years old, her hair blond and her eyes bright blue, peered into the corridor next to her mother. "Get out!" Jack Gardiner shouted again, and the woman grabbed up their child and ran toward the back of the house.

"Jack?" Mary Terror's voice had a broken sound, the tears streaming from her eyes and all but blinding her. *You were always dumb,* he'd said. "I *love* you."

"YOU CRAZY BITCH!" Spittle spewed from his mouth and hit

both her and Drummer in their faces. "YOU'RE RUINING EVERY-THING!"

"Police!" Mary heard the woman cry out on the telephone. "Operator, get me the police!"

"Take him," Mary urged. "Please . . . take our baby."

"That's all over!" he shouted. "It was a game! A play! I was so high on acid all the time I didn't even know what I was doing! We all were!" Realization hit him, and rocked his head back. "My God . . . you mean . . . you still *believe?"*

"My . . . life . . . was yours," Mary whispered. "It *is* yours!"

"Police? This is . . . this is . . . Sandy Cavanaugh! We've got . . . somebody's in our house!"

"I don't want you!" he said. "I don't want that baby! That was a long time ago, and it's all over and gone!"

Mary stood very still. Drummer was crying, too. Jack pressed his back against the wall in front of her, his hands up as if to ward off something filthy.

She saw him, in that awful moment.

There had never been a Lord Jack. There had been only a puppet master, pulling heartstrings and triggers. Lord Jack had been a fiction; before her stood the real Jack Gardiner, a trembling, terrified bag of guts and blood. His power had always been a lie, a deft juggling of counterculture slogans, acid dreams, and war games. He had lost the faith because he had had no faith to lose. He had sewn the Storm Front together with deceitful hands, built towers of clay and painted them as stone, merged horses with lions, called them freedom fighters, and thrown them to the flames. He had created a coat of many arms whose purpose was to clothe himself in the threads of glory. And now he stood there in the uniform of the Mindfuck State, while Gary and Akitta and Janette and CinCin and all the rest of the faithful were ghosts. He was allowing a woman who knew nothing of fire and torment to call the pigs. And Mary knew why. It crushed her soul, but she knew. He loved the woman and the child.

Lord Jack was dead.

Jack Gardiner was about to die.

She would save him from the pigs as her last act of love.

She held Drummer in the crook of one arm, and she drew the revolver from her shoulder bag and aimed it at point-blank range.

Jack jammed himself into a corner. Next to him on the wall there was a framed coat of arms: a castle on a cloud, bordered by stags and swords. Beneath it was the name Cavanaugh.

Mary gritted her teeth, her eyes dark with death. Jack made a whimpering sound, like a whipped dog.

She pulled the trigger.

The noise was terrible in the hallway. Sandy Cavanaugh screamed. Mary fired a second time. Then a third shot rang out, all the rich red love gushing from the punctured body as Jack lay crumpled and twitching. Mary pressed the barrel against his balding scalp and delivered a fourth bullet that burst his head open and flung brains all over the wall and her sweater. Blood and tissue flecked her cheeks and clung to the Smiley Face.

Two bullets left. The woman and the child.

She started after them, but paused in the doorway.

Two bullets. For a woman and child. But not the ones who cowered and cried in that room. And not in this house where the pigs would leer and pick at the corpses like hunters with big-game trophies.

As Mary limped to the front door, she passed God skulking in a corner. "You know where," he said under his floppy-brimmed hat, and she answered, "Yes."

She left the house with Drummer, the two of them against the world. She got into the Cherokee and reached for her roadmap as she backed along the driveway in a storm of gravel.

Her finger marked the route and the place. It wasn't far, maybe twenty miles along the coast road. She knew the way. She wondered if Jack had ever gone there, to sit and dream of yesterday.

No, she decided. He never had.

A police car, its lights flashing, passed her as she turned onto Overhill. It took the curve to Muir Road and kept going. She drove on, heading home.

The door opened, and a white-haired man in a green robe with sailboats on it said, "Yes?" as if he resented the intrusion.

"Nick Hudley?" Laura asked, her nerves jangling.

"I am. Who are you?"

"My name is Laura Clayborne." She searched his face. He was too old to be Jack Gardiner. No, this wasn't him. "Have you seen a woman—a big woman, stands about six feet tall—with a baby? She might've been driving a—"

"Dark blue Cherokee," Hudley said. "Yes, she came to the door but I didn't see a baby." His gaze took stock of her dirty clothes and her bandaged hand. "She knew my name, too. What the hell's this all about?"

"How long ago was that? The woman. When was she here?"

"It wasn't over fifteen minutes ago. She said she was trying to find Muir Road. Listen, I think you'd better explain—" He suddenly looked toward the street, and Laura turned in time to see a police car speed by, going west with its lights flashing but no siren.

Muir Road was to the west, Laura realized.

She turned away from Nick Hudley and ran to the Cutlass. She started the engine and left rubber on the pavement as she sped west along Overhill, looking for Muir Road. Somehow, Mary Terror was only fifteen minutes ahead of her instead of three or four hours. There was still hope of getting David back . . . still hope . . . still . . .

A dark blue vehicle roared around a curve in front of Laura, hugging the center line, and Laura saw the face of the woman behind the wheel. At that same instant Mary Terror recognized Laura, and the Cherokee and the Cutlass slid past each other by no more than three inches.

Laura fought the wheel with her hand and elbow, taking the car up onto somebody's lawn, skidding it around and back onto Overhill but now going east. She put her foot to the floorboard, the Cutlass coughing black smoke but gaining speed. The Cherokee was flying in front of her, and in another few seconds they passed Nick Hudley's house, the scream of engines scaring birds out of the birdbath.

On the next curve the Cherokee went up over the curb and knocked a mailbox into the air. Laura got forty feet behind Mary and stayed there, determined not to lose her again. She didn't know if David was in the vehicle or not, or why the police car was on its way toward Muir Road, or if Jack Gardiner was in Freestone, or how Mary's lead had dwindled to forty feet, but she knew Mary Terror would not get away from her. Never. No matter how long it took, no matter where she went. Never.

The Cherokee and the Cutlass swerved onto Parkway, roared under the caution light and past the WELCOME TO FREESTONE sign. Mary's eyes ticked back and forth from the winding road to the car in her rearview mirror. The shock of seeing Laura had been only a further kink in the warp of Mary's mind. Everything was karma, after all. Yes, Mary had decided, it was karma, and karma could not be denied. Let the bitch come. Before Mary took the baby's life and her own, she would execute the bitch who had killed Edward and Bedelia.

Mary's tears had stopped. Her face was a ruin of smeared makeup, her eyes bloodshot and deep-sunken. Her heart had reached its final evolution. It was empty now; there was nothing to dream on anymore. She was the last survivor of the Storm Front, and she would end it where it had begun.

Six miles out of Freestone, she turned onto a country road that led west to the Pacific. Laura kept with her. The miles flashed past, the road deserted. Mary took a turn to the left, following the route on her map, and Laura stayed close. Mary smiled to herself and nodded. The baby was quiet, his hands grasping the air.

The road wound through dense woods. A sign said POINT REYES RANGER STATION, 2 MI. But before a mile had passed, Mary whipped the Cherokee to the right onto another narrow dirt road. She put on speed, dust billowing back into the windshield of the Cutlass as Laura took the turn, too. "Come on!" Mary said, her voice a husky rattle. "Follow me! Come on!"

Laura sped after the Cherokee, her tires bouncing and jubbling over potholes. After a mile or so there was no more dust, but the woods on either side of the road were cobwebbed with mist. Laura could smell the salt air of the Pacific leaching into the car. She followed Mary Terror around a curve, mist swirling between them, and suddenly she saw the taillights flare.

Mary had just stomped on the brake. Laura wrenched the wheel to the right, her shoulder muscles shrieking. The Cutlass missed a collision, but went off the road into the pine woods. The tires plowed through a mossy bog, blue mist hanging between the trees. Laura's foot was on the brake, and the Cutlass grazed a treetrunk and stopped in swampy, rim-deep water.

Laura picked up her pistol. Through the mist she could see the Cherokee sitting there, its taillights no longer flared. The driver's seat was empty. Laura opened the door and stepped out into a bog that claimed her to her ankles. The Cherokee's engine wasn't running. In the silence, Laura heard the thudding of her heart and the cries of sea gulls.

Where was Mary? Was David still with her, or not?

Laura crouched down, moving through the muddy water, and got a treetrunk between herself and the Cherokee. She was expecting a shot at any second. None came.

"I want my baby!" she shouted. Her finger was poised on the trigger, her broken hand throbbing with renewed pain. "Do you hear me?"

But Mary Terror didn't answer. She was too smart to give herself away so easily.

Laura would have to move from where she was. She scurried behind another tree, closer to the Jeep wagon, and waited for a few seconds. Mary didn't show herself. Laura worked her way closer to the Cherokee, mist drifting around her and the sunlight gray through its canopy in the treetops. She gritted her teeth and ran to the vehicle's rear, where she hunkered down and listened.

She could hear distant thunder.

Waves, she realized in another moment. The Pacific, beating against rocks.

The air was cool and wet, moisture dripping from the trees. Laura peered around the Cherokee's side. The driver's door was open. Mary was gone.

Laura stood up, ready to crouch again if she saw movement. She looked into the wagon, saw the clutter of Mary's journey, the smell of sweat and urine and soiled diapers.

Laura walked past the Cherokee, following the dirt road. She went at a slow, careful pace, her senses sharp for any hint of an ambush. The flesh rippled on the back of her neck, the smell of salt in her nostrils. The sound of thunder was getting louder.

And then the woods fell away from both sides of the road, and a house stood before her overlooking the Pacific and its wave-gnawed rocks.

9.

The Thunder House

It was a two-story wooden house with a gabled roof, a widow's walk with broken railings, and a wide porch that went around the lower floor. A path of fieldstones, overgrown with weeds, led from the road to the porch steps. The house might have been beautiful once, a long time ago. It was past saving now. The salt breeze and Pacific spray had long ago scoured off what paint there had been. The house was dark gray, its walls covered with green moss and lichens the color of ashes. What looked like cancers had taken hold on the wood, grown tendrils and linked with other tumors. Part of the porch's supports had collapsed, the floor sagging. Vandals had shown their hand: every window in the house was shattered, and spray-painted graffiti was snarled like gaudy thorns between the lichens.

Laura started up the steps. The second one was already broken, as was the fourth. Laura touched the banister, and her hand sank into the rotten wood. There was no front door. Just beyond the threshold there was a hole in the floor that might have been the size of Mary's boot. Laura walked inside, the smell of saltwater thick and the inner walls dark with growths. Moss hung from the ceiling like garlands. The decorations for a homecoming, Laura thought. She walked toward the staircase, and her left foot slid through the floor as if into gray mud. She pulled free, little black beetles scurrying out of the hole. The first riser of the stairs had given way. So had most of the others. The house was decayed to its core, and the walls were about to fall.

"I know you're there," Laura said. The saturated walls muffled her voice. "I want my baby. I'm not going to let you have him, and you know that by now."

Silence but for the thunder and the noise of dripping.

"Come on, Mary. I'll find you sooner or later."

No answer. What if she's killed him? Laura thought. Oh Jesus, what if she killed him back in Freestone and that's why the police were—

She stopped herself before she cracked. Laura walked carefully into another room. Its bay windows, long broken out, gave a majestic view of the ocean. She could see waves crashing against the rocks, spume leaping high. Mist, a silent destroyer, was drifting into the house. On the cratered floor lay beer cans, cigarette butts, and an empty rum bottle.

Laura heard what she thought at first was the crying of a sea gull on the wind.

No, no. Her heart kicked. It was the crying of a baby. From upstairs, somewhere. Tears burned her eyes, and she almost sobbed with relief. David was still alive.

But she would have to climb the stairs to get him.

Laura started up, over the broken risers. David was still crying, the sound ebbing and then strengthening again. He's tired, she thought. Worn out and hungry. Her arms ached to hold him. Careful, careful! The staircase trembled under her weight, as it must have shaken under the weight of Mary Terror. She climbed into the gloom, moss glistening on the walls, and she reached the second floor.

It was a warren of rooms, but David's crying guided her. Her right foot slid down into the floor, and she nearly fell to her knees. On this second level, much of the floor had already given way, the rest of the boards swollen and sagging underfoot. Laura eased around the rotten-edged craters, where black bugs swarmed, and followed the sound of her child's voice.

Mary could be anywhere. Lurking around a corner, standing in the darkness, waiting for her. Laura went on, step after careful step, her gaze wary for the big woman suddenly appearing in a doorway. But there was no sign of Mary, and at last Laura came to the room that held her son.

He was not alone.

Mary Terror was standing in the far corner of the room, facing the doorway. She had David in the crook of her left arm. Her right hand held a revolver, aimed at the baby's head.

"You found me," Mary said. A smile flickered across a face tight with madness. Her eyes were burn holes, beads of sweat like blisters on her skin. A patch of blood and pus had soaked through the thigh of her jeans.

The hairs had risen on the back of Laura's neck. She'd seen the gore spattered on the woman's sweater and the Smiley Face button. The revolver's hammer was cocked and ready. "Let him go. Please."

Mary paused. She seemed to be thinking about it, her eyes staring off somewhere beside Laura. "He says I shouldn't do that," Mary told her.

"Who says it?"

"God," Mary said. "He's standing over there."

Laura swallowed thickly. David's crying waxed and waned. He was calling for his mother, and her legs wanted to carry her to him.

"Throw your gun down," Mary commanded.

She hesitated. Once the gun was gone, she was finished. Her brain was smoking, trying to think of a way out of this. "In Freestone," she said. "Did you find Jack Gardi—"

"DON'T SPEAK THAT NAME!" Mary shrieked. Her gun hand trembled, the knuckles white.

Laura stood very still, her lungs rasping and cold sweat on her forehead.

Mary's eyes closed for a second or two, as if she were trying to shut out what she'd seen. Then they jerked open. "He's dead. He died in 1972. Linden, New Jersey. There was a shootout. The pigs found us. He died . . . saving me and my baby. I held him while he died. He said . . . he said . . ." She looked to God for guidance in this. "He said he'd never love anyone else, and that our love was like two shooting stars burning bright and hot and people who saw it would be blinded by that beauty. So he died, a long time ago."

"Mary?" Laura kept her voice steady with a supreme effort. If she didn't do something in a hurry, her infant was going to die. The thought of a police sniper and a madwoman on a balcony whirled through her mind in a horror of flashing blue lights. But that woman had killed the baby because of the death reflex. If Mary had to make a sudden choice, would she kill Laura first, or David? "The baby is mine. Can you understand that? I gave birth to him. He belongs to—"

"He's mine," Mary interrupted. "And we're going to die together. Can you dig it, or not?"

"No."

It was the only way. Laura's eyes calculated the inches as her mind measured the dwindling seconds. Time was almost gone. She lunged forward and dropped to her knees, the quickness of her movement catching Mary Terror by surprise.

A single memory passed through Mary's fevered brain, like a cool balm: Drummer's small hand, tightening around her index finger as if to stop it from pulling a trigger.

The revolver didn't go off.

As Laura lifted her pistol and took aim, the gun in Mary's hand left the child's head and began to turn toward Laura.

But Laura got off the first two shots.

She was aiming at the woman's legs, from a distance of ten feet. The first shot missed, hitting the wall behind Mary, but the second bullet grazed Mary's wounded thigh and burst it open in a hot spray of blood and pus. Mary screamed like an animal, her legs buckling and her gun firing before it could train on Laura. As Mary's knees hit the floor, Laura scrambled toward her and swung the automatic at the woman's head, striking her a blow across the left cheekbone. Mary's gun hand began to spasm uncontrollably, and the revolver fell to the floor. Then Laura grabbed hold of the green parka David was zipped up in. She wrenched him out of Mary's grasp, and then she kicked the revolver through a hole in the floor and backed away.

Mary fell onto her side, grasping her ruined leg and moaning.

Laura began to sob. She pressed David against her and kissed his face. He was squalling, his eyes bright with tears. "It's all right," she told him. "It's all right. Oh God, I've got you. I've got my sweet baby, thank God."

She had to get out of there. The rangers' station wasn't far. She could go there and tell them where Mary Terror was. Her heart was beating wildly, the blood rushing through her veins. She felt faint, the ordeal about to smash over her like the ocean on the rocks. She held her baby close, and staggered out of the room. "I've got you, I've got you," she kept saying as she carried him toward the stairs.

She heard a *whuff.*

Behind her.

She turned.

And Mary Terror took one last hobbling lurch and hit her in the face with her right fist, the blow snapping Laura's head back. As Laura fell, her mind ablaze with pain, she hugged David close and swiveled her body so the impact would not be on him but on her right shoulder. The gun left her fingers, and she heard it thud down somewhere in the gloom.

Mary was on her, trying to pull David away. Laura let go of him and clawed at Mary's eyes, her broken fingernails raking across the big woman's face. Mary hammered a punch into Laura's chest, cheating her lungs of air, and as Laura gasped for breath she felt David being taken from her again.

Laura hooked an arm around Mary's throat and squeezed. Mary let go of the baby to beat at Laura's ribs, and then she swung Laura up and around with fierce strength and both the women crashed together against a wall with David on the floor beneath them.

The rotten wall gave way. They went through the soft insect-eaten boards and onto the floor of another room. As they fought, Mary's knee slammed against Laura's splinted hand, and the pain was like incandescent light, startling in its power. Laura heard herself moan, a bestial sound. She struck out with her right fist, hit Mary's shoulder, struck out again, and got her jaw. A blow from Mary hit Laura in the stomach, and then Mary had her by the hair and was trying to slam her head against the floorboards.

Laura fought back with the raw strength of the doomed. She got her fingers in Mary's eyes and tore at them, and then Mary cried out and was pulling away from her. Blood was spattered all over them from Mary's thigh wound, splattered all over the floor. Laura kicked out, hit Mary in the ribs, and drew a grunt from her. Another kick missed, and Mary Terror was crawling away, blood dripping from the corner of her right eye. Laura staggered to her feet, and suddenly Mary turned on her again and grabbed her legs, lifting her off the floor and throwing her back into another wall. Laura went through it as if it were damp pasteboard, and then Mary burst after her through the rotten timbers and sodden plaster with a strangled bellow of fury.

Blood was in Mary's eyes, her face a crimson mask. She kicked at Laura, who got to her knees and desperately tried to protect her face and head with her arms. She warded off one kick, was struck in the shoulder by another. Freighted with pain, she fought to her feet. And then Mary—half-blinded, her right eye white in its socket—clamped her arms around Laura's body, trapping her arms at her sides. She began to crush the life out of her.

Laura thrashed, couldn't break free. Her vision was fading. When she passed out, Mary would beat her to death. Laura rocked her skull back and brought it forward, smashing her forehead as hard as she could against the woman's mouth and nose.

Bones snapped like twigs. The pressure on Laura's ribs eased, and she slid down to the floor in a heap as Mary staggered across the floor, her hands pressed to her face. She hit a wall, but this one was solid. And then she shook her head, drops of blood flying, and she leaned over and breathed like a bellows as red drooled from her mouth.

Laura was shaking, her nerves and muscles almost used up. She was about to pass out, and when she put her hand to her face it came away smeared with blood.

Mary snorted gore, and came at her dragging her mangled leg.

The big woman reached down for her, grabbed her hair with one hand and her throat with the other.

Laura came up off the floor like an uncoiling spring, her teeth gritted, and she grasped the front of Mary's sweater with her good hand and kicked with her last reserve of power into the woman's bleeding thigh.

A howl of pure agony burst from Mary's mouth. Mary let go of Laura's throat to clutch at her leg, and she toppled backward off balance, her shoulders slamming against a wall five feet behind her.

Laura saw the gray wall break open, rusted nails popping like gunshots, and Mary Terror kept falling.

There was a scream. Mary's bloody hands clawed at the edges of the hole she'd gone through, but more of the rotten wood gave way beneath her fingers. The scream sharpened.

Mary's hands disappeared.

Laura heard a moist-sounding *thump.*

The scream had stopped.

She could hear sea gulls. Mist, the silent destroyer, drifted through the broken wall.

Laura looked out. Mary Terror had gone through the side of the house and fallen to the ground forty feet below. She lay on her stomach, amid rocks and weeds and broken bottles, the detritus of someone's party. A graffiti artist had been at work on the larger rocks, adorning them with names and dates in Day-Glo orange. Twenty feet from Mary's head was a spray-painted peace symbol.

There was something in Laura's right hand. She opened it, and looked at the Smiley Face button that had been ripped from Mary Terror's sweater. Its pin had pricked her palm.

She shook it out of her hand, and it clattered facedown to the floor.

Laura staggered out of the room, and near the staircase she knelt down on the floor beside her son.

His gaze found her, and he shrieked. She knew she was no beauty. She picked him up—a major effort, but a pleasure she would not be denied—and rocked him, slowly and gently. Gradually, his crying subsided. She felt his heart beating, and that miracle of miracles broke her. She lowered her head and sobbed, mixing blood and tears.

She thought she must've passed out. When she awakened again, her first thought was that Mary Terror was coming after her, and God help her if she got up and looked out and saw that the woman was no longer lying where she'd struck.

She was afraid to find out. But the thought passed, and her eyelids drifted shut again. Her body was a kingdom of pain. Later—and exactly when this was she didn't know—David's crying brought her back to the world. He was hungry. Wanting a bottle. Got to feed a growing boy. *My* growing boy.

"I love you," she whispered. "I love you, David." She zipped him out of the parka and inspected him: fingers, toes, genitals, everything. He was whole, and he was hers.

Laura held him close against her, and she crooned to him as the ocean spoke outside.

It became time to think about what she was going to do.

She believed she could get the Cutlass out of the bog. If not, maybe the keys were still in the Jeep wagon. No, she couldn't bear to drive that. Couldn't even bear to sit in it, because that woman's smell would be in there. If she couldn't get the Cutlass out, she would have to walk to the rangers' station. Could she do that? She thought so. It might take her a while, but she'd get there eventually.

"Yes we will," she told her baby. He looked at her and blinked, no longer crying. Her voice was froggish, and she could still feel the pressure of that woman's fingers on her throat. "All over now," she said, shunting aside the darkness that kept trying to claim her. "All over."

But what if she looked out and Mary Terror's body was not there?

Laura attempted to stand. It was impossible. She had to wait awhile longer. The light seemed brighter. Afternoon light, she thought. Her tongue probed around her mouth and located no missing teeth but some blood clots. Her ribs were killing her, and she couldn't take deep breaths. Her broken hand . . . well, there was a point in pain where pain no longer registered, and she had passed that. When she got back to civilization, she was going to be a doctor's delight.

Getting to the rangers' station was not the real test. The real test involved Doug, and Atlanta, and where her life would go from there. She didn't think Doug was in her future. She had what belonged to her. He could keep the rest.

And there was another question, too. The question of a woman who did not want to be forgotten, and who feared strangers might pass her grave and never know her story.

Laura would make sure that didn't happen, and she would make sure Bedelia Morse got home.

She thought Neil Kastle of the FBI might take her calls now, too.

Laura got her legs under her, held David against her, and tried to stand. She almost made it. The next time, she did.

Moving slowly and carefully, she descended the staircase. Downstairs, she had to rest again. "Your mama's an old lady, kid," she told David. "How about that?" He made a gurgling noise. She offered him a finger, and his hand curled around it with a strong grip. They had to get to know each other again, but they had plenty of time. There were scrapes on his face; he wore his own medals. "You ready to try it?" she asked. He offered no judgment, only a curious blue-eyed stare.

Laura hobbled out of the house into the afternoon light. The mist was still drifing in, the Pacific thundering against the rocks as it had for ages. Some things were steady, like a mother's love for her child.

The road beckoned.

But not yet. Not just yet.

Laura went around the house, her heartbeat rapid in her bruised chest. She had to see. Had to know that she could sleep again without

Robert R. McCammon

waking up screaming, and that somewhere in the world Mary Terror was not driving the highways of night.

She was there.

Her eyes were open, her head crooked. A rock was her pillow, red as love.

Laura released her breath, and turned away with her son in her arms.

Both of Thursday's children had far to go.